Ashyn closed her eyes and reached out to the spirits. After a moment, she could feel them pulling at the edge of her consciousness. It wasn't like the gentle plucks of the ancestral spirits; these were harsh, like needle jabs.

She repeated the words Ellyn had taught her.

"I'm here to give you peace," she said. "You want peace."

No, they wanted revenge.

SEA OF SHADOWS

KELLEY ARMSTRONG

HARPER

An Imprint of HarperCollinsPublishers

Sea of Shadows

Copyright © 2014 by KLA Fricke Inc.

All rights reserved. Printed in the United States of America.

No part of this book may be used or reproduced in any manner whatsoever without written permission except in the case of brief quotations embodied in critical articles and reviews. For information address HarperCollins Children's Books, a division of HarperCollins Publishers, 195 Broadway, New York, NY 10007.

www.epicreads.com

Library of Congress Cataloging-in-Publication Data

Armstrong, Kelley.

    Sea of shadows / Kelley Armstrong. — First edition.

        p.   cm.

    Summary: "Twin sisters Ashyn and Moria must embark on a dangerous journey when the spirits they're charged with protecting turn vengeful"— Provided by publisher.

    ISBN 978-0-06-207125-5

    [1. Adventure and adventurers—Fiction. 2. Twins—Fiction. 3. Sisters—Fiction. 4. Spirits—Fiction. 5. Supernatural—Fiction. 6. Fantasy.] I. Title.

PZ7.A73362Se 2014   2013032809

[Fic]—dc23   CIP

                                        AC

Typography by Anna Christian

       17 18 19 PC/RRDH 10 9 8 7 6 5 4 3 2

❖

First paperback edition, 2015

To Julia

SEA OF SHADOWS

PROLOGUE

After three days of tramping across endless lava fields, Ronan quickened his steps at the sight of the forest. He swore he could feel soft earth under his feet, hear birds in the treetops, even smell icy spring water. If one had to pick a place to die, he supposed one could do worse.

He glanced over at his father and uncle, but their gazes were fixed straight ahead. Even the guards weren't paying attention. Still Ronan didn't consider escape. There was a reason the exiles weren't bound or chained. They were in the Wastes. There was no place to hide except the Forest of the Dead, and they'd be there soon enough.

Ronan sat around the campfire with the others, eating their final dinner in the livestock enclosure. Once they passed the canyon walls, they'd be expected to fend for themselves. Without weapons. In a forest rumored to be bereft of life.

For their last meal, they got water, dried fish, and overcooked rice. At least the water was clean, which was more than he could say for the murk he'd been drinking.

Beside him, his father sat motionless, staring at the fire. Two of the exiles eyed his untouched food. As soon as Ronan's uncle turned away, one snatched a chunk of fish . . . and found his wrist pinned to the ground.

"Drop it," Ronan said.

"You little—"

The convict didn't get a chance to finish the curse. Ronan's fist slammed him in the throat. The man gasped, eyes bulging as he struggled for breath. The other exiles laughed. Ronan knew they weren't cheering his victory; they'd have laughed just as much if he were lying there with a makeshift blade in his gut. On the road, he'd watched three prisoners die, their killers goaded on by the others, who cared only that the deaths lifted the monotony for a moment or two.

He didn't glance at his uncle. He knew he'd be pleased. He also knew that he wouldn't have interfered if Ronan *had* faced a blade. If Ronan wasn't strong enough to survive, then he shouldn't. It was that simple.

Ronan set the fish back in front of his father, who hadn't moved during the entire incident. His uncle shook his head, reached over, and took the untouched meal. He divided the fish and rice and pushed half toward Ronan.

"Eat."

Ronan took it, only to press the fish into his father's hand. It fell to the rocky ground. His uncle snorted. After another try, Ronan kept the food, and his uncle grunted in satisfaction.

A single-word exchange. That's what passed for conversation with his uncle. Ronan's father had been the loquacious one, always talking, always laughing, always charming. And

4

yet, somehow, Ronan had always felt more affection in his uncle's grunts and glares than in the false and easy charm his father used on marks and family alike.

After eating the rations, Ronan walked to stretch his legs. As he neared the barn, he noticed something perched on the enclosure fence. He slowed to let his eyes adjust to the dark.

The shape looked like a cat, but it was almost half as tall as him. Blacker than the surrounding night, with a swishing, thick tail that kept it balanced on the thin wall. Its massive paws seemed too large for its body. Its tufted ears swiveled and twitched. A wildcat? Ronan recalled seeing one in the imperial zoo, but it hadn't been much bigger than a house pet.

This cat was looking off to the side. Ronan took a few cautious steps. Then he noticed what the cat was watching—a village boy had climbed the fence and was slinking along the barn to get a look at the exiles.

Ronan's practiced eye slid over the boy, taking in his size, his demeanor, and most of all, his clothes. He was half a head shorter than Ronan, with his hood pulled up around his face. Perhaps thirteen summers, given his size. An easy mark. A rich one, too, considering his attire—woolen breeches, a fine cloak, and laced leather boots. Both the cloak and the boots were fur trimmed and likely fur lined. So the boy came from a family of power. That made him valuable.

As Ronan watched the youth, a plan formed. It was not a good plan or even a reasonable one, but he was a single night from exile in the Forest of the Dead. A plan no longer needed to be good or reasonable. If he took the boy, perhaps he could barter him for something—food, a weapon, anything that might help Ronan survive the winter.

He needed to survive. He had a sister and brother back in the imperial city. Aidra was six summers old and Jorn was not yet ten. Ronan knew it wouldn't be long before his aunt decided they needed to work for their keep—filching in the marketplace and scouting marks for their older cousins. Ronan would do whatever it took to get back to them.

He crept after the village boy, his worn boots making no sound. When he heard a noise, he glanced to see the cat's yellow eyes fixed on him. Ronan supposed that ought to be some cause for alarm, but the beast only stared at him balefully. Then it made an odd chirping sound. The village boy didn't seem to hear it.

Ronan slid closer, measuring the distance. The boy had crouched to peer around the barn. Defenseless. Oblivious. A perfect mark.

Ronan sprang. The moment he was in flight, the boy twisted and dove at him. As he did, his hood fell back and red-gold hair tumbled out. *Long* red-gold hair. Later Ronan would tell himself that *this* was why he ended up on his back, with a girl on his chest and a blade at his throat. Not because she'd bested him, but because he'd been caught off guard realizing *he* was a *she*.

The dagger didn't help matters. That threw him as much as her gender. Only the warrior caste was permitted to carry edged weapons, and she wasn't dressed as a warrior. And he could see enough of the dagger to know it was relatively new, not a warrior's ancestral blade.

He grabbed the girl by the back of her cloak to wrest

her off—and got a knee jab in the stomach, so hard it made him very glad she hadn't aimed lower. The dagger bit into his neck, and he felt blood well up. Still, that might not have been enough to deter him. But the cat was.

The wildcat had appeared beside them, silent as a wraith. It padded closer, as if witnessing a dull game of capture-my-lord, plunked itself down, and stretched, its front paws coming so close Ronan could see the tips of its giant claws. Then those claws shot out, razor-sharp talons as long as finger joints, barely a hairbreadth from his face.

The girl turned to the cat. She made a noise in her throat, a cross between a grunt and a growl. The cat sighed, then straightened and proceeded to clean a forepaw. Yet it kept its gaze on Ronan.

A hunting cat? He'd heard of such things, in the deserts to the south, where the climate was ill suited to shaggy hounds. But the girl was clearly Northern-born, with her pale skin and blue eyes.

"Are you the youngest of the damned?" the girl asked. To Ronan's surprise, her voice was low, almost rough. With her red-gold hair and finely cut features, she looked like she ought to speak with a teasing lilt. Of course, she didn't look like she should be able to send him flying either—or knock out his breath with a well-placed knee.

"What?" he said.

"The damned. The exiles. Are you the youngest?"

He was, but he had no idea what it mattered, so he stared at her.

"They sent me to find the youngest. Are you he?"

"*Who* sent you?" he asked carefully.

Her free hand fluttered, but she said nothing, only asked the question again, sounding impatient now.

"And if I *was* the youngest?" he said.

She looked around, as if waiting for someone. "Do you know what would truly help?" she said, speaking to the air. "Clearer communication."

The cat chuffed and seemed to roll its eyes.

"I know, I know," she muttered under her breath.

She's mad, Ronan thought. *I've been taken by a madwoman.*

That would have been cause to resume struggling if she weren't already sliding off him. She sprang to her feet, as gracefully as her cat, and pointed the dagger at his chest. "Keep your distance, boy."

Boy? She was older than he'd estimated at first, but she still had to be a summer his junior.

She gave one last look around, muttered, "This was a waste of time," and began backing away. After a few steps she stopped, and her head swung to the side, as if she'd heard something.

"What?" she said.

"I didn't—" he began.

She silenced him with a wave, then focused on the air to her left.

Spirits. She hears the spirits.

No, that didn't make sense. True, there were spirits, all around them, all the time. Everyone knew that. But only the spirit talkers could hear them, and those were mystics who'd sacrificed every other sense to earn that one. Blinded, tongues cut out, nostrils seared, forbidden to touch anything except the paper on which they scribbled messages from the second world. This girl was clearly not one of them.

He looked at the cat. The sight of it triggered some memory. Yes, there was an answer to this riddle, and he should know it, but he'd relegated it to the refuse heap of things he didn't need to remember.

Or the girl was mad. That seemed more likely.

"Are you mad?" she said, as if echoing his thoughts, and he jumped, but she was still addressing the air. "What good will—?"

She paused, then muttered, "Clearer communication. Is it too much to ask?"

She turned to Ronan. "Stay there."

"What?"

She looked back at the air. "He's simple. You do realize that, don't you?"

"Simple? I am not—"

"Stay!"

Still walking backward, she retreated to the fence and climbed on top of it. The wildcat jumped up beside her. She whispered something to it, and the beast dipped its head, as if agreeing.

Then, without another word, she hurled the dagger. It hit the barn, embedding itself in the wood.

"There," she said. "Now, let's hope you have the intelligence to keep it hidden."

He stared at the blade. "You're giving me . . ."

"Not by choice. It won't do any good anyway. If the

9

swamp fever doesn't drive you mad, the spirits of the damned will. You'll probably end up using that blade on yourself. Not much else in the forest you can use it on. A dagger won't kill the fever. Won't kill the spirits." She turned. "But good luck anyway."

She jumped down, the wildcat leaping beside her, and they were gone.

It was barely past dawn when the exiles were marched to the forest. Beside Ronan, Cecil—a young man a few summers his senior—gaped at the fierce village guards who accompanied them. Had he expected farmers and craftsmen armed with cudgels? Edgewood guarded the only passage from the Forest of the Dead. Of course its guardians would be warriors.

Ronan's family had been warriors once. Until an ancestor backed the wrong imperial heir, and they'd been stripped of their caste, expected to beg for a living. Yet while the empire could confiscate their blades, it couldn't rescind generations of martial training. So Ronan's family had found other ways to keep themselves fed. Which had ultimately led to this.

As they walked, Ronan eyed the youngest village guard. He wasn't much older than Ronan. Intricate tattoos covered his forearms. In them, Ronan saw a nine-tailed fox. The totem of the Kitsune clan, family of the disgraced former marshal, who'd been exiled to this forest himself. Apparently *his* clan hadn't been stripped of its caste. They just wound up here, guarding the forest.

The exiles left the village guards behind at the watchtower and continued on with the ones who'd brought them here. As they walked, the convicts stared into the endless verdant sea ahead. Even with the trees shedding their leaves, the forest was still green, thick moss covering everything.

The guards urged them forward. They'd have two days of walking to reach the middle of the forest. Behind them, a guard unspooled a bright red ribbon in their wake. Once they entered the dense woods, that ribbon would be the only chance for the guards to find their way out again.

Ronan glanced over his shoulder at the village.

"Take a good look," a guard said, smirking. "It's the last you'll ever see of it."

Ronan shifted and felt the cold steel of the hidden dagger against his leg.

Perhaps, he thought. *But not if I can help it.*

Four Moons Later

ONE

A shyn sat by the fire, eating pork rolls while feeding meat scraps to Tova, the giant yellow hound that never left her side. She gazed out the window and watched the spring sun burn away the lace of frost.

Her twin sister, Moria, sauntered in, late for breakfast as always. Moria's wildcat, Daigo, appeared out of nowhere and snatched a scrap from under Tova's nose. As Ashyn scolded the wildcat, Moria whisked the pork roll from her hand.

Ashyn sighed and Tova sighed, too. Then they just helped themselves to more food and moved over to let Moria and Daigo sit with them.

When their father came in a moment later, he said, "Moria, you'll be pleased to know that your new dagger will arrive on the next supply wagon."

"Finally. I lost it before the first snow fell."

"Then perhaps, in future, you ought to be more careful with your belongings."

"I can't help it. I'm forgetful."

Father shook his head. "You've never forgotten anything in your life, Rya. Who got your blade this time? Another woman needing protection from her husband?"

"That would be wrong. Blades are for warriors. Ash and I are the only exceptions." She took a bite of her pork. "But if I did give it to some poor soul in need, it would be the spirits' fault. They speak, and I must obey."

Their father shared an eye roll with Ashyn. While it was true that the girls served the ancestral spirits, it was an excuse Moria used too often.

"Waiting so long for weapons isn't reasonable," Moria continued. "We need a smith. I'm sure there's a strong young man who could take up the task, for the greater good." She chewed. "How about that Kitsune boy?"

"What's Gavril done now that you're volunteering him for smithing?" Ashyn asked.

"It was merely a suggestion. He's young. He's strong. He's in need of a trade."

Ashyn sputtered a laugh. "He's a *warrior*, Moria, from a line of warriors stretching back to the First Age."

"Then his ancestors have forgotten him, because he isn't very good at it."

Ashyn shook her head.

"Since I won't have my dagger by morning, I'll need a knife," Moria said, her voice deceptively casual. "I'm going lizard hunting."

"Are you?" Father mused. "Perhaps I'll come along."

"You scare the lizards."

"No," he said. "I'll scare *you*—away from the forest. Which is where you truly plan to go."

Moria made a face. "Why would I want to go into the forest?"

Neither Ashyn nor their father replied to that. They both knew what Moria had in mind. Tomorrow was the Seeking. Ashyn was the Seeker. Having passed her sixteenth summer, she would enter the Forest of the Dead for the first time, where she would find the bodies of the damned and put their spirits to rest.

"I don't see why I can't go," Moria continued when no one answered. "I'm the Keeper. I protect the empire from unsettled spirits, so it should be my duty to help with the Seeking."

"No," Ashyn said. "It's your duty to stay here and guard the village *during* the Seeking." She lowered her voice and whispered to Moria. "I don't need my little sister to protect me."

Moria grumbled. Ashyn knew she hated the reminder that she'd been born a half day later. Twins were so rare that their mother had gone that long before realizing the ongoing labor pains weren't merely the aftereffects of Ashyn's birth.

"I'm trained with a blade," Ashyn continued evenly. "Besides, I have Tova. He wouldn't let anything happen to me."

On cue, the hound laid his head on her knee.

"I still don't like it," Moria said.

Ashyn leaned against her twin. "I know."

Tomorrow Ashyn would conduct the Seeking—her primary role as Seeker of Edgewood. There were four pairs of Seekers and Keepers in the empire. Two traveled where they were needed, and one stayed at court. The last pair was permanently stationed at the most spiritually dangerous place in the empire—Edgewood—where they guarded the only break in the box-canyon wall that surrounded the Forest of the Dead.

Their forest had always been thick with spiritual energy, from the old practice of elder abandonment. After that ended, the empire began exiling its criminals here, and the ancestral spirits had fled to the village at its mouth. That was what made Edgewood so dangerous that it needed its own Keeper and Seeker. The village was filled with ancestral spirits in constant need of appeasement, and the forest was filled with angry spirits in constant need of restraint.

Before the Seeking, there was a full day of rituals to be conducted. As they followed the rocky lane to the sanctuary, Ashyn looked at her twin sister. Two of the village children walked backward in front of Moria. A half dozen more followed behind her. The children were not coming along for the ritual, of course, but merely tagging along after Moria. If they got too close or grabbed at her cloak, she'd snap and Daigo would growl. They'd dance away, grinning, only to come right back, chattering like Healer Mabill's pet magpie. *Tell us a story, Moria. Show us a trick. Teach us something.*

Moria would scowl at the younger children and lob insults at the older ones. They still adored her, still followed her through the village like stray dogs, knowing a scrap would eventually come. They'd get a story or they'd get a trick or they'd get a lesson, and they'd get smiles, too, and kind words, if they earned them.

"Better run home," Moria called as they continued down the lane. "You know what happens if you get too close to the sanctuary and see the rituals."

"Our eyes will pop!" a boy shouted.

"Yes. They'll explode like dried corn in a fire, and you'll be left with holes in your head for your brains to leak out."

"Eww!" one of the girls said. "And then what?"

"Then you'll be walking around with only half your wits, drooling and gaping." She pointed at the oldest boy. "In other words, you'll end up just like Niles over there."

The children giggled.

Moria continued, "If you behave yourselves and stay away from the sanctuary, I might tell some stories tonight. But you must stay away. Ashyn needs complete silence outside or she'll forget the words to all the chants." She lowered her voice to a mock whisper. "I think *she* might have gotten too close to a ritual when she was little."

Ashyn made a face at her. Moria tossed back a grin. Despite the insult, Ashyn knew Moria was doing her a favor—a quiet sanctuary would indeed help today. It was the first time she'd conduct the Seeking rituals alone.

"Now, what kind of creature do you want for tonight's story?" Moria asked. "Thunder hawks? Sand dragons? Water horses?"

As the children called out suggestions, a small voice whispered beside Ashyn. "Are you scared?"

She looked down at the girl, walking so close Tova had to give her room. There were always a couple frightened by Moria's stories and scowls. This one was Wenda, just past her ninth summer. Ashyn stroked the girl's black curls.

"I've assisted with the rituals many times," Ashyn said. "It's not frightening."

"I mean the Seeking. Finding the"—Wenda shuddered—"bodies. And the spirits. Momma says when the damned die, they become the forsaken and can hurt us." She looked up, dark eyes glistening. "They can hurt *you*."

"But they won't. I'm there to calm them and make sure they are buried properly. That takes away their anger. They'll go to the second world and be happy."

Moria glanced over, her rough voice softening. "Ashyn's been training for this since she was smaller than you. She's ready."

Ashyn wished she shared her sister's confidence. It was true they'd been training most of their lives. The Seeker and Keeper from the imperial court had come every season to train them and conduct the rituals. Ashyn was not fond of the harsh old Seeker, but she wished Ellyn could be here now to guide her, even if she could not enter the forest with her tomorrow— only one Seeker was permitted in at a time.

Ashyn couldn't even appeal to the ancestral spirits for guidance. While she often heard their wordless whispers, their actual communications were little more than a few words. From that, she had to interpret what they wanted—and it was all about what *they* wanted. She was their servant. They did not assist her.

"Who wants Ashyn's fortune today?" Moria asked.

The children clamored to be chosen. Then Wenda whispered, "I think Ashyn should take it. For luck."

Ashyn shook her head. Anyone who left an offering was welcome to a fortune, but she never took hers because there was a chance it could be a curse. It seemed an unnecessary tempting of fate. So Moria let the village children take it, which was fine, because a curse didn't count if you weren't the one leaving the offering.

The children ran to the offering tree. It was set just under the eaves of the sanctuary, sheltered from the rare rains. Made of metal, the tree had fortune scrolls in place of leaves and a slotted hole for the offering. The shrine caretaker replaced the scrolls with shipments from the court priests.

Ashyn knelt beside the metal tree and dropped in a copper coin, hearing it clink at the bottom. Then she closed her eyes, selected a scroll, and handed it to the little boy Moria had chosen. He shoved it into his pocket to be opened later, so he wouldn't miss the next part.

Moria waved the children away from the tree and stepped back five paces, coin in hand. She measured the distance. Then she pitched the coin. It sailed squarely through the slot and rang off the metal like a bell.

The children cheered, but the show wasn't over. They went quiet as Moria pulled a dart from her cloak. She turned around and threw the dart over her shoulder. It flew straight through a scroll and pinned it to the wooden sanctuary wall.

The children whooped and cheered. Ashyn shot her sister a grin. Moria smiled and went to retrieve her prize.

"Leaving an offering is a sacred act, Keeper," said a deep voice behind them. "It isn't a child's game."

TWO

Ashyn winced as Gavril Kitsune stepped from behind the children, but Moria only said, "Yes, it is a sacred act, and so I honor the spirits by demonstrating the skills I have developed for the protection of my village."

Ashyn swore she heard the whispery chuckle of the ancestors.

One of the older boys turned to Gavril. "The Keeper protects us from the spirits of the damned. Like your father—"

Moria laid her hand on the boy's shoulder, silencing him. Gavril's mouth tightened. One could think he was reacting to the insult, but Ashyn suspected Moria's defense bothered him more.

When Gavril first came to Edgewood, the village had recognized the uncomfortable irony of sending a young man to guard the forest where his father had been exiled to his death. They'd tried to welcome him. But Gavril was as hard as the lava rock of the Wastes. He did his job and asked for nothing, expected nothing, gave nothing. Still, he wasn't rude to the villagers . . . with one exception—the person who'd been the most outraged by his predicament and had tried most to befriend him.

Gavril goaded Moria, challenged her, and caught her when she was up to trouble. Moria forbid Ashyn to complain. "It's practice," she'd say. "He pokes at me and insults me and watches me, and I learn to be tougher, quicker, and stealthier."

Now Gavril walked close enough to Moria to make Daigo growl. He towered above her by a head, his dark braids brushing her head as he leaned over to whisper to her. His muscled arms glistened with sweat, as if he'd just left his morning drill. The perspiration made the green eyes on his nine-tailed fox tattoos glitter.

"Remember what I said," he murmured. "If you try tomorrow, I'll do it. I swear I will."

Moria's hand tightened on the dart. "I don't need to be told twice."

"I just want to be sure we understand each other, Keeper."

"What's going on?" Ashyn said.

Gavril didn't even look at her. "This is between your sister and me."

Unrolling her fortune, Moria walked toward Ashyn. She glanced down at the paper, then stopped midstep. It was only a moment's pause before she wrapped her hand around the tiny paper, her expression neutral. But Ashyn noticed.

"It's a curse, isn't it?" Gavril said, striding to catch up with her.

Ashyn braced for his next words. He'd say she deserved it after disrespecting the spirits with her performance. Instead, he swung into Moria's path and said, "Go put it on the statue behind the sanctuary."

Moria's brows shot up. "Is that an order?"

"Now is not the time to take a curse—" Gavril began.

"I'm not going on the Seeking. That has been made very clear." She gave him a look. "If I accept my good fortunes, then I must also accept my curses."

"Ashyn, tell her to put the curse on the statue."

Ashyn jumped at the sound of her name. It was quite possibly the first time he'd ever said it. And definitely the first time he'd looked straight at her. She decided she much preferred being ignored. His eyes were discomfiting enough. Green. A rare color in the empire. Kitsune eyes, her father said, the mark of Gavril's illustrious family. A sign of sorcery, others said, whispering old stories about how the Kitsunes first gained their power.

"You know I won't, so don't ask." Moria took Ashyn's arm. "Everyone's waiting inside. Father keeps peeking out. We're late."

As they walked to the door, Moria glanced over her shoulder. Ashyn did the same and saw that the children were still there, quiet now, their faces tight with concern. They'd overheard enough to know Moria had picked a curse.

"What are you waiting for?" she called to the children. "You know what happens if you see the rituals."

Silence answered her.

Moria reached into her pocket and pulled out a handful

of coppers. "Huh. Seems I have extra. What should I do with these?"

That got a few smiles and whispers, but most of the faces stayed solemn. Moria opened her hand under the fountain water. Then she clenched her fist around the wet coins.

"Grant me a boon, o spirits," she said. "Twice-bless these coins for the children. May they have nothing but good fortune until the Seeking is done."

Wind rustled through the fortune scrolls, making them whisper, as if the spirits themselves were replying. Moria kept one of the coins and threw the rest to the children. As they scrambled after them, shrieking, she tossed the remaining copper to Gavril.

He made no move to catch it, letting it fall, clinking. Then he turned on his heel and marched away.

Ashyn's knees ached. Which was exactly the wrong thing to be thinking about in the middle of a spiritual ritual, and it only made her feel all the more ill prepared to lead the Seeking tomorrow. This was not the first ritual she'd ever done—she'd been assisting Ellyn since she was old enough to recite the words. It was not even the first one she'd conducted alone— lately, Ellyn had left the minor seasonal rituals to Ashyn, only coming back in the spring for the Seeking. And yet Ashyn was not prepared. She simply wasn't.

The Seeking rituals took the longest by far, and by this point her knees always ached from the cold stone floor. In the past, any guilt at fussing over discomfort had been mitigated by the knowledge that her participation didn't matter. She'd do better when Ellyn was gone.

How? she wondered now. Had she expected that her knees would miraculously toughen as she passed her sixteenth summer? That the endless chants would suddenly flow without stammers and stutters?

When something brushed her hand, she jumped, eyes flying open.

"Shhh." Moria laid a hand on her shoulder.

Her sister held out a cloth, and Ashyn thought she'd read her mind. She was about to refuse—she wasn't allowed a kneeling pad—but then she saw the bowl of steaming water.

"It's time for your purification." Moria kept her voice low. The others—the governor, their father, and the shrine caretaker—had retreated outside long ago, but might still be close enough to overhear.

Ashyn shook her head. "I need to finish the Song for the Fallen first."

"You did," Moria whispered. "You started it over again."

Ashyn's cheeks warmed and tears prickled. *I can't do this. I truly can't.*

"I'm sure no one noticed," Moria whispered. "I only did because I woke up when you got to the interesting part." Ashyn knew Moria hadn't truly fallen asleep, but the thought made her smile.

As Moria helped with the ritual bath, Ashyn tried to cleanse her mind as well. She opened her mind to the spirits—all the spirits. While the ancestral ones of the village were her primary concern, there were many, many others. Spirits were everywhere, inhabiting everything—spirits of hearth and fire, of wind and rain, of plant and beast. She did not hear those. They were not the sort that spoke. There were other human spirits, though, ones she might hear, if they passed her way. The hungry dead. The lost and the angry.

Like the spirits in the forest. The forsaken. The vengeful—

She inhaled so sharply that Tova lifted his head and whined.

Moria rubbed the steaming cloth over Ashyn's aching knees. "Did I tell you that Levi wrote me a poem? I can recite it if you like."

"You memorized it?"

"Of course. It was truly memorable. I've never heard anything so terrible."

Ashyn sputtered a laugh.

"Do you want to hear it?" Moria asked.

"Please." Ashyn leaned back, closing her eyes and relaxing as Moria finished the purification ritual and recited Levi's poem.

As for whether the rituals went well or not, Ashyn couldn't say. That evening, as promised, Moria entertained the children with stories, but Ashyn knew they were truly for her. Distracting tales of legendary beasts and wild adventures.

There were some creatures that didn't find their way into Moria's tales that night. Monsters of the spirit world, like fiend dogs and shadow stalkers. Those would not calm Ashyn's fears as she headed into the Forest of the Dead.

"You'll do fine," Moria said later as they slid onto their sleeping mats.

"What if I don't?"

Moria sighed. "Nothing ever goes wrong, Ash. If it did, we'd hear the stories. The only thing people love more than a good story is a bad one. Tales of tragedy and woe and bloody entrails, strung like ribbons, decorating the battlefields."

"I could do without that last bit."

Moria grinned. "That's the best part. You know what I mean, though. There are no bards' tales about Seekings because they are boringly predictable. You find the bodies. You purify the bodies. You bury the bodies. No one's ever done it wrong before."

"What if I'm the first?"

A coin thumped off Ashyn's forehead.

"Oww."

"Don't complain. That's one of the twice-blessed coins. I kept it for you. Put it in your pocket tomorrow, and you'll be protected from evil spirits and snakebites and Faiban." Moria paused. "Unless you don't want to be protected from Faiban. I hear he *volunteered* for the Seeking."

Ashyn's cheeks heated. She lay in the darkness, feeling the copper warming in her hand.

"What kind of curse was it?" she whispered finally. "A minor one?"

Moria groaned. "What does it matter? It was one of many I've taken. It only means I'll suffer some small misfortune. Daigo will probably get gas tomorrow night. You'll be thankful you missed it."

The wildcat growled softly beside her sister.

"So it *was* only a minor curse?"

"Good night, Ashyn."

Moria flipped onto her other side, ending the conversation.

Ashyn waited until her sister began to snore. Then she slipped from her sleeping mat and tiptoed to Moria's cloak, left thrown over the chair. As she reached into the pocket, Daigo watched her but did nothing. She pulled out the curse scroll. Then she tugged on her own cloak and headed for the door with Tova padding along behind her.

THREE

During the day, it was clear that spring had arrived—the sun bright, the air warm. But the nights still seemed determined to cling to winter. An icy wind blew off the north, freezing Ashyn's nose and cheeks. As she pulled her hands under her cloak, the scroll rustled against the fur lining. She clutched it tighter.

The village was particularly dark tonight. There were always lanterns left blazing, holding off the endless black of the Wastes. Tonight they were a necessity, with the moon hidden behind clouds. When Ashyn peered up, the sky looked faintly red.

The color of blood.

She shivered, cursing her sister's stories.

As she walked, the scent of burning wood wafted around her. She could see the lazy trails of smoke over the houses and inhaled deeply, letting the familiar smell calm her.

The sounds were familiar, too, like the lonely yips of Blackie, the carpenter's dog, never let into the house, even on the coldest nights. Ashyn rested her hand on Tova's head as he stiffened in sympathy with the poor beast. She could pick up the distant squawk of chickens, the low of cows, and the grunt of pigs. No horses—they produced nothing edible, so the village couldn't afford to waste feed on them when there was so little soil for growing and so few wagon trains bringing supplies.

As she drew close to the sanctuary, she thought she heard the scuff of a boot against the lava rock. Tova confirmed it by glancing in that direction. He gave no sign of alarm, though. Other girls might need to worry about a guard who'd had too much honey wine and been too long from court. But the penalty for touching the Seeker or the Keeper without her permission was . . . well, it would ensure he never had any urge to touch a woman again. No amount of honey wine would addle a man's brains enough to risk that.

Ashyn reached the sanctuary and ducked around back, where the statue waited. It was a small wooden figure, so battered by the elements that she could only make out faint grooves to show it once had a face. Instead of clothing, it wore a cloak of scrolls pinned over its entire body, some yellowed, others nearly disintegrated with time.

Ashyn bent and took out Moria's scroll. She looked down at it, still tightly rolled.

What type of curse was it?

She didn't want to know. She just wanted to pin it to the figure and run. But that was cowardly. After all, she was getting rid of it, so it didn't matter what sort it was.

She unfurled it, a half roll, and then . . .

She stopped. At her side, Tova whined.

Even in the darkness the lines on the white scroll were easy to read. The symbol seemed blacker than most, and she swore she could feel it under her finger, as if the writer had pushed the quill into the paper, hoping the ink would soak through enough to warn anyone who thought of choosing it from the tree.

Not a major curse, but a *great* one. The worst there was. Something terrible was about to befall her sister.

Fingers trembling, Ashyn rerolled the scroll and pinned it to the statue, in the rear, as if that could hide it from whatever powers governed fate.

As Ashyn hurried from behind the sanctuary, she could feel someone watching her. She glanced at Tova. He noticed, but was simply watching.

When Ashyn turned the corner, a boot squeaked. She glanced back. A figure stood in front of the sanctuary, his back to her. A guard's heavy coat cloaked his figure. Then he bent, braids falling forward, and she knew who it was.

The braids didn't give him away—many of the warrior caste wore them. Almost all warriors, though, tied theirs with bright beads. Only one used dull, black leather.

Gavril crouched, reaching for something on the ground. When he picked it up, copper glinted in the moonlight. The twice-blessed coin Moria had thrown to him. He shoved it into his pocket. Then he stood and gazed at the sanctuary.

He made a noise, like a grunt of satisfaction, and she knew he'd watched her take the curse to the statue. Had he mistaken her for Moria? Thinking she'd slunk back to discard it in private, like a coward? Ashyn was ready to stride out and disabuse him of any such notion. Then Tova brushed her hand, and she looked down at him, his pale fur glowing in the darkness.

There was no way Gavril could have mistaken her for her sister. So why did he seem pleased that the curse was discarded?

She shook off the thought. Moria always said that there was no use trying to make sense of anything the young Kitsune did.

As Gavril crept away, Ashyn took one last look at the sanctuary. She'd gotten rid of her sister's curse. Was she too late?

She whispered her question to the spirits. They didn't answer.

At dawn, Ashyn met with the rest of the Seeking party—the governor, the healer, four guards, and six villagers who'd volunteered. The party gathered by the first tower, a wooden structure as tall as four men, yet still not cresting the forest's trees. The top was open to the elements, so as not to impede the vision of the warrior within as he guarded the sole break in the canyon wall.

Most people in the empire believed that the box canyon explained how the forest had survived the Age of Fire—that the lava had simply run around it. As Ashyn knew from her books, that wasn't true.

When the volcanos erupted, everyone fled or died under the flood of lava. After it cooled and hardened, they returned and found the Forest of the Dead, now ringed by stone, as if some invisible force had shielded it and the lava had flowed upward, forming walls around the wilderness.

Ashyn had always looked on those canyon walls and seen safety. They kept the forest inside. They kept the damned and their vengeful spirits inside. And now, for the first time in her life, *she* was going inside.

"Everyone comes back."

Ashyn turned to see Moria there, having snuck up unnoticed as the others milled about, preparing to go. Ashyn looked up at Gavril in the tower. Even from that distance, she could see his hawkish gaze fixed on her sister.

"I'm tempted to run into the forest, shrieking and cackling, just to see what he'd do." Moria waggled her foot over an imaginary line. Gavril scowled and turned away to look out over the forest.

"As I was saying, everyone comes back," Moria said. "Every Seeker. Every hound. Every volunteer. Every guard. They do their duty and they return, and all is well. You can't tell me that every Seeker has been perfect. They must make mistakes. It doesn't matter. I'm not even sure if the rituals matter at all. It is a kindness to the spirits of the damned, but would they truly rise up and attack? If it's never happened before, I'll wager it can't."

"Don't be blasphemous, Rya."

"If you don't fret, I'll not say scandalous things." Moria paused. "Which would be rather difficult, but since I'm quite certain you'll never stop fretting, I do believe I'm safe."

Ashyn threw her arms around her sister so abruptly that Moria let out a yip of surprise. Ashyn smiled and hugged her until that rigid steel melted and Moria embraced her, whispering, "You're ready, Ash. I know you are."

Ashyn hung there feeling her sister's arms around her, wishing she didn't have to leave. Then the governor cleared his throat, and she opened her eyes to see her father, back by the path's edge, waving that Ashyn needed to go and Moria needed to come back.

"Off with you, then," Moria said as they parted. "Tova? Watch out for her. Or I'll set Daigo on you."

Ashyn wasn't sure which beast looked more affronted. She managed a laugh, pushed her sister toward their father, and joined the party as it headed into the forest.

As a Seeker, Ashyn was as much a part of Edgewood as the village wall, and no more able to leave. Yet she read books from every part of the empire. She knew what a forest ought to be like. There ought to be burbling streams and twittering birds. Rabbit and deer tracks should crisscross every path. If you were lucky—and quiet—you might catch a glimpse of a wolf or a wildcat. The air ought to strum with the very energy of life.

There was none of that in the Forest of the Dead. No birds. No rabbits or deer. No wolves or wildcats. Even insects didn't buzz past. She'd heard it was like this, but now, experiencing it was something different altogether.

She gazed up at the trees. They were lush and rich, covered in vibrant green leaves and moss. Yet when she touched one, the bark was as cold and dead as the lava rock of the Wastes.

Some said there *was* life deep in the forest—twisted life, revealing itself only in a flash of fur or feather or scale. Even when Seeking parties spotted more, they could never quite say what they'd seen. Her sister swore those parties had seen not living things but monsters. Shadow stalkers and death worms and fiend dogs.

Today, Ashyn wouldn't care if her twin spent the whole Seeking tormenting her with stories of monsters. She just wanted her there, at her side. Without her, Ashyn felt smaller. Weaker.

Tova bumped her hand, as if to say, *I'm still here.*

"Yes, you are," Ashyn said, smiling as she patted his head.

She took a deep breath and continued into the forest.

FOUR

They were heading into the true forest now, beyond the second tower. As the trees closed in around them, Tova whined. Ashyn put her hand on his massive head. Normally that was enough to calm him, but his whine grew steadily louder until the governor glowered back at her.

"Silence your cur, girl," he said. "Or he'll bring the forsaken on us."

Ashyn bristled. Tova was a Hound of the Immortals, almost as much a creature of legend as those in her sister's tales. Raised in a secret location and given only to Seekers, a Hound of the Immortals lived as long as a human and was said to be the reincarnation of a great warrior from the First Age. Clearly *not* a cur.

Moria said the governor saw them as threats. He was a highborn warrior—tattoos covered him from neck to foot, leaving only a bare strip down his chest. The girls were merchant-born, which would place them in the lowest caste, except that caste laws did not apply to the Seeker and the Keeper. Moreover, Ashyn and Moria had a direct connection to the only force in Edgewood that superseded the governor—the spirits of the ancestors.

Still, Ashyn wasn't convinced of any ill will on the governor's behalf. Yes, he was brusque and sometimes rude. But he treated everyone that way. He was simply not a happy man, growing old and realizing he'd never be more than governor of this empire-forsaken outpost.

Ashyn was so wrapped up in her thoughts that she didn't notice when Tova blocked her path—not until she stumbled over him, landing on all fours on hard earth. Before she could rise, the hound grabbed the hem of her cloak and yanked. Her limbs shot out and she was suddenly facedown on the ground, being dragged back along the path.

She sputtered a laugh and twisted to see the governor bearing down on them. He was *not* laughing.

"This isn't the time for play," he said.

"I know. I'm sorry. The forest is making him uneasy."

Tova's snort denied the charge. Legend said that bond-beasts could speak to the Seekers and Keepers, but it wasn't true. It was simply that, having been with Tova almost since birth, Ashyn could read her Tova as well as she could read her twin sister.

When she turned back to the forest, Tova raced into her path and planted himself there again. He lowered his head and a noise bubbled up from his deep chest. It took a moment for Ashyn to realize what the noise was. Tova was growling. At *her*.

Something's wrong here.

She rubbed down the goose bumps on her arms. Tova whined in apology. When she moved forward, though, he stayed in her path. She stepped left. He lunged to block.

"Bring him to heel," the governor said.

A Hound of the Immortals did not obey commands like a common dog. Ashyn would never dream of giving him one. Instead, she knelt, coming to eye level with him.

"I need to go into the forest, Tova. No matter how horrible it feels, this is our job. Our duty. Yours and mine."

He laid down in the path.

"Tova, please."

Again he whined in apology. But he would not move.

"Faiban," the governor snapped. "Help the girl move her dog along."

The young guard looked at Tova and shook his head. "It's a Hound, sir. We aren't to interfere."

The governor strode forward. Tova stayed where he was, growling. The governor grasped Ashyn's elbow. He only seemed to be trying to get her attention, but he startled her and she yelped. Tova sprang and his teeth clamped on the governor's arm.

The governor reeled back. His sword arm swung up, as if in self-defense. The blade flashed. Tova let out a howl and dropped.

Ashyn saw the governor pull back his sword, his eyes wide with shock. Blood flecked from the blade and oozed from Tova's rear leg. Ashyn crouched beside him. The sword had cut to the bone. Someone pressed a scarf into her hand. She looked up to see the village healer.

"Thank you," Ashyn said.

Healer Mabill helped her bind Tova's leg. Tova tried to walk but lurched and whimpered until Ashyn made him stop, and he collapsed at her feet.

"I need to take him back," Ashyn said. "He'll be fine tomorrow. Hounds heal quickly." Even as she spoke the words, she knew what the others would say.

"We can't delay the Seeking, child," Healer Mabill whispered. "It always takes place on this day, when the veil between the worlds is thin. Someone will need to go back for help while we push on."

Ashyn wanted to argue. Moria would snarl and spit like her wildcat. That's why she was the Keeper, and Ashyn the Seeker. Like Tova, Ashyn's world was ruled by duty. That duty lay with the spirits waiting for peace.

"I'll run for help," Faiban said. "I'll tell them to come for the hound, then rejoin the search."

The governor shook his head. "We need all the guards." He turned to the bard, who'd joined the group to soothe their difficult task with music. "You go. Hurry to the village and then run back to us."

The bard—a portly man who likely hadn't run in twenty summers—stared at the governor.

"We can spare you," the governor said. "If you do not go, we must bind the hound and hope someone in the village hears its howling. I know the Seeker would not want that."

The bard nodded with some reluctance and took off back toward the village as fast as his thick legs would carry him.

Ashyn tried simply to leave Tova on the path. But as soon as she'd start walking away, he'd limp after her. So, for the first time in his life, he had to be bound. Ashyn knelt and explained it as she tied him, but he kept lunging against the rope until he collapsed in pain and exhaustion.

Even then, Ashyn looked back to see him trying to crawl after them, and it took Faiban and another guard to keep her moving forward. When he began to howl, the tears started.

"He'll be fine," Faiban whispered. "He's a good, strong dog. But we can't do this without the Seeker."

Duty over self. The spirits over Tova. She only hoped he understood.

It wasn't long before the forest was so thick that Faiban had to walk ahead of Ashyn and let the other guard follow her. Although they could still hear Tova's howling, the path was nearly gone. That's when one of the rear guards took out the spool of red ribbon and tied the end to a tree.

Without a ribbon, it would be nearly impossible to find the way out. Until now, Ashyn hadn't fully understood that. It always had seemed odd that so few of the damned ever managed to find their way back to the village. Now, surrounded by endless trees, she understood.

Most exiles never traveled far from the marked place where they were always left. That made Ashyn's job easier. It would take all day to reach that spot, though, even with guards at the fore, hacking through saplings and vines.

While they wouldn't want a road to lead exiles out, it made little sense to cut an entirely new path each spring. They all knew that. So, too, had the first governor of Edgewood. The tale of the path was one of Moria's favorites, and Ashyn could hear her voice telling it as she walked.

The governor had sent extra guards on a Seeking to prepare the path properly. They'd made it wider and laid out the discarded branches and vines to keep down new growth. That way, the path would last for many summers. But by the time the Seeking party headed out the next spring, the forest had swallowed the makeshift lane entirely.

The governor had not been a man accustomed to having his will thwarted, even by nature. So he'd asked his warlord to provide men to clear a path as wide as a road. The village guards watched from the tower as the passage was cut until the party could no longer be seen. The next day, one of the men came racing back along that path, gibbering nonsense.

Certain the man had swamp fever, the governor quarantined him and sent a search party after the others. But the man soon recovered and told his tale. They had been working on the road, and he'd been sent back to camp for water. When he'd returned, he'd looked ahead to see the men hacking through the forest. Then, without even a change in expression, they'd turned and begun hacking one another, as calmly and diligently as if they were still chopping trees and vines.

The man had run to his fellow workers, screaming for them to stop. They hadn't uttered a sound, just kept chopping at one another, stone-faced.

Eventually the search party returned to report the scene exactly as the survivor had described it. The governor declared it had been a mass outbreak of swamp fever. However, in light of the tragedy, there would be no more attempts to create a permanent road. And so the forest swallowed their work, leaving only the initial stretch.

Ashyn looked out ahead, thinking of that worker and what he'd witnessed. She started to shiver.

"Are you cold, my lady?" Faiban asked.

She managed a smile for him. "Unsettled."

"The forest does that," he said, nodding sagely, though she knew he'd never passed the second tower himself. "Shall I tell you a tale?"

"Can you make it a happy one?"

He smiled, his plain face lighting up. "Of course. I am not your sister. Let me tell you a story of a fair maiden of the North, who tamed a snow dragon. . . ."

At noon, the Seeking party ate, and sent the signal. A few had whispered uneasily when the governor fired the green flare, which meant all was well. The bard had not yet rejoined the party.

At least Tova was fine. Ashyn would know if he wasn't. The hound must have gotten back to Edgewood, and the bard would come panting and wheezing down the path at any moment.

When they finished the noon meal and the bard still hadn't arrived, she *did* start to worry. But what could happen? Yes, there were vengeful spirits. Yes, there was swamp fever. But it took days for spirits to drive a person mad. And one could only contract swamp fever by drinking contaminated water or being bitten by the infected. The Seeking party had brought its own water, and any infected exiles would have died over the winter. The bard would come soon enough, and if he didn't, then he must have returned with Tova and stayed in the village.

FIVE

By late afternoon, the Seeking party reached the marked site where exiles were abandoned . . . after their guards had led them there on a circuitous route so they'd think they were farther in. The guards left the exiles under the largest tree in the forest, but the Seeking party could not see it from the ground, and had to send a scout to scale trees as they walked.

While the village volunteers stayed to make temporary camp, the governor waved for Ashyn and the guards to follow him. It was time for the Seeker to begin her work.

With every step, Ashyn's heart beat harder. Tova ought to be here. No matter what the governor said, the Hound of the Immortals was supposed to help the Seeker find the bodies. Now she was on her first Seeking, without her hound, and if she failed . . .

I won't fail. I must not.

When the governor stopped walking, Ashyn continued past him. Twigs cracked behind her, and she turned to see Faiban following, sword in hand. She smiled at him, and he hurried to get in front of her, murmuring, "Just tell me where you want to go, my lady."

She pointed with another smile and he tripped over his feet to cut her a swath deeper into the forest. Ashyn followed slowly, letting her mind shift to the second world. Since entering the forest, she'd heard no whispers. The spirits of the ancestors stayed out. This was the domain of the damned.

She was here to help them find peace. It sounded like an act of mercy. It was not. The unsettled dead who roamed the forest were dark, demented forces bent on blind revenge against every living thing. They drove the exiles mad, and they made the forest uninhabitable for man and beast. By giving them peace, the Seeker kept their number at bay.

When Ashyn was far enough from the others, she asked Faiban to retreat a little. Once he'd backed down the path, she lowered herself to the ground. The earth was damp beneath her fingers, and she could feel the chill of it seep through her breeches. The air down here smelled fetid as the breeze blew off a nearby bog.

Ignore that. Concentrate.

Ashyn closed her eyes and reached out to the spirits. After a moment, she could feel them pulling at the edge of her consciousness. It wasn't like the gentle plucks of the ancestral spirits; these were harsh, like needle jabs.

She repeated the words Ellyn had taught her.

"I'm here to give you peace," she said. "You want peace."

No, they wanted revenge.

The empire's laws forbade execution, and this was supposed to be a kinder alternative. It wasn't. She stopped herself from imagining what happened to the exiles. *No. That isn't right.* She took a deep breath and instead let herself imagine it. Let herself feel their pain. Feel their rage.

As she opened herself up to the spirits, she kept repeating her promises of peace. She needed to persuade them that they stood no chance of avenging themselves on those who'd exiled them here, and the best revenge would be the happiness they'd find in joining their ancestors.

She could hear them now, grumbling and muttering. Their anger flared, like flames licking her face. Then their ghostly fingers reached into her mind, and she began to see images, as Ellyn had warned she would.

She saw a man crouched by a stream, scooping water. Another came up behind him and slammed a rock down on the crouching man's head. He fell face-first into the stream. The killer calmly took the dead man's pack and left him there as the stream ran red with blood.

"I see," she whispered. "I'm sorry. That shouldn't have happened to you. Now show me where you are, and I'll give you peace."

She followed their wordless whispers. Faiban saw that she was moving and tried to clear the way, but she waved him back. Finding the dead was *her* duty. Her promise to them.

As she pushed through the thick woods, vines snagged her hands and feet. Branches poked and prodded. Once or twice, she swore the branches and vines moved, as if the forest itself was rising to stop her.

Leave us our dead.

She continued on until she reached the stream she'd seen in her vision. She walked along its edge, staying away from the murky water. But with every step, the muddy shore sucked at her boots.

Leave us our dead.

"No," she whispered. "You have enough. This one is mine."

The wind whipped through the trees, as though in answer. She shivered and pulled her cloak tighter.

Finally, she saw the man, still lying where he had fallen, his body nothing but bone, covered in scraps of leather and cloth. His boots were gone. So was his belt and anything else that could be used.

She walked up beside the dead man. Then she took a bright yellow sash from her pack and tied it to a nearby tree. She put her fingers in her mouth and whistled as loud as she could. That would bring the volunteers to collect the body. They would take the exiles' corpses to the camp. When they were all collected, Ashyn would conduct the rituals to put the spirits to rest, and the bodies would be buried.

Ashyn knelt beside the dead man. "I'm sorry," she whispered. Then she rose and went to find the next.

It was Faiban who saw the man first. He shouted, "Who's that?" and Ashyn jumped, having been lost in the second world. Then she spotted the man—walking upright—and nearly jumped again, thinking, *Shadow stalker.*

The man was actually a living being, though he looked ready to pass into the second world—so gaunt his skin seemed stretched over bone. He shuffled, as if the act of fluid locomotion took more energy than he possessed. Dirt encrusted his clothing, and his brown skin looked gray with it.

"Stay back," Faiban said, flourishing his sword.

The filthy man fell to his knees, hands to the ground, stretching toward Ashyn.

"My lady," he said. "I have survived."

"And you will keep your distance," Faiban said, his voice dropping. "He may have the fever, my lady. I must call for the governor."

Ashyn nodded distractedly. She stared at the man, hearing his words again. *I have survived.* An exile who had lived through the winter? It happened, of course, but she'd not seen one in her lifetime. And no wonder, looking at him. She swore that by morning his spirit would have been leading her to his corpse.

"I don't have the fever," the man said. "My name is Cecil. I was exiled for the crime of—"

"Enough," Faiban said. "If you are not sick, you will be freed. For now, keep your distance, or your freedom"—the young guard brandished his sword again—"will be short-lived." He put his fingers in his mouth and whistled for the others.

"He's mad," Healer Mabill whispered as Ashyn watched the governor interrogate the survivor. A guard stood at either side of the man. One held a sword at his throat.

"He doesn't look mad," Ashyn said.

"The fever sometimes hides. But the governor can tell."

"How?"

Healer Mabill shrugged. "The eyes. The manner of speech. Little things."

"Are there often survivors?"

Another shrug. "Perhaps one every third Seeking. But they're always infected. They've been in the forest too long."

Something moved deep in the trees. When Ashyn turned, she thought she saw a last ray of sunshine reflecting off a blade. But all the guards were here, and when she squinted into the woods, she saw nothing.

"Ashyn?" Healer Mabill said.

"I thought I saw someone."

"It might be the two men we left with the first body. I hope so. If the fools got themselves lost, the governor will leave them here."

"They haven't returned yet?" Ashyn said.

Healer Mabill shook her head.

No matter how far Ashyn had wandered with Faiban, they'd been able to see the torches at camp, burning bright in the dim forest. If the villagers somehow could not see them, all they had to do was shout for help.

The bard hadn't returned either.

Ashyn shook off the thought. No one else seemed worried. She turned her attention back to the survivor, Cecil.

"He truly does not look mad," she said.

"Don't let that fool you, child. It's a good thing Faiban was there. If you'd been alone, you might have ended up like my grandmother."

"Your grandmother?"

"She was a healer in the Seeking party. She came across a

survivor who seemed well. Being a kindly woman, she knelt to give him fresh water . . . and he ripped out her throat with his teeth."

Ashyn's gaze swung back to the survivor.

"Yes, take a better look, child. I know he seems like a poor wretch, but don't trust your own eyes. You can't trust *anything* out here."

"What happens if the governor thinks—?"

A gasp cut her short. She turned to see the survivor kneeling there. His head seemed bowed. Then his body fell forward, and the others staggered back out of the way, and she realized that he had no head. That it was lying in the moss. That one of the guards was wiping his bloodied sword.

"He was infected," the governor announced.

"But . . ." Ashyn whispered, barely able to draw breath. *I'm seeing a man's head. Sliced from his body.*

My lady, I have survived.

"But . . ." she whispered again.

Healer Mabill put her arm around Ashyn's shoulders and turned her away. "Let's walk, child. That wasn't a sight for you. The governor ought to have given warning."

"How could they know so quickly?"

"Speed is mercy, Ashyn. And it must also be quickly because a simple bite is all it takes to pass on the fever."

"But what if he wasn't—?"

"Remember who these are, child. The worst criminals in the empire. If the governor suspects they are infected, he is not going to risk the life of a lawful citizen waiting to see if the fever manifests."

"Back in the woods with you, girl," the governor said as he walked over. "The sun is falling, and we'll lose what little light we have. You can set this wretch's spirit at ease with the others." He waved Faiban to her, then turned to two of the villagers. "You go with her as well. It'll soon be too dark to fumble in the forest, following her whistle."

Ashyn set out to continue the Seeking, and tried not to think about the dead man in the grove, still leaking his life-blood into the soil.

SIX

Of course, Ashyn did keep thinking about the dead man. *Cecil*, she told herself. *He had a name. Use it. Remember it.*

One moment, he was there, talking. And then he was lying beside his severed head. How could she *stop* thinking about that? How could anyone?

Yet as she looked into the forest, she wondered what sort of crimes he had committed. The empire said only the worst came here, and yet . . . She swallowed. And yet she knew better, didn't she? Her own parents had nearly ended up in this forest, for a crime no greater than trying to protect their infant daughters.

At first, their mother had told no one she'd borne twins. She'd kept the girls hidden and told the neighbors that she wished to take her newborn daughter to her own village. She'd sent a note to her husband, on a trade mission.

While most twin girls were simply ordinary children, there was the chance they could be divinely blessed. The Seeker and the Keeper. In order to learn that, though, they had to be tested. That test . . . it was a parent's worst nightmare. And failure to inform their governor of the birth meant both parents would be exiled to the Forest of the Dead.

Before their mother could leave, the midwife came to call. Their mother brought out one of the girls—and the other, never separated from her wombmate, began to wail. When the twins were discovered, their mother took her own life and left a note absolving her husband from all responsibility. Their father was allowed to live.

Ashyn was quite certain Cecil had no such tragic story behind his exile. As much as Ashyn tried to hold on to what she believed, that image wouldn't go away. Of the man who'd been there. And then was not.

It was nearly dark now. As Faiban held the lantern, Ashyn knelt beside the corpse of a man past his sixtieth summer. Too old to be exiled.

The body was better preserved than most of the others. He must have lived into the winter, frozen until spring, just beginning to rot now. He still looked human. White hair. Lined and weather-beaten face. His dark eyes stared up in shock.

This man had seen death coming, as Ashyn knew from the vision he'd sent. She knew how he'd felt teeth rip into his throat. How he'd tried to fight. How his spirit had hovered there, watching his killer tear into his flesh, devouring it. His spirit had still been watching when his killer had died, choking on a finger bone.

Ashyn looked over at the second body. It lay only steps from the first. A woman. The fever had taken her. Ashyn had seen that in her vision. Wild-haired and crazed, she'd ripped the man apart, mumbling about venison, sweet venison, thanking the spirits for their mercy, and Ashyn realized she hadn't seen a man at all—she'd thought she'd killed a deer.

"My lady?" Faiban whispered.

She looked up at him. *How am I supposed to handle this?* she wanted to ask.

Ellyn had warned her that death in the forest was not pleasant. Healer Mabill had said the same. Ashyn had paid little mind. Of course it wouldn't be pleasant. Death never was.

Moria had understood. That's why she'd insisted on coming along. *I don't need protection,* Ashyn had said. *I have my dagger.* But that wasn't the kind of protection Moria had meant. She'd understood what Ashyn might find, and she'd known her sister wasn't prepared to deal with it. Not alone.

"My lady?"

Ashyn took a deep breath and rose. "Can you take both?" she asked the two volunteers.

"We'll try," one said as he pulled on his thick gloves.

"Good. Stay at the camp afterward. We'll look about a little more before joining you."

The villagers began to wrap the first body. Ashyn motioned to Faiban, and they headed into the growing darkness.

So far, Ashyn had located eleven bodies. There had been sixteen exiled since last spring's Seeking, plus two that hadn't been found then. So she had seven left to find. There was also the possibility of locating the remains of long-dead exiles whose spirits haunted these woods. But if she found the seven, she would be done. She'd have one more day to do it. Then they headed home. It was too dangerous to be in the forest longer, and they had brought only enough supplies for two days.

She was calculating this as she moved away from the bodies.

"It's growing late, my lady," Faiban said.

"Just one more try," she said. "There's still light."

He squinted into the near-darkness. "The governor expects—"

A shriek cut him short. He wheeled, sword raised.

"Night birds," he said, but he kept the sword up, his gaze sliding from side to side.

There are no birds here.

Another shriek, this one clearly human, sounding as if it came from the direction they'd left.

Ashyn started running back. Faiban swung into the lead. When they neared the clearing where they'd left the bodies, Faiban lifted his hand for her to stay back. She waited a moment and then crept close enough to see him standing in the clearing, looking around with his sword lowered and his lantern raised.

The bodies were still there. The old man lay on the blanket the villagers used for transporting them. The woman's corpse seemed to have been lifted and dropped, crumpled now, one arm askew.

"Why did they leave them?" Ashyn asked.

"I don't . . ." Faiban adjusted his grip on the sword and pointed it at the woman's body. "I think they realized two

55

would be too heavy to drag back. They must have gone to get help."

"Why not take the old man and return for the woman?"

"It's too dark," he said. "They'd never find the way back if they weren't quick about it."

That wasn't true. They'd marked the site, and the hacked path wouldn't grow in by morning.

A twig cracked to the east. When they turned, the forest had gone silent. Eerily silent. Travelers always marveled at the silence of the Wastes, but if you'd lived out there long enough, you could hear the sounds of life—beetles and lizards and snakes and birds. In the forest, there was none of that. Even the wind had died, leaving a silence so complete she could hear Faiban's breathing.

"We need to head for camp, my lady."

Faiban started along the path. As Ashyn turned to follow, her hand brushed something wet and warm and she fell back with a yelp. She looked over to see a dark shape on a low tree limb. She lifted her lantern. It was a piece of meat, almost like a ball, but . . .

She realized what she was looking at and covered her mouth to keep from crying out again.

"It's a heart," she whispered.

"What?"

She pointed. "A *heart*."

Faiban raised his lantern for a better look, then let out an oath. It was indeed a heart, impaled on a branch.

"How could—?" He took a deep breath and stepped back. "It came from the woman's corpse." He looked at it, lying just below the tree. "Yes, that's why they dropped her. They were lifting her to the blanket and she was impaled by the branch. Her heart popped out."

Ashyn's dagger training had included lessons in anatomy, using a pig, and she was quite certain that a heart impaled on a branch would not "pop" out.

"Yes, that's what happened," Faiban continued before she could speak. "It popped out, and it startled them. That explains the cries we heard. The forest was already making them anxious. This was all it took for them to flee."

"But it's warm."

"What?"

Ashyn pointed at the organ. "I brushed the heart, and it was warm."

"You were mistaken, my lady."

"No, feel it." She steeled herself and reached out. "It's—"

Faiban snatched her hand. "Do not touch it again. It could be infected."

"But it *is* warm. And wet. If the heart came from that corpse, it wouldn't be—"

"Enough." He swallowed and softened his tone. "I'm sorry, my lady, but it's late and it's dark and we must return—"

Another twig cracked. Faiban went rigid. Then came the distinct sound of a murmuring voice, and some of the fear left his face.

"Who's there?" he said.

"Who's *there?*" the voice called back.

Faiban opened his mouth, but footsteps began heading away from them as the voice called, "Hello? Who's that?"

Faiban sighed. "Wait here. I'll be right back."

Ashyn looked at the corpses and then the impaled heart. "No, I'll—" She started after him, but tripped over a root. By the time she recovered, the forest had swallowed even the glow of his lantern.

"I'll wait here," she muttered.

She glanced at the heart, shuddered, and turned away, only to find herself looking at the old man's partly devoured corpse. That was no better.

She backed up to a fallen tree and settled on it, lantern at her feet. She stared out into—

Pain exploded in the back of her head. The forest spun into blackness.

SEVEN

Ashyn awoke feeling cold ground under her fingers. She leaped up, only to feel another jolt of cold— this one from a blade at her neck.

"Don't," a voice in front of her murmured.

"You'd better be talking to *her*, boy," said an older voice behind her—the man holding the blade.

Her eyes adjusted to the semidark and she saw the first speaker. He was her age, perhaps a little older. He looked like a typical Edgewood villager, with light brown skin, and dark hair curling over his ears and tumbling down his forehead. She'd never seen him in the village, though. She tried twisting to see the older man, but the blade tip pressing into her neck stopped her.

"I didn't expect to see you out here," the boy said.

"Who are you?" she said.

When she spoke, he frowned as if her voice sounded odd.

"You knocked me out—" she began.

"Payback." The boy grinned. "You aren't nearly as alert as the last time."

She stared at him. "The last time?"

"When you . . ." He looked over her shoulder, presumably at the man behind her. "Um, when I got the blade."

She blinked, clearing her head, throbbing and still fuzzy from the blow. "I don't know what you mean."

He only smiled. "Ah, so that's your story." He winked. "I'd stick to it. Something tells me you'd get in trouble for letting this go."

He pulled a dagger from his belt. The blade shimmered in the lantern light, but it wasn't the steel that caught her attention—it was the filigreed handle.

"That's . . . that's my sister's dagger." She glared up at the boy. "You stole the Keeper's blade? Do you have any idea what the penalty is for that?"

Behind her, the man laughed, and the steel finally moved from her neck. She twisted to see her other captor, and when she did, her breath seized in her chest. He was at least twice the boy's age and almost double his size, with thickly muscled arms and a barrel chest. Scars crisscrossed his face. It wasn't the scars that stopped her breath, though. It was the look of him—the tangled hair and beard, the dirt creasing those scars. He was bigger and healthier than poor Cecil, but seeing that filth, there was no doubt *what* he was. One of the exiles. One of the damned.

Ashyn turned back to the boy. He wasn't nearly as filthy, but on closer inspection, she saw dirt on his clothing and under his nails. There was a gauntness to his cheeks, though, as if he hadn't been quite so thin a few moons ago.

She remembered the noises she'd heard when the governor had been interrogating Cecil. She remembered seeing a blade flash, deep in the trees. These two had been watching. Seeing what happened to Cecil, they'd realized that they weren't getting out of this forest by prancing over to the governor and saying, "I survived."

So they'd taken a hostage. A valuable one.

"I'll not mention the dagger," she said quickly. "Moria told our father she lost it. That's all that needs to be said if you treat me kindly."

"Treat you kindly?" The man laughed again.

The boy didn't smile. He was watching her with that same look of confusion he'd had when she spoke earlier.

He lifted the dagger. "You say this is your sister's?"

"Yes."

"You lie. Why?"

"What's this?" The man lifted the blade to Ashyn's neck again.

"It's the same girl," the boy said. "I swear it. She's making her voice sound different, and she's acting different, but it's the girl I got the dagger from."

"No, I'm Ashyn. You met Moria. My twin."

"Twin?" He said the word as if it was foreign.

"Born of the same mother, at the same time. My womb-mate. We look exactly alike."

Now the man stepped around her, getting a better look at his captive. He slid the blade around, too, the tip digging into

61

her throat. Ashyn tried not to wince.

"Boy's right. You lie. Twins are curse-born. Not allowed to live. Unless . . ." He turned to the boy. "She said you stole someone's blade."

"The Keeper," Ashyn said. "He stole the Keeper's blade." She looked down at her bare dagger sheath. "And now you've stolen the Seeker's, too."

The man stared at Ashyn. Then he shook his head sharply. "You cannot be."

"No? A Seeker hunting for the spirits of the vengeful dead, to give them peace? Isn't that a Seeker's task?"

"The dog," the man said quickly. "You don't have a hound."

She plucked pale hairs from her breeches. "These are his. He's back at camp. He was injured on the way in." She turned to the boy. "If you met my sister, I'm sure you saw her wildcat, Daigo."

The boy nodded, still looking confused.

She turned to the man. "You've kidnapped a Seeker. That is not—"

Her gaze fell on the blade in his hand. She'd presumed it was her dagger, but now she could see the long, curved blade of a sword. It had a boar's head just above the hand guard, marking it as a blade of the Inoshishi clan.

"That's Faiban's sword!" she blurted, startling the man. When the blade fell from her throat, she leaped forward. "What have you done with Faiban?"

"Who?" the boy said.

"The guard you took that sword from. He—" She stopped. "It was you."

"What?"

"You killed the bard. And the volunteers who were recovering bodies. The heart." Her knees weakened at the memory. "By the spirits," she whispered.

"Heart? What are you talking—?"

"She's mad, Ronan," the older man said.

He stepped toward her, but the boy—Ronan—blocked. The man let out a low warning growl. Ronan moved closer to Ashyn. As she turned away, she spied her dagger in the moss. She aimed toward it while she backed away from Ronan.

"I don't know what heart you're talking about," he said. "But that guard with you is fine. We knocked him out and bound him."

"And the two villagers who just disappeared? Or the two by the stream earlier, collecting the first body? They never returned. First the bard, then—"

"Body by the stream? We passed that. It was still there, on a blanket. We wondered what had happened."

"You know exactly what happened," she said. "You killed the villagers and the guards. Picking them off so they couldn't fight—"

"The only people killing anyone are the ones who came with *you*. We saw what happened to Cecil." Ronan's voice took on a growl, not unlike the older man's.

"He wasn't infected, and they knew it," Ronan continued. "That's why we took you hostage. To make sure we get out of here alive. So, yes, we knocked out your guard, but he's right over there. We have no cause to kill the others."

Ashyn took another step toward her dagger.

63

"Don't argue with her, boy," the older man said. "We're wasting time."

"No. It'll be easier if we're not fighting her every step of the way. And if something *is* killing the villagers—"

"Nothing's killed them. They got spooked and—"

Ashyn dove for her dagger. Ronan was closer and lunged with her. She managed to get her fingers on the handle, but he slapped his hand down on the blade, pinning it there. She looked up. Their eyes met. Then he drew his hand across the blade and fell back with a yelp, cradling his fist. She snatched the dagger and scrambled up.

As Ronan shook his hand, she could see a small line of blood on his palm. Too tiny to excuse the cursing he was doing. He clenched his fist against his chest and, grimacing, turned to the other man.

"Sorry, Uncle. I—"

The older man cuffed him hard enough to make Ashyn wince. But Ronan shook it off and looked at Ashyn.

"You have a blade, but so do we." He waved Moria's dagger and gestured at Faiban's sword. "So don't bother running. Now, bring your lantern. We'll go find your guard, and you'll see he's fine."

EIGHT

Faiban was gone.

"Where is he?" Ashyn demanded.

"Not here, obviously," Ronan said as he prowled the clearing. "You said some of your party vanished. What—?"

His uncle cut in. "The guard escaped, boy. Vines must have been weak. Or someone freed him."

"Then where are the vines?"

His uncle waved at the forest. "Everywhere."

As they argued, Ashyn glanced at her hands, one holding the dagger, the other the lantern. She was armed and she had a light. She could fight or she could run.

Her sister would attack the moment she got the opportunity, whatever the odds. How many games of capture-my-lord had Ashyn lost after composing the perfect strategy, only to have her sister make some bold, mad move?

Now, watching the boy and his uncle argue, Ashyn wanted to make that bold move. They were distracted, having decided she wasn't a threat.

As she considered it, a drop fell from the treetops, hitting a leaf with a soft *plop*. The droplet shone red in the lantern light.

"Blood," she said.

The two stopped arguing.

Ronan walked over just as another drop fell from above. He touched the leaf.

"You're right," he murmured. "It's blood." He peered into the dark branches. "There must be something up there."

Ronan took her lantern. While he lifted it overhead, the light blinded them to everything beyond its glow. His uncle snatched the lantern and held it up. It reached a little higher, but that didn't help.

"There's nothing there," his uncle said.

Another drop fell, landing squarely on the lantern and dripping red down the glass.

"It's from a dead squirrel," he said. "Or a bird."

He handed the lantern back to Ashyn, who stared after him as he walked away.

"Is he mad?" she whispered to Ronan. "There are no birds here. No squirrels. What's going on?"

"I don't know," Ronan said. "We saw things last night, and again today. In the forest. Shadows. Noises. After the blood moon."

"Blood moon?"

"When the moon turns red. It signifies—"

"—a breach in the spirit world. I know." She remembered

last night's cloud-covered moon, the tinge of red in the sky. Then she shook her head. "If there was truly a blood moon, someone would have noticed. Moria and I have to perform a ritual."

"We saw a blood moon last night. Didn't we, Uncle?"

At first, his uncle pretended not to hear. When Ronan repeated the question, the older man shrugged.

"You said you saw it, too," Ronan pressed.

"Then perhaps I did. It's a nanny's tale. Doesn't signify."

"I think it—"

"Doesn't signify. We need to get the girl to her camp. Move out."

Ashyn looked around the camp. A clearing had been cut in the forest, and four small tents had been erected for the villagers. Sleeping blankets lay on the bare ground for the guards. In the middle, the campfire still smoldered; the smell of it had led them the final stretch. Packs lay against tents. But that was all she saw: objects. No people.

"Must've gone looking for the girl." Ronan's uncle stamped through the clearing. "She was late. They went searching."

"All of them?" Ronan said.

"She's the Seeker. Valuable."

"They'd leave someone to guard the camp," Ashyn said. "That's the rule."

"Doesn't signify."

Ronan turned on his uncle. "Stop saying that."

His uncle raised a hand to cuff him, but Ronan ducked out of the way and lifted Moria's dagger. His uncle looked at it, blinking, as if his nephew had rammed the blade into his back.

Ronan lowered the dagger. "It *does* signify. You know it does. Something happened to the villagers. *All* the villagers."

"What do you want to do about that?" Ronan's uncle stepped toward him. "If there's someone—or something—out there, then there's not a blasted thing we can do except be careful. Now grab supplies. We'll follow the ribbon back to the village."

Ronan's uncle rooted through packs, grabbing food while Ronan stood at the clearing edge.

Ashyn stepped closer and lowered her voice. "You said you've seen things in the forest. I ought to know what I'm watching for."

"Shadows, mostly. Sometimes a noise. It's always gone when you look."

Ashyn nodded and reached for her pack. That's when she heard a sound in the woods. A soft whisper like the wind. Except she felt no wind.

Then the ground vibrated beneath her feet.

When she glanced over, she saw Ronan looking up into the trees, frowning as the noise came again, closer now.

"Do you feel that?" Ashyn whispered.

"I heard—"

"No. *Feel.*"

She bent and put her fingers to the ground. When she lifted them, she could still sense the vibrations strumming through the air.

"What is she—?" Ronan's uncle began.

Ronan motioned for quiet. Ashyn closed her eyes, her fingers out as the air thrummed. The sound in the woods whistled around them, darting closer, then away.

It's watching us, she thought. *Whatever's out there is watching us. Stalking us. But something's keeping it back.*

She was keeping it back. She had no power to banish evil spirits, as Moria did, but her very presence was supposed to keep them at bay.

"What do you sense?" Ronan's voice startled her.

"I . . . don't know. The air. It's . . . vibrating. Something's here."

"Grab the packs. The lantern—" his uncle said.

A dark shape shot from the trees, so fast Ashyn had only time to yelp and fall back. It went straight for the lantern, swirling around it, and for a moment, she saw black smoke. And eyes. She was sure she saw eyes. Then the lantern went out, plunging them into darkness.

"Run!" Ronan's uncle bellowed.

Ashyn looked toward him. In the dim light of the smoldering campfire, she saw his sword flash as a shadow swirled past. The blade cut through the smoke, dispersing it for a moment.

Ronan stood there, staring. He lunged toward his uncle, but she caught his elbow, yanked him back, and gave him a shove toward the marked path.

"Run!" his uncle shouted again.

Smoke encircled the man. As Ashyn dragged Ronan, he tripped and staggered, looking back as if transfixed by the sight of the sword cutting through the smoke. That's all they could see—the occasional flash of a blade. Ronan turned, starting back for his uncle even as Ashyn yelled no, they had to go.

Then his uncle roared. A terrible roar of rage and pain. Blood sprayed from inside the smoke.

Ronan stopped. He gave a choked sob. Then he stumbled back to Ashyn, pushing her ahead of him as they fled.

MORIA

NINE

Moria sat cross-legged on her sleeping mat, listening to the chatter from the main room, each burst of laughter raking down her spine.

"I wish they'd go away," she muttered to Daigo.

He grumbled his agreement.

"Father doesn't want them here. He's only being polite. They ought to see that and leave."

If her mother were here, would she send them scattering with a snapped word, a snarl? Was that where Moria got it from?

Don't think of her. Not today.

The villagers had come to distract them with companionship, candied fruits, and honey wine. Moria took another gulp from her cup. The wine did seem to help. Less so the companionship.

In the next room, her father said something and the women laughed. It didn't take much to bring them. At one time, even the imperial court had sought to provide their newest Keeper and Seeker with a mother. They'd sent a pretty nursemaid of marriageable age with each supply train. Each had been summarily returned. Finally, the court had stopped trying. The village women had not.

Their father was kind and healthy and strong, a good provider who loved his daughters and helped his neighbors and made people smile. Moria often heard the women whisper about how handsome he was, though she couldn't see it herself. She wished they'd leave him alone. He clearly did not want to marry. He did have "friends," and Moria was old enough to know that when he went to visit one of the widows, he was not playing capture-my-lord. That didn't bother Moria. It was a perfectly sensible solution.

She scowled as the women tittered again. Then she noticed Daigo looking toward the window.

"You're right," she said. "We should be going."

She hopped up and knelt where Tova lay. He was sleeping now, thanks to a brew from Healer Mabill's husband. Still, it was a fitful sleep as the big hound twitched and moaned, worrying about Ashyn.

"I'll watch for the flare," Moria whispered to him. "I'll make sure she's all right."

She walked into the main room, where everyone sat around a blazing fire. As tempting as it was to stamp through with a grunted "Going out," she couldn't quite manage it—too much time spent with her father and sister. She murmured vaguely polite greetings as she passed. When she reached the front room, her father appeared, closing the door behind him.

"I'm going out," she said.

"To wait for the flare."

She shrugged and pulled on a boot.

"She's fine, Moria. The flare will come. It always does."

She'd caught *him* at the fence at midday, watching for the signal. He'd pretended otherwise, of course—just out for a stroll. That's the excuse she used now, which only made him sigh.

She leaned over and hugged him. It was a slightly awkward hug—she wasn't nearly as good at it as Ashyn—but he never seemed to notice, embracing her back and whispering, "Stay on the ground, all right? Please."

She nodded and slipped into the night with Daigo.

Moria did walk on the ground—all the way to the end of their street. But the road was crowded. She had to pass at least two people and a cart. So when she reached the village wall, she climbed onto it and Daigo hopped up beside her.

True, she had fallen before—once from the wall, once from the roof of the village hall. She'd broken an ankle the first time, a wrist the second. But she regretted neither because they had been lessons. Her father didn't see it that way, and he swore his heart would fail him when he saw her running atop the high wall.

She didn't run today. There was no need. The flare wouldn't come until the moon reached its zenith. So she strolled along the fence top, lifting a hand each time a villager called a greeting. *They* never worried—she was the Keeper, as sure-footed as her wildcat.

"Off to watch for the flare?" The chicken-keeper's wife peered from her window. "You needn't fret, child. The flare will come."

"I know."

Before Moria could move on, the woman came out, apron drawn up. "I heard you thrashed the miller's boy for tormenting the little ones."

Moria shrugged. "He needed a thrashing; I needed the exercise."

The woman smiled and held up a wineskin. "Chicken soup. To keep you warm while you wait." She plucked two eggs from her apron and passed them up. "I didn't forget you, Daigo."

The wildcat chuffed. Moria thanked her and continued on.

Moria paced alongside the first tower. By now even Daigo had grown weary and was lying down, paws tucked in, feigning boredom. Yet at every flicker, he looked to the sky. The flare was late. And no one seemed to notice except her.

"It's warmer up here," the guard called from the tower. "I have furs."

Moria bet he did. Levi was one of the youngest guards, just past his twentieth summer. After the Fire Festival, when she'd had a few too many sips of honey wine, he'd taken her behind the hall and offered to "make her a woman." He apparently made the same offer to Ashyn after the autumn dance, perhaps hoping to double his chances.

74

In theory, Moria was not opposed to his proposal. She understood his offer didn't come with heartfelt promises of undying love. Ashyn was the one who dreamed of romance. Moria's interest in men was far more practical.

Although the Keeper and the Seeker were not permitted to marry, they could take lovers. While Ashyn envisioned ardent romances, Moria didn't quite see the point. She did understand the *physical* allure, though. When she watched the guards strip off their tunics in the summer heat, she could feel her own body temperature rise. Sadly, given Levi's fumbling embraces, he didn't quite seem suited to the task. That hadn't stopped him from trying. Nor had it stopped Moria from allowing the occasional kiss or fondle, in hopes that, with practice, he might get better at it. So far, though, he'd shown no aptitude for learning.

"Moria," he called. "Come up. It's too cold down there."

"I have my cloak," she said, pulling it tighter.

"It's too dark."

She lifted her lantern in answer.

"It's too dangerous."

That one wasn't even worthy of reply.

"Quit your caterwauling, Levi!" yelled a voice behind her.

The newcomer was almost invisible under cover of night, dressed in a dark tunic, breeches, and boots, his skin no lighter. The only color came from his bare forearms, the ink-black tattoos spotted with green, like emerald-studded sleeves.

"No, Gavril," she said. "I am not trying to sneak into the forest after my sister."

"You'd better not, Keeper. I meant what I said."

Daigo growled as anger warmed Moria's wind-chilled face. "You told me once. That's enough."

Two days before the Seeking, Gavril had caught her on the other side of the first tower investigating a possible blind spot that would let her slip past the canyon wall. Gavril hadn't simply warned her against going into the forest. He'd reminded her about the last party of the damned to enter the forest. How a young man carried her sacred blade. A non-warrior. An exile.

Gavril had been guarding the exiles that night, and he'd seen her give her dagger to the boy. Then he'd held on to that knowledge . . . to use against her.

She'd asked him to let her go into the forest. No, not asked. Shame heated her cheeks as she remembered. She'd begged him. Moria would only follow the party—she wouldn't interfere. She would let Ashyn know she was there, so Ashyn could relax and do her job. That was all.

He'd refused. If she went, he'd tell the governor about the dagger, and her father would be punished. That's how it worked—they couldn't punish the Keeper, so her father took it in her stead. For such a crime, he might even be exiled.

How could Gavril make such a threat when his own father had been sent into the forest?

"You'd best hope your sister finds that boy's corpse," he said. "And that she has the sense to hide your blade."

She looked at him, stone-faced. "You can leave now, Kitsune. You've done your duty, checking on me."

"I'm here to make sure you stay within the walls and don't go flitting after butterflies."

She fought the urge to shoot her fist at him. She'd used that excuse once, when he caught her up to trouble. *I was only chasing butterflies.* Now he kept bringing it up, and she wasn't sure if he knew she'd been lying or if that was truly how he saw her—a child chasing butterflies.

"The flare isn't coming," she said. "I'm going to speak to the commander."

TEN

oria hadn't been the only one watching the sky. When they reached the barracks, her father was coming out, the commander at his side. They were assembling a search party.

By the time the party was ready, there was little doubt that something had gone wrong with the Seeking. The moon was halfway from zenith to the treetops now.

"I'll need a blade. I couldn't find mine this morning," Moria lied as she adjusted her boots. "If there isn't an extra dagger, I'll take a sword."

The commander shook his head. "The Keeper is not permitted a sword until she passes her eighteenth—"

"Then a dagger will do." She walked to Gavril. "I'll borrow yours. The spirits demand it."

He looked at her, as if surprised that she'd dare single him out when he knew she'd not misplaced her blade that morning.

What she truly meant, though, was: *If you're going to tell them what happened to mine, then do it.*

"I can't give you my dagger, Keeper, because I'm going into the forest." Gavril turned to one of the sleep-woken guards. "I'll take your place."

"Then I'll take *your* blade," Moria said to the same guard.

The sleepy guard handed it over. Moria looked at her father and held her breath until he gave a slow nod. She hugged him and whispered, "I'll bring her back." Then she hurried after the others.

Moria strode through the dark forest, holding a frayed length of red ribbon.

"The rest has to be here." She turned to see Levi, Oswald, and the other guard—Jonas—clustered around, watching her. "You have lanterns. Look for it."

"We have." Levi's voice took on a whine. "The ribbon is gone. We need to head back."

"The village is that way." Moria pointed into the darkness. "Anyone else who thinks saving the Seeker and the governor is too much work can go with him."

Gavril had not stopped searching for the ribbon. After a moment's pause, the other three joined him, while following the trail of cut and broken branches.

It should have been dawn by now. The others were probably telling themselves that the rays of weak light were the rising sun, but Moria knew it was the moon. Night was her time. The Keeper. Bond-mate of the cat. Protector of the night. Daughter of the moon.

Moria had been in the forest before. Not far. It was the Seeker who ventured in while the Keeper guarded the mouth. But those short trips to the second guard tower had told her what to expect. The cold, hollow weight of death.

They kept walking until Levi said, "Does anyone else hear that?"

Before Moria could reply, something darted through the trees. She glanced at Gavril. His grip tightened on his sword. Daigo's growl rose until it vibrated through the air.

A shadow bolted past, so close that Daigo spat, fur rising. Two of the lanterns flickered. The third sputtered out.

"Everyone back!" Moria said. "We just passed a clearing. Retreat to that. We can fight there."

Fight shadows? With what? Swords?

When Gavril opened his mouth, she tensed for argument, but he barked, "Get back! Move!"

Moria and Gavril herded the others to the clearing. There they clustered in a ring, backs together, blades out. Shadows wove and dodged through the forest around them.

Moria channeled her energy and commanded the spirits to be gone. The men shifted and muttered under their breath. When one of the shadows passed close, Levi lunged at it.

"No!" Moria shouted. "Stay in formation!"

Oswald yanked Levi back. Then, from deep inside the forest, came a voice.

"Moria!"

"Ashyn," she breathed. She started to take a step in that direction, then stopped herself and looked back at the others.

"You think it's a trick?" Levi whispered when she hesitated.

No, but I think if I leave this clearing, you'll all be dead.

She could hear someone crashing through the bushes. She looked down to see Daigo leaning toward the noise, ears up, tail swishing, poised to run.

"Go," she whispered.

The wildcat shot off noiselessly through the woods. Moria waited, her heart thumping. *Please, please, please.*

"Daigo!" Ashyn called.

The sound of running footsteps resumed, and Moria had to fight to stay where she was. When she saw her sister's pale hair, she relaxed. Then she saw her sister's eyes, wide with terror as she ran. There was a shape right behind her. A dark shadow—

No, *not* a shadow. A flesh-and-blood being with a blade in his hand. Chasing Ashyn.

The moment Daigo and Ashyn stepped into the clearing, Moria hit her sister's pursuer square-on, knocking him to the ground, pinning his arms as a blade flashed.

Her gaze flew to that blade first. It was her dagger.

"This feels familiar," said a voice below her.

She looked down to see the young exile she'd given her blade.

"Moria," he said, grinning, as if she'd knocked him down in a game of catch-me.

She wrested her dagger from his fingers. "Is this how you repay me, boy?" When he tried to get up, she pressed the tip to his throat. "You used my blade to attack my sister?"

"Moria, no," Ashyn said. "He's with me. We were fleeing whatever's out there."

"And you just happened upon him?"

Ashyn seemed as if she'd like to say yes, that's what happened, but she could not lie to her sister. "His uncle captured me. Briefly. No one harmed me, though, and his uncle is dead. Now let him up. Please."

Daigo padded over and stood guard as Moria rose. Her sister fell into her arms, head on her shoulder. Moria didn't ask if she was all right. Physically, she seemed to be. In other ways? No, she would not be all right. Moria held her sister until Ashyn sniffled and stepped back, dry-eyed and fighting for composure.

"Save the tears, Keeper," Gavril said, though she'd given no sign of crying herself. "We need to go."

As much as his words and tone grated, he was right. Moria turned to the exile. "My wildcat is watching you, boy. No sudden moves."

"My name is Ronan."

She snorted as he rose and brushed himself off.

"May I have that dagger?" he asked.

"I think you've had quite enough use of it," she said.

"Not yours. That one." He pointed at the one she'd been using.

"No. Now walk in front of me."

He sighed and started around her. Then he stumbled on a vine, his hand shooting out to brace himself against her. As she shoved him away, the lantern light glinted off a dagger in his hand. Her fingers shot to her belt, and she cursed.

"Give that back," she said.

"Don't, Rya," Ashyn said. "You have yours. Everyone ought

to be armed out here. He knows how to use it, so obviously he's a warrior. He ought to have a blade."

Ronan's expression confirmed that, as Gavril had guessed, the boy wasn't warrior caste. Yet even if she didn't think a blade would help against the shadows, no one should be defenseless.

"What about the others?" Levi said. "The governor and the rest of the Seeking party."

"They're gone," Ronan said. "Your governor. Your guards. Your villagers. They've vanished and all that's left is blood."

"Who attacked them?" Gavril asked.

"Those . . ." Ashyn waved at the shapes flitting through the woods. "Those things."

"Shadow stalkers," Moria whispered.

Ronan shook his head. "They're black smoke."

"Which is one form that shadow—" Moria began.

"It doesn't matter what they are," Ashyn cut in. "The Seeking party is gone."

"Can we stop talking and start walking?" Ronan looked out at the forest. "Running wouldn't be a bad idea either."

Moria hesitated, then nodded. "Form a line. Gavril at the end. Daigo and I will— No, you—" She pointed at Ronan. "Get in front, where you can't stab anyone in the back."

His face darkened. "I wouldn't—"

"I'm not taking that chance. Now move."

ELEVEN

The sun still hadn't risen. If anything, the forest had grown darker and the air colder. Moria's breath puffed as she walked.

Shadow stalkers.

Did she truly believe that's what she'd seen? She wasn't sure. As much as she loved chilling tales, they were simply delicious paths for the imagination to wander.

And yet . . .

She peered into the forest and gripped her dagger tighter. She was still scouring the woods when one of the lanterns flickered. The light wavered again . . . and went out.

Oswald called for the procession to halt while he relit it. Moria gazed out into the surrounding grayness. The swirling shadows were gone. They had been since they'd begun the return trek. While the forest beyond wasn't a pleasant sight— gnarled trees, hanging moss—it was empty.

"It won't ignite," Oswald said.

"Here," Jonas said.

As he tried to light Oswald's lantern, his own went out.

"That happened to us earlier," Ashyn whispered to Moria.

Moria nodded. "If you can relight them while you walk, then do so. Otherwise, keep moving and—"

Jonas pitched forward, the lantern sailing from his hands and crashing to the ground. Then the guard disappeared, flat on his stomach, arms flailing as something dragged him into the undergrowth.

Moria and Daigo charged after him.

Moria raced through the forest as she clawed vines aside.

I shouldn't have left Ashyn. I know it's my duty to protect everyone, and Ashyn can keep the spirits at bay. But I shouldn't have left her.

Her foot caught on a vine. She didn't have time to even break her fall before she went down hard, chin hitting the ground, blade flying from her hand. She leaped up, but the vine held her fast. Daigo fell on it, snarling, pulling it so hard she fell again, tears springing to her eyes.

Tears? Truly?

She pushed Daigo away and managed to sit up, swiping at her eyes and cursing.

When she heard a noise, she looked up to see Gavril hacking his way through the vines.

"Here!" she called.

As she struggled to cut herself free, Daigo hovered anxiously and Gavril had to shove him out of the way. The wildcat snarled but backed off.

Gavril dropped to his knees and slashed the vine so angrily she expected the blade to go right into her leg. When she was free, she leaped to her feet, looking in every direction, straining to listen.

The forest was silent. Jonas had been taken. She'd been his only hope and she'd lost him. Because she'd tripped. Over a vine.

She bent to Daigo. "Where is he?"

The wildcat looked back the way they'd come.

"*No.* Where is Jonas?"

Daigo butted her legs, again in Ashyn's direction. When Moria ignored him, he caught her breeches and tugged, growling.

"Your wildcat is telling you that your duty is back there, Keeper," Gavril said. "With the others. Protecting them. Not chasing after—"

She spun on him. "If you tell me I'm chasing butterflies, I swear I'll stake you to a tree and leave you for the shadow stalkers."

"Is that what you think they are? Shadow stalkers?"

His tone had softened, and she deflated. "I don't know."

"Your duty is to protect the group, not the individual. The group is back there with your sister. That's what your cat is trying to tell you. You can't help Jonas."

"I was too slow. I should have grabbed him before they dragged him off."

He exhaled, almost a sigh. "No one else could either."

"I'm supposed to be better than that. I need to be."

She found her blade and let Daigo lead her back the way they'd come. As they walked, Moria caught Ashyn's voice.

"Ignore it," Ashyn was saying. "Stay close to me and don't—"

"They're closing in! We need to run!" It was Levi. The fool.

"Not without my sister."

"Then *you* wait for your sister."

Running footfalls sounded. Levi had bolted.

Moria started to run. Gavril leaped in front of her and barreled along the path.

"No!" Ashyn's voice. "Oswald! Don't go after him!"

Moria heard Oswald's and Levi's pounding footsteps as they took off, deeper into the forest.

"By the spirits!" The snarled shout came from the boy, Ronan. "Are you both mad? Get back—!"

A scream cut him short. Moria had once heard a terrible scream once when a guard lost his arm during a drunken sword fight. This was beyond that. And it was Levi's voice.

Moria tried to push past Gavril as they ran. When he wouldn't move, she ducked, but his arm shot out and she ran into it with an *oomph.*

"It's too late," he said.

"It's not. You go to Ashyn and take care of her. I—"

"No."

She let out a hiss of frustration and dodged past him. He grabbed for her, but she was too fast. She ran, as Daigo cleared the way so she wouldn't trip again.

When she stumbled, Gavril grabbed her cloak, but she'd

already recovered. She'd simply tripped in surprise as the forest opened into a small clearing.

They didn't have a lantern. The only illumination was that sickly gray moonlight. But when Moria stepped into that clearing, she could see, and what she saw was blood.

It was everywhere. Small pools on the moss underfoot. Droplets coating the ferns and saplings. More dripping from leaves.

Moria stood in the middle and turned in a slow circle.

"It can't be," she whispered.

"It is."

She shook her head. "That's not possible. There's so . . ." Her voice hitched. "So much."

Daigo butted against Moria's legs, growling under his breath.

"Your cat is right," Gavril said. "You should get back to Ashyn. Levi and Oswald are—"

He stopped. She turned to see him staring down at a patch of brush. In it, she could see a boot, so polished the leather shone in the faint light.

"Do you like them?" Levi asked, pointing at his boots.

"They're very . . . shiny."

"The best your father could procure. My family sent me money, and they said I ought to spend it on my uniform. Father says it makes an impression, and I need to do that if I'm going to advance—"

She grabbed him by the tunic and pulled him into a kiss, mostly just to make him stop talking, but ever after that, he was convinced it was the boots, and wore them even in the summer's heat, always polished to a gleam.

Now she looked down at that boot, at his leg above it, at the blood—

Gavril pulled her back, his grip so tight it hurt. She tried to pull away.

"I need to make sure he's—"

"I will." He yanked her behind him as he checked. "He's dead."

Beside her, Daigo let out a strangled yowl. Moria dropped her hand to his head to comfort him.

"We need to go," Gavril said.

She nodded and returned to her sister.

Whatever was in the forest let the four of them leave. Even the path was open and clear, almost . . . helpful. That made Moria uneasy. What could she say, though? That some Keeper instinct told her she *shouldn't* leave? Daigo understood. He kept up a low, growling hum as they walked.

We should find out what's in here. That's my job. To fight, not to flee.

But flee she did. She had to. Get Ashyn to safety. Tell the village what had happened. Then go back in. Find survivors— or the bodies. That was the sensible order of things.

"The sun," Ashyn whispered. "At last."

Moria looked up to see shafts of sunlight piercing the canopy.

"I see the second watchtower," Ashyn said.

As Moria passed, Ronan caught the back of her cloak. She spun, but Gavril was faster, knocking the boy's hand off her.

Ronan glowered. "I was getting her attention, Kitsune."

"My name is Gavril. If you wish to speak to her, use words.

89

You do not touch the Keeper. Not if you'd like to keep your hands intact." He turned to Moria. "Call out a greeting. To warn the guards."

"So they can come and kill me?" Ronan said. "No one survives the forest. Do you know why? Because you don't allow—"

"*We* have nothing to do with it." Ashyn's voice was soft, but it silenced him. She turned to Moria. "There was another survivor. The governor said he was infected, and the guards killed him."

"He was *not* infected," Ronan said.

"Did he *seem* to be?" Moria pressed.

"He did not," Ashyn said after a moment.

Moria turned back to Ronan. "You can tell the rest of your story to the commander. I will make sure you are allowed to do so. If they claim you are infected, I will ensure that you are properly quarantined, not killed." She cleared her throat and called to the guards.

TWELVE

Ronan was being taken into the prison cells where they kept the damned when conditions weren't right for the exile journey. Clearly he wasn't pleased.

"Think of it as quarantine," Moria said as they climbed down the ladder to the subterranean cells.

Ronan shot a look at the dripping earthen ceiling, then down at the scattering rats.

"At least the vermin are running," she said. "We had some in the livestock sheds that weren't afraid of man or beast. They bit a farmer, and we realized they were infected with the fever. They're gone now, though. Just vanished. We've always wondered where they . . ." She looked at the fleeing rodents. "Oh."

Ronan jerked back as if bitten. The guards laughed.

"She's having fun with you, boy," one said.

"Of course I am," Moria said. "We'd hardly quarantine

you someplace with infected rats. Although that would be rather clever, in a diabolical way. . . ."

Being sent down here was partially his own fault anyway. When the commander had asked about his crimes, he'd said nothing. So they had no idea how dangerous he was.

The guards reached the cells. They waved Ronan into the first one.

Two of the guards had left; only the third remained, taking up his post at a chair in the hall. The cell had a heavy wooden door, reinforced with metal, only two window squares cut in it—a low one for passing food and drink, and a higher one to see the occupant.

When Moria and Daigo began to withdraw, Ronan moved to the window and said, "What do you think the search party will report back?"

I'm not sure they will report back. She was trying not to think of that. She was already furious with the commander for sending a party of warriors to search for survivors. At the very least, she should go with them, using her power to protect the men. But the commander was convinced what they faced was not shadow stalkers, but exiles who'd survived.

"You're worried about the Kitsune boy going back in there," Ronan said when she didn't answer.

"Gavril isn't going . . ." She caught his expression and said slowly, "What do you mean?"

"The commander sent him. He needed someone who'd been in there."

Moria's hand grasped the damp wood of the door to steady herself. "When did he say that?"

"While you were talking to your father, after everything was decided."

Moria turned and ran before he could say another word.

There was nothing Moria could do. Gavril was gone, and she couldn't leave Ashyn and their father behind to go after him. All she could do was help her sister perform the rituals of spiritual protection. Moria didn't know what good they would do against shadow stalkers, but they had to try.

Moria also appealed to the spirits for guidance. This was an emergency. Surely the rules did not apply. But there was no answer. She'd barely felt the spirits since returning to the village. Were they angry with the girls for not stopping what had happened in the forest?

After dinner, their father had to attend a village meeting. Once he'd left, the girls took food to the prisoner. Ashyn also brought a box of stones to play black-and-white. They could not enter Ronan's cell—it merely latched on their side, but the guards would not permit them to open the door. They had to pass the food through the hatch, then set out the game board in the hall, with Ronan watching through his window and calling his moves.

When Ronan had said he wasn't very good at the game, Moria had insisted Ashyn play against him. Her sister was a master strategist and would win the game quickly, so they could leave. But the boy had lied. Shocking, truly, for a criminal.

It was not, then, a short game. Worse, as it stretched on, he decided he wanted to talk—to Moria. She tried to dissuade him by sharpening her blade. When he didn't take the hint, she used a piece of rock to draw on the door of the farthest cell, and began target practice.

"You're good," he said when her dagger struck the center of the target.

"She's just playing," Ashyn said. "She can hit at twice that distance."

"I've thrown a few daggers myself," Ronan said.

"Were there people in front of them?" Moria asked as Daigo brought back her blade.

"Not that I recall." A soft creak sounded as he leaned against his door. "Even if there were, I doubt I would have hit them. It's clearly a skill that requires practice. Perhaps if you were to teach me how to improve my technique . . ."

"Huh." She threw the dagger again. "That's a fine idea. I'll let you out so I can . . . Wait. Ooh, you almost got me."

"I meant when I'm released, of course."

She glanced back. He was looking out the window, grinning.

"You're in a fine mood now," she said.

He shrugged. "I realized you were right. I ought to be grateful that I'm safe. You defended me, and I truly appreciate—"

She cut him short with a burst of laughter.

"Moria!" Ashyn said.

"He's playing us." Moria sauntered to his cell. "We brought him food and a game, so he sees opportunity. Perhaps even a couple of foolish girls he can charm with his city manners. I brought you stew because I consider you my responsibility. Ashyn brought you a game because she's kind. We'd do the same if you were old and toothless."

94

Daigo growled. Moria thought he was just echoing her annoyance, but he kept up a low, humming growl until Tova whined and rose.

She glanced at the guard. He was in his chair, trying to stay awake. No sounds came from above. Considering everything that had happened, though, it seemed unwise to ignore any sign of trouble, however slight.

"Daigo's telling me we've been down here much too long," she said. "Our father will be back from his meeting and beginning to worry. Ashyn can finish the game. She almost has you beat. I'll check in with our father and return."

Ashyn hesitated, but Moria insisted. If she had concerns about what might be happening above, her sister was safer down here.

"I'll be back," Moria said. "Don't leave without me."

As she passed the guard, she murmured, "Don't *let* her leave without me."

He nodded, and Moria and Daigo headed for the ladder. When she climbed from the cells, she found the barracks still and silent. That gave her pause. Then she remembered that half the garrison was in the search party, the other half on duty. No one would be in here until the searchers came home.

As she stepped into the hall, she heard footsteps.

"It's Moria," she called.

A door slapped shut. Then silence. Someone must have snuck back for a few stolen moments of rest. She glanced into a barrack room and saw dark red droplets sprayed across the sheets. Even as she hurried over, though, she could see it wasn't blood. Too dark and too thin. She bent to sniff the drops. Berry wine. A guard sneaking back for a drink, then spilling it when he heard her coming.

Daigo was already at the door, growling again. She pushed it open. The wildcat walked out, his nose lifted, ears twitching.

She peered around. Darkness had fallen. Complete darkness. It was much later than she'd thought. The day had been so chaotic that they hadn't eaten dinner until night was falling, and it was well past their usual bedtime now.

"Where are the lights?" she murmured.

She looked up into a gray-black sky, devoid of stars or moon.

Dark and quiet. No, not quiet. Silent. The village was absolutely, utterly silent. When she sucked in breath, the whistle of it startled Daigo.

"Something's wrong," she murmured.

He chuffed in agreement. Moria glanced back at the barracks. If there was trouble, Ashyn should stay right where she was. And just because the village was dark didn't mean anything was wrong. People would have gone to bed, and with half the garrison away, the village was bound to be quiet. She wouldn't panic Ashyn for nothing.

As she walked along the barracks, the carpenter's dog, Blackie, howled. A normal sound of night. She exhaled. Then the howl stopped. Midnote. The hair on her neck rose. Daigo growled.

"We're going home. We'll speak to Father and make sure everything is all right, then we'll return for Ashyn."

Daigo grunted, approving the plan. As they continued on, Moria slowed, rolling her footsteps so she walked as silently as her wildcat. When something moved to the left, she wheeled but saw nothing. Still she stood there, watching the spot until she was certain it'd been a trick of the eye.

A few more steps. Then a low groan sounded to her right. Moria looked over at the village square. She saw only an empty patch of rocky ground with a few precious beds of dirt, fresh turned, seeds planted for summer flowers.

Another groan. She followed the noise to the village hall behind the square. A board had come loose under the eaves and seemed to be groaning in the wind.

As she turned back, a shadow darted across the square. This time, there was no mistaking what she was seeing—a dark shadow twisting and writhing as it skittered across the square.

Shadow stalker.

Her fingers tightened on her blade.

"Begone," she whispered. "By the power of the ancestors, I command you to leave. You trespass on blessed ground."

The shadow—smoke, fog, whatever it was—just kept twisting lazily, making its way across the square.

"Spirits," she whispered. "This is your home. Protect it."

The spirits didn't answer. When she went still and focused, she could find no trace of them.

It felt like the forest. Empty and dead. Dark and silent.

Moria broke into a run. The shadow made no move to chase her, just swirled off toward the forest. She raced across the rocky ground until her boots slid on something slick. She tried to catch herself, but she'd been going too fast and fell, hands out, dagger clinking against the rock. When she smelled and felt the warm dampness, she knew this was not berry wine.

Daigo circled, trying to get to her while staying clear of the blood, but it was everywhere. Like in the grove. The rocks were slick and wet with it. More pooled in every divot and dip. Finally, Daigo charged through, grabbed her cloak in his teeth, and pulled.

Moria got to her feet and looked around. Blood. So much blood. No other sign of anyone, anything.

She moved forward, sure-footed now, slower. A noise sounded to her right. She glanced over to see something dripping from the village hall roof. A body lay on it, one arm draped over the edge, blood dripping to the stones below.

"We have to get home," Moria whispered.

Daigo leaped forward, and Moria tore after him.

Where were the guards? The remaining garrison was supposed to be on alert, watching the forest. Where were they?

Gone. Dead. Whatever was in the forest had come, and the warriors' blades had been powerless to stop it.

The guards didn't even have time to sound the alarm.

She tried to understand that. There was a bell right at each guard tower. Within arm's reach. If they'd rung, though, she would have heard them even down in the cells.

As she raced past a house, she heard a moan. She looked over. The door was open. Through it, she could see a body on the floor. Someone was inside, alive, injured. Still, she didn't stop. She'd come back.

There was more blood ahead. Splashed over the road. Speckling the houses. She refused to process the implications, and let Daigo lead her through the village until, finally, she was home.

THIRTEEN

The front door was closed. She wanted that to be a good sign, but she knew her father might not have made it back at all. Perhaps he'd been at the meeting when . . .

She opened the door. Inside, the house was as still and silent as the village. Daigo edged past her, growling softly as if to say, *I'll handle this.* He bounded straight to the back of the house. To her father's bedroom.

Did he smell him there? *Please, please,* she begged the spirits. *Let Daigo smell him there.*

She raced through after the wildcat. In the near-dark, she could see a figure on her father's sleeping mat. Pale hair glistened on the pillow. She exhaled as relief shuddered through her.

Daigo let out a strange noise, like a strangled yowl.

"He's fine," she whispered.

She went to the chest and picked up the lantern, then fumbled in the dark with the flint and firestone. The lantern sputtered before casting its pale glow over the room.

Daigo yowled again.

"Stop that," Moria hissed. "We'll check on the others next. I want to speak to Father."

As she walked to the mat, her fingers trembled. Despite what she'd said to Daigo, his yowl worried her, and she half expected to see blood-soaked blankets pulled up over her father's corpse. But he lay there under clean sheets, his eyes closed.

"Father?" she whispered. "It's Moria. Something's happened."

He didn't move. She rubbed the back of her neck, almost nicking herself with her dagger. She sheathed it, reached out, and shook his shoulder. His head lolled.

"No," she whispered. "No."

Her hand flew to his cheek. It was cool.

Because it's a cold night. That's all.

She shook him harder, calling him. Then she touched his chest, his neck, searching for some sign of life, finding none.

When Daigo jumped up on the mat, she snarled at him. She would have shoved him if he hadn't leaped off first. When he gave a long, plaintive yowl of pain and grief, she spun on him, hand raised. Then she realized what she was doing, let out a strangled cry, and dropped to her knees.

Daigo rubbed against her, his sandpaper tongue licking her cheek. She put her arms around him and collapsed against his side. A sob caught in her chest. Her eyes burned and stung, but tears wouldn't flow. She just hung there over Daigo, gasping.

He's . . . Father is . . .

Her mind wouldn't even finish the thought. Like the sob and the tears, it clogged up inside her, stabbing through her chest and her head.

I didn't take care of him. Didn't take care of any of them. Levi, Gavril, Father . . .

Father . . .

She doubled over, convulsed in pain.

Then she heard a soft moan. From the sleeping mat. She scrambled up and leaned over to touch her father's shoulder. He just lay there, head lolling, eyes closed.

"Father?"

He made a sound. Like breath exhaled through clenched teeth. Now the tears came, springing to Moria's eyes as her hands flew to his chest.

Still no sign of life.

No, you're mistaken. He is alive. You heard him.

As if in answer, his chest moved. She climbed onto the thick padded mat, leaning down and hugging him as tight as she could, tears flowing free now.

"It's me," she said. "It's me, Fath—"

A noise sounded deep in his chest. A strange, unnatural gurgling, and she released him, falling back, apologies spilling out.

A hiss. Then a noise, unlike anything she'd ever heard before, part moan and part snarl. She caught a flash of claws swiping at her, and pain ripped through her arm.

Claws.

Not Daigo. Not a paw. A misshapen hand with talons as long as the fingers themselves.

She grabbed her father's shoulders to haul him to safety. His eyes were open. Those blue eyes she knew so well, the whites shot with blood. Then she saw his face.

With a cry, she released him and fell back. She hit the floor. Daigo leaped onto her, facing off with whatever . . .

Father. It's . . .

No, it wasn't. Couldn't be.

Then the cry came, a moaning, snarling screech that set every hair on end. The claws swiped at Daigo. The wildcat pounced and caught the thing by the wrist. The other hand slashed Daigo's back. With a howl, Moria yanked out her dagger and leaped up.

Then she saw it. Truly saw it.

It was her father. She tried to tell herself it wasn't—couldn't be—but it was. Her father's blue eyes. Her father's fair hair. But not her father's face. The face of something from a nightmare, gray skin stretched over bone, jutting chin and nose and cheekbones. No lips, just a slash of a mouth. And teeth. Fangs. So big his mouth couldn't close. He let out another of those terrible cries, his jaw stretching open until all she could see were the fangs. They shot toward Daigo.

Moria broke from her shock and lunged at him. Her blade was raised, but she couldn't swing it down, her arm refusing to move, her mind telling her this was her father, no matter what she was seeing. All she could do was swipe at him with her free hand. It was a feeble blow, but enough to surprise him. He turned on her. Daigo dropped between them, fur rising as he spat.

Moria made a noise. She wasn't even truly sure what it was, but Daigo understood. He backed up to her side.

The thing on the sleeping mat—*not my father, not my father*—pushed its gnarled legs from beneath the covers. Its gaze stayed fixed on her, head bobbing, nostrils flaring. Drinking in her scent. Thinking. Considering. Planning.

"Father?" she said. Her voice came out so low she barely heard it. She tried again. "Father? You're in there. I know you are."

He's not. You can see that. Look in his eyes and you'll see it. He's gone. This is a . . .

No, no, it's not.

It is.

Shadow stalker.

This was the missing piece. The one part that had made her think it wasn't shadow stalkers in the forest. Because they hadn't seen this. The risen dead. The manifested form.

Her father was gone. This . . . thing was a twisted spirit inhabiting his body. He was . . .

Her breath caught, and it stayed caught, and she stood there, unable to draw air, chest burning, vision blurring.

Dead. My father is dead. This thing killed him.

She let out a howl, flew at the creature, slashing at it with her blade. She had no compunctions now. This wasn't her father—it was a killer, a parasite. It had murdered her father, and now it was using his body, and she would not let that happen.

Her blade slashed its leathery skin. The bloodless cut only made the thing shriek in rage. Talons sliced through her cloak. Daigo leaped on its back, fangs sinking into its neck. It tried to claw at the wildcat. When it couldn't reach, it swung at Moria instead.

This time, the talons caught her side, under her cloak. Pain ripped through her. Daigo snarled, shaking the thing, his teeth biting in until she heard a snap. Its neck broke, head falling to one side, but still it kept scratching at her.

She stabbed it in the heart. It grabbed at her and caught her by the cloak. She tried to wrest free, but its claws were embedded. She yanked the clasp and broke away, leaving the thing fighting with her cloak. Then she spun, dagger raised, as Daigo leaped to her side. They dove at the thing together and . . .

A gust of wind knocked them back. As Moria fell, she saw the creature, in shadow form now—that twisting, writhing smoke rising from her father's body. It rose, then shot past her, and it was gone.

Moria walked to her father's body. No, not her father. Not truly. It still looked like that twisted thing. A mockery of her father, lying on the floor, clutching her cloak, blood everywhere.

She ought to lift him back onto the padded mat. She ought to kiss his cheek and weep. But this wasn't her father. She could no longer see it as her father. Ashyn would. Ashyn—

Ashyn.

Moria spun and ran out the door.

Moria stood in the junction between two lanes. She looked toward the barracks, then the forest. The choice ought to be simple. Everyone was gone. Dead. Massacred by the shadow stalkers. She needed to get to Ashyn right away.

And yet, when she listened, she heard voices in the forest. Not the screeches of the shadow stalkers, but actual voices. Was it possible some guards had lived? The shadow stalkers could have slipped past them in shadow form.

She looked at Daigo, but the wildcat was doing the same thing, his attention swinging from those voices to the barracks and back.

Ashyn. It had to be Ashyn. Her sister was all she had left now that—

Moria's knees buckled as pain washed over her. Daigo slid beneath her outstretched hands.

"I have you, too. I know." But it wasn't the same, because he was almost an extension of herself.

As she turned toward the barracks, she caught a flash of red-gold hair, streaming behind a figure darting between buildings.

"Ashyn?"

Of course it was. They were the only fair-haired Northerners in Edgewood now that their father . . .

Moria stifled the thought and raced after her sister. When she reached the end of the road, she caught sight of yellowish fur running around the next corner.

She whistled, but Tova didn't come back. She ran after them and again she got to the road's end just in time to see a flash—of both figures this time, her sister and her hound, running like the spirits of the damned were chasing them. Running toward the forest.

"Ashyn! Tova!"

They didn't stop. Behind her, she heard that now-familiar snarling, moaning shriek, and she turned to see a twisted figure in an open doorway. A shadow stalker in human form. It lunged at her. She wheeled and tore off after Ashyn.

FOURTEEN

"She's not coming back, is she?" Ronan said as he moved his playing piece. "She doesn't want anything to do with me."

Because you used her blade to kidnap me, Ashyn wanted to say. She'd forgiven him. Moria would not until he proved himself worthy.

"Is she worried about the Kitsune boy?" he continued. "I mean, yes, of course she is. But that's what she's thinking about. Him."

Ashyn stifled a sigh and pretended to miss the question.

After a moment, he said, "They're courting, aren't they?"

Ashyn choked on a laugh. "No, definitely not."

"But there is someone, isn't there? A girl like that . . ."

A girl like that.

Ashyn loved her sister. And yet . . . It was not that Ashyn particularly *wanted* any of the young men who trailed after her sister. It was simply . . . well, simply that she wouldn't mind a boy's attention, if only to prove that she wasn't completely invisible next to Moria.

It had started two springs ago, when a young bard came with the supply wagons. Ashyn still remembered him, with his dark eyes and long braids and quick smile, his pretty words and lilting voice. He'd seen Ashyn first and stopped midsong to stare. Then he'd begun to sing about her. He'd followed her from the village square, still singing as she blushed. That had felt . . . new. Wonderful and warm.

She'd walked all the way home with the bard singing her praises. Then Moria came swinging out, blade in hand, and told him to quit his caterwauling or she'd use him for target practice. He'd stopped singing about Ashyn then. And started singing about Moria.

Her sister had made good on her promise, whipping her dagger and pinning his cloak to the wall. And that was it. One throw of that blade, and he'd completely forgotten Ashyn. He'd followed Moria for the rest of his visit, composing ballads about the flaxen-haired warrior girl of Edgewood. By the time he left, his cape was so full of holes it looked like a fishing net. Yet he wore it as proudly as if Moria had covered it in kisses instead.

Then there was Levi. Again, Ashyn hadn't been truly interested; he was a braggart and a bit of a fool. After he kissed her behind the village hall, she'd hurried home to tell Moria. She'd expected they'd laugh over it. Moria had indeed laughed . . . because he'd done the same to her. The next day he'd awkwardly apologized to Ashyn, and she realized he had drunkenly mistaken her for her sister.

Now Moria had caught Ronan's attention.

"It's getting late," Ashyn said as she stood. "We'll pick up the game tomorrow."

"No, stay. My apologies. I was just . . ." He leaned to peer through the window and down the hall.

I know, she thought. *And I don't blame you.*

"You can't go anyway," he said. "Moria said to wait until she gets back."

"Yes, she does that. But I'll be fine. I have Tova."

The hound rose at his name. Ignoring Ronan's protests, Ashyn put the game aside and said her farewells. Before she could take a step down the hall, though, the guard appeared in the flickering lantern light.

"I cannot permit you to leave without your sister," he said. "I'm sorry."

Theoretically, Ashyn's authority matched her sister's. But in martial matters, particularly with the guards, it was Moria's voice that rang the loudest.

"She seems to have forgotten me," Ashyn said.

Anyone who truly knew Moria would realize that was impossible. Most likely, Moria had been waylaid and simply delayed. But Ashyn was tired and not particularly eager to wait.

The guard looked up at the hatch, as if considering. Then he shook his head. "I'm sorry, but she was very clear."

"Can you get someone to find her, then?"

He hesitated.

"The barracks are right above us," she said. "Someone must be near."

He nodded. She followed him down the hall. He climbed the ladder, opened the hatch, and called out. When no one answered, he called again, louder. Then a third shout, one that made her ears ring.

Something's wrong.

The thought seemed to leap from nowhere, but it didn't, of course. It had been there since they'd run from the forest. *Whatever happened out there isn't over.* She'd felt that in her gut, in the cold silence of the spirit-empty village. When they'd met with the commander, she'd wanted to tell him to run. *Everyone run.*

That was foolish, of course. Run from what? Run to where?

Ashyn had watched her sister marching around, giving orders, and making plans, and thought, for perhaps the thousandth time since their birth, *Why can't I be more like her?* Instead, she'd sat quietly to the side, fear strumming through her, ashamed of her cowardice, consumed by guilt.

Moria insisted that what happened in the forest was not Ashyn's fault. It was not possible that a mistake in the Seeking could have caused that. While Ashyn knew she hadn't raised those spirits, she could not help but feel she had still failed. That Ellyn would have been able to stop the spirits.

Now, as the guard came back down the ladder, that tamped-down fear and guilt ignited. She stifled the first licks of true panic and said calmly, "With the search party gone, they must all be on duty. Would you go out and check, please? I'll wait here at the hatch."

He nodded and climbed out.

"I'm going to step outside," he said.

She fought a prickle of impatience as his boots scuffed across the floor. A distant door creaked.

"Hello?" he called.

No answer.

"What's going on?" Ronan asked from his cell.

She silenced him with a wave and kept listening as the guard's voice got farther and farther away. Tova whined. She waved him to silence, too.

"You there!" the guard's distant voice called. "Yes, you! Come back."

Boots pounded rock as the guard gave chase. When he spoke again, his voice was louder, as if he'd come closer to the barracks.

"I'm not going to report you for breaking curfew. The Seeker asked me to—" The guard stopped short. "Who are you? What's wrong with—?" A wordless shout of surprise. "Stay back. You have swamp fever. I don't want to hurt you, but I can't let you touch—"

A curse. Then an inhuman shriek. The click of a blade against stone or steel. Ashyn gripped the hatch opening, ready to race out fighting, as Moria would.

But you aren't Moria. You aren't the Keeper.

Moria . . . Oh, goddess. Moria. Their father. The villagers.

She scrambled down the ladder so fast she missed the last rung and tumbled, her ankle twisting, pain shooting through her leg.

"Ashyn!" Ronan called.

Tova pushed under her arm, supporting her as she rose. She limped to Ronan.

"Something's happened," she said. "I need to find Moria."

As she turned away, his arm shot through the window and grabbed her cloak.

"Wait!" he said.

She tried to yank free, but his grip was too tight.

"Don't leave me here," he said as she struggled. "Whatever's out there, I can help. I can use a blade. My family were warriors once. I'm trained."

She fumbled to undo the clasp on her cloak and escape.

"Ashyn, please. I'm locked in a cage. If anything comes, I don't stand a chance."

She hesitated, then threw open his cell latch and raced down the hall.

FIFTEEN

Ashyn and Ronan crept along the barrack wall. Ashyn could barely see—the village lights were out and the moonless sky offered little help. But Ronan seemed as surefooted as Daigo and equally adept at seeing in the dark. He padded along as quiet as a thief.

She tried to emulate him but kept stepping on pebbles and stumbling in the dark. Tova's nails clicked along the stone.

As they moved, Ashyn squinted into the night and listened, but there was nothing to see, nothing to hear.

She focused on Ronan's back, tapping him with directions as they moved. They passed the barracks and two more buildings before he stopped. Something lay on the road ahead. Ashyn squinted, then swallowed.

It was the guard. Facedown on the road.

Ronan knelt a few paces away, as if he could check the guard's condition from there. Ashyn started forward. Tova caught her cloak in his teeth, and when he did, she saw why

Ronan hadn't gotten closer. The guard lay in a pool of blood. His face was turned toward them, his eyes wide and empty. His throat . . .

He was dead. There was no doubt of that.

It couldn't have been those smoke spirits. You don't try to converse with smoke.

As they circled the blood, she saw footprints leading away from it. Bloody bare footprints.

Ronan followed her gaze. "Someone must have stolen from the body." He said it casually, as if looting a corpse was a natural occurrence. "His blades are still there, though. Both of them."

Ronan skirted the puddle and picked up the sword. He hefted it. Then he leaned over the guard again and eyed the dagger. It lay under the guard, covered in blood. He took a careful step into the pool and snatched it up. Then he wiped it clean on the guard's back as Ashyn stared, horrified.

Ronan slid the dagger into his belt, and pointed the sword. "Onward."

When they neared her house, Ashyn darted ahead. Ronan caught up at the door, and shot his hand out to stop her from opening it.

"I'll go first," he said, lifting the sword.

"You've seen Moria throw her dagger. If anyone but me opens that door . . ."

Ashyn expected he'd square his shoulders and say he'd take that risk. Apparently, she'd been in a garrisoned town too long, with warriors who'd never let her step first into danger. Ronan waved for her to go ahead.

As she reached for the door handle, Tova whined. She looked down to see his nose twitching.

"It's all right," she murmured. "If they aren't here, we'll find them."

She opened the door. It was dark inside. Tova pushed past hard enough to nearly topple her.

"Father?" she whispered. The closing door stole the gray glow of the overcast night, plunging them into black. "Moria?"

She felt her way to the table and lit a lantern. It hissed, then flared. Ronan cast an anxious look at the window.

"Cover it," he whispered.

She frowned at him.

"Hide the light."

She turned the lantern down as much as she could. Tova was at her father's bedroom door, his nose at the base, whining louder. She walked over and grasped the handle. Tova spun, hitting her hard and knocking her back. Then he planted all four feet and growled. Warning her back, as he'd done in the forest.

She stared at the door, her heart thumping.

Ronan came up behind her and snatched the lantern. He opened the bedroom door just enough to squeeze through. Ashyn tried to follow, but Tova knocked her down, then planted himself over her, growling.

She stared up at him in shock. He ducked his head, whining, as if in apology, but when she tried to rise, he pinned her cloak with one massive paw.

Ronan stepped from the bedroom. The door clicked shut behind him. He held the lantern low, and she couldn't see his face.

"We have to leave," he said.

"What?" She scrambled up, knocking Tova aside. "Where's my father? Moria? Are they gone?"

A pause. Then, "Yes."

"All right. We'll find them. I have a few ideas where—"

He caught her cloak as she turned to the door. "We need to get out of the village."

She stared at him. "What?"

"We have to leave. *Now*."

"We . . . we can't. We're in the middle of the Wastes. I'm not permitted to leave. I'm the Seeker. And . . . and Moria, my father." She took a deep breath. "You can go. I'll tell no one you've escaped. You'll need to grab supplies." She waved at the kitchen. "Take what you want. Tova and I will find my—"

He stepped in front of her as she turned. "There's no one to find, Ashyn."

"What?"

He laid his hand on her shoulder. "When I said they're gone, I meant—"

She didn't let him finish. She pushed past him, yanked open the bedroom door, ran inside, and tripped over something. She fell face-first, her chin striking the floor, teeth catching her tongue with a sharp blast of pain. She flipped around to see what she'd tripped over.

An arm. There was an arm stretched from a dark heap on the floor. She struggled for breath as she scrambled over, still on her hands and feet, getting closer.

When she saw the misshapen fingers and thick, claw-like nails, tears sprang to her eyes. She looked at that ugly, monstrous hand and thought she'd never seen anything more beautiful in her life.

"It's not them," she whispered. "It—it's a—"

"Shadow stalker," Ronan finished as he reached down for her hand. "I didn't want you to have to see it, but now you have, so come on and we'll get out of here."

"But you said my father and Moria—"

"They're gone. Not here. We should go. This one is dead, but the light might attract others."

He took her shoulders and steered her past. "Don't look at it. You've seen enough."

If it was a shadow stalker, she should see it, know exactly what she faced. She looked. Ronan pulled the lantern away quickly. Not quickly enough. Not before she got a look at the face. It was horribly disfigured, but not disfigured enough to disguise the features. Features she knew well. A nose that had been rendered permanently crooked when a warrior tried to negotiate a better price with his fists. A mouth always quirking at the corners, ready to burst into laughter.

"F-Father?" She dropped to her knees and yanked at the thing's tunic, ripping it open to see the scar on his chest bone. Then she screamed, a wail of horror and grief wrenched from deep inside her.

Ronan grabbed her, his hand slapping over her mouth to silence her. She fought him, kicking and twisting. Tried to bite him, too. But he held his hand there, tight, whispering, "I know, I know. But you can't scream. You can't. Shhh."

She caught sight of Tova now. The hound was lying beside her father's body, his muzzle on her father's arm, not interfering with Ronan, just waiting, eyes pleading with her to stop screaming.

She did. And the moment Ronan released his grip, she shoved him aside and looked around. There, next to her father's body, was what seemed like another figure. As she fell on it, she felt the soft fur underside of a cloak identical to her own.

Moria's cloak.

She would have screamed again, if she could. But when she opened her mouth, the pain doubled her over and stole her voice.

It can't be. If she was hurt, I would have known.

The cloak was sticky with blood. She snatched it up and—

There was nothing beneath the cloak. She scrambled over on all fours, looking about wildly. Then she raced to the sleeping mat. She looked all around it before turning to Ronan.

"She's not here."

He paused, then said carefully, "There's blood on the cloak, Ashyn. Quite a lot. It was clutched in his hand. He must have attacked her."

Her heart stopped as she imagined the scene, their father going after Moria. Attacking her. Trying to kill her. Moria going through that, alone.

No, not alone.

"Daigo wouldn't leave her," she said as she walked back toward the door.

"He might have gone with her, if she turned into one of those."

It took a moment for his words to process. He thought Moria had become a shadow stalker. That's why he hadn't questioned the lack of a body.

No. There was an equally logical explanation. Her sister had been injured but escaped, shucking her cloak and running.

Running where?

There was no question where she'd go.

"She's headed back for me, and we've missed her."

She started for the door. Tova finally rose from his place beside their father.

"Ashyn . . ." Ronan said. "There's a *lot* of blood."

"Then take supplies and go. I'm finding my sister."

SIXTEEN

Everyone's dead.

 The thought looped through Ashyn's mind as she walked down the dark and empty lanes.

 As they'd made their way to the barracks, she'd insisted on checking each house they passed. She listened for survivors while Ronan looked.

"One man in his third decade and a younger woman," Ronan reported as he walked from a bedroom of the last house.

"You don't need to spare me. I asked for a thorough accounting, and you haven't given one yet."

"What?"

She marched to the second bedroom. He didn't make a move to stop her. She threw open the door to see two small sleeping mats. Unmade but empty.

She turned to him. "Where are the children?"

He looked perplexed for a moment, then he nodded. "I haven't seen any. That's odd . . . Unless . . . Are children more susceptible? More likely to become shadow stalkers? Or perhaps they've been taken—"

Now he paused, obviously realizing what he was suggesting. Shadow stalkers were predators. If they took the children, it would be no different from a bear carrying off what it could easily drag back to its den for . . .

"We'll figure that out later," he said. "We're almost at the barracks."

Moria wasn't in the barracks. There was no sign she'd been there in their absence—the door was ajar, as they'd left it.

"She's rescued the children," Ashyn said as they stood in the empty barracks hall. "They escaped and ran to her. They trust her. She'd take them someplace safe."

"Without fetching you?"

"She must have had a reason. I know a few places she might hide with them."

Ronan stepped into her path. "That doesn't make sense, Ashyn. If she was looking for a safe place, why not bring the children to us, in the cells?"

She skirted past him. "There's no escape route down there. If the shadow stalkers came, we'd be trapped. And she might lead the stalkers there. She'd take the children someplace else and return for me when she could."

Ashyn kept going until she reached the wall of the livestock enclosure. From within, she heard silence. No cackle of chickens or grunt of pigs.

She ran along the fence, past the village's main gate. On reflex, she looked for the guard on duty. Of course there wasn't one. She could see his empty post. No trace of him. Not even blood. Just . . .

Empty.

She ran around the livestock enclosure. The heavy gate was closed. Ronan helped her push it open, all the while muttering, "She's not here, Ashyn. You know she's not."

Ashyn squeezed through. Behind her, Tova whined. She turned to see him trying to push his massive head through the narrow opening. Ronan heaved the gate a little more.

When Ashyn tried to run again, Ronan caught her. He motioned for silence as they looked and listened. Nothing. Then, as they were about to move, a whisper came from the barn. Ashyn smiled at Ronan, but his expression stayed grim, and his grip on her cloak only tightened.

"Slowly," he whispered. "Get behind me and stay there."

She didn't appreciate being given orders, but he *did* have the sword.

They crept along the fence until they reached the barn. The sounds from within became clearer: first rustles and whispers, then finally voices.

"I heard something," a young girl murmured. Someone shushed her quickly, but Ashyn smiled. She'd been right. The children were here. Moria was here.

Ronan nudged her into the lead, whispering, "They ought to see you first. I'll wait here until you can explain."

Before she could argue, he slid off into the night. Ashyn opened the barn door. An excited cry. A scrabble of shoes. Tova tensed. A small figure shot out from the darkness as someone whispered to stop, to come back. The figure launched herself at Ashyn. It was Wenda, the girl who'd walked with Ashyn to the temple.

Ashyn hugged her and motioned her back farther into the barn, where a woman leaned out. Someone closed the door behind Ashyn, making her jump. A lantern swung up. A guard stepped forward. Ashyn didn't recognize him—he looked like many of the others, around thirty summers, brown-skinned, dark braids, no tattoos. A warrior, but not from the highest families.

Ashyn *did* recognize the woman. One of the farmer's wives. Beatrix. She was older—her children had grown and left Edgewood for something better, as many did.

"Where's my sister?" Ashyn asked. "Did she leave to look for me?"

Silence. Another figure shuffled from the shadows. An elderly man, past his days of working. Quintin was his name, as he reminded her. The guard was Gregor.

"My sister," Ashyn repeated after the introductions. "She was here, was she not?"

"No, miss," Beatrix said. "I haven't seen her."

"But the children. They're here?"

Ashyn already knew the answer. If there were children here, they would not be so silent.

"Where are the children?" she asked. "They aren't in their homes. There are no . . . signs they were hurt." She started for the door. "They must be with Moria. I need to find—"

"You won't, miss." The old man moved into her path. "The little ones were taken."

"With Moria," Wenda piped up. "That's what I said,

and no one believed me, but if you're here and she isn't, then I was right."

Beatrix cut in. "The child thought she saw the Keeper, but we did not. The children were taken, miss. Rounded up and taken. There was naught anyone could do. There was naught anyone could do about any of it. It happened so fast."

"*What* happened? What did you see?"

"Nothing. My husband was here, in the barns, so I was alone. I woke when Wenda came to my door. I went out and . . . and the village was . . ." She swallowed. "Silent. Empty."

Ashyn turned to the child as Tova padded to the door to stand watch.

"I heard a noise," Wenda said. "I woke and went to see my parents, but they were gone. Everyone was gone. It was so dark and quiet. I ran next door. Beatrix was there. We went to her other neighbor and . . ."

"They were dead," Beatrix whispered. "All of them. I didn't let the child see, of course. I took her, and I was running to the barracks, and that's when we heard old Quintin, coming out his door, gibbering about monsters."

"Then I found them," the guard said. "I was patrolling the road outside the village. I came back and found the gate unguarded. I ran into the village, but whatever had happened was over. I met these three. Then we heard the children."

"They were being taken down the road," Wenda said. "They hardly made any noise. Like they were walking in their sleep."

"They were alone?" Ashyn said.

"No, there were men," Wenda said. She paused. "I think they were men."

Ashyn glanced at Beatrix. "Did you see . . . other things in the village? Not men."

"Shadow stalkers," Quintin said. "I saw one. I live with my son and his wife, and I heard her cry out. I walked from my bedroom and . . ." He inhaled sharply. "My son. He was . . . one of those things. He'd killed her and he was eating—"

Beatrix cleared her throat loudly. He mumbled an apology and withdrew, his gaze dropping.

"It all happened so quickly," he said. "We'd barely gone to bed and then . . ."

"They weren't shadow stalkers with the children," Beatrix said. "They were riders on horseback. Wenda meant that we couldn't tell for certain they were men, but I'm sure no woman would steal the children."

She turned to Wenda. "You saw Moria?"

The girl nodded. "She was hiding behind the rocks. I think she was trying to save the children. But the men captured her and took her along."

Ashyn turned to the others. "You saw none of that?"

"There *was* a commotion," Beatrix said. "I heard it. But my eyes are not good. Nor his." She gestured at Quintin.

"And yours?" Ashyn turned to the guard, Gregor.

"I had gone back to the barracks, looking for more survivors."

"*After* you saw riders stealing our children?"

Gregor squared his shoulders. "There were many riders. Only a fool would chase them."

Only a coward would not try, Ashyn thought. Her sister was not a coward. Moria wouldn't be foolhardy enough to engage the entire party, but she would have tried to follow them. That's how she'd been spotted and taken.

"Which way did they go?" she asked.

"Following the road across the Wastes," Beatrix said.

"Then so will we. I'll need you to gather what you can while I conduct a quick ritual for the dead. They deserve more than that, but it's all the time we can afford."

As they left the barn, Ashyn remembered she needed to warn them about Ronan. When Gregor saw that she'd brought the exile, armed, he would—

Before she could explain, she saw paper pinned to the barn wall. A note? Ashyn hurried over and pulled it down.

The characters were written in a neat, precise hand, almost as good as her own. Not Ronan's, then. Most of the empire was illiterate, leaving books and writing for the priests and scholars. She read the note. Blunt and simple, despite the perfect calligraphy.

Follow the road. Take care.

It was signed *Ronan.* She read it twice, to be sure, as if there were any mistaking his intent. There was not. She'd freed him. He'd repaid her by helping her find other survivors. Then he'd left.

Ashyn crumpled the note. As she did, though, it made her think of something she should do before they left the village.

SEVENTEEN

Moria ran into the forest chasing her sister. She could still make out Ashyn's and Tova's forms, but they were getting fainter.

Blast it, how could they be pulling away? Ashyn wasn't nearly as sure-footed as Moria, and Tova was as graceful as a newborn calf.

Daigo glanced back, his yellow eyes glowing. Then he let out an unearthly wildcat scream.

"Well, they ought to hear that," Moria murmured.

"Stay there," she called, as loudly as she dared. "I'm coming."

Her sister seemed to stop. With every few steps, Moria would lose sight of Ashyn, and her heart would pound, but then she'd catch sight of her again.

Then, without warning, she plowed into something. Her hands hit soft, sleek fur.

"Daigo? Blast it! Don't do that."

He didn't chirp an apology. Moria moved up beside him as he stared at the pale forms of Ashyn and Tova.

"Ashyn?" Moria called softly.

No reply.

A little louder. "Ashyn?"

The figures just stood there.

What if that's not truly Ashyn? What if she's become . . . ?

Her mind refused to finish the question.

But why else would Ashyn run *into* the forest? In all the time Moria had been chasing her, she hadn't paused to wonder that.

Moria crept forward, gaze fixed on her sister's face. She could see the shape of it but not the features. Not enough to know that it was still her sister's true face.

"Tova?"

Daigo let out a soft snarl, as if also calling the hound.

Even if her sister couldn't hear them, Tova should, but he stood straight and unflinching at Ashyn's side.

Daigo and Moria skirted a dead tree. As they rounded the roots, the figures of Ashyn and Tova disappeared behind it. Then Moria stepped out the other side and—

They were gone.

Moria shoved through the dense woods, squinting into the darkness until Daigo stopped and nearly tripped her again. He glanced over his shoulder, not at her, but behind them. Then he backtracked. Moria hurried after him. This time when he stopped, she halted in time. He looked up at her and made a noise deep in his throat.

They must have passed the spot.

"Where are they?" she said, her voice echoing.

Daigo grunted and started into the forest. When Moria tried to follow, he growled softly, telling her to stay. As soon as she stopped moving, the silence prickled at the back of her neck, as if someone was creeping up behind her. She spun and saw nothing.

She strode to the nearest tree, rammed her dagger into her belt, and grabbed the bottom limb. She swung up from branch to branch, not slowing until there weren't any more that would hold her weight. Then she stretched out and peered down to see . . .

Nothing. She saw nothing.

Moria's boots squelched in mud. She could not see well in the ink-gray night, but she could make out obstacles before she smacked into and stumbled over them. There were no trees in this barren strip. There were rocks, though, and the gurgle of water, so faint it was as if a tiny underground spring was trying to hide beneath the stagnant, fetid water.

She walked to a large rock. There was a smaller one attached, like a baby on his mother's back.

"We've been here before," she said, casting an accusing glare at Daigo. "I thought you were leading us out."

He harrumphed, as if to say, *What do you expect? I'm not a tracking hound.*

They needed to find out what had happened to Ashyn. Moria had no idea what she'd seen—a hallucination, a phantasm? It didn't matter. What was important was that it had not been Ashyn. She had to get back to the village to find her sister . . . but they were lost. Hopelessly lost.

Moria collapsed on the rock. Daigo put his front paws on her knee, the dampness of them seeping through her breeches. He rose until he was looking her in the eye, his whiskers tickling her cheeks.

They said the Wildcats of the Immortals possessed the spirits of ancient warriors. Moria had never given that much thought. She tried not to, if she was being honest. It seemed demeaning to be trapped in the body of a beast and bonded to a mortal girl.

"It doesn't matter, does it?" she whispered. "Even if you were a great warrior, there's nothing here for either of us to fight."

He sighed, his breath warming her face. Then he backed off her and looked around. As he did, his gaze stopped on something behind her. She turned to see a dagger stuck in the shallow streambed, point up.

Moria took off her boots, unwrapped her feet, and stuffed the silk into her boots. Then she rolled up her breeches and stepped into the stream. It was like breaking through winter's ice on the cistern, and she bit back a gasp as she walked.

The blade was buried up to the collar. When she crouched and reached into the water, her fingers brushed something oddly soft. Then she felt the ridges of the carved handle. She yanked. The dagger flew up . . . with a hand wrapped around the haft.

Moria fell, splashing as she landed on her backside, icy water shocking her again. A man's hand still clutched the dagger's haft. An arm was attached to the hand. A dark-skinned arm covered in tattoos. When she made out eyes in the inking, her breath jammed in her chest. She was sure of what she was looking at—the nine-tailed fox. Then the design became clear. A dog's head. The Inugami clan.

It was Orbec. A substandard warrior from an elite family. He'd been sent to Edgewood to toughen up, and he'd stayed there by choice. It was easier in Edgewood, where his tattoos meant something and where no one expected him to be more than average. He was above average in one skill, though. Throwing a dagger. He'd been the one who'd taught Moria.

Moria stood there, looking at his body. *I let the commander send him into these woods. I got them all killed—everyone in my village. I was supposed to protect them, and I was underground, entertaining a convict, throwing daggers at a wall.*

That was the fact she'd been struggling to ignore. The shadow stalkers had come and the Keeper had not been there to stop them. That her village—her father—died because she wasn't there.

I failed.

Her legs gave way and she fell to the ground, shaking and gasping for breath. Daigo yowled and rubbed against her, but she barely noticed. She tried to cry, to let it out, but no sound would come. She just kept shaking.

When something struck her hand, she looked to see Orbec's dagger on the ground. It was an ancestral blade, with the stylized dogs engraved along the handle. Daigo bent and nudged it toward her.

"I don't want—"

He snarled, cutting her off, then glowered at her, telling her to stop being dramatic. Gather her wits. Take action.

He nudged the blade toward her again.

Fight. That's what he meant. *You missed your chance before. Take it now. Fight back any way you can.*

She took the blade. Then she put on her wraps and boots.

EIGHTEEN

"The sun." Moria laughed. "The *sun*, Daigo. It came."

He grunted and walked behind her, prodding as if to say, *Yes, yes, that's all very nice, but it won't come down here and rescue you, will it?*

That's when she noticed blood on the rocks.

The blood drops continued over the rocks. Then the drops became smears, as if the wounded had fallen. Furrows were raked in the soft ground by the creek. Someone dragging himself along. Near death but trying to escape it.

When she rounded a boulder, she saw a man's body downstream, his arms over his head. A sword lay beside one hand. His hair was in braids. His forearms were covered with tattoos.

There were only two guards with braids and ink. She'd already found one and left him in the stream.

"Gavril," she whispered.

Daigo leaped over and started nudging Gavril's corpse. She wanted to call to him. Tell him to leave the body. She'd had enough—enough of looking upon the spirit-fled corpses of people she'd known, people she had cared for. There is a point when the mind says, *I've had enough. Strike me again and I'll shatter.*

She took a deep breath and walked slowly toward him. Daigo nosed away his braids to show a gash in the back of Gavril's head. Moria took a moment's pause to brace herself, then she bent and laid her hand on his inked forearm, and—

She yanked her hand away and bit back a yelp.

Gavril's skin was warm. She pressed her hands to his upper arm, as if there might be some sorcery in the tattoos that warmed the skin. When her ice-cold fingers touched warm flesh, her hands flew to his neck. She felt a pulse. A strong one.

Daigo huffed as if to say, *I told you.*

"Yes, yes," she muttered.

While she'd been trained in battle healing, Ashyn was much better at it. Moria had spent most of her lessons grumbling that, in a battle, she was supposed to be on the front lines with the warriors, not tending to the wounded. That was woman's work, and it seemed that's why she was being trained in it—a sign that they might give her a blade, but they didn't truly expect her to be much use on the battlefield. So to prove them wrong, she'd thrown her focus into fighting instead of healing. A foolish choice, motivated by pride.

She dragged Gavril by his tunic to drier ground. Daigo tried to help, but when she snapped at him for ripping Gavril's breeches, he stomped off, offended. As she reached the edge of the mud, it seemed to make one last effort to keep Gavril, and she had to dig her boots in, hands wrapped in his tunic, and heave—

Gavril's arm shot out and struck her, the blow so unexpected she let go as he scrambled to his feet, his hand going to his empty sword scabbard. Only as he pulled out his dagger instead did he look up.

He stopped. He squinted. He brushed a hand over his face, smearing mud.

"Moria?"

Beside her, Daigo chuffed and rolled his eyes. *Who else would bother?* he seemed to say.

Gavril staggered up, dagger raised. "You're a spirit."

"A spirit couldn't have hauled your arse out of the mud."

"You followed us." He cursed under his breath. "You child. Your duty is with the village, Keeper—"

"The village is—"

"Your duty, one you're far too immature and foolish to—"

All the fear and the grief poured out again, and she whipped her daggers. They whistled through the air, one on either side of Gavril, no more than a hand's span away, embedding themselves in trees.

"The village is gone," she said, her voice thick with rage and tears. "Everyone's dead."

"Dead?"

"Dead and turned into shadow stalkers. Now go on back to the village. Do your duty. Bury them. And then tell me what a foolish child I am."

His mouth worked. Nothing came out. Then he shook his

head sharply and retrieved his fallen sword. As he pushed it into its sheath, he said, "You've drunk infected water. You're fevered—"

"I'm fine," she snarled. "The villagers are dead. My father is dead. Turned into—" She stopped fast. "He's gone now. I freed him."

"Freed him . . ." Gavril stared, as if he couldn't quite comprehend her meaning. "If you thought you saw shadow stalkers, then I'm sure that was terrible, but your father cannot be dead."

His eyes held something she'd never seen there before. Genuine concern. His voice was soft, and she wished he would shout. She wished he would snap and yell and call her a foolish child again, because somehow this was worse. Giving her hope where there was none.

"My father is dead. I watched him rise as a shadow stalker and try to kill me. I expelled the thing from his body, and then I ran through my village and there was nothing but bodies and blood, and that was no nightmare."

"Then why would you come back into the forest?"

"Because my sister—" She inhaled. "I thought I saw Ashyn and Tova, and we followed, but they were some sort of phantasm."

She steeled herself for Gavril's arguments, but he only stood there, an odd look on his face.

"A phantasm of your sister led you into the forest?"

"Yes, and don't tell me I was sleep-blind. I never went to bed. Ashyn and I were at the cells with the captive, Ronan. I went up and . . . I found what had happened to the village. To my father. I saw Ashyn and Tova running. Daigo saw them,

135

too." She looked at Gavril. "He's a Wildcat of the Immortals. My bond-beast. If I were fevered or running from a nightmare, he'd know it. Now I need to get back to the village. I need to help Ashyn. I left her in the cells, and I can only pray she's still there, safe, and—"

"Moria . . ."

Her back tightened as he used her name. *Call me Keeper,* she thought. *Shout at me. Curse me. It suits you better. This . . . It feels like pity. You called me a child before. Now you're treating me like one.*

"Your breeches are wet."

"What?"

He eased back on his heels. "You've gotten wet in the stream. You should dry off. Build a fire. Rest a little. You're tired. You haven't slept since the Seeking. You're cold and you're wet and you think you've seen—"

"I *have* seen."

He coughed, as if physically choking back a response, then winced as if the cough hurt his head. "All right. But whatever has happened, you need to get through this forest, and for that, you must be dry and rested. Let me build you a fire."

She looked up at him. His words were kind, but his face was unreadable, as if he was struggling to be nice. Why?

Because he needed her. He was lost and wounded.

"I can't stop," she said. "Ashyn—"

"Whatever has happened, Ashyn needs you to get out of this forest. You can't do that if you collapse from exhaustion. I'll start a fire. It'll take a moment. Wash that mud from your face. You'll feel better."

NINETEEN

Gavril had gotten the blaze going faster than she expected. She didn't see what he'd used—he'd put it away before she arrived. Now he poked at the fire to get it higher, but it was as if the dense forest devoured all the air. It was still blessedly warm. Daigo agreed, curled up so close he'd singed his fur.

"The path was still clear enough for me to lead them to where the other guards perished," Gavril said. "Levi—his body—was gone. I saw something moving in the woods. I saw those blasted boots of his and someone called his name. And then . . ." Gavril gripped the hilt of his sword. "There was a scream, and I didn't see anything until they had Levi on the ground. But it wasn't Levi at all. It was . . ."

"A shadow stalker."

He grunted. "That's what the others said. They killed it . . . or expelled it, I suppose. Then the forest erupted with smoke and shadows. It wasn't like with Levi. There wasn't even time to scream."

"Levi was their decoy. They're predators, not mindless—"

"I don't know what happened. I was at the back with Orbec. The shadows fell on everyone and . . . Orbec told me to run. I saw an arm in the fray, and I grabbed for it and . . ." He stopped, his gaze unfocused, trapped in the memory. "By the time I pulled, that's all there was. An arm. Orbec dragged me out of there. We ran. It felt like cowardice, and I know . . ."

He trailed off then. Moria knew his father had been exiled for cowardice. Instead of ordering his men to retreat, he'd supposedly escaped alone under the cover of sorcery.

Gavril poked the fire with a stick. "We found the stream. And then the shadows came and fell on Orbec. I ran to help him, but I slipped. I hit my head on the rocks. When I woke up, he was dead. I knew I had to get away, in case he came back as one of them. I crawled until I passed out."

After a few moments of silence, he said, "You're wrong about the village."

"Can we not talk about that?"

"You seem upset—"

"*Seem* upset? My village is gone. I know you didn't care about anyone there—"

His eyes darkened. "Of course I cared. I lived there for—"

"No, you *existed* there. You made no effort to get to know—"

"Shhh."

"Are you shushing me? I—"

138

He lunged and grabbed her, his hand clamping over her mouth.

While the temptation to bite him was overwhelming, this did seem an extreme measure to stop her talking, and thus suggested something else was wrong. Also, he smelled. Of filth and sweat and blood. She didn't want to discover what he tasted like. When he relaxed, she peeled his fingers away.

"I heard something," he whispered.

She glanced at Daigo, who seemed not to have noticed his Keeper being grabbed and silenced. Something else occupied his attention. Something in the forest.

Gavril quickly put out the fire. Daigo's tail was lowered, swishing. His whiskers were pricked, his pupils dilated. One ear was flattened, the other forward. Uncertain, listening. He looked back at her. He wanted to investigate, but he'd like her to follow.

She nodded and nudged him forward. When Gavril caught her tunic, she half lifted her blade. Then she pointed it at the forest and began easing forward, crouched behind her wildcat.

Behind her, Gavril made a noise. A rumble, almost like a growl. He didn't stop her, though. When a twig crackled, she looked back to see him following. She motioned for him to stop. He pretended not to notice.

When they reached the forest's edge, she heard something moving in the undergrowth. The sound was soft. Was that how shadow stalkers moved?

Daigo had stopped, muzzle lifted, nostrils flaring. She raised a finger. Yes, the wind was blowing their way, meaning Daigo could smell whatever was out there.

His nose kept twitching, like a dog's. His body language had changed little. Apprehension. Concern. He smelled something. He thought it might be a threat, but he wasn't sure.

He started forward, slower now, slinking. She did the same. The noise continued. It sounded familiar. Like rats in the hay barns. The scuttling of their feet over the boards and through the dry straw.

Daigo stopped again. His growl rose, then he choked it back. She slid up beside him.

His tail whipped against the back of her legs, as if in warning. *Come closer, but stay low.* Behind them, Gavril crept forward. When he snapped another twig, whatever was out there squeaked.

She slid along, staying as low as she could, making her way through the cluster of trees between her and the noise. She passed the largest and—

She stopped and stared. Daigo slunk up alongside her. Gavril snaked up on her other side. When he saw what she did, he exhaled a curse. Then they all just crouched there, staring.

The thing was a little larger than the rats in the barn. It had the same humped form and snakelike tail, but otherwise it was like no creature she'd seen. Long brown fur stuck up in every direction. Its eyes were huge and grotesquely bulbous. Fangs jutted down below a misshapen jaw. When it rose onto its hind legs, she saw long, curved claws. She could smell the thing, too, a rank odor that made her stomach churn.

It started toward them, head bobbing as it snuffled, teeth gnashing. Daigo sprang.

140

The thing rolled into a ball, and its fur seemed to shoot from its body. Moria lunged on top of Daigo, her eyes closed as she shielded him. The "fur" rained down like arrows. One jabbed her hand like a needle. Daigo yowled as another struck him. She heard Gavril's boots as he thundered past. A noise, like a snarl of rage. Then a high-pitched squeal.

Moria opened her eyes. Gavril stood over the beast. His sword skewered it.

"Don't move," he said when she started to rise.

There was a long dark pin stuck in the back of her hand. She looked to see more embedded in her tunic, hanging there harmlessly.

"What are those?" she asked.

Gavril pulled his sword from the creature. "If you don't know, then you shouldn't have leaped out. Were you going to protect your cat's life with your own?"

"It's the same thing."

He snorted. "You don't believe that superstitious foolishness, do you? That your lives are bonded? My father said—"

He stopped abruptly. She'd never heard him mention his father before.

Gavril bent and fingered the long needle embedded in her hand. "It's called a quill. It's barbed, and if you move when I'm pulling, it'll only make it worse."

"What did your father say?"

He worked at the quill. "Just that my grandfather once met a Keeper whose bond-beast died in battle. She was fine."

"She lived?"

"For a while. Then she took her own life. Apparently,

she decided that would make a more tragic tale. You ought to appreciate that."

"Perhaps that means we don't die if the other does, but we cannot bear to go on living."

Another derisive snort.

"So you've seen those things?" she said.

"Quills? Yes. In the south there are creatures that bear them on their tails. But that's not the same beast. It's . . ." He glanced over at the dead thing. "Not like anything I've seen."

"Sorcery," she whispered. Then, "Oww!" as he jerked the quill free.

"I told you to be still."

"It must be sorcery," she murmured. "To make such a creature."

"You're as superstitious as an old nanny. Sorcery didn't make such a creature. Necessity did."

"Necessity?"

"Quills for protection? Jagged teeth for tearing? Claws for climbing? Large eyes for seeing in dim light? That makes the beast perfectly suited for living in a place like this." He eased a quill from her tunic. "Anything new is frightening to the superstitious mind. There are villages in the south that have never seen a Northerner. They would think pale skin and reddish-yellow hair a sign of sorcery. Your coloring is a product of your climate. As are your slow wits."

She twisted to snarl a protest and yelped as a quill jabbed into her side.

"Didn't I tell you to be still?"

She swore there was a lightness in his voice. *Nothing pleases him so much as mocking me.*

142

She glared at him. "If you're book-read enough to know why my skin is pale, then you know that Northerners' wits are *not* dulled by the cold climate."

"True. Your sister seems bright enough."

She resisted the urge to shoot her fist at him, and lay there, still on Daigo, fuming quietly.

Yes, that was the typical view of Northerners. Slow thinking, slow moving, lazy, as if they had ice in their brains and their veins. Her father had made himself wealthy using that to his advantage as a merchant. It worked best on the lower castes, those who'd never met people beyond the empire's middle realms. For Gavril, highborn and court-raised, such a belief would be as quaint a notion as her superstitions. He was goading her, and she was foolish for letting him.

As for the beast, it could indeed be an adaptation to an inhospitable environment. The exiled boy—Ronan—had survived the winter. He must have eaten something.

When a distant branch cracked, Moria's head snapped up. Daigo shot an accusing glare at the dead creature, as if it had brought friends.

As they listened, Moria heard the distinct clomp of boots on hard earth. She started to ease forward, but Gavril grabbed her collar and whipped her back so fast she gasped. He shoved her hard, pushing her to the ground.

"Down!" he whispered, as if she had some choice in the matter.

She hit the earth with Gavril practically atop her back as he held her there. When she opened her mouth, he slapped his hand over it.

"Quiet and stay down."

She wrenched his hand off. "If you want me to do something, try *asking*—"

"Shhh!"

He glowered, but there was fear in his eyes. Genuine fear. He leaned against her, hand between her shoulders, pinning her there, and she could feel the thud of his heart.

He thinks it's shadow stalkers.

They lay in a cluster of trees, nestled in undergrowth now. Daigo stretched out, his gaze fixed on the distant source of noise. She could still hear the clomp of boots, the rhythmic sound broken only by the occasional rustle of dead leaves or the crack of a twig.

How many are there? It sounds like an army.

An army of the dead.

TWENTY

Moria shivered. Gavril's hand rubbed between her shoulder blades. She glanced over at him, startled. His gaze was fixed forward, straining to see whatever was coming, rubbing her back absently, as if in reflex to her shudder. When he realized what he was doing, he stopped and scowled, as if it was her fault he'd shown a moment's kindness.

You're always so angry, as hard as you try not to show it. Furious at being sent here, to guard this forest—the insult of it.

That *tramp-tramp* vibrated through the earth. *The thunderous drumbeat of an army on the move.*

It was a line from many a tale, but Moria herself had never heard the sound. The empire had been at peace ever since the desert hordes were vanquished in the war that had sent Gavril's father here.

But now, listening to the drumbeat of footfalls, the line

came to mind, as did an image from another tale. The army of the night. A thousand shadow stalkers raised by a hundred sorcerers, long before the Age of Fire. The dead rose, and they moved across the land like a plague, killing army after army, the warriors falling, only to rise again. An unstoppable force.

But it had been stopped. By the warriors of the North on their snow dragons. They'd ridden over the battlefields and blasted ice on the shadow stalkers, freezing them so the armies of the living could shatter their corpses with a single blow, giving the shadow-stalker spirits no place to hide.

It was a story often singled out as proof that bards' tales were foolish nonsense. People would laughingly debate which part of the story was the most ludicrous: shadow stalkers, snow dragons, or clever Northerners. All three were equally mythical beasts.

As the footfalls drew closer, Moria calculated the distance to the stream. Could they outrun them on more open ground? In legend, shadow stalkers were relentless, moving with speed, yet never running, as if their broken bodies couldn't quite manage that. But they had a second form, too—the fog, their spirit form.

She moved her lips to Gavril's ear. "Would you fight shadow stalkers? If they're in manifested form?"

"Of course." He looked offended and a little bewildered, as if there was no question.

"Good. If they come this way and there are fewer than it sounds, we'll fight."

He frowned. "You think those are shadow stalkers?"

"Don't you?"

He turned his gaze forward again. "It sounds like boots. But the search party is dead."

Or it was . . . and is risen again.

As the footfalls grew louder, the drumming lost its rhythm and became scattered boot clomps, as if distance had made it sound synchronous. Fewer feet than she'd thought, too. Perhaps a half dozen men.

"It was near the fresh stream," a voice said. "I heard a girl talking, then a shriek."

She began to rise. Gavril's hand on her back slammed her down.

"It isn't shadow stalkers," she whispered. "They don't speak—"

"Shhh!"

"It must be guards, from the village. They're searching—"

"Shhh!" His lips came to her ear, warm breath filling it, his voice harsh with anger. "Be still and be quiet, Keeper. For *once.*"

Another voice, from the forest. "Do we even know this is the way to the fresh stream? Liam has already led us astray once."

Moria knew all the guards by name. All the villagers, too. There was none named Liam.

"Do *you* want to try leading us through this forsaken place?" a third voice said. "You should thank the spirits I'm here."

They heard many accents in Edgewood, which drew guards from all corners of the empire. She'd only heard this particular one once, from a tradesperson. It was a guttural accent, not soon to be forgotten.

147

So who were these men? Not a rescue party. Even if someone from the village had escaped across the Wastes, it would be many moons before help returned.

"I told you I heard a girl's voice singing," the first voice was saying again, as the others complained about tramping over rough terrain.

"I think you've been away from women too long," another replied. "You're hallucinating. Next you'll see a pretty maid skipping along the stream."

"Mmm," another said. "Is she swimming in the stream, too? Unclothed? If he is imagining that, I don't blame him. It has been too long. They should have let us loose on that village before—"

"Enough." A man she hadn't heard yet, his voice quiet but firm. "All of you. If one of those guards did survive, we won't hear him with all your jaw flapping."

Gavril shifted, his hand on her back, his leg tensing over hers. On her other side, Daigo squirmed closer, too, leaning against her, one paw resting on her outstretched hand.

"Don't move," Gavril whispered in her ear. "Whatever happens, don't move."

It's not like I could anyway. With you and Daigo practically on top of me.

She made a noise of agreement. Gavril eased back. Then he let out a curse. He looked around frantically, and began wriggling out of his tunic. She didn't avert her eyes. He'd told her not to move.

He winced as he tugged it over his head wound. Then he handed it to her.

"Cover your hair."

"What?"

"Your—" The crack of a twig, telling them the men were almost on them. Gavril cursed and grabbed her hair, twisting it up over her neck, then slapping the tunic down over it. He adjusted it until her face was shadowed under the folds.

Moria lay still and tried not to breathe too deeply. She could smell the tunic. It wasn't pleasant. However, the brief sight of Gavril without it had been quite nice, so she remembered that and ignored the rest.

She saw a flicker of movement through the trees. Then all went dark as Gavril fussed with the tunic, pulling it farther over her face. She waited until he turned away, then tugged it back enough to see again.

The men were, it seemed, not coming directly toward them, but off to the side, taking a clearer path. Still, as a figure took shape, Moria lowered her chin to the ground, her face better hidden by the tunic's shadow. She'd pulled her hands into her own tunic. Gavril had tucked his forearms under him. Even Daigo had slitted his yellow eyes. No flash of color would betray them.

She could see figures now. Five of them, heading for a gap in the thick forest. They stepped into the light, and she watched them troop past, single file. Strangers, as she expected. Men from all corners of the empire, skin tones ranging from the light brown of oakwood to nearly black. One man's head was shaven. Another wore warrior's braids. The last man was the palest, with hair the color of copper.

For someone from Edgewood, accustomed to new guards and traveling merchants, the diversity was expected. It wasn't until she truly thought about it that the regional variance seemed odd. If these men were responsible for somehow raising the shadow stalkers, it would make sense for them to come from the same area. A strike against the emperor meant one region in revolt.

Is that what you think this is? A strike against the emperor?

I don't know.

What also startled her was their manner of dress. Or, more aptly, their swords and daggers, given their manner of dress. They wore the heavy boots favored by guards, and similar sleeveless tunics, leaving their arms bare to swing a blade freely. Two had cloaks over their shoulders. Their breeches were simple and more form-fitting than was the fashion.

While guards were allowed to commission their own clothing, there were severe restrictions on color and cut, so they would present a uniform image. These men's clothes came in a variety of shades and cuts. Moreover, that clothing was filthy and ill kept, tears left unmended, boots scuffed and worn. Their own appearances were just as unkempt—with untrimmed beards and unshaven faces. If any guard showed up in such condition, he'd be on toilet-cleaning duty for a moon.

"Mercenaries," Gavril whispered in her ear. "Hired blades."

Moria had heard of such a thing. Not every warrior in the empire lived in a barracks, of course. That would hardly befit members of the highest caste. The guards they saw in Edgewood were usually from low-ranking families.

Other warriors owned property or became warlords or climbed the ranks in court itself. But there were those of lower ranks who had no hope of property or position and no interest in service. They hired their swords to whoever would purchase them.

The stories she'd heard about mercenaries were not flattering. True warriors considered them a stain on the caste; warriors were supposed to serve the empire. Mercenaries served only themselves. Perhaps even worse, they did not follow the warrior code.

Sometimes bards would sing heroic songs of the lone warrior, the blade without a warlord, a noble and dashing hero. Looking at these ragged men and hearing them talk, Moria would now place those stories alongside those of snow dragons, as products of a romantic—or optimistic—imagination.

The men filed past. Moria craned her neck to follow, making note of everything from their faces to their clothes to the cut of their weapons. The last part was, unfortunately, most impressive. Whatever care they neglected to give their bodies and garments they seemed to have paid to their weaponry. Their swords were clearly new—not ancestral blades—but they were the highest quality. True and strong steel, free of the adulterated metals and nicks and scrapes one saw on the purchased weapons of the lower-born guards.

They had more than blades, too. Two mercenaries bore bows. Another had a quiver of darts. Yet another wore a whip coiled on his belt. True warriors were forbidden such weapons; they were left to hunters and farmers.

Today the goddess showed some modicum of mercy, and the men continued on to the streambed. She could hear them sloshing and slopping in the mud. She and Gavril had walked on the firmer ground, but she still tensed, certain they'd spot a stray footprint.

The mercenaries split up, going both ways along the stream. Then came a cry. A body had been spotted.

Moria strained to listen as they seemed to decide Orbec was newly dead, and that's what their comrade had heard—the warrior shouting or cursing, and then his death scream.

She listened as the footsteps retreated the way they'd come—after the mercenaries had stripped anything usable from Orbec. Still, she and Gavril stayed where they were until Daigo nudged her and rose, meaning even he could no longer hear the men.

Moria plucked the tunic from her head as they crawled out and stood. She handed it to Gavril.

"You ought to wear a hood," he said. "Something to cover that hair and skin. I don't know how you Northerners survive outside your land of ice and snow."

He pulled his tunic on. She watched. He didn't seem to notice, his gaze distant, looking toward Orbec's body.

"I took his dagger," she said.

"So I saw." Still no expression.

"I thought I should. It's an ancestral blade. I'll return it to his family."

He nodded curtly. "Good. Might as well use it, too, while you have it."

Was he mocking her? His voice lacked the edge that usually crept in when he did.

"I wasn't sure if I ought," she said. "It seemed wrong, but it also seemed wrong to leave it. What does the warrior's code say?"

She expected him to snap some retort. But he only shrugged.

"Nothing specific. You acted out of respect. While carrying another warrior's sword is forbidden, the code allows for necessity, too, under the circumstances. You'll honor his memory. They—" He hooked his finger toward the departed mercenaries. "They'd sell it to the first merchant they found."

"What were those men?"

"Mercenaries," he said, as he turned in the direction of the stream.

"You said that. I mean what are they doing out here? They mentioned the village. They must be connected with what happened—"

"We don't know what happened. But if you stop talking and start walking, perhaps we'll live long enough to find out."

TWENTY-ONE

As they'd hoped, the stream ended at the swamp, less than a hundred paces from the canyon wall. The very air seemed different here. Warmer. Easier to breathe. Daigo bounded ahead, leaving them clamoring to keep up.

When Moria reached the canyon wall, she put her hands on it outstretched, eyes closed, as if communing with its spirit. She expected Gavril to make some sarcastic comment. He only mumbled that they ought to get into the village while there was still light to see.

They walked along the wall, Moria keeping one hand on the cold stone, until they reached the opening. Gavril stood at the base of the first tower, peering up as if he expected to see someone there.

"It's empty," she said. "Everyone is—"

"This *guard tower* is empty," he said, and strode ahead

into the village proper.

She wanted to be wrong. She prayed to the spirits that she was. Prove that she'd exaggerated the danger. That people had survived. They'd been sleeping or hiding, and they were alive and fine.

As Moria passed through the gates, she stared out at the dark, silent village and knew she'd not been wrong. She wanted to drop to her knees and weep. Ashyn would. Moria stared out, dry-eyed, and felt . . .

A little less than human.

When Gavril returned with lanterns, she knew he'd seen no sign of life. He'd be quick to tell her otherwise, to prove her wrong.

I wish you could. You may forever afterward call me a child, a careless girl who flits after butterflies. Just prove I was mistaken.

They continued on, walking side by side to the barracks. Gavril stopped inside the door and shone his lantern about. Moria headed straight for the ladder down to the cells. The top hatch was open. The guard's chair at the bottom was empty. So, too, was Ronan's cell. She ran her light over the walls and down to the floor. There were no signs of blood or struggle. Daigo stalked up and down the hall, then grunted in satisfaction, as if reaching the same conclusion.

"They're gone," Moria said as Gavril came down the ladder.

He did his own inspection. Then he said, "They're not *gone*, Keeper. They've left. Of their own volition."

He glanced over, as if expecting her to argue, but she only nodded before heading back to the ladder. She didn't ask what he'd found upstairs. Again, he'd tell her if it was good news.

They went out. He followed now, letting her and Daigo lead the way.

She should go home. That wall in her head quivered at the thought, but she pushed on. It would be the first place Ashyn would go.

They found blood just past the barracks, where the public buildings ended and the private homes began. A pool of crimson with an empty spot in the middle. A spot where someone had lain . . . then risen again.

They were about to pass the blood when Daigo stopped. His nose was to the ground, sniffing something. He lifted his head and grunted, calling Moria back.

She shone the lantern light on a bloodied print. A massive paw.

"Tova," she whispered.

There was another, fainter print heading away.

"They passed here," she said. "They saw the blood. Tova stepped in it."

Daigo rolled his eyes. *Dogs. Such clumsy beasts.* Moria managed a half smile and slung her arm over his neck in a quick embrace. When she stood, Gavril was there, looking relieved.

"See?" he said. "I told you—"

"Stop telling me," she said. "Please."

"I'm only—"

She looked up at him. "Do you think I want to be proven right?"

He had the grace to dip his gaze and waved her on.

She began searching houses as they reached them. The doors were unlocked. That wasn't unusual in Edgewood, where people only latched doors when a trade wagon was in town. Last night, though . . . After what happened in the forest? They would have locked their doors.

The first house was empty. So was the second. In the third, they found death. A woman, so bloodied and torn that Moria couldn't be sure who it was, and preferred not to struggle to recall.

When Moria turned to leave, Gavril was blocking her path. She thought he was going to give some explanation for what they'd found, but his gaze was fixed on the corpse. She circled past, and he made no move to stop her. Only when she reached the road did she hear his boot steps behind her.

They found more bodies. More blood where there were no bodies. Sometimes the condition of the corpses meant Moria could pretend it wasn't someone she'd known all her life. Other times, there was no doubt. Faces so familiar she knew them even in the half light. Faces fixed in looks of agony and horror, each one chipping a block from that wall, letting her feel a little more.

Most who remained were women. A deliberate choice, she was sure. That's why they found no guards. The warriors had been killed and had risen again, as had the other able-bodied men.

Building an army.

The men had risen, and their wives . . . Moria knew that the men were responsible for the corpses she'd found. They'd risen, possessed by shadow stalkers, and slaughtered their own families.

But the children . . . ? That's what she didn't understand. There were no children. She was blessedly glad not to find them horribly murdered, like their mothers. But what had happened to them? Had they died and risen again? Perhaps the older boys, even the older girls. Yet they were all gone, down to the baker's daughter, barely able to toddle.

Again, she had to brush past Gavril in the doorway. He'd been better after the first house, but now he seemed frozen in the baker's home. She pushed on. The next house was hers. When she neared it, her head started to throb. She rubbed the back of her neck. It didn't help. Nothing would help but getting past this.

As she pulled open the door, she heard a soft flutter, like the wings of a moth. She lifted the lantern and saw a note pinned to the door with a needle. A note in her sister's handwriting.

Moria grabbed it and smoothed it as she turned to sit on the front stoop, lantern perched on her lap, light leaping over the paper.

> *Moria,*
>
> *Wenda says you're with the children, long gone, but in case she is wrong, I ought to leave a note.*
>
> *Everyone is dead or missing. I do not know what has happened, only that I am certain you are safe, because I would feel it otherwise. Father is . . . You know what has happened. I will speak no more of it until I see you, which I pray will be soon.*
>
> *Men took the children. Men on horseback. I do not know why. Wenda believes she saw you with them, so we follow. The horses head east. There is nowhere else to go, I suppose.*
>
> *If you find this note, come, but take care. Ronan has left us, but I am with Tova and Gregor of the guards, and I have my dagger, which I am quite capable of using, however much*

you insist otherwise. We are safe and we are fine, and I do not wish you to kill yourself rushing to my rescue. I do not need rescue. I need my sister, alive and unharmed.

Ashyn

"They're safe," Moria whispered to Daigo, sitting beside her. "Ashyn and Tova. They're safe."

He chuffed, as if this was never in question. She looked up to tell Gavril but found herself staring into the night.

She hurried back to the baker's house and strode into the bedroom to see the baker's wife on the floor. She was turning to leave when she spotted Gavril. He stood in the corner, his back against the wall, lantern out, staring at the body.

She walked to him. She wanted to comfort him. But she didn't know the words, and even if she did, she didn't think she could speak them. In refusing to accept her account of the massacre, he'd denied her any comfort, and she could not find it in herself to offer some to him. Ashyn would.

But Ashyn isn't here. All you have is me, and I can't grant you anything that you wouldn't grant me.

"We need to—" Moria began.

"I knew her."

"You knew all of them." She heard the snap in her words and wished she regretted it. She didn't. She wanted to shout at him. To pound at him. *They're dead. My village—our village—they're dead. Do you see that? Do you finally see it?*

"She brought our bread," he said. "Every day. When she had honey cakes, she always kept one for me. 'In your father's memory,' she'd say. She remembered seeing my parents' wedding, when she was a child. There was a parade, and my father waved to her, and my mother tossed her a honey cake. She remembered that." He paused. "She was kind to me."

"They all were. You just didn't care to notice."

He dipped his chin, and she did feel guilt then, just a twinge.

"They've taken the children," she said.

His chin shot up, gaze swinging to her. "What?"

She lifted the note. "It's from Ashyn. She's with a few others. They're following men on horseback who took the children. A girl saw me with them. Or saw another phantasm, I suspect."

"I don't understand." He looked at the baker's wife. "It's all . . . I don't understand. This isn't . . . Something's gone wrong."

"Yes. Our village is gone. The women massacred, the men turned to shadow stalkers, the children stolen. I believe that qualifies as 'something gone wrong.'"

She expected her tone to rouse him to anger, to slough off his shock. But he only stared at the dead woman.

"We need to go after my sister," she said. "Find her."

"Yes."

"And we need to tell someone. Out there. Warn them."

"Tell . . . ?" His voice faded to a whisper. "Yes, I suppose that's all that can be done. My duty . . ." He swallowed. "Tell someone. Warn them." He pushed to his feet so fast Daigo jumped. Then he turned on Moria, and in a blink, the old Gavril was back, his face stone, his eyes harder still. "Let's see that note."

TWENTY-TWO

Moria left Gavril there, reading Ashyn's note. She got as far as the street before he came after her.

"Where are you running?" he said, striding up beside her.

"To find my sister, obviously. Find her, find the children, warn someone. That's the plan, isn't it?"

He swung in front of her. "It's not a half day's jaunt, Keeper. Night has fallen. It will be just as dark until morning, so there's little point in rushing. We'll need more lantern oil, fire-starter, warmer clothes. . . . My cloak is in the barracks and you need yours. If you can recall where you dropped it."

"I know exactly where I *dropped* it. At home, where it lies in my dead father's hand. It's still there, I'm sure. Where he tried to kill me and I had to kill him. I will freeze before I go back for that cloak."

As she spoke, the annoyance fell from his face and by the time she finished, she saw . . .

Empathy. Shared pain and understanding and contrition. She saw that and she turned away.

"I'll find something at the barracks," she said.

"Can you go into your father's shop?" His voice was low, the undertone of compassion making her anxious, and she wanted to brush it off. Make him angry again.

You fault him for being unkind in your grief, and you fault him for being kind. What do you want, Moria?

"If you don't feel you can go into his shop, I will," he said. "But that is the best place to find supplies."

She answered by veering in that direction.

Gavril suggested she tell him what she needed from the shop. His tone said he would see it as no sign of weakness if she stayed out. She still saw weakness in the choice. Moreover she saw a lack of respect for her father.

He'd been proud of his shop. Proud to be a merchant. The empire would have let him take on a higher-ranking position in Edgewood. He was the father of the Keeper and the Seeker. He ought not tend shop. Yet he did, and while Moria knew he enjoyed his profession, it was also a quiet rebellion. The empire had cost him his wife and could have cost him his children. Now they'd "allow" him to rise from his caste-bound occupation? No, they would not. He wouldn't risk rebelling loudly, as Moria would, but he did so with a quiet resolve that seemed so much braver. She would honor that bravery by going into his shop for the last time.

The mental wall stayed up as she went in, and she was

glad. It let her look around the familiar tables and shelves, inhale the familiar scents, and commit it all to memory. She started gathering everything they'd need along with packs to put it in.

Her father's entire selection of clothing fit on one shelf. There was a separate room given to the raw materials—furs and leathers and fabric and buttons and clasps and threads and baubles. The people in the empire viewed ready-made clothing as emergency wear only. It might be cheaper, but only because the tailor fashioned it from ends and scraps. The one cloak they found was for a man—too large, made of patchwork leather without fur.

"You'll need a sleeping fur if you take that. Otherwise, you'll freeze. The deeper you go into the Wastes, the colder it gets at night." Gavril looked around. "Does your father keep orders anywhere? Perhaps something waiting to be picked up?"

He did. While it might make sense for a person to buy the raw material and take it to a tailor, that wasn't how it worked. A tailor was an artisan, two castes above a merchant. He ought not soil himself with matters of trade. So the merchant gave him the order and materials, then sold the finished item back to the customer, and returned a portion of the cost to the tailor. Which meant that the tailor was still *selling* his goods—just to the merchant instead of the client—*and* losing money in the bargain. A ludicrous arrangement to Moria, though it seemed perfectly reasonable to everyone else.

She took Gavril to where her father kept commissioned goods awaiting pickup. There were no cloaks. Nothing that could substitute either. She was about to take the plain leather one when Gavril said, "Moria?"

He held out a parcel wrapped in paper. On the top of it, in block writing, it read: *This is NOT your Fire Festival gift, Moria, so do NOT peek in it.*

It was her father's writing. Gavril put the parcel in her hands. She opened it carefully, as she'd never opened a gift in her life. First the string. Then the paper. She laid the parcel on a table and opened it to find . . . a cloak. A magnificent butter-soft leather cloak with a removable fur liner.

As she lifted it, a note fell to the table. In her father's neat, precise handwriting, it read:

> *Fire Day blessing to my Fiery Child*
> *I know you haven't quite outgrown your old one yet, but it is starting to look rather ragged. Please do try not to get any dagger holes in this one. And tell Daigo the hem is not for claw sharpening.*
> *All my love, always,*
> *Father*

Moria read the note twice. Then she dropped to her knees and she wept. Finally, she wept.

TWENTY-THREE

As Ashyn climbed the pile of rock, she banged her knee—the same one she'd banged twice already. She hissed in pain as tears sprang to her eyes. Tova whined from the base and put one tentative paw on the rocks, but she motioned for him to stay down and then waved to the others, assuring them she was fine as they made camp.

The outlook was man-made, rock piled by an age of travelers along this road, using a rare rise in the landscape for a base and adding to it. The stones were volcanic, like everything around them. Sharp as broken glass, if you grabbed the wrong piece. Ashyn already had a cut on her hand to prove it. But she kept going until she reached the top. Then she found her footing and looked out.

There was little to see. One could argue that these lookouts were a tribute to the endless—and foolish—optimism of the human spirit. Or to their equally foolish determination to conquer everything in their path, including nature itself.

In the Wastes, nature won. There was no contest, truly. Ashyn stood on that pile of rock and looked out at . . . more rock. In places the land was smooth and swirled, like a quiet river. In others, it was as rough and choppy as a stormy sea. There were patches, here and there, of scrubby trees and moss, improbable islands of life. Yet most was rock.

They'd been walking for two days now, and every time she saw a possible lookout, she'd run ahead. After the first day, she no longer even needed to search for them herself. Tova would see one and bound off with a bark.

While she was scouting for danger, she was also looking for Ronan. At first, she'd scoured the landscape, furious with him for abandoning them. Then, as her temper had settled, she'd begun to look with less anger and more hope. By the second day, though, the hope had vanished.

He was long gone. She tried to understand that. Given the way the village had treated him, she couldn't blame him for leaving. But it still hurt. She took one last look around, then scrambled down to rejoin the others.

Ashyn crawled from her sleeping blanket. She could hear the soft snores of Wenda beside her. Beatrix was on Wenda's other side, and the two men were about five paces away. Only Tova was up, having woken as soon as she did.

Ashyn followed his pale form through the rocks, stumbling as she went, her body aching from a third night sleeping on stone. She shivered as she walked. Even her fur-lined cloak did little against the bitter nights. If her bladder weren't full to bursting, she'd have stayed in her blankets until the morning rays warmed the rocks. By midday, she'd be cursing that same sun. It was like living in an oven, nestled among stones that were bitingly cold until the flame made them unbearably hot.

Tova was anxious to return to bed, too, and they'd gone barely ten paces before he found a place to lift his leg. When Ashyn continued on, he grumbled.

"You can go back," she whispered.

His grumble bordered on a growl, annoyed and offended that she would suggest such a thing. Normally, she'd have patted him in apology. But their even tempers were both fraying out here in the Wastes. It wasn't simply the poor sleep or the inadequate food, or the heat or the cold or even the boredom. They were lonely. They had each other, but that was no different from having your arm or your leg. You couldn't imagine life without it, but it was, after all, a part of you. They missed Father and, even more, they missed Moria and Daigo. In sixteen summers, they'd never spent more than a night apart.

When Ashyn insisted on finding more privacy, Tova laid down as if to say, *I mean it.*

"Wait there, then," she said.

His grumble warned her to come back and argued she didn't need to go so far. As the distance between them grew, Ashyn could feel it, like a rope going taut. She *was* being unreasonable.

Ashyn turned. "I'm just going there, behind those rocks."

Tova chuffed and pushed to his feet. As he padded toward her, Ashyn jogged to the rocky outcropping, swung behind it, and—

She heard the sound of something scratching against rock. She wheeled, and it was right there, perched nearly at eye level. A scorpion. Or so her eyes told her, but it was unlike any scorpion she'd ever seen. In Edgewood, they were less than a hand long. This one was a leg's length from clicking claws to raised tail.

As she stood there, paralyzed, Tova tore around the corner and the scorpion rose up, claws waving, tail poised. She could see the stinger now, as long as a finger, venom glistening on the tip.

She took a slow, careful step backward. Her gaze stayed fixed on the creature as she prayed to the goddess that it would let her leave, just let her—

It sprang. She tried to twist out of the way, knowing it would do no good, seeing Tova leaping forward, knowing that wouldn't help either. The scorpion was coming right for her and—

My dagger.

Her hand shot down and hit the folds of her cloak. Yes, she had her dagger—uselessly hidden under her cloak.

Her hands flew up to ward off the scorpion. It struck her, knocking her off balance, its armored body ice-cold against her fingers, and then—

It gave an earsplitting shriek. A spray of something cold and wet hit her. Venom. It wasn't simply going to sting her. It had sprayed her with—

Fingers wrapped around her arm and hauled her upright before she hit the ground.

"Where in blazes is your dagger?" a voice said, sharp with irritation.

She looked up to see a dirt-smeared face and blazing brown eyes. *Ronan*.

She stared at him, then down at the scorpion. It was cut in half, still twitching on the rock. She stared at it and felt not relief but shame. She was armed with a dagger and hadn't even had the sense to draw it when walking into the Wastes at night. She might be her sister's wombmate, but clearly they shared little beneath their outward appearance. That's what he must be thinking.

Moria would have huffed that she'd been relieving herself, which did not usually involve being attacked by giant scorpions. Ashyn said, "You're right. I ought to have had my blade out."

"Yes, you should have. And your hound ought to be at your side, not lying ten paces away like a stubborn mule."

Tova whined and moved closer to Ashyn, butting his head under her hand.

Ronan sighed. "You need to be more careful, Ashyn, but I lay most of the blame at the feet of that guard who accompanies you. I'm starting to wonder if he's a farmer who stole the sword and boots. He ought to be arranging a nightly watch schedule and choosing safer campsites, preferably ones with a pissing spot nearby."

"A guard isn't expected to lead. I'll help him."

Ronan motioned her away from the rocky outcropping. "You've been through a great tragedy, and I ought not to have left. That shames me, Ashyn, but I hope to make up for it now." He looked into her eyes. "I was worried about you."

She blushed. "I understand why you—"

169

"No, there was no excuse. I told myself I was doing the right thing, going ahead to send help back, but you needed me. I failed you. I have barely slept these last three nights, thinking of what I'd done." Another look, deep into her eyes. "Thinking of you."

Ashyn felt her insides flutter. Was this not the stuff of bards' tales? The maiden who captured the heart of a rogue, who inspired him to rise to the role of warrior, devoted to her protection? Such pretty words. And they would be so much prettier if she didn't hear them in that same soft voice he'd used when he'd meekly thanked Moria for helping him get locked up in a dungeon cell.

"Do you play the lute?" she asked.

He blinked, that soulful look evaporating. "What?"

"The lute. Lies and false flattery go so much better with the strains of a lute. You ought to consider becoming a bard. You have a certain rakish charm. An eye patch would help, too."

His face darkened.

"Yes, definitely an eye patch," she continued. "You can concoct some tale of tragic bravery to explain how you lost your eye. Wait—I know one. You were maimed when you rescued a Seeker from the ruins of her ravaged village and escorted her through the Wastes. Then you heroically delivered her to court while expecting nothing in return." She paused. "You do expect nothing in return, I presume?"

"More gratitude and less mockery would be nice. But yes, if you insist, I will admit that I do hope for something. I hope to survive the Wastes, and I realized we both stand a better chance of that together."

"And that is all?"

"You may not wish to believe I came back for you, but I did, Ashyn. I was concerned. For you. A Seeker is a very valuable member of the empire."

"Valuable?"

"I meant important," he said. "It's the same thing."

"Not quite. You came back because you realized you had walked away from an opportunity that could turn you from pauper to lord, from exile to hero."

"I came back for you, Ashyn."

He said it with breathtaking sincerity, and she looked at him there, silhouetted against the pale moonlight, sword in hand, a scratch across his dirty cheek only making him seem more raffish.

Truly, Ashyn? Truly?

She heard her sister's voice and imagined Moria shaking her head. Ashyn silenced her. Just because she was admiring the scenery did not mean she would step blindly into the quicksand.

"Yes, I'm sure you did come back for me," she said. "Except I would word it differently. You came back for the *Seeker*. And I don't care. If you get me to the nearest town, you deserve that reward."

He eyed her, wary now.

"I mean it," she said. "I understand your situation. You might return to the imperial city only to be thrown into another cell, awaiting a fate as dire as the forest. If you return with me, and I say that you rescued me, at the very least you will be free. You would also likely receive some sort of more tangible reward. I don't begrudge you that. I would simply ask that you are honest with me."

He paused, still searching her face, as if for a trick. Finally he said, "I apologize."

"Good. Now, I'll need to explain the situation to the others. That would be best done in morning's light."

He bent and wiped his blade on the sand, cleaning it. "While I understand why you don't wish to frighten them by disappearing, I'm not sure that discussing the matter will help."

"Disappearing?"

"With me." He stopped. "You expect me to *join* them?"

"I will say that you are my chosen guard. Gregor cannot argue with that."

"It's not arguing that concerns me. You can't continue at their pace, Ashyn. The woman and child are slow enough, but the old man? I left Edgewood just ahead of you, and I had to walk back half a day to find you."

"I'll not leave them."

"I know you feel responsible, but I also have respons . . ." He trailed off and resumed checking his sword. "I wish to get back to the city as quickly as possible. I've been in the Forest of the Dead for four moons. I'd like a soft sleeping mat and clean clothing, and I'll not get that out here."

"I understand, but the matter isn't open to discussion. My duty is to my village—those few who still live. If you wish to join us, you may. Otherwise . . ." She looked up at him. "I hope to see you again someday."

He shook his head. "I'll not join them."

"Then that is your—"

"I can't. The guard won't stand for an exiled convict bearing blades. It would be disruptive for no purpose." He returned his sword to its sheath—he must have taken one from the bodies in Edgewood. "If you insist on staying with the others, I'll do what your guard does not—watch out for you. Would that be sufficient?"

He meant would she still vouch for him, to say he "rescued" her. Someday, perhaps, a young man would give her that soulful look and not want anything more than her kind regard. Ronan wasn't that young man. But he was what she needed right now. So she agreed and returned to camp with Tova.

TWENTY-FOUR

When Ashyn didn't see Ronan the entire next day, she began to wonder if he was there at all. It would be a clever scheme. Promise to guard her from a distance, then hurry on ahead and find his soft mat and hot food, and wait for her to arrive. She trusted, though, that he wanted his freedom and a reward enough not to risk it. To be honest, she only suspected him of ill intent because she was disappointed not to see him. The others were hardly spirited conversationalists.

The next morning she sought Ronan out. For very good reason. They'd woken to find Quintin's sleeping blankets empty. Empty and cold. Worse, she'd had to prod Gregor to hunt for him.

"He's missing," she'd said. "Possibly injured, out there in the Wastes."

"My responsibility is with you, Seeker."

Which he was doing a poor job of, as Ronan had said. She'd ordered him out to hunt and then gone looking herself—both for Quintin and for Ronan.

Finding Ronan turned out to be simple enough. She walked straight to the biggest outcropping of rock and he was there, settled into his sleeping blanket. He roused at her footsteps, as if he'd only just gone to bed.

"Quintin is gone," she announced as he stood.

He peered at her, feigning sleepy confusion as if trying to determine what reaction would best suit the situation.

"You knew that, I presume?" she said.

A flicker of anger. "If you are accusing me—"

"Of harming him? Of course not. Of seeing him walk away and doing nothing? Yes." She pointed at the rocks. "You were sitting guard up there last night?"

"I was, and yes, I saw him, and yes, I did nothing. He was not attacked, Ashyn. He walked away. He knew he was a burden, and he made his choice."

She stared, stunned at the casual way he said it. "Abandoning elders is the mark of a primitive society. We've moved past that. *Long* past it."

"Because we can afford to. Because we have an organized system of trade and communication that means a village never needs fear passing a winter without sufficient supplies. Do you think they used to drag the elders off to the forest as they kicked and screamed for mercy?"

"Sometimes."

He paused, then nodded. "Yes, I'm sure sometimes they did. But for most elders, it was a part of life. A final sacrifice for their families. A way to die with honor."

When she didn't answer, he moved toward her, his voice lowering. "Every time you needed to stop for Quintin to rest, the entire group was at risk of being bitten by rattlesnakes or attacked by nomads and bandits. You were all at risk of running out of food and water because the walk was taking twice as long as it should. He knew that."

"And you gave no thought to going after him?"

A pause. "Yes, I did. To offer a quick death."

Ashyn stared at him.

He stepped back, his face hardening. "Did you want me to lie to make you feel better, Ashyn? Or are you hoping to make *me* feel worse? You've told me to be honest. So don't ask a question if you don't care to hear the answer." A brusque wave. "Now, if you'll leave me be, I might get a little sleep before I need to catch up with your party."

That night, Ashyn lay shivering on the hard lava, her cloak and sleeping blanket wrapped tightly around her. It was still not enough to fend off the savage chill of night. She peered around. Under the moonlight, lava fields stretched to the horizon itself.

There was an end. They were following the "road"—a smooth, winding strip of lava, marked by piles of rock. It was not the fastest route through the Wastes, but it was the only safe one.

Safe *being a relative term,* she thought as she peered into the night.

Besides the poisonous snakes and giant scorpions, the Wastes were home to roving bands that called themselves nomads. There were only two reasons anyone would choose to live here. First, it was beyond the reach of the empire's law, at least from a practical standpoint. Second, trade wagons passed through once a moon in the warmer seasons. So, too, did travelers or scholars who wished to see the Wastes for themselves. All were such easy pickings for "nomads," there was almost an unspoken arrangement that wagon trains would bring extra goods and toss them out like honey cakes at a festival. Road tax, they jokingly called it.

They'd seen no one since leaving Edgewood. Ashyn had detected no spirits either. She could feel the lack of them, chilling the air. She supposed that made sense—what spirits would exist in a desolate land of rock?—but it still unsettled her. She longed for their whispers and their warmth and the soft buzz of their energy.

That's not all I long for.

She blinked back the prickle of tears. She'd spilled enough of them onto the rocks at night. Tears for her father. Tears for her village. Tears of worry for Moria, thinking of her with the children, a captive.

Please, don't do anything foolish, Rya. If I lost you . . .

Tova shifted, pressing his shaggy body against hers. She nestled into it, face buried in his fur. Then she lifted her head and peered around. Ronan was out there somewhere, watching over them. Protecting his investment—she understood that, but it didn't change the fact that he was sacrificing his own safety for them. Just as Quintin had sacrificed his life.

If she'd gone ahead with Ronan, Quintin wouldn't have walked into the Wastes. He could have slowed down, knowing they would have sent help when they reached the first town.

I failed him.

But it's not too late for the others.

She pushed up from her sleeping spot, Tova rising beside her.

"Can you find him?" she whispered.

Tova grunted, as if understanding. She would go speak to Ronan now. She'd tell the others at dawn and then leave with Ronan.

TWENTY-FIVE

Soon after Ashyn returned from talking to Ronan, she awoke to a scream. She leaped up. Tova was already on his feet, fur bristling.

It was Wenda. The girl stood by her blanket, sobbing as Beatrix held her.

A nightmare, Ashyn thought, sinking down again. The girl had held up so far, but bad dreams had to come eventually.

As Ashyn settled, though, she noticed Gregor standing in front of Beatrix and Wenda, motioning frantically, saying something she couldn't hear over the girl's sobs.

Ashyn pushed up again. Wenda raced over and threw herself into Ashyn's arms, head buried against her as she cried.

"What happened?" Ashyn asked.

Gregor turned to her. "The girl had a nightmare. She dreamed—"

"It was not a nightmare!" Wenda pushed from Ashyn's

179

arms and swiped at her tears. "You touched me."

"Touched . . . ?" Ashyn began.

"He came into my sleeping blanket. I felt someone there, and I forgot where I was and thought it was my sister. I moved closer to get warm, and then I felt his hand on my leg. It was moving toward my . . ." She leaned and whispered the rest to Ashyn.

Ashyn sprang up. "Gregor!"

"No!" His face filled with what looked like genuine horror. "I swear on my ancestors I did not do this, Seeker. I could . . . I could not imagine such a thing. The girl is mistaken. She's had a nightmare. I swear—"

Wenda howled and ran at him. Ashyn grabbed her, and the girl sobbed that she had not dreamed it. Beatrix took her, and she collapsed against the older woman.

"I did not do this," Gregor said. "I am not saying the child is telling tales, only that she is mistaken."

"How would she even imagine such a thing?" Beatrix said.

As Ashyn thought it through, the arguing and accusations gradually ceased, and she glanced up to see everyone looking at her. Waiting for her to give her opinion.

No, they don't await your opinion. They await your verdict.

With neither the commander nor the governor in their party, the weight of authority fell to her.

She looked from Gregor's horror to Wenda's anguish, both seeming equally certain of what had—or had not—occurred here. Then to Beatrix, her glower and stiff back placing her firmly on Wenda's side.

Ashyn was not qualified to make this decision. Yet they expected it of her. They needed it.

I can do this.

I must do this.

"Wenda," she said. "I need you to tell me again what happened. Gregor? Please don't interrupt her. You'll have your turn."

And so she proceeded, exactly as she'd seen the governor conduct trials. Each party told their story. The witness—Beatrix—told hers.

Wenda's story did not change. She'd awoken to find Gregor in her sleeping blankets, his hand moving up her leg. Gregor simply said it did not happen. He was asleep in his own blankets. He awoke to Wenda striking him with her fists. Beatrix woke to see the two of them on their feet. She said they were nearer Wenda's blankets than Gregor's, but the two were separated by only a few paces.

There was, then, no easy answer. Gregor looked genuinely horrified; the girl genuinely traumatized. Could it have been a misunderstanding? Gregor rolling in his sleep, thinking it was a woman by his side? Or Wenda having a nightmare that seemed real?

Ashyn carefully suggested the possibility of an accident or misunderstanding, avoiding blame, but they vehemently denied it. Wenda said it happened; Gregor said it did not. Beatrix could add no evidence. The decision rested on her.

If she had any personal feelings on the matter, they sided with Wenda. She knew the girl to be good and honest. She barely knew Gregor at all, even after four days together. Yet that did not seem a valid criterion for such a judgment. Even were she to find Gregor guilty, his punishment would be imprisonment in the town where they now headed. She could insist he wait until the sun was high, then follow the same road, but if they were to encounter trouble, they would have no warriors to aid them. To punish Gregor could punish them all.

"I am not qualified to preside in a court of legal matters," she said finally. "I must commend Gregor to the court in Fairview, where we now head. He will accompany us, but staying in the lead to scout our path. Wenda will sleep in Beatrix's blankets. And Gregor shall give the child his dagger."

The last part was, as she expected, the most contentious. Wenda was thrilled to have the blade. Beatrix was concerned and offered to hold on to it for her, but Ashyn said she'd show her how to carry it properly.

As they prepared to set out early, Ashyn excused herself to tell Ronan that they would not be leaving together.

The next morning Ashyn woke to Ronan's voice whispering her name. She opened her eyes to see his face over hers, his eyes looking into hers, his lips over hers. She thought . . . Well, she supposed it was obvious what she thought. Not, she corrected later, that she actually believed he'd come to her in the night, driven by an overwhelming desire to kiss her. Such things happened often in songs, but Ashyn suspected they rarely did in real life.

What she truly thought was that she was dreaming.

"Ashyn?" he whispered. "Can you hear me?"

She felt a dampness on her cheek. Not a kiss, but a . . . lick. Tova nudged Ronan aside. At the same moment that she realized it was not a dream, she noticed the anxiety in Ronan's dark eyes and the tightness in his voice.

She started to scramble up, but he grasped her shoulder and whispered, "Shhh," motioning for her not to wake the others.

She blinked and looked around. Tova was sitting beside her now, wide awake. Gregor's snores said he was sleeping soundly. Across the campsite, Wenda seemed to be doing the same, in the blankets she shared with Beatrix. Except the older woman wasn't there.

"Bea—" Ashyn began.

Ronan shushed her again. "I saw her go to relieve herself. But it's been too long. I thought it better if you checked on her. It could be a . . . female problem."

Ashyn suspected Beatrix was well past any such "problems," but in any event, he was right—Beatrix would panic if a stranger came after her in the night, particularly after what had happened with Wenda. Remembering that, though . . .

"I can't leave Wenda alone with Gregor," Ashyn whispered.

Ronan cursed under his breath.

"I'll go," she said. "You wait here."

He peered into the night. Even the moon's light seemed to shun this place. They'd used the lanterns judiciously, but the last one had run out the night before.

"I'll follow a bit, while staying close to camp," he said.

She nodded and stood.

"You have your blade?" Ronan whispered.

She nodded again, and withdrew it. Then she set out with Tova.

TWENTY-SIX

Ashyn headed across the plain. When her foot touched down on sand, the change came as such a surprise that her boot almost slid out from under her.

Yes, she remembered now—they'd stopped at one of the rare sandy areas, setting up camp on a patch where scrubby cacti had taken hold. It'd been two days since they'd passed the last oasis, and Wenda had spotted red flowers on the cacti nearly fifty paces off the road. She'd insisted they stop early so they could camp there, where the ground was soft. Ashyn had known she ought to refuse—they had to use every moment of sunlight, but the girl had been so entranced by the flowers, and Beatrix's old bones had ached so much from sleeping atop rock. Ashyn hadn't had the heart to refuse.

She adjusted her stride for the sand. It did feel better. Softer. Slower, though, too, as each step slid a little. There were patches of rock, and she found herself steering toward them, to pick up the pace. Tova figured out what she was doing and led the way across the rock.

As they walked, Ashyn squinted around for Beatrix. There were no cacti here, no piles of stones, so the old woman—standing or squatting—should be easy to spot. But Ashyn saw nothing. She tried calling to her. Her voice carried in the silence and no one replied.

How far did she go?

There was no need to go far. Since the scorpion episode, Ashyn had chosen camps carefully. Tonight, there'd been no obstacles to hide behind, so she'd told them to simply walk far enough that smells wouldn't waft back to camp.

Ashyn sighed. Soon she wouldn't be dreaming of dangerous boys, but of hairbrushes, and hot water, and toilets with doors that latched. And as long as she had none of those, she suspected there was little use in dreaming of the other either. She was rather grateful they hadn't passed a still body of water in two days, so she'd been spared the horror of her own reflection.

She was so caught up in her thoughts that when Tova growled, she only reached out and absently patted his head. He grabbed her fingers in his teeth. She stopped abruptly to look around.

"Beatrix?"

No answer.

As Ashyn looked, she caught a rustle. No, not a rustle. This was just as quiet, but more of a rasping, sliding sound, like something moving across sand.

185

Tova's growl drowned out the noise. She tried to shush him, but when he finally stopped with a snort of satisfaction, the sound was gone.

A snake. That's what it had sounded like. They got them in the village sometimes, coming in from the edge of the forest. Little green ones, harmless, children scooping them up as pets. But the snakes of the Wastes could be dangerous. She'd seen men bitten by them, their fellow travelers rushing them to Edgewood for treatment. Some were merely ill, easily treated. Others . . . others were not.

"Beatrix," she whispered. She reached for Tova. "Can you help me find her?"

He grunted, lifted his muzzle, and made a show of sniffing the air; then he shook his head and grunted again.

I've been trying all along, he seemed to be saying, *but wherever she is, I can't smell her.*

"I'm sorry," she murmured. "I know you're already helping. I'm just . . ."

He walked behind her and butted her legs gently.

"And I won't find her by standing here in the dark, worrying about *not* finding her."

Tova took the lead again, steering her another way, sniffing the air more obviously now, as if to make sure she knew he was working on it.

Perhaps Beatrix was taken. That's why we can't find her. Bandits. Or something else.

What else? They'd seen no sign of shadow stalkers, bandits, or anything that moved on two legs.

Ashyn walked faster, calling louder. When she heard her

own name on the wind, she broke into a run, jogging toward a distant figure—

It was Wenda, running barefooted across the rocky plain. Ashyn could make out Ronan following. Ashyn hurried over to Wenda, who ran into her arms with a sob.

"I woke, and you were gone and Beatrix was gone and Tova—"

"It's all right," Ashyn said, patting her back as she hugged her.

"But I was all alone with *him*."

Ashyn hesitated. Time to end this ruse. "No, you weren't. Someone was watching."

The girl's face screwed up in confusion as Ashyn waved for Ronan to join them. He approached with reluctance.

"I'm sorry," she whispered over Wenda's head. "It's better this way."

She introduced him as quickly as she could, keenly aware that Beatrix was still missing. Luckily, Wenda was still sleepy enough to simply accept that this boy was here and Ashyn knew him and he would help.

"No sign of Beatrix?" Ronan whispered as they began walking.

"Not yet." Ashyn lowered her voice, so the girl wouldn't hear. "I think I heard a snake."

Ronan cursed. Wenda said something, but Ashyn's attention was divided between scanning the empty landscape and watching for signs that Tova had scented the old woman.

Ronan and Wenda were talking when Tova stopped, his fur bristling. He was looking to the side, and Ashyn shushed the others as she strained to peer into the night.

The moon slipped behind clouds and the darkness seemed to wrap around them. Wenda crept closer. Ashyn put her arm around the girl's shoulder. A gust of wind brought a blast of sand and icy cold. Wenda shivered and whimpered.

Then Ashyn heard it again. That dull rasp. Like scales on rock.

"Wh-what is that?" Wenda said.

Ronan lifted his sword and tracked the sound as Tova did too. Both halted, facing the same direction.

"We're going to walk that way," Ronan whispered, pointing his sword in the opposite direction. "And don't be quiet about it. As I've said before, with snakes, you run the biggest risk if you startle them."

As he said the words, something deep in her gut flared up, telling her no. She tried to push the feeling aside, but it only grew stronger.

"Ashyn?" Ronan whispered.

"I—I think we ought to be quiet," she said. "I feel . . ." She swallowed.

"Is it the spirits?" Wenda whispered.

Ashyn shook her head. "I haven't heard any out here. I just— I feel . . ."

"She's the Seeker," Wenda said to Ronan. "We ought to listen."

Ashyn suspected that carried little weight with him, but then the noise came again, closer now, and when Ashyn looked over—

She stifled a gasp. Ronan wheeled, sword up.

They could see a dark shape moving along the ground

188

twenty paces away, too far for them to make out any more than that. Far enough that they should not have been able to see a mere snake. This looked as big as a man, a creature slithering across the rock.

"Move!" Ronan whispered, pushing them ahead. "Go!"

TWENTY-SEVEN

As they ran, Ashyn fumbled to get her dagger out of the sheath. She'd put it away to hug Wenda. Now she was so preoccupied with removing it that when Tova bounded over a small fissure, she didn't notice until she was already tripping.

Her hands shot out to stop herself, and they managed to touch down just in time to keep her from bashing her face into the lava rock. Except she wasn't touching rock. Her forearms rested on something soft. *Tova*, she thought . . . until she felt the hound yanking her cloak. That's when Wenda started to scream, and Ashyn looked down at her forearms, resting on green worsted wool. Beatrix's cloak. With Beatrix's plump body beneath it.

Ronan silenced the child as Ashyn crawled quickly toward Beatrix's head, her fingers ripping the older woman's cloak apart, her hands going to her heart. She felt wet fabric and thought it was blood. Then her fingers began to burn and, as she fell back, she saw Beatrix's own hands, covering her face and . . .

Bone. Ashyn saw bone. Skin, too—and flesh and bone. Her own fingers continued to burn, and she wiped them brusquely on her cloak as she moved up for a better look. Beatrix's hands were . . . damaged. Chunks of skin and flesh were missing, bone showing through. Her throat was the same. And beneath Beatrix's hands, Ashyn could see parts of the old woman's face. Holes in her . . .

She turned and emptied her stomach onto the sand. Ronan's hand closed on her shoulder, tugging her up. He didn't bend—he was holding the child's face against his tunic, hiding the sight from her.

"She's gone," he said as he pulled Ashyn up.

"But what . . . what could do that?"

"Fire, perhaps? She looks burned."

She doesn't smell burned.

Her stomach lurched again at the thought. Her fingers still stung and she rubbed them harder. Ronan whispered for Wenda to stay where she was, facing her away from Beatrix's body, then he caught Ashyn's hand and pulled it up into the moonlight. Her fingertips were red and raw.

"Did you touch her?" he asked.

"Just her cloak. It was wet. Her blood, I suppose, but . . ." There was no blood. Looking down now, she saw that. But she could also see damp patches all over Beatrix's cloak.

"Venom," Ronan whispered. He spat on her fingers and rubbed furiously.

She jerked her hand back. "It's worse if it breaks through the skin." Her voice sounded so calm. As if she were treating a stranger on a battlefield. "I need to wash it off."

"There's water at camp."

"I brought a healing bag, too. There might be something there."

This isn't calm. It's shock.

She looked again at Beatrix's maimed body, and it was like a smack, snapping her out of her stupor. She broke into a run heading for camp, Tova leaping in front to lead her down a clear path.

I'm all right, she thought as she ran. *My fingers sting, but that's it.*

Was that calm reason talking? Or shock? Either way, it kept the panic away. Whatever poison affected Beatrix had been horrific, but it seemed to have happened quickly. It must have, if she hadn't had time to scream.

Because it burned her throat. She couldn't scream. That doesn't mean she didn't—

No, Ashyn had barely touched the poison and had wiped it right off. She'd be fine.

"You'll be fine," Ronan said as he and Wenda caught up. "We'll fix it. You'll be fine."

She stifled a laugh as his words echoed her thoughts. *Yes, it's probably shock, but it's keeping me calm, so I'll take it. Just keep moving. Don't let it dull my senses and—*

A curse rang through the night, so sudden and loud that it seemed to be right beside them. Ronan spun, blade raised with one hand as he tugged Wenda back. He swung between them and the noise, with Tova at his side.

Ashyn pulled Wenda against her. The girl seemed to be in shock, too, uttering not a word, shaking under Ashyn's hand. Ashyn rubbed her shoulder, trying to comfort her.

Ashyn gripped her blade and looked around. She thought she detected a scuffling sound, so distant it was only a whisper.

Then another wordless shout, and this time, there was no question of where it came from. That's when Wenda spoke, so loudly that her whole body jerked under Ashyn's hand, as if she'd just woken from sleep.

"Gregor!" Wenda cried. "At the camp!"

They ran. Ronan scooped up Wenda and swung her onto his back. It wasn't easy—the girl wasn't a toddling child—but it was faster than dragging her along with them.

Gregor shouted a challenge at some unseen attacker. Then they could see him on his feet, waving his sword at the air.

"I heard you!" he shouted. "Show yourselves, cowards! Do not slink in shadows!"

He whirled as if he'd heard something.

"Where have you taken them, cowards? If you've harmed the Seeker, you will be cursed. Do you understand that? *Cursed*."

"We're here!" Ashyn called. "We're—"

Something reared up a few paces from Gregor—like a snake lifting its head, but too big by far. It must be a man, crawling on the ground, starting to rise.

Gregor saw it and let out a shout. He staggered back, his sword held awkwardly, as if it were a shield. Then he screamed. A terrible scream, like Levi's in the forest, that high-pitched shriek of agony that seemed as if it should not come from a human throat.

Ronan dropped Wenda from his back and ran. Tova stayed with Ashyn as she raced toward the camp, clutching the girl against her.

Gregor dropped to his knees, his sword clanking against the rock as it fell from his grip. His hands shielded his face, and he kept screaming that terrible scream. Then he began to gurgle, his body shaking. That thing—whatever it was—stayed in front of him, reared up.

Ronan skidded to a halt about ten paces away. He let out a curse, a blasphemous commentary on the goddess's anatomy that, at any other time, would have had Ashyn slamming her hands over Wenda's ears. But she just kept running as fast as she could, while holding the girl against her.

Then she saw the creature, and she stopped, too. She may also have cursed.

It was not a snake. It was a worm. A long, reddish, segmented cylinder of a creature, at least as long as a man and just as wide. She could see no features—no eyes, no earholes, nothing. It was reared up, pointing one end at Gregor. Then that end sprang open in a giant circle of teeth, and it spat a stream of liquid.

Acid. It spat acid.

"That—that's a death worm," Wenda whispered, her thin body quaking. "From the story Moria told after the earth moved."

Moria said that each time they felt the spirits of the earth shift, blaming "death worms" for the amusement and horror of the children. Now Ashyn stood there, watching a worm the size of a man spitting acid at Gregor. Killing Gregor. Right before their eyes.

I'm asleep, she thought. *Or I've gone mad. Moria's tales have come to life, and that is not possible, which means I've gone mad.*

Or the world has gone mad, and we're simply trapped within it.

She looked at Ronan. He stood there frozen, blade raised. Gregor was on the ground now, writhing in agony, his screams garbled as the acid ate away his throat.

Ashyn turned Wenda away. Then she ran forward, dagger raised. Behind her, Ronan shouted. He lunged at her. Yelled for her to stop. She kept going, covering the distance between her and the worm—

It turned with lightning speed, twisting its body. She saw that terrible mouth open, the teeth flicking out like blades. A stream of acid shot straight for her face. Then the ground disappeared under her feet as Ronan whipped her back. She heard the patter of the acid hitting her shoulder. Heard the sizzle as it burned through her cloak. Heard Wenda scream, and twisted to see the worm seeming to fly at them across the rocks, so fast it was a red blur—

Ronan threw her aside. She hit the rock and scrambled up just in time to see his blade flash. The worm reared, spitting. Wenda screamed. The blade sliced through the worm, and its head fell, cleaved clean off.

TWENTY-EIGHT

Ashyn was on her feet and running to Ronan. He shoved his sword bladefirst into the sand, and was fumbling to get out of his tunic. Holes dotted the thin fabric. As she helped him out of it, she saw the acid had passed through, a line of it across his chest, holes searing to the skin.

She fetched water, and splashed it on his wounds. As she did, she heard a little voice in her head telling her to be more careful, not to waste it; this was all they had. But she didn't care. She'd use the whole waterskin if she needed to. Finally, it was Ronan who stopped her, fingers clasping her arm as he said, "That's enough," through teeth gritted against the pain.

She looked at the wounds, raw and ugly, a line of spots across his chest where the skin had burned away.

"I need to bind them," she said. "Keep them dry and clean. I have an extra tunic—"

"Later," he said. "You need to tend to your own wounds."

She shook her head. "They're only minor burns."

"Then we have to get out of here, in case that wasn't the only one."

He looked at the worm, and she was sure he shuddered. Then they heard a faint gurgling sound. They looked over together.

"Gregor," Ashyn whispered. "He's still alive; I need to tend to—"

Ronan caught her by the wrists. "Take the child. Start walking. Stay off the sand."

"But I need—"

"You can't," he said, lowering his voice. "You know you can't."

She looked at Gregor's mutilated hands. Listened to his gurgles as he tried to scream through his ruined throat. She thought of Beatrix. Of her face beneath her hands.

"Take the child. Now, Ashyn."

He pushed her toward Wenda, and she was about to refuse when she saw the girl staring at Gregor, her thin chest heaving.

She's watching a man die horribly. And I'm letting her.

Ashyn scooped Wenda up and held the girl's face against her shoulder as she hurried away. Tova followed. She could still hear Gregor's agonized gurgling. And then, she couldn't.

Ashyn looked back to see Ronan standing above Gregor's still body. He stepped aside and plunged his blade into the sand to clean it.

He killed Gregor.

No, he ended Gregor's suffering. Would you have him leave the man to die a slow, tortured "natural" death?

Ronan looked over. He saw her watching. He hesitated. Then he motioned that he'd gather their belongings when a shape reared up behind him.

"Ronan!" she shouted.

He turned sharply. Too sharply, slipping in the sand, one foot shooting out. She dropped Wenda and raced toward him. Ronan was on one knee, frozen in place. The worm was poised in front of him, swaying back and forth, as if it somehow couldn't see him.

She heard her sister's voice, telling her tale to the children.

"Death worms have no eyes. They spend so long in the dark that they have little need of them. Instead, they sense the vibrations of the earth and the currents in the air. So, if you ever meet a death worm—"

"Don't move!" Ashyn shouted. "It can't see you if you don't move."

She raised her dagger as the distance between them closed. She'd stab it behind the head so it couldn't whip around and spray her. Use a downward stroke, driving its head down, so it wouldn't spray Ronan.

Yes, see? I can do this. I just need to think it through—

The worm whipped in her direction.

Think it through . . . and forget the fact that I'm thundering toward a creature that can feel me coming.

The worm shot straight at her. She threw the dagger—a move that would have been so much smarter if she'd accepted any of those dagger-throwing lessons Moria had tried to foist on her.

The dagger sailed harmlessly off to the side as the worm

sailed toward her. She froze then. Went completely still and sent up a prayer to the spirits—

The worm seemed to rear up suddenly. Then its head flew, hewed from its body, with Ronan standing behind it, still swinging his blade.

Ashyn watched as the two pieces of the worm twitched on the sand. When they went still, she took a deep shuddering breath as Ronan cleaned his blade.

"We need to go," she said. "Quickly. Before another comes."

"That was the same one," he said, gesturing at the worm.

"What? No. You killed . . ."

She moved forward, being careful not to step in whatever was seeping from the worm's torso. That torso had both ends cut clean.

She heard Moria whisper, *Beware if you chop off a death worm's head. It has another in its tail, teeth and all, and it'll come back. And then you'll have an even bigger problem, because the part you chopped off? It will—*

Across the campsite, she could see the first head segment twitching. Regenerating.

She pointed. "It's coming back. This one will, too. We need to—"

"Take the girl. Start moving."

"You can't kill—"

"I'm not going to try," he said. "Now move."

There was even less time for Ashyn to perform a ritual for the dead now. She had to do it as they ran, moving as fast as they could while staying far from the sand. Ashyn suspected death worms could not truly gnaw through rock, as her sister claimed. By this point, though, she wasn't taking any chances.

First shadow stalkers. Then death worms. Both had featured prominently in her sister's stories, along with snow dragons and thunder hawks and fiend dogs—

Perhaps it's best not to recite the entire list. While she was quite certain she could not conjure the beasts merely by imagining them, she was not going to tempt fate.

Finally, around midmorning, they had to stop. Wenda's legs had given out long ago, and neither Ashyn nor Ronan could carry the child another step. They rested past midday, then started off again.

They said little as they walked. Ashyn wanted to talk to Ronan about the death worms, but she didn't dare in front of Wenda, for fear of frightening her all the more.

Beatrix and Gregor were dead. They were truly the only survivors of Edgewood.

No, she reminded herself each time the thought surfaced. The children were alive. And Moria.

They ran out of water before nightfall. They'd tried to drink sparingly, but the sun beat down on the lava plains. So they'd drunk what they needed, and soon it was gone. After they made camp, Ronan set out in search of water, but Ashyn knew there was little chance he'd find it. They'd been scouring the horizon all day for any sign of greenery.

When Ronan returned with nothing, they decided to sleep and make an early start of it. Ronan thought they were only a day or two from Fairview. They'd try to travel in the morning and evening, resting under the midday sun.

She stayed with Wenda until the girl fell asleep. She'd spent the day reassuring and calming the child. Once Wenda slept, Ashyn went over to where Ronan sat guard atop a boulder.

"You'll wake me so I can take a turn?" she said as Ronan patted Tova's head. "When the moon reaches its zenith?"

He nodded unconvincingly.

"You must," she said. "We need you to be rested. In case anything else happens. I'm not . . ." She looked down at the dagger, held awkwardly at her side. "I didn't follow my lessons the way Moria did. As I'm sure you could tell."

"You did fine."

He said it easily, empty reassurance. She hadn't done fine. She knew that.

"Perhaps you could teach me," she said.

"Not tonight. We shouldn't expend the energy."

Her cheeks heated. "I didn't mean tonight. Just . . . sometime."

Another absent nod.

"I wanted to thank you," she said. "For saving me. Again."

He shrugged, his gaze surveying the empty plain. "You saved me, too."

It wasn't the same. She'd simply alerted him to danger.

He continued looking about the plain. Ending the conversation. He was tired, and she was distracting him from guard duty with meaningless chatter.

She started walking away.

"You seemed to know what that thing was," he said without turning, as if he hadn't noticed her leaving.

"A death worm," she said.

He glanced at her, his expression blank.

"Like in the old tales?" she said.

He eased over, as if making room for her. When she took a cautious step closer, he shifted more.

"Not many bards in my life," he said. "Or time for tales."

"Moria's the expert. Shadow stalkers, death worms, corpse dragons, fiend dogs, thunder hawks . . ." She lowered herself beside him. "She loves monster stories and grisly stories, and she tells them to the village children. She says she does it to get rid of them, but she knows they love it, and they love her for it. They follow her around hoping for more."

"I wager they do," Ronan said, as if he, too, would follow Moria for a story. "So she's the one who told you about these . . . death worms? That's what they're called?"

Ashyn told him what she knew, then said, "I've never heard any other story mention the part about chewing through rock. I suspect that's one of Moria's embellishments. It doesn't make nearly as good a tale if the monster can't actually get you where you live."

He chuckled, then sobered. "The Wastes are lava. The rock doesn't go down forever. They must be living under it, and they come up in the sand if they hear someone."

Ashyn shook her head. "Death worms aren't real."

"That one looked real to me. Felt real, too." He touched his chest and winced.

"I mean they aren't supposed to be real. Just like shadow stalkers. Something or someone has brought them to life."

Ronan frowned. "How?"

"Sorcery."

The corners of his mouth twitched. "Ah. Of course."

"Are you laughing at me?"

"That depends. Are you serious?"

She started to stand up, but he caught her arm.

"I didn't mean to mock you, Ashyn. It's just . . . sorcery? I suppose in a place like Edgewood they still believe in that sort of thing. Old superstitions."

She glowered at him. "And how would *you* explain it?"

"Do we know for certain that these creatures don't exist? Perhaps it's just that no one—"

"If you say that no one who sees them ever lives to tell the tale, I'll scream. That's what my sister always says."

He laughed. "I'll not say she's right, but think of it this way: What if there were things like death worms in past ages? That would explain the tales. Since then, most of the creatures have died, but there are still a few, in far-flung places like the Wastes. So few that they're rarely spotted, and when they are, some *might* live to tell the tale, but who would believe them? Such creatures aren't supposed to exist."

"And the shadow stalkers?"

"Spirits are real. Everyone knows that. Shadow stalkers are a twisted form of them. The Forest of the Dead is an unnatural place. It's filled with the spirits of the damned, however hard the Seeker works to put those spirits at rest. Does it not make sense, then, that that bad spiritual energy could warp itself into shadow stalkers, waiting for the right opportunity?"

"Waiting for me," she whispered. "A weak Seeker. One who can't hold them back."

"I meant the blood moon. I saw it, even if you didn't."

"But it's true that I'm a weak Seeker. In past springs, the court Seeker came. She's powerful. I'm not. I wasn't ready. I tried, but—"

"This wasn't your fault."

She said nothing, but sat there, her stomach twisting. Tova rose from his spot behind her and nudged her face.

"Tova's agreeing with me," Ronan said. "You're too hard on yourself."

She said nothing.

"Ashyn . . ."

"I don't think I *caused* it. I just think I ought to have been able to stop it. I ought to have been stronger. Moria . . ."

"Your sister couldn't stop it either."

"But she tried. She came for me, and she got us out. She fought every threat."

Even our father. I fear I'd have stood there and let that thing kill me.

He moved closer. "You don't need to be like your sister. You didn't break down when faced with death worms. You remembered what they were and how to deal with them. You tended my wounds. Don't forget, you found Beatrix."

"I tripped over Beatrix's dead body."

His lips twitched. "Ah, yes. Sorry. But you still found her."

She gave him a look, and he laughed softly, then he leaned closer until she could see the sparkle of his eyes in the darkness, feel the warmth of his breath on her cold skin, and then he was right there, his face in front of hers.

"You did fine," he said.

She nodded, scarcely able to draw breath as she waited, her gaze locked with his. He leaned closer. His lips parted.

"Now go to bed," he whispered. "You need your rest."

He backed away, giving Tova a pat, and then shooing them both off.

"I'll call you for a shift later," he said. "Get some sleep."

And that was it. She hung there feeling confused and cheated. Then embarrassed and annoyed with herself.

"Ashyn?" he called as she began walking away.

She looked back.

"You *are* doing fine," he said. "We're going to make it."

She nodded and hurried to her sleeping blanket.

TWENTY-NINE

They found no water the next morning, and the sun seemed hotter than ever. Ashyn remembered tales of travelers to Edgewood, those who'd come late in summer, when some of the oases had gone dry. They'd told of having to drink their own urine. *I could never be so desperate,* she'd thought at the time. By midday she was reconsidering.

They'd found an outcropping of rock that provided some shade for a rest. Wenda was so weak she'd fallen straight asleep. Once the sun started to drop, they'd headed off again, but Wenda could barely walk, and when they prodded her, she'd vomited, losing what little liquid her body had retained. Neither had the strength to carry her. As for Tova, the hound was the worst off of them all, trapped in his heavy coat.

After Ashyn settled Wenda into her sleeping blankets, she found Ronan sitting guard.

"How is she?" he asked.

Poorly. That was the truth, but he didn't need to hear it. "Well enough."

He shifted as if restless. When he noticed she was still standing, he waved for her to sit, but as soon as she did, he stood and peered out across the lava plains.

"I know you want to keep moving," she said.

He looked down, as if startled. Then he gave a short laugh. "No. Well, yes, I would but . . . Do you know what I'm truly doing?"

"What?"

He lowered himself again. "Promise not to laugh?"

"Of course."

"I'm looking for water to steal."

She choked on a laugh.

"You promised," he said, waggling his finger. "Yes, I know, it's ridiculous. Obviously there's no one here to steal water from. I just can't shake the urge. That's how I was raised. If you need something and you don't have it, you take it from someone else."

She nodded and watched Tova as he settled in beside her.

Ronan's gaze slid her way. "You've never asked me why I was condemned to the forest. I'll presume that means you'd rather not know."

"No," she said. "I don't ask because that would be rude."

Now it was his turn to sputter a laugh. Then he leaned his shoulder against hers, briefly, but enough to make her cheeks heat.

"I ought to have guessed you were simply being polite," he said. "I'll tell you my crime, then. Selfish of me, but I'll feel better if there are no illusions for me to shatter." He sobered. "We killed a minister. He wasn't supposed to die. It was a robbery. We ran a . . . a scheme. With a woman my father . . . spent time with. She used to . . . entertain men."

He cleared his throat. "That part isn't important. The point is that we had a scheme for robbing rich men while they were . . . otherwise occupied. It had worked many times. This time, something went wrong. We were caught."

He went quiet then, for so long that she thought that was the end of his story.

"No," he continued. "*I* was caught. Things went wrong and I didn't get out quickly enough, and my uncle . . . It doesn't matter *who* killed the minister. We were all responsible. So we were all exiled."

"Including your father?" she asked.

He nodded.

"So he perished in the forest?"

"He hung himself shortly after we arrived. He . . . was a man given to extremes. Life was wonderful or life was hopeless. Once we were abandoned in the forest, he gave up."

And abandoned you. That's what she thought, and the anger that flared in her gut had nothing to do with Ronan for his thievery or his uncle for killing the minister. His father had committed the worst crime. He had brought his son into that life, and when things went wrong, he abandoned him in the Forest of the Dead. Ronan might joke that he was selfish, but *that* was true selfishness.

As she judged Ronan's father, she was well aware that her mother had also taken her own life. But it was not the same. It could not be *less* the same.

When Ashyn and Moria were born, their mother had kept their twin birth a secret for a very good reason. Because when the girls were discovered, their local governor would inform his warlord. The warlord would tell the marshal, who would, as soon as possible, dispatch a nursing Hound of the Immortals and nursing Wildcat of the Immortals.

This great hound and wildcat would be deprived of food from the moment they left their kennels. When they reached the twins' village, the babies would be placed in a room. The starving beasts would be put in with them at dawn. The door would be closed and not reopened until dusk, no matter what terrible sounds emanated from within.

If the babes were truly a Seeker and Keeper, they would be found nestled with the beasts, suckling, the Seeker with the hound and the Keeper with the wildcat. Then they would be given the best pup and kitten from the hound's and wildcat's litters, as their bond-beasts, and the family would be transported with much pomp and circumstance to their future post.

If the twins were not a Seeker and a Keeper? Then the starving beasts would do what all starving beasts did when left alone with defenseless prey. It was said that the chance of twins being blessed was one in a hundred. Those were the odds her mother had faced. That was why she had tried to run with her daughters. When she'd been caught, she'd taken her own life not in despair, but to ensure the girls' father would not be implicated. Take all the blame on herself. Let their father live, for his sake and their daughters'. There was nothing selfish in that.

Ashyn realized then that she'd been quiet too long after Ronan's confession. He was fussing again, obviously uncomfortable now, as if her silence judged him.

"I'm sorry about your father," she said.

He glanced over sharply, as if that was not the answer he expected.

"I'm sorry about your father and your uncle. I can't imagine how difficult that was."

He met her gaze. "I think you can, Ashyn."

She nodded and looked away.

Ronan reached over and squeezed her hand. "We'll get you out of here. You and Tova and Wenda. And we'll find Moria." He paused. "I'm going to keep walking."

"What?" She stared at him. "Tonight?"

He nodded. "We can't be far now. I'll get water and come back."

"How will you see your way?" She waved up at the cloudy sky.

A tired smile. "I'm a thief, remember? I see very well in the dark. The road is clearly marked. Waiting until morning will only mean we've gone that much longer without water. With luck, I'll be heading back before you wake."

"I shouldn't have used up the water."

"You were worried about my wounds." He managed a strained smile. "I can't fault you for that." He brushed off his breeches and leaned over to give Tova a pat. "I should probably leave now. I was planning to as soon as we'd spoken." He waved at what she'd thought was a rock. It was his pack. He stood. "I'll find us water, and I'll see you soon."

He hefted his pack, offered her one last smile, and set out across the lava plains.

Ashyn woke to Tova growling. When she lifted her head, she could see only his pale shape, so close she could smell his fur. The sky was dark gray.

As Wenda stirred beside her, Ashyn looked up at Tova. His big head moved, as if tracking something. She tried to listen, but all she could pick up was Tova's growling, growing louder until she could feel the vibration of it.

"What's wrong?" Wenda asked.

Ashyn shushed her, then softened it with a reassuring pat.

Tova was turning his whole body now, his nails scratching the rock as he moved, his gaze fixed in the distance.

Another death worm?

Ashyn sucked in air, but reminded herself that they hadn't seen sand or soil in a day.

As she sat up, she heard a scraping to her left. She caught movement. When she glanced over, it stopped, but she could make out the faint outline of a human figure.

Tova started walking slowly in that direction. Ashyn crawled from her sleeping blankets, staying on all fours, ready to follow Tova—

She heard a crack behind her. Something struck her, fast and hard, searing her skin, wrapping around her neck and yanking her up as Wenda screamed. Ashyn's hands flew to her neck as the cord tightened, cutting off her air. Tova let out a roar and raced behind Ashyn. The cord tightened again as if he'd grabbed it in his teeth. Then it slackened, and as she yanked it off, she fell to the hard rock.

She heard another roar and lifted her head to see Tova leaping onto a dark figure. Both went down. A man screamed. Then Tova threw the man aside, his body falling limply as Tova stood there, snarling, his legs planted, fur on end.

"The dog!" a man shouted. "Shoot it!"

"No!" Ashyn screamed.

She ran for Tova and threw herself over him. Something hit her shoulder, piercing right through her cloak and tunic. Then another, this one catching in her cloak before clattering to the rock. Arrows.

"Get off the dog, girl!" a man shouted.

"It's not a dog!" Wenda shouted. "It's a Hound of the Immortals. And that's the Seeker."

Laughter echoed seemingly from every direction. Ashyn's heart pounded, but she stayed on Tova and slid out her dagger, keeping it hidden under her.

"All right, *Seeker*," a man's voice said, mocking, drawing closer.

He stepped from the darkness. He had the coppery skin and eyes of one from the distant desert lands. His head was shaven and he stood at least half a head taller than any man she knew, with broad shoulders and burly arms, bare despite the cool night air. His filthy clothing was covered in silver beads, an odd display of wealth on such shabby apparel. When he smiled, his teeth shone, too, his front ones silver-coated.

A bandit.

Another man sidled up behind him, smaller, with lighter skin and braids.

"Look at that hair," he said, his voice breathy. "The color of the setting sun."

The big man snorted. "Have you never seen a Northerner? Skin pale as a fish belly. Hair like dirty straw." His lip curled in distaste. "We'd be lucky to find a man willing to take her to bed."

"Oh, I'd be willing," the smaller man chortled. "I think you need spectacles, Barthol, if you think that hair resembles straw. And those eyes? Like a summer sky."

The big man—Barthol—shook his head. "On your feet, girl. Mind your cur."

"It's not a cur," Wenda said. "It's a Hound—"

"Yes, yes," Barthol said. "It's a poxed Hound of the—"

He broke off as Tova rose. Then he stared at the huge hound. Behind him, the smaller man whispered, "By the spirits . . ."

"His name is Tova," Ashyn said, as loud as she could while keeping her voice steady. "I am Ashyn of Edgewood. I am the Seeker who guards the Forest of the Dead. He is my bond-beast."

The smaller man dropped to his knees. "My lady. I meant no offense with my joking—"

"Oh, don't grovel," Barthol muttered. "She's a girl, barely old enough to be sold to a whorehouse."

"Barthol!" the other man said.

Another man stepped forward, still hidden in the dark.

213

"Fyren's right, Barthol. Our customs may not be yours, but you ought to show some respect. The girl is blessed by the spirits."

"I know what a Seeker is. A rare and valuable creature." Barthol smiled, teeth shimmering. "The empire will pay well to ransom her."

"Ransom?" Fyren choked on the word, sputtering. "A Seeker? They'd exile us all to her forest . . . after they burned out our tongues for blasphemy."

Noises of assent came from the darkness.

"It's true," Ashyn said. "You cannot ransom me. But if you found me and the child—the last survivors of our village, dying of thirst in the Wastes—and you gave us water and escorted us to Fairview, you would be handsomely rewarded."

"Last survivors?" Fyren said.

"I can explain," she said. "When you bring water for the child."

As Ashyn soon realized, the bandit leader—Barthol—was not a stupid man. One doesn't rise to that position without at least a feral intelligence. He dismissed her stories of shadow stalkers and death worms as the panicked ravings of a girl who'd spent too long in the sun without water, but her suggestion of a reward struck him as rational and sensible. They would escort Ashyn and Wenda to Fairview.

The bandits had plenty of water and food, and strong men willing to carry the child. Fairview was less than a half day's walk, they said, and they set out immediately, lighting the way with lanterns.

As they walked, Ashyn watched for Ronan. She did not mention him—the bandits might fear competition for that reward and send a runner ahead to make sure he didn't reach Fairview alive. Wenda took the hint and stayed silent as well.

THIRTY

It was barely midmorning when they reached Fairview. Wenda had seen it first, from her perch on a bandit's shoulders. She'd cried out so suddenly that the man nearly dropped her. Ashyn looked up and there it was, the white-washed clay buildings shimmering under the sun.

The bandits sent a runner ahead, before the village guards trooped out with their blades flashing. When the party drew close enough to see warriors in the guard stations—and the runner hadn't returned—Barthol sent another. Both came back escorted by armed guards.

Ashyn had her speech prepared. She didn't need it. The guards took one look at Tova and a second at her, and they ordered the bandits back. The warriors surrounded her like a shield and took her to the village.

The governor was waiting at the gate when they arrived. When she drew close enough to see his jowly face, he dipped his chin and bent one knee in a stiff bow.

"Ashyn of Edgewood," he said. "It has been many summers, Seeker."

She remembered him then. He'd visited Edgewood nearly ten summers ago.

"Sir." She gave a slight bow, as taught by the court Seeker. *Always show respect but never genuflect. Remember who you are. Remind them who you are.*

"I bring you news of Edgewood," she said. "The village is no more."

The governor shifted his bulk and glanced at Barthol. "I heard something of that from the runner these men sent. I need to hear more, of course. After you have rested and been fed." He waved to the guards to bring her inside.

"Wait," Ashyn said. "There were children, from my village. They were taken by men. Are they here?"

"No, Seeker. We have seen no one but your party in a fortnight."

"And my twin sister? You have not seen the Keeper?"

He dropped his gaze and shook his head. "No."

He said something else then—platitudes and reassurances, from his tone—but she didn't hear the words. He'd said the only thing that mattered.

Moria was not here.

Ashyn let the guards lead her through the gates.

Fairview was not like Edgewood. Ashyn realized that as soon as they entered. Of course, it looked different, with rounded, whitewashed buildings instead of squared, rough-hewn wood.

217

And they were close enough to the edge of the Waste that villagers had brought in plenty of soil for yard gardens. But it was more than that. The people were . . . not the same.

They looked the same, of course. Mostly native to the region, though it was hard to tell because she saw few villagers as she was escorted through. In Edgewood, by this time of day the streets would have been humming with voices and laughter, footfalls and cart wheels, everyone off and about on their daily chores. Fairview was so quiet that her heart almost stopped, stricken by the irrational fear that she was walking into another empty town, decimated by shadow stalkers. That passed, of course. There were guards and a governor and villagers, just very few of them, most hurrying inside.

The windows along their path were battened shut. As they passed, she'd hear one open, and glance over to catch a flash of a face before it banged shut again.

"Do you get sandstorms here?" she said.

"We do," panted the governor as he struggled to keep up. "Thankfully, they are rare. But the people have retreated because I sent a messenger to clear your path, Seeker. You do not need to be gaped at."

She murmured her thanks and continued on down the empty street.

Seeker, a voice whispered, so faint she could barely hear it. *It is a Seeker.*

It had been so long since she'd heard and felt ancestral spirits that her eyes filled with tears.

"I am Ashyn of Edgewood," she murmured, too low for her escorts to hear. "Seeker of the Forest."

The forest. Ashyn of Edgewood. Seeker.

They seemed merely to repeat her words, voices running together.

"I'm looking for—" she began.

"Who are you talking to?" Wenda asked.

Ashyn smiled and patted Tova. "Just Tova. He's not used to new places. I'm reassuring him."

The hound chuffed, supporting her lie. When Wenda's attention turned away, Ashyn listened for the spirits, but they'd slipped away. She was alone. Again.

The governor left Ashyn and Wenda in his guesthouse. It was unlike any house either of them had ever seen, with silk drapes and cushioned chairs piled with embroidered pillows.

The governor had said he'd return at midday. Soon after they'd arrived, two women had come with food and drink, richer than either girl was accustomed to. Not just honey cakes, but peach jelly and green-tea biscuits and dried persimmons and fruits they'd never seen. Wenda chattered endlessly about the food and the room and the village and the bandits until Ashyn longed to say, "Be still, please, just be still." She wanted to retreat into her thoughts and ponder their situation, but the girl had been so strong during the trip, never complaining. Now, as the ordeal ended, her grief and fear must all be rushing in, and she was dealing with it through girlish chatter.

After the meal, the two women returned with clothing— dresses of linen and silk. Any other time, Ashyn would have delighted in the gifts. Right now, she was only glad that they were clean.

Soon she'd be clean, too. They'd brought buckets of hot water for the tub. Wenda was in no hurry to wash, which gave Ashyn an excuse to retreat into the next room for a quiet bath.

It was then, as she stood by the steaming tub, that she broke down and cried. A silly thing to bring tears. But she saw that tub, and she thought of all the times Moria had drawn a bath for her. She'd come all this way, and she'd been so certain Moria would have at least come through.

Perhaps the kidnappers had passed by Fairview in the dark of night, so as not to be caught with their captives.

But why had they taken the children captive at all? If for ransom, would they not have stopped here? The governor could send a fast horse to his warlord or straight to the court.

Ashyn slid absently from her tunic and breeches. Still in her silk shift, she checked the water. It was a little hot. The women had left a bucket of cool water, too, and she was pouring it in when a hand slapped over her mouth, another grabbing the bucket. She fought, but her attacker dropped the bucket silently into the water-filled tub, and his other hand went around her waist to hold her still.

Why wasn't Tova attacking—?

"It's me," a voice whispered. "Ronan."

As she relaxed, he released her slowly, as if still expecting her to struggle. She turned and, without thinking, she threw her arms around his neck and whispered, "I was worried about you."

"No need to be." She moved back and his gaze dropped. "But with a welcome like that, perhaps I ought to disappear more often."

She blushed, snatched up her tunic, and tugged it on. He motioned for her to stay quiet.

"I'm sorry I startled you," he whispered. "I was waiting until you were making noise pouring the water, so you wouldn't cry out and alert the guards."

"Guards?"

"There are two at every door. One at every window. I had to come through the roof."

"Because of the bandits?"

"Those men aren't bandits, Ashyn. They're mercenaries. They didn't just happen upon you in the Wastes. It was their mission to bring you here."

"What—?"

He covered her mouth again. "Shhh. I don't know exactly what's going on. I only overheard enough to know that whoever they work for has this whole town terrified—the governor, the guards, and the villagers."

She remembered the governor's lowered gaze, the villagers fleeing before her, the closed shutters.

"An entire town?" she whispered. "How?"

"Again, I don't know. But the children of Edgewood are here, too."

This time he seemed to anticipate her exclamation, and covered her mouth.

"I don't know how or why. Moria isn't with them. That's all I could tell. They're being held captive. The whole town seems to be held captive. But I'm going to get you and Tova out."

The door opened. Wenda walked in. She saw Ronan. Ashyn flew across the room before she could cry out.

"Yes, it's Ronan," she said. "He had to sneak in. Something's wrong. The children are being held here."

"How?" Wenda asked.

"I don't know, but Moria isn't with them."

"Then he lies," Wenda said, turning on Ronan. "The boy lies."

The boy? Ashyn had never heard Wenda call him that. Nor had she heard that hard edge in the child's voice.

"I saw Moria. I know I did." Wenda's tone changed now. Childish indignation.

Ashyn relaxed. "I'm sure you did. She must have escaped. Now, Ronan's going to lead us out—"

Wenda looked alarmed. "Out? Why?"

Ashyn explained as quickly as she could.

"And you believe him?" Wenda said when she finished. "He's a thief."

Ashyn felt a surge of anger. "Who helped us through the Wastes."

"Because he wanted a reward. Which he doesn't think he'll get because he abandoned us out there."

Reward? When had the child heard that? They'd never discussed it. Nor had they told Wenda that Ronan was a thief.

Ronan had moved forward and was watching Wenda, his eyes narrowing.

Wenda went on. "If these bandits stole the children, why wouldn't they have taken us captive at Edgewood? Why let us come across the Wastes alone?"

Now Ashyn stared at Wenda. This did not sound like the words of a child, nor the reasoning of a child.

"We can't go!" Wenda said suddenly, childlike again, tears springing to her eyes. "We can't! Ronan's wrong, Ashyn. He must be. He's made a mistake." She looked up at her. "We're safe now. We have food and water, and they're taking care of us. We can't go back out there."

"Then you can stay," Ronan said. "Ashyn?"

She looked from Ronan to Wenda. Outside, she heard voices.

"They're coming," Ronan said. "We must go. The child will be safe." He turned to Wenda. "I'm sorry."

"So am I, boy," she snarled. Her eyes turned orange, a bright, glowing orange, even the whites suffusing with color. Then she opened her mouth and let out an inhuman shriek as she launched herself at Ronan.

THIRTY-ONE

Moria and Gavril had been walking through the Wastes for three days now. They were moving quickly, rising early, walking until they needed lanterns, and then stopping to conserve fuel.

They'd found signs that others had passed that way—a campfire by an oasis, footsteps in a sandy patch, an abandoned waterskin by the roadside. Signs of Ashyn and at least four others, including what looked like a child's small footprints and an elderly villager's shuffling ones. Moving slowly, then. Good. They would catch up before the party reached Fairview.

The third night, they stopped earlier than usual. Moria wanted to push on, but Gavril refused.

"You're getting tired," he said. "Keep this up, and you'll fall by the roadside. I'll not stop for you, Keeper."

"Of course you won't. You'll carry me."

He hadn't even favored her with a scowl for that one.

"I'm stopping now," he said. "If you go on without me, and if I find you collapsed by the roadside—"

"Yes, yes. You'll leave me to die of thirst and let the buzzards and corpse dragons pick my bones."

"There's no such thing as corpse dragons."

"Or shadow stalkers. Don't worry. I'll stay and protect you. I'll let you rest, too. If you need that, you have only to say so, Kitsune."

He stalked off. She smiled and set about finding a place to camp. She knew he wasn't truly angry or even annoyed. It was a long walk, with little amusement to be had beyond needling each other, and the barbs had lost their poisonous tips after Edgewood.

As the sun began to drop, she found another amusement—practicing her dagger throws. They'd stopped at a spot that might be an oasis after one of the rare rainfalls in the Wastes. For now, it was only a patch of sandy soil big enough for two houses. No grasses or flowers. Just moss-covered rocks and a few stunted, gnarled trees. One of those trees was already dead, having been almost entirely debranched for firewood. So she felt no guilt using it as a target.

She practiced with Orbec's blade to get used to it. There was far more variety in warrior daggers than swords. Some were almost as small as kitchen knives. Few warriors used those. Most preferred a blade nearly two hand spans long, similar to the short swords warriors had once paired with their long blades. Moria's and Ashyn's daggers were somewhere between the two, a model more suited to small hands—with a longer handle for throwing. Orbec's dagger blade was slightly longer than hers, but not much, and the handle was perfectly weighted. It was, in short, a superior throwing weapon, suited to both the short distance technique—with rotation—and the more difficult non-rotational long-distance technique. Moria practiced both.

When Gavril returned, she saw him watching a rodent scamper past. They'd seen many of them—brown ratlike creatures with powerful back legs that sent them hopping over the lava plains.

"If you were better with those"—he pointed at her blades—"you'd get us some dinner."

The challenge could not go unanswered, and she set off with Daigo toward an outcropping of rock that appeared to be a likely home for the rodents. It seemed Gavril did not expect her to actually return with a meal. Or so she presumed from his expression when she came back with two of the rodents, tails tied, slung over her arm.

"I'm hoping you know how to dress these," she said as she dropped them in front of him.

"Hardly," he said. "I didn't grow up in this spirit-forsaken place. And you'd best not think you're going to make me do it because it's man's work. If you didn't wish to bloody your hands, you ought not have killed them."

She scooped the rodents up. "I simply thought that if you knew how to dress them, then you should, or we'll be eating hacked meat for dinner. I'll figure it out while you gather wood and start the fire."

"Fetch wood? I—"

"You're a grand warrior, from a line of grand warriors. Fetching wood is, I'm sure, beneath you."

"Give me the beasts."

"Too late." She started strolling off. "Make sure the fire is ready when I am, Kitsune."

He said nothing for a moment, then called after her, "Take them back to that rock to clean them. I don't want to sleep beside a pile of offal."

Skinning rodents was rather like removing a too-tight garment—slit the beast from from nape to arse and then peel. She had no idea how to cut it up, though, so she left the beasts whole. They could put them on a stick, roast, and eat.

Daigo watched the process with a complete lack of interest. When she showed him the final result, he sniffed, unimpressed.

"Yes, I know, I ought to have gotten a third for you. A little help in that matter would have been appreciated."

Another sniff, as if to say he was not a mere hunting cat.

As they neared camp, she could see Gavril ahead, with his back to her as he bent over a fire pit. They had materials to light it from the lanterns, and he'd managed with less in the forest, but he was obviously struggling now. The moss wasn't dry enough to act as tinder. She could have told him that but . . . well, again, there was little enough entertainment to be had in the Wastes. So she hunkered down with Daigo behind a boulder and watched the show.

It was not a silent performance. There was plenty of cursing involved. Finally, as she was about to advise him to use his blades to trim strips from the dried wood, he stopped cussing.

He crouched there, staring at the pile. Then he glanced over his shoulder. She ducked behind the boulder.

When she looked again, he was hunched over the fire pit, talking to it. That's what he seemed to be doing—whispering a string of words so softly that she struggled to make sense of them. Then she realized why. They were not spoken in the common tongue.

The words came faster and stronger. Then his hands lowered over the pit. He crouched there, shoulders quivering slightly, as if with exertion. Finally, he lifted his hands. And there was fire.

Moria pushed to her feet and padded toward him. Daigo followed, equally silent. By the time they arrived, the blaze was devouring the dried wood.

"You started the fire," she said.

He jumped. "That was my task, wasn't it?"

She nodded and crouched beside it, warming her hands. Without looking his way, she said, "I saw you start it."

Silence. Then, belatedly, "So?"

She looked over. "I saw how you started it. Not with tools. With sorcery."

Panic lit his green eyes, but only for a moment before his face set. "Watch your words, Keeper. If you were a man, that accusation could earn you a blade between the ribs."

"It's not an accusation. It's a statement. I wondered how you started the fire in the woods. Now I know."

"You know nothing," he said.

She straightened. "Your father was rumored to be a sorcerer. Apparently, it was more than rumor. I care not whether you are one or not. Whatever you may think of me, I'm not an ignorant village girl. I am the Keeper. My world—"

"—is filled with childish nonsense," he said. "I've heard your stories. You fill your head with monsters and magic and—"

"I *saw* monsters," she said. "And now I've seen magic."

"You saw nothing." He stepped closer, towering over her. "If you claim otherwise again, Keeper, you'll wish you'd held your tongue."

"Are you threatening me?" Her voice was edged with a growl that he seemed not to notice.

"I am warning you against spreading lies about me. I am suggesting you hold that tongue of yours or—"

Before he could finish the sentence, her blade tip was digging into the bottom of his jaw.

"I am the Keeper of the Forest, *boy*," she said. "Do you think those pretty patterns on your arms give you the right to threaten me? They do not. Even if your father was still marshal, they would not. I will take your glowers. I will take your insults. I will take your warnings that you'll abandon me by the roadside if I do not keep pace. But you will not call me a liar. And you will not threaten me."

He'd gone still, his expression unreadable. She tensed, ready to defend herself if he reached for his sword. Even the spirits would not know if he left her here, gutted, in the sand. So she waited. But after a moment, he dropped his gaze.

"My apologies, Keeper." His voice was low, his tone hard to read. It was not obviously mocking. Perhaps it was even genuinely contrite, though she doubted it.

She lowered her blade and stepped back. Gavril reached as if to rub his throat, before stopping himself. A bright red drop of blood fell on his tunic, but he didn't look down at it.

"We have both seen things no one should see," he said finally. "It is difficult for me and an immense tragedy for you. We are anxious and wary. You clearly thought you saw me light the fire by sorcery. I did not, but I accept that is what you believe you saw. I am overly sensitive to the charge, given the rumors about my father. With this situation and my current state—yes, I am tired, I'll admit it—I overreacted. I do apologize. There is no excuse."

On the scale of apologies, none was considered greater than that: *I have no excuse.* She made a noise that he could take as acceptance, though she intended no such thing. Then she lifted the rodents from where she'd dropped them by the fire.

"We'll need sticks."

"I'll roast them," he said.

"You only need roast your own. But save some for Daigo. He doesn't eat scraps. He isn't a house pet."

"I know. I'll share mine."

He reached to pat Daigo, but the wildcat snapped at his fingers and then stalked off with Moria to find a roasting stick.

THIRTY-TWO

After that, Moria was quite willing to drop the subject of sorcery. Gavril would not. As they ate, he felt compelled to explain his reaction to the charge by detailing his father's experience. How the accusation had dogged the Kitsune family even before his father became marshal. How it arose from the fact that their family came from the Katakana Mountains, said to be the birthplace of sorcery, so the charge was as inaccurate and offensive as saying all Northerners were stupid and lazy.

He explained how his father's enemies had used the slander to belittle his accomplishments by saying he'd used enchantments to gain his position. How those same enemies whispered the rumor in the ears of all the court, season after season, and the Kitsune clan believed it was those rumors that had led to his downfall. Given all that, could Moria blame Gavril for reacting too strongly?

231

Yes, she could. Because she'd seen what he'd done, so she knew the rumors were not baseless. He insulted her intelligence by denying it. She ate as quickly as she could, saying little, then retired for the night.

The next day, their walk began in awkward silence. It did not last, though, no more than his angry silences would. They were too much effort to maintain, and as the day passed, he would usually reach the point where he forgot that she was the last person in the empire he'd wish to traverse the Wastes with.

That did not mean, of course, that he would launch into friendly conversation. Moria had begun to suspect that particular social skill was one he'd never mastered. Instead, their discussions would be much like the current one, which had begun when she'd noticed a flock of birds winging past and wished aloud that she were skilled in archery.

"Arrows are for hunters, not warriors," he said. "Attacking an enemy from afar is cowardice."

"And that includes the throwing of blades, I presume?"

"It depends on who's throwing it. For a warrior in battle? Yes. That is why Orbec was not valued for his expertise. For you, though, it's a wise choice."

She was going to comment, probably sarcastically, but he continued.

"The dagger is a poor hand weapon. Most warriors rarely use theirs for anything more than cutting meat. It's good for self-defense against an unarmed man, but otherwise nearly useless. The Keeper and Seeker aren't warriors, though, and it isn't as if they could properly handle swords."

"Give me yours and we'll see whether I can handle it."

"You can wield it, but not well. It's too big for you. That's no insult, Keeper. It's a simple fact. The sword"—he took his out and cut a loop in the air—"is intended for a man's size and strength."

"*That* sword is better suited to a man. Women warriors have thinner and lighter ones, which I will handle quite adeptly when my time comes."

"Adeptly, perhaps, but against a true sword?" He lifted his. "A smaller one is like a dagger, an inferior weapon, which is why so few women become warriors."

For Gavril, even discussion was a form of warfare. The trick, she'd learned, was not to take offense at his strong opinions.

She watched yet another flock of birds fly past.

"Ceding my point, Keeper?" he said after a moment.

"The birds," she murmured. "We've scarcely seen any and now two flocks have passed within a hundred paces."

"If you are unable to counter my point, have the courage to say so. Distraction is a coward's gambit."

A tremendous crack exploded in the distance, and they both froze. Moria looked down to see Daigo plastered against the ground, ears to his head. When she laughed, he gave her a baleful look, rose, and shook himself.

"Thunder," Gavril murmured as he scanned the sun-bright sky.

"Is that what it sounds like?"

"Of course. What else—?" He paused. "I suppose you haven't heard thunder before."

And that, Moria reflected, was the difference between normal Gavril and good-tempered Gavril. There was still a snap to his words, but he skipped the ripe opportunity to mock and insult her.

"We do get rain in the Wastes," she said. "Rarely, though. I suppose that's what had the birds fleeing and the beasts cower—" Daigo cut her off with a growl.

Gavril made a noise that could be a laugh. "He does understand you, doesn't he?"

"When he chooses. Usually only when there's excitement or insult involved."

"Like his Keeper."

She glanced over. She wouldn't say that Gavril was smiling. The curve of his lips was far too slight for that. But his eyes glowed with a rare light, one he did not extinguish when he caught her looking, though he did rub his mouth, as if to temper that sign.

Are you ever happy? Can you be? Or will you just not allow it?

She shook off the thought. Trying to understand Gavril's moods was like trying to gauge the direction of whirling sand to avoid getting blasted.

"Speaking of excitement," she said. "I wouldn't mind getting a glimpse of the storm, if we're close enough."

He squinted up. "Looks like we might be, if that sky is any indicator. See how dark it is?"

"That means a thunderstorm is coming? There's lightning, isn't there? How dangerous is it?"

"It can kill a man if it touches him. It rarely does, though. Just don't lift your sword over your head. I saw that once. We were having a mock battle in the plains and a storm blew in. They made us keep fighting, but told us not to lift our swords. It's a challenge to the storm spirits. So of course one warrior had to issue that challenge. He lifted his sword clear over his head. A bolt of lightning shot from the sky. It hit the sword, lighting with a blast that blinded the two warriors standing beside him."

"Did he die?"

"Exploded in a cloud of ash."

"Truly?"

A twitch of his lips. "No, not truly. Nor were the others actually blind—"

She lifted her hand. "I'll keep the first version."

The twitch grew to a half smile. "I thought you might. Lightning is deadly, though, so—"

A blast of sand hit them, seeming to come from nowhere. Gavril let out an oath as he coughed.

"These thunderstorms come with wind?" Moria asked.

Gavril nodded, spitting sand.

"Then we'd best prepare for more than rain and lightning. I've been out in a sandstorm and—"

The wind whipped up again, and she quietly shut her mouth and eyes. It wasn't just a single gust of wind this time. It swirled around her, blasting from all directions, and she fumbled with her pack, yanking out her cloak and putting it over her face. She peeked out to see Gavril circling, trying to get his back to the wind.

"Cover up!" she shouted. "You can't avoid—"

A gust sent her stumbling. The wind howled now, sand

battering them from every direction.

"Down!" she shouted. "Get down!"

She fell to her knees as Gavril struggled to get his tunic up over his face.

"Down!" she yelled. "Before—"

The wind caught him and knocked him clear off his feet. Moria crawled over. He tried to rise, but Daigo pinned him there. Moria reached him and slung her cloak over both their heads. She tried to stretch it to cover Daigo, too, but the wildcat snorted and burrowed between them, telling her he'd rather just keep his eyes shut.

The wind continued to whine and howl like a wild beast, ripping at their clothes and blasting every bare piece of skin. She tried to see Gavril under the tented cloak, but could only make out the whites of his eyes, then a flash of teeth as he hissed in pain.

"Who'd have thought sand could hurt so much," she said.

He grunted and shifted, as if yanking his tunic down more.

"Is this part of the thunderstorm?" she asked, raising her voice to be heard.

He said something, but she didn't catch it. The whine of the wind hurt her ears, and she gritted her teeth against it. While the wind seemed to grow stronger, she swore the sand wasn't blasting as hard.

She was about to say so when a tremendous crack sounded again. Rolling thunder. She'd heard the expression and it seemed appropriate—great cracks of thunder, one after another. They grew louder and louder, as if the storm was closing in on them. Then she couldn't just *hear* the thunder—she felt it, too—huge vibrations that seemed to push down from above with each crack.

Gavril's head shot up. "That's not—"

Daigo screamed, like a woman's shriek, a terrible sound that ripped through Moria. His claw caught her in the side, tearing through her tunic as she grabbed for him. Her fingers brushed his fur. Then he was gone.

THIRTY-THREE

Moria threw off her cloak and leaped up. Wind beat down, waves of it buffeting her as if trying to push her back to earth. Only a smattering of sand still swirled around, and she squinted, daggers out.

"Daigo!"

He screamed, and she looked up and there he was, suspended in the air, all four paws lashing, tail lashing, too. Moria saw what had hold of him, and yet it took a moment to believe what she was seeing.

Huge yellow talons stretched clear over Daigo's broad back, as if he were a newborn kitten in the grip of a hawk. She didn't try to see the rest of the beast. She didn't care. She ran and slashed the talons. Above her head, a deafening shriek rent the air. Again, she didn't look, just slashed again until whatever had Daigo dropped down enough for her to get a better swing.

Her dagger hit bone, but the blade wasn't big enough to do serious damage, and stayed buried in the talon, wrenching it from her hand. Dimly, she heard it clank to the rock as it fell free. The injured talon released its hold on Daigo. The other kept a grip, though, and the beast started climbing as Daigo struggled wildly, his blood flecking Moria's face. She jabbed upward with Orbec's dagger. She saw then what she was hitting. A feathered body. Green feathers. That was all that fit in her field of vision. A green-feathered stomach, two yellow talons, and Daigo.

She jabbed upward, but the beast was too high and her blade too short. As she swung for the other talon instead, the beast lurched suddenly, giving another earsplitting cry. Blood spurted from the beast's gut, and Moria twisted to see Gavril there, his blade thrust deep in the creature. It dropped Daigo. As it did, its talons scraped the back of Moria's head. They caught in her loosely braided hair, and then began shaking her wildly, trapped by her hair. Moria's body flailed, pain cracking through her neck as she frantically reached up to free herself. She did—or the beast got itself free—and she fell to all fours on the lava rock below.

She saw Daigo spitting and snarling. Her fallen blade lay beside him. She grabbed it, clawed her hair from her face, looked up, and saw the very sky darkened by a bird. It had the shape of a hawk, but was covered in bright plumage, shimmering greens and reds and blues that nearly blinded her. She could just barely make out its head, with a long, curving beak and bloodred horns. With each flap of its massive wings, the air cracked like thunder, the force as mighty as a gale.

Thunder hawk.

A creature of legend, sending storms of wind and sand and rain in its path and in its wake, clapping thunder from its wings and shooting lightning from its eyes.

The huge head turned her way. She saw the glowing, yellow eyes, remembered the stories, and started to drop, her head under her arms, but knew it was too late and there was no place to hide from its gaze—

The beast shrieked again. She glanced up and saw it looking straight at her. No lightning bolts, just those yellow eyes.

She bounded up. Gavril was wrestling to pull his blade from the bird's guts, but it wouldn't budge and he was hanging from it. As she ran over to help, the bird's talons headed for his raised arm.

"Drop the sword!" she shouted. "Let it go!"

Perhaps he didn't hear her over the thunder of the bird's wings. But she was sure he did. Yet a warrior never releases his weapon in battle. Apparently, not even to save his life.

The talons wrapped around Gavril's arm as Moria struggled to get to him, fighting against the tremendous wind, loose hair whipping in her eyes. A black blur passed her. Daigo, leaping at the bird as it flapped its wings to ascend. Moria jumped, too. Daigo caught the bird in the side, all his front claws digging in. Moria did the same, using her daggers for claws, ramming one in as she jumped, and the other on the upswing.

The bird screeched. Daigo swung his rear legs up. They found purchase in the bird's belly. As he dug in all four sets of claws, the bird began to flap its wings madly. Moria glanced down to see the earth dropping away beneath them.

She yanked one dagger free and stabbed the bird's breast. It screamed and dropped a little, losing momentum. Daigo pulled back one giant paw and imitated her with a vicious slash. Blood sprayed. The bird shrieked. Another strike with her dagger. This time, she aimed it into the leg holding Gavril. She pulled it out and plunged it in again. A third time and the talons flexed. The bird didn't release Gavril, but that flex was enough. He fell free, sword still gripped in his hands. She heard him gasp as he hit the rock below.

"Daigo!" she shouted. "Go!"

He understood her just as well as Gavril had. She was sure of it. But he was just as stubborn, turning away as if he hadn't heard, and slashing the bird again. Then Daigo looked over and snarled, fangs flashing. Telling *her* to drop. When she hesitated, he aimed one of those swipes her way. She scowled but yanked out one dagger, braced herself, and pulled out the other. Then she fell.

Daigo dropped, too. He landed on top of her. Which, she reflected, might have been his plan all along, to soften his own fall. It hadn't been as long a drop as Gavril's, though—Daigo's attack had made the hawk dip low enough. She supposed she owed him thanks for that. But she still booted him off her.

The bird was beating a fast retreat, its wings flapping up uneven spurts of wind that buffeted them as they stood. As they watched the beast ascend into the sky, the thunder and the wind became a mere distant boom and a strong breeze that whipped about their legs.

Moria stood there, heaving breaths, her arms aching. She

glanced over to see Daigo twisting to lick at his back. His black fur gleamed wet. *Blood. The talons.*

She raced over and pushed him down. She carefully moved the fur aside to see his skin. It was dark in color, but lighter than his fur, and she could see a puncture as wide as two fingers and as deep as . . .

She swallowed. She had no idea how deep it was, but when she remembered those talons digging into him, she knew it wasn't a shallow gash. And it wasn't only one wound. There were four on this side and, she was sure, a matching four on the other.

When a shadow passed over them, she jumped, but it was only Gavril.

"He's hurt," she said, struggling to keep her voice steady. "Badly hurt. The talons—"

She remembered then that Daigo hadn't been the only one gripped in those terrible claws.

"Your arm," she said. "Are you—?"

"Only scratched," he said.

She could see long, bloody gashes through the tattoos on his right forearm. She started to rise. "Those aren't *scratches*—"

"Little more," he said, waving her down. "They're shallow. Are his . . . ?"

"Not shallow," she whispered as she turned back to her wildcat.

"Can he stand?"

"He shouldn't. He needs—"

"Moria, there's no healer here. If he can walk—"

Daigo answered by struggling to his feet. Three of his wounds gushed fresh blood.

"No!" she said, pushing him back down. "He'll hurt himself more. They need to be sewn. I didn't bring— Blast it, why didn't I bring—?"

Tears sprang to her eyes. She wiped them away. "You go on ahead. Send someone back."

"It'll be days before I reach Fairview, Moria. Then someone has to return—"

"By horse. They'll return by horse. We have water. I can hunt for food. We'll be fine."

"No, you won't. Not with that creature hunting for *its* food. We need to go before it comes back. We have to find shelter."

She sprang up. "And abandon Daigo? I do not leave him. Anywhere. Ever. If that monster comes back, it comes back for both of us, because—"

"Moria, calm yourself." He put his hands on her shoulders. "I know you won't leave him. I wouldn't ask you to. I meant that we need to figure this out."

She took a deep breath, then peered over the landscape. There were piles of rock here and there, and gullies, too, where the earth had shifted. Were any nearby ones enough to shelter the three of them from the thunder hawk?

"They taught me battle healing," she said. "Why didn't I pay more attention?"

As she cursed herself, Gavril said hesitantly, "I might be able to help."

She looked up sharply. Sorcery. Healing magic.

"I also had lessons in battle healing," he said quickly, as if reading her thoughts.

And you didn't mention this when your head was injured? Or when that beast shot quills in us? No, Gavril, that is not what you mean at all.

It didn't matter. He could help Daigo. That was all that counted. She backed away.

"You ought to gather the packs," he said. "Some items may have fallen out. You should go look."

You want me to leave so I don't see you use sorcery.

"I need to keep him still and clean his wounds. I don't care what you do, Gavril. I'll tell no one."

He broke eye contact and shook his head, his jaw setting. "I don't know what you mean, but if you don't go and look around . . ."

He didn't finish the threat, but she heard it clearly. *Leave me or I'll let your bond-beast die.*

She walked away, and she kept walking until she heard only the distant murmur of his voice, casting his spells. Then she lowered herself to the rocky ground, pulled up her knees, and waited.

THIRTY-FOUR

Whatever Gavril did, it didn't miraculously cure Daigo. Moria expected that. She knew a little about sorcery. When villagers told hushed tales of evil men who would murder infants and mutilate children, their father would take the girls aside, particularly Moria.

"I know you enjoy such tales, Rya," he'd say. "But you must never soil an entire people with twisted lies. There are sorcerers. I've seen them. I've traded with them. They know small magics, helpful magics."

"And nothing more?" she'd ask.

When she was young, he'd say no, nothing more. As she grew older, though, he'd said, "There are dark uses for sorcery. It is a tool. It can be a simple one, used for simple things, like a blade for cutting meat. It can also be more dangerous, like a sword, but even then, it is intended only to defend oneself

245

against one's enemies. Yet not every man who wields a sword is honorable, and so, too, with sorcerers."

Whatever Gavril had done to Daigo, it had been that simple kind of sorcery. A magical stitching of his wounds. But it was enough. Daigo was on his feet and moving.

Moria kept scouring the landscape for places to hide, but they'd seen no sign of the thunder hawk, and as she grew more certain that the danger had passed, she sank into thoughts of her father, spurred by those reflections on his words.

She would never see him again. Never hear his voice. Never sit and listen to him gently instructing her, guiding her in the right direction. Had she appreciated that? Perhaps not. He'd had stories, too, endless tales of his adventures as a traveling merchant before they came to Edgewood. She'd liked those better.

She would never see him again. Not in this life. The thought seemed too much for her mind to even approach. It was like in winter, when they'd go to the spring to slide on the ice. Daigo would circle the edge, sometimes putting a paw on the ice, only to back off quickly. That's what the truth of her father's death felt like—her mind endlessly circled it, evaluated, considered, perhaps took a step toward acceptance, only to retreat quickly.

"So that beast . . ." Gavril's words shattered her thoughts. "It was a thunder hawk?"

She made a noise he could interpret as assent.

He replied evenly, as if fighting the urge to snap at her, "I'm trying to understand the threat, Moria. If it comes back again, we need to be ready."

She wheeled on him. "You would have let him die."

"What?"

She waved at Daigo. "You were willing to let him die if I didn't walk away back there."

"I would never—"

"We jumped on that bird. Daigo and I. For you, because you were too blasted stubborn to let go of your sword. Daigo made his injuries worse fighting for you, and you would refuse to heal him to protect a secret that is not a secret at all?"

"I did not mean I wouldn't treat him."

"And if I'd stayed?"

He pushed his braids behind his ear. "You wouldn't."

So it had been an idle threat, knowing she'd never risk her wildcat's life to simply prove a point.

She resumed walking. "We can't keep doing this. If you have skills that can help—"

Thunder rumbled in the distance. They looked at each other.

"Was that . . . ?" Moria said.

"It sounded like it." He turned quickly, scouring the landscape. "We need cover. Rocks. Or a narrow chasm."

"I saw a pile of rocks over there." She pointed left, in the direction they'd come. "But it didn't look big enough."

Daigo nudged her to continue forward and she ran alongside him. Gavril's boots thumped as he followed. The plains looked flat, but the lava rose and fell in waves often too gentle to see. Moria crested one of those waves and looked out to a see a hillock in the distance, the sun shimmering off the rock, nearly hiding it.

As they raced toward it, the wind picked up, sand swirling from every seemingly barren nook and cranny in the rocky plain. Moria slitted her eyes and shielded them. Another roll of thunder, closer now. Then the sun vanished. She glanced over her shoulder to see a dark shape blocking it. The thunder hawk swooped over the plain, searching for its lost prey.

They reached the rise. It was nearly as tall as Moria. When the lava had swept over the land, it had plowed down almost everything in its path. Sometimes, though, it had met an obstacle unwilling to fall, even under molten rock. The lava had done its best here, but the obstacle remained—a heap that may have been a stone hut, one side crumbling now, as if it was finally giving way under the weight.

As Moria and Gavril scooped out the debris, Daigo paced and watched the sky. Finally, they'd removed all they could, leaving a cave-like hole. It narrowed in the back, better suited for Daigo's flexible form. He wriggled in as best he could.

Moria and Gavril hid their packs under the debris. Then Moria went in. It was a tight fit, with barely enough space to crouch.

"Are you going to make room for me, Keeper?"

"I'm trying."

Another long roll of thunder. The sky was so dark she could barely see. The sand whipping about didn't help, especially after they'd unsettled it moving rocks.

"Come out," he said. "There's more room in the middle. I ought to be there."

She shielded her eyes and slipped from the hole. Gavril

crawled inside and turned around. Once he'd settled, Moria backed in and promptly bashed into him.

"Move back," she said.

"I can't. Just sit."

He tugged her down, and she landed in his lap.

"Not there," he said, his voice muffled as if he was talking through gritted teeth.

"Is there someplace else?"

He didn't answer. She was still uncomfortably close to the cave mouth, so she shifted to get farther in.

"Stop wiggling."

"My knees are sticking out. And I'm getting sand in my face."

"Then cover it. Just stop—" He drew in a ragged breath, as if she was crushing him. "Stop wiggling."

"I'm not that heavy. I just need to move—"

"I said, stop. Now." His breath was coming harder and she could feel the thump of his heart against her back.

"Do you have a fear of small places?" she said.

"No."

"It's nothing to be ashamed of. I know—"

"Yes, I have a fear of small places. Now stop—" He put his hands on her hips, as if to hold her still, then quickly pulled them back. "Stop moving. Please."

"Fine. There. Better?"

A moment's pause. "Not truly."

"And you call *me* difficult."

He made an odd noise, and she realized her hair was probably in his face, which may have explained his continued difficulty drawing breath. She leaned to the side, feeling him tense as she moved, then he relaxed as she swept her hair over and rested her head against his shoulder. He lifted his arms and seemed to be trying to figure out where to put them.

She grabbed his wrists and set his hands on her knees. "There. Now if the thunder hawk sees anything, it'll be your hands. You'll be taken again, and this time, I might not save you."

"I don't think the bird will get me out without taking you along."

"Oh, I'll find a way."

He began to relax, his hands resting on her knees, his body shifting slightly, getting comfortable, his chin moving to rest on her head. Then a sniff, as if he was about to sneeze, and he reached up to move a stray piece of her hair aside.

"I know," she said. "I ought to cut it off. It almost got me killed by that bird."

"You can't cut it off."

Keepers and Seekers were not permitted to do more than trim their hair to elbow length. Ashyn said they ought to be grateful they weren't like the spirit talkers, who weren't ever allowed to cut their hair or their nails. Personally, Moria would be more concerned with the "eyes plucked out, tongues cut off, and nostrils seared" part of being a spirit talker, but she could see that the uncut nails might be inconvenient as well.

Even when Moria and Ashyn trimmed their hair or their nails, it had to be done at the shrine, and the leavings imme-diately burned, the ashes scattered. Otherwise supposedly they could be used against the spirits—and the village—by sorcerers.

"I don't care what they say. As soon as we get out of here, I'm cutting my hair off."

"No, you're not," he murmured.

"Care to wager on it? There are no spirits here to offend."

"And no sorcerers to steal it?"

"Is that true, then? Do they use hair and nail clippings?"

He tensed. "I have no idea."

"Then don't bring it up."

He relaxed again and she did, too, settled in against him, listening to the storm rage outside. He shifted his shoulder, making her more comfortable, and she felt the muscles of his chest, hard against her back, and saw his arm flex, too, muscles moving under his dark skin.

Her eye traveled down to the Kitsune tattoos. Perhaps it was their association with warriors, but they were, for her, as a woman's jewels might be to a man. Gavril's were among the best she'd seen, beautifully wrought, the dark-inked artwork amazingly intricate, the spot color bright green. There were few physical shortcomings a man could possess that could not, in her mind, be compensated for by good warrior ink.

She glanced over at him and had to admit there were blessed few physical shortcomings that needed compensating for. It was a shame to waste such a face and physique on such a surly—and, yes, exceedingly difficult—boy. Although, she supposed it was probably for the best, or being alone with him on this long journey might have pushed her to seek distractions they could ill afford. As it was, she'd be safer wooing a rock adder.

Speaking of rock adders . . . they did like to inhabit damp, rocky holes. She glanced over her shoulder.

"Stop that," Gavril hissed.

"I moved my *head*."

"Shhh!" Then, "Listen."

She did, and picked up the distant *crack-crack* of the thunder hawk's wings.

THIRTY-FIVE

"Now hush," Gavril whispered. "Before it hears us."

Though she was not the one who had instigated or perpetuated the exchange, she said nothing, which was usually the best course with Gavril.

The wingbeats grew louder. The beast seemed to be heading straight for them. Could it smell them? Did birds *have* a sense of smell? It wasn't anything she'd ever needed to ponder.

Then it landed. They couldn't see it—the cave mouth dipped down, and they were looking at rock. But she heard a thud that set the earth trembling.

The thunder stopped. The wind stopped, too. Then talons scraped against rock. A thump. Another one. The bird was walking, and the earth quaked with each footfall.

It stopped. Silence. Then the beast let out a deafening shriek . . . right outside the cave.

"No," Gavril whispered. "No, no, no."

His hands went around her knees, as if shielding them, yanking and tugging as he tried to shift backward, to get them farther into the cave. She could feel Daigo moving, too, trying to give them room. It was no good. They were in as far as they could go. And her legs were a hand's breadth from the mouth of the cave.

Thunder cracked as the bird flapped its wings. The wind swirled up. Gavril kept pulling her, trying to shift her, get her off to the side. But there was no room.

She took out one dagger, gripping it, then pried his fingers from her knee and tugged his hand to the hilt of his blade. He hesitated as if, for one moment, he wasn't sure what it was. Then he eased the sword from the sheath and up, over her lap, blade ready, if awkwardly held. Though he tried a few angles, she could tell it was no good—with Moria on his lap, he couldn't do more than feebly jab.

Moria unsheathed her other dagger. They sat there, holding their weapons in the dark, sand swirling in as the bird beat its wings, each crack of thunder punctuated by an earth tremor, as if it was hopping more than walking, using its wings to help itself along.

It's injured. Remember that. We hurt it and—

The bird stopped. Everything stopped.

A beak thrust into the cave, so fast that they both jumped. Gavril's free arm wrapped tighter around her legs, but the beak was right there, so massive it barely fit through. It opened just enough to reveal rows of small, blade-sharp teeth. The beak slashed at her legs as the bird worked itself in farther, rock crumbling to give it room. Gavril tried his sword, but only succeeded in enraging the bird, making it fight harder, those tiny teeth slashing and biting Moria's leg.

"Can you use anything else?" she said as she struggled to keep back from those teeth.

"I'm trying—"

"No, something else." She twisted, gaze meeting his. "Do you know anything else? I'll cover my ears. I'll hide my eyes. If you know any magic—"

"I would use it." He held her gaze. "Truly, Moria. I have nothing more to fight with than my blade, and I can't get enough leverage—"

"Then we'll have to fix that."

She raised both her boots and slammed them into the bird's beak. The beast let out a tremendous roar and fell back. As she rushed from the cave, she felt Gavril grab for her feet and heard him shout. She lunged out and leaped up, daggers still clutched in her hands. The bird was there. Right there. Towering above her—that head diving toward her, a head as big as a horse cart, beak opening, that massive beak with those terrible teeth.

I'm dead, she thought.

The head slashed down, and she leaped at it. Straight at it. Blades raised. One made contact, slicing into the bird's eye. It screamed then, a shriek that seemed to open the skies. Thunder and lightning and a sudden torrent of rain battered her as the bird yanked back, her blade coming free, her body falling, realizing only then that she'd been lifted clear off the ground by her strike. She hit the rocky ground so hard the air flew from her chest.

She saw a blur. Black fur raced past. Daigo launched himself at the bird. Then she heard a snarled shout and lifted her head to see Gavril there, in front of the bird, thrusting his sword up into its throat.

The bird let out a gurgling scream and whipped its head back, sending Gavril flying to the side, still clutching his sword. The thunder hawk's giant wings lifted as it prepared to take flight, blood pumping from its torn throat. Moria squinted through the torrents of rain to see Daigo still hanging from the bird's side.

"Daigo!" she shouted. "Jump!"

He did, but not before one last slash. He dropped, twisting and landing on all fours just as the bird took flight. It rose. Then it stopped and hovered there, bright, rain-soaked plumage shimmering as the sun pierced the clouds. Then it started to fall. Moria looked to see Gavril, still struggling to his feet, dazed. The bird was right above him, dropping fast.

"Gavril!" she shouted as she ran at him, sheathing her daggers.

He looked up and started to lunge. Moria caught him by the tunic and yanked. The thunder hawk landed, glancing off Gavril as it did, knocking them both off balance. Gavril recovered and raced to the bird, slipping and sliding on the wet rock. He raised his sword, ready to stab the beast in the breast. Then he stopped.

He stood there, rain pouring off him in sheets, the sun bright now, strangely shining through the rain, the light glinting off his sword. Moria could see him breathing hard, his green eyes seeming to glow as bright as his sword, bright with fury and determination and fear. Yes, fear. She could see that, in his face and in his stance, holding himself fast, gulping air, watching the bird, ready to strike the fatal blow. But it lay there unmoving.

Moria unsheathed her daggers as she walked over. Daigo followed her, creeping through the rain, head down, as if he could avoid getting wet.

She walked to the bird and looked down at its ruined eye and bloody throat. She kicked its beak. It fell open, but the bird didn't move. Another kick, just to be sure, then she sheathed one dagger and turned to Gavril.

"It's dead," she said.

"You . . ." He looked toward the cave. "You just ran out . . . you could have been killed."

She sheathed her other dagger. "Yes, it was foolish. Exactly what you expect, I'm sure."

"No, not foolish. It was . . ." He seemed to search for a word, then looked down at the bird as if in shock. His gaze turned to her. "You don't fear anything, do you, Moria?"

She gave a short laugh. "Oh, there was plenty of fear. I'm glad it's raining, because I'm not completely sure my breeches would have been dry."

A quirk of a smile. "A warrior isn't supposed to admit fear."

"Then I suppose it's a good thing I'm not a warrior."

"No, you are." He paused, meeting her gaze. "You truly are."

She felt her cheeks heat and covered it by kneeling beside the bird. The rain was easing now, and with the sun shining, the colorful plumage glittered.

"Sadly, I can't claim the killing blow," she said, ducking to look at the bird's throat. "Good work, Kitsune."

He didn't answer. She could sense him walking up behind her, but she kept examining the bird.

"I meant what I said in the cave, Moria. I don't know anything that could have helped."

"I know."

More silence. He was right behind her now. She swore she could hear him breathing.

"You were right. I don't need to tell you that, but . . . yes, my family . . . " He trailed off. "I only know simple things, though, like how to start a fire or close a wound."

She nodded and then glanced over. He was frozen there, braced for a reaction, for questions.

"I'll tell no one," she said, and then she turned back to the bird.

She plucked out three feathers—smaller ones from the chest and one large one from the wing plumage.

"Trophies?" Gavril asked.

She gave him a look. "That would be dishonorable. A warrior—or a Keeper—is not supposed to take pride in the kill. It's proof. Otherwise, no one will believe we met a thunder hawk."

He nodded. "Here, I'll carry the large one. My pack is bigger."

He reached out. His fingers were trembling slightly. He gave a soft, nervous laugh. "As you see, you weren't the only one frightened by that thing."

"I thought a warrior wasn't supposed to admit fear."

He met her gaze. "I know you'll protect my secrets, Keeper."

"I will." She pushed to her feet. "Now, let's see if we can find dry wood somewhere to build a fire. Rain was perhaps the last thing we needed."

"At least your face is clean now."

"Perhaps, but it did absolutely nothing for this." She lifted a handful of her knotted, soaked hair.

"We'll get that fixed. Come on, then. Gather your pack and we'll go."

THIRTY-SIX

Moria had argued most strenuously for the obvious solution to her hair issues: chop it off. Gavril refused to permit it. Ashyn would be upset, and Moria would have to answer to the court Keeper and Seeker, perhaps even the emperor. Clearly, the emperor had far too little to do if he'd concern himself with a Keeper's hair, but she ceded Gavril's point. Or she did when he offered to help come up with an alternate solution.

The basic methods—a single braid or tie—were perfectly acceptable for daily life, but did not control her locks when battling anything of substance. Additional braids would help, but took time, and would likely give her welts when they whipped about in battle.

"I fail to see how you'd think I'd be an expert in this matter," he said as she finished brushing out the snarls.

"You've been to court. You've seen the women's styles."

He snorted. "I'm not sure which is more amusing, Keeper: to think you believe I spent much time in court, or to think you believe I'd waste any time there looking at women's hair."

"True," she said. "There are probably far more engaging sights if the rumors are true, about how little some of the court women wear."

"The women of court are not to my taste."

"You have a taste?"

A glare. "No, I have better things to occupy my mind, in and out of court."

And that, she mused, was truly a shame, but sadly not unexpected.

He continued. "If I have any knowledge of women's hair fashions, it comes from my mother, which won't help you at all. Your hair could not be more dissimilar." He paused, then hunkered down, tilting his head. "There is a style I have seen some men wear, those with your sort of hair. Men too vain to cut it short."

"Vanity is not my issue. I would gladly—"

"Yes, yes, I know. Which is why I'm devising solutions. What the men do is braid the sides, perhaps a hand's span of hair, then tie them together. The back stays untethered, but as long as the sides are held, it seems to work."

"Unless I get caught in a thunder hawk's talons again."

"I'm trusting that's a once-per-lifetime experience. Now, take the hair . . ."

"If you ever tell anyone of this . . ." Gavril warned as he worked on the second braid.

"Is that a threat, Kitsune?"

"Yes." He tightened the braid. "Yes, it is."

She'd attempted to do her hair herself, and thought she was doing a fine job, but apparently, it hadn't been to his standards. After several fruitless attempts to correct her technique, he'd taken over.

"Given that I promised not to tell anyone you're a sorcerer—or that you admitted fear in battle—I'm certainly not going to tell anyone you braided my hair. And truly, can you imagine any conversation in which the subject would arise?"

He tugged a braid and grumbled under his breath, but it was a good-natured grumble—or as close to good-natured as Gavril seemed capable of. They'd had to trek out of the storm-struck area to find dry wood for fire, and he hadn't said an unkind word in all that time. He was still prickly, of course, and argumentative and difficult, but that was to be expected.

When he finished, he pulled back the braids and surveyed his work. "Now we need to find something to tie it with. You had a band . . ."

"Which came out when the thunder hawk decided to restyle my hair. I can pull a strip of fabric off my other tunic—"

"No, it'll unravel." He took one of his own braids and pulled off the band.

As he fastened it in her hair, she asked, "Why don't you have beads, like other warriors? Is it a family custom?"

"No. I don't see the need. Colored beads are for show. Like a peacock's plumage."

"Like those?" She gestured at his tattooed forearms.

A scowl, more mock angry than serious. "That's not the same, Keeper. Those are—"

"Ancestral devotion markings for high-born warriors," she said. "I know. I'm only teasing." She shifted for a better look. As long as the subject was being discussed, it gave her the excuse. "I've heard it's done with needles and ink. Is that true?"

"Yes."

"When I asked Orbec about them, he said it doesn't hurt."

"He lied."

She laughed softly and looked up. "Truly?"

"*Very* truly. I am extremely glad they only do one section at a time, with many moons between."

She smiled and shifted onto her stomach, her feet over Daigo. Gavril was sitting, leaning back on his elbow, letting her examine the tattoo on his left arm. His eyes were almost closed, as if basking in the fire's heat. He looked more at peace than she'd ever seen him.

"When do you get the upper arms done?" she asked.

"Soon. They were supposed to be done on the eighteenth anniversary of my birth, but winter is hardly the time for travel in the Wastes."

"Are you glad for the delay?"

He paused. "Not particularly. Getting inked is hardly pleasant, but . . ." He shrugged. "It means something that's important to me."

"It's beautiful work."

He hesitated. Then, "Thank you." Another pause. "I'll remember that when they're doing the inking, and I'm trying very hard not to cry out."

She laughed. "If you fell from a thunder hawk without so much as a gasp, I think you can handle inked needles."

She rolled onto her back, staring up at the dark sky, feeling the fire's heat against the top of her head. Gavril reached forward and she felt a faint tug on her hair. She tilted her head back to see him moving her hair away from the fire pit.

"Before it catches alight," he said.

"See? It's a menace. We may have escaped a thunder hawk, but ultimately, we *will* perish . . . killed by my hair."

A chuckle. He settled in again, and silence fell, broken only by the snapping of the sparks and the crackle of burning wood. When the clouds shifted, stars lit up the sky, brighter than they'd ever seemed in Edgewood.

"I know you're curious," Gavril said after a while. "About the sorcery. You're trying very hard not to ask about it."

"Given how difficult it was for you to admit to it, I can hardly imagine you'd welcome questions."

A few moments of silence. Then, "What I said yesterday, about the rumors of my father, how his enemies used that against him: it was true."

"Except that they weren't mere rumors."

She heard his boots scrape the rock as he shifted. "That we can do sorcery? Yes, that was true. But they said he stole babies from their cradles, Moria, and cut out their hearts in dark rituals. Murdered children. Defiled women. Mutilated warriors. All the worst that has been said of sorcery, they accused him of doing to further his fortunes. The same rumors have dogged my family since the first Kitsune became a warrior. Is it any wonder we deny having powers? Admit to anything, however simple, and the rest would be presumed true as well."

"So you use it for nothing more than lighting fires and closing wounds?"

Silence. Her tone had been curious, not accusatory, but clearly he seemed to have taken it that way. When she glanced over, though, he didn't seem angry or offended, just contemplative.

"There is . . . more," he said. "I haven't the skills or the training for it, but there are more . . . martial applications." He moved to look at her. "It is a skill we are born with, Moria. A gift from our ancestors. Like caste. Would you argue that a man born a warrior should not lift a sword against an unarmed enemy because it gives him an advantage?"

She considered that as she stared into the night sky. "But if your enemies do not know your skills, is that not unfair? If you are a warrior, other men see your blades and know not to challenge you or they'll taste your steel."

He said nothing for a long while. Then, "Perhaps. But we do not hide our sorcery by choice."

"True."

He paused, as if he'd been preparing to add further arguments.

"Will you learn more?" she asked.

"Yes. My training has been . . . slow. My mother blames sorcery for my father's exile and wouldn't allow my uncles to train me. So they did it in secret."

"Against her will?" She looked back at him.

He shrugged. "I am my father's only son. To deny my abilities would be an insult to our ancestors."

She flipped over. "His only son?"

"You did not know that?"

"No. I was a child when your father was exiled. When you arrived, I only recall my father saying you were the child of Marshal Kitsune's third wife. I presumed you had older brothers. Your father was not a young man."

"True, but he was not blessed with fertile wives."

"Oh, so clearly it was *their* fault. All three of them."

He gave her a stern look. She reminded herself that in the warrior code, there was only one thing more important than loyalty to one's emperor: filial piety. To suggest that a man's father lacked virility was to ask for a drawn sword and spilled blood.

"I'm sorry," she said.

He shrugged and leaned back, getting comfortable again. "I'm hardly an expert in such matters. I was told that his first two wives could not bear children, so he wed my mother. I'm his only son. Only child, as well." A sidelong glance her way. "Which may suggest you're correct about my father being the problem, but I did not ever say such a thing."

"I still apologize."

He dipped his head. "Thank you."

"You were his only child, then. I can see why your mother would want to protect you." She paused. "And why your uncles would wish you trained in their ways. You must have been close to your father. I suppose I hadn't realized that. An only son is much different from a late-born child to a third wife. You must—" She stopped. "Now I am being too curious. I'm sure your father is not a subject you like to discuss."

"I . . ." He stopped and stretched out on the rock. Daigo grunted as Gavril rested his bare feet against him. "I do not often discuss it. In court it is a subject best avoided. To most citizens, I am the son of a traitor. My father still has supporters in the army, though. Warriors who swear he did not flee that battlefield. To them I am the son of a martyr. Neither position is . . . comfortable."

"No, it would not be." She went quiet for a moment, then she said, carefully, "I know my father believed the empire had not done right by your father."

"He was betrayed." He spat the words, laced with bitterness. Quiet rage, too. "Accused of a crime he did not commit. Betrayed by men he thought he could trust, including the one he trusted more than any other, his closest friend, the emp—"

He clipped the word short. "I speak rashly. I apologize."

"You needn't apologize to me. I have no reverence for a man I've never met."

"You should, Keeper." His voice was firm. "Or, at least, have care enough to feign it. You cannot be careless in court. Ever."

"I would prefer not to go to court. Ever."

"I know. And I agree. But I fear, after this, neither of us will have a choice in the matter."

"As long as it's a short visit."

He paused, then murmured, "Yes, let's hope it's a short visit," and they lapsed into peaceful silence again.

THIRTY-SEVEN

They had been on the road for five days now. Gavril believed they were approaching Fairview. Moria hoped so. She still worried about Daigo's wounds.

As for Gavril, he'd been a better companion since the thunder-hawk fight. That sense of calm had, for the most part, stayed. He still confused debate with conversation, but if Moria was being honest, that was her preference as well. She had little patience for idle chatter, and a lively discussion kept her entertained on the mind-numbing walk.

It was nearly midday when she spotted it, shimmering in the sun. A city of white.

"Is that . . . a mirage?" she asked.

"No, that would be Fairview. They whitewash the buildings. A beacon for the weary traveler on the Wastes."

"Ah, a fair view indeed." She tried to smile, but her heart pounded too hard. "So this is it, then. If Ashyn—*when* Ashyn made it through the Wastes, this is where she'd go."

"It is, and she did. You know she did. We saw no signs otherwise, and as you said many times, you'd know if she was gone. She's there—or she was there and you'll have news of her."

"And the children?"

He paused then. "I still . . . I do not see the point in men taking the children."

"Does evil need a purpose?"

Another pause. "If the children were taken, perhaps that proves that what happened at Edgewood was not evil. That the massacre at Edgewood was a mistake, one that could not be reversed but could be mitigated by saving the most innocent."

Even after all they'd seen, he could not accept it. Should she blame him, when she still skirted around the treacherous ice of her father's death?

Gavril cleared his throat. "I doubt the children would be here, though. Those men would push on to Riverside, where the warlord resides. Fairview does not even have a proper garrison."

"I'll worry about the children later. Ashyn will be here." She found her smile then, a blazing grin as her heart lifted. "I'll race you."

She wheeled and took off, Daigo at her side.

"Keeper!"

She turned, still moving. "Yes, only children run. I don't care. You can be mature and walk."

He gestured to the sword hanging at his side. "It's not about maturity. Run and I end up with bruises."

She laughed. "Then you must walk, Kitsune." She started to turn away again, then looked back. "Is my face clean?"

"Yes, Keeper. Your face is clean. Your hair is tame. Your clothing looks as if you've been walking for five days in the Wastes, but if you don't stand too close to anyone, you'll be fine."

She made a face at him and took off.

Guards met Moria as soon as she drew close. She stopped running then and walked with all the dignity she could muster, one hand resting on the handle of a sheathed dagger, the other on Daigo's head.

"I am Moria of Edgewood," she called as the guards walked out. "Keeper of the Forest of the Dead."

Like her, they had their hands on their sheathed weapons. Caution devoid of disrespect. Now they dipped their heads.

"Welcome, Keeper."

Gavril walked up beside her.

"I am the Keeper's guard," he said. "From the Edgewood garrison."

He'd pulled on his spare tunic, with sleeves that covered his forearms. As he'd pointed out last night, he could never be certain just how welcome Gavril Kitsune would be.

Three guards had come out at first—two from the towers, and one from inside. Now, the gates opened and four more approached. And when they did, Moria knew something was wrong. A town without a garrison would likely not have seven warriors in the entire community. Also, these new men were not warriors. Yes, they dressed in plain tunics and breeches, and they were clean-shaven, as required of warriors in service. They also wore the traditional blades hanging together on their left side, the dagger above the sword. But there was a food stain on the collar of the smallest man. The large one—a bald, copper-skinned desert dweller—had a tiny tattoo on the side of his neck. A third had shaving-blade nicks along his chin, as if he'd recently cut away more than mere stubble. Small things, which would go unnoticed by anyone who hadn't grown up scampering through a garrison.

Daigo began to growl. Not loudly, but she could feel the vibration. Gavril started to step in front of her before stopping himself. He moved behind her instead, so close she could feel his sword hand on his hilt, brushing her back.

The big bald guard waved at the gates. "Come, Keeper. Fairview welcomes you."

"No," Gavril said. "We'll not be stopping. The Keeper wished merely to greet Fairview and bless it. We're pressing on to Riverside."

The smallest man stepped forward. "Fairview wishes to welcome the Keeper. This is a rare honor, and we would like to celebrate."

"I fear that is not possible," Moria said. "I beg the forgiveness of Fairview's spirits, but we have urgent business in Riverside." She dipped her head. "I'll take my leave."

She turned, Gavril and Daigo moving with her. The small man lunged into their path, sword drawn. Gavril swung around her so fast she didn't realize he'd even moved until she heard the clang of steel. Gavril's sword knocked the small man's hard enough that Moria swore she heard the man's wrist crack. He held his blade, though, smacking it back against Gavril's, both stepping forward, swords crossed.

"Lower your weapon, Kitsune," the biggest man rumbled. "I know who you are. My scout spotted you before you hid your ink."

The others surrounded them, blades drawn, all pointed at Gavril. Moria's hands flexed on her sheathed daggers, and she felt Daigo tense. Seven armed men against one young warrior, one even younger Keeper, and a wildcat. In a fight for their lives, the odds would be worth taking, but until then . . .

Her hands relaxed on her blades and she whispered, "Gavril . . ."

"Sheathe your sword, Kitsune," the big man said. "Do you wish to begin a sword fight with the girl in the middle?"

"The girl is a Keeper." Gavril took a deep breath and lowered his blade. "Remind your men who she is and the disrespect of pulling steel on her."

"My men are not good with respect," the big man said. "But they will not harm your Keeper. Our lord wishes her safe, so she will be safe, as her sister is."

"Ashyn?" Moria said in spite of herself. "You have Ashyn."

The big man smiled and she caught a flash of silver teeth. "She is a guest of Fairview. Now come along inside."

"No." Moria lifted her chin. "Bring her to the gates. I will see her before I enter."

The small man stepped past Gavril, who rotated, gaze locked on him.

"Is that how it works, girl?" he said. "You give us orders?"

"I will not enter until I see—"

The small man's blade shot up. Gavril leaped forward, and she saw his sword arm swing out, and was about to shout a warning, tell him not to provoke them with his blade, but there was no blade in his grasp. He'd caught the man's sword with his bare hand.

"You do *not* raise your weapon against the Keeper."

Moria stared at Gavril's hand. Blood seeped through his fingers as he held the blade. Her heart pounded. A warrior's sword was unbelievably sharp—new ones were tested on dead men, and a blade that could not pass through at least two cadavers with one slice was discarded. With a twitch of that sword, Gavril could lose his fingers. She stepped forward, touching his back, but he kept his gaze locked with the other man's. Gavril pulled the blade down, then he released it.

"Warriors." The small man spat to the side. "It's a wonder they haven't all died out from their own reckless stupidity." He turned to Gavril. "You think you're brave, boy, but all I see is a coward hiding behind a girl. Hiding who he is." He nodded at Gavril's covered arms. "Or are you ashamed of your family?"

"I am not. I stand here only as the Keeper's guard. That is my duty: subsuming my own identity until she is safe."

"How noble." The man sneered and spat again. "Warriors."

The big man stepped forward. "Do you still insist on seeing your sister before you'll enter, Keeper?"

Moria straightened. "I do."

He whispered something to a man near him. The man loped off into the village. Moria and Gavril waited in silence.

When the man returned, leading two women with hoods hiding their faces, the true guards stiffened. The big man shot them a look, and they dropped their gazes and shuffled back.

The man pushed the two women forward. The big man yanked back the hood on one. It was a middle-aged woman.

"Is this your sister?" he asked.

Moria's mouth tightened. "Of course not. My sister is my twin. We look alike. If this is a game—"

"So it is not your sister?"

"No."

The man's dagger shot out. Before anyone could react, he sliced the woman's throat. Moria leaped forward, but Gavril caught her, his hand gripping her cloak, holding her fast. The big man held the woman by the hair, her throat split, eyes rolling as her hands frantically grasped her throat as if she could hold it shut while blood gushed over her fingers.

He's making me watch her die.

Moria tried to pull away from Gavril, but his arm went around her waist now, his lips to her ear, whispering, "No, Moria. You cannot save her."

The big man dropped the woman. Just dropped her, still writhing, still gasping, still dying. He yanked down the hood on the second woman, a girl barely older than Moria, tears streaming from her wild, terrified eyes.

"Is this your sister?"

Moria glared at him as hate bubbled in her gut.

Someday I'll slit your throat and watch you die.

"Will you come in the village now?" he said. "Or do you still wish us to find your sister first?" He stepped toward them, ignoring Daigo's snarl. "She is in there, Keeper. This is but a lesson. I am in command here. You will obey me or you will get another lesson. There is a whole village waiting to help me teach you. Now, will you come?"

She brushed past him and strode toward the gates.

ASHYN

THIRTY-EIGHT

Ashyn crawled across the rafters. Dust filled her nose, and her mouth, too, when she forgot to close it. She had to bite her cheek to keep from sneezing. She couldn't even stifle herself with her sleeve. She was dressed only in her shift, so she wouldn't get her clothing dirty and tip off their captors to their escape plan.

Escape *plan* was an exaggeration. Escape *hope* was closer to the truth. Or, if she was being realistic, escape *fantasy*.

Ronan had come in through the roof. Naturally, their captors had figured that out and plugged the hole. It stood to reason, then, that Ashyn and Ronan would not attempt to escape through there. Except there was no other way out. The windows were battened shut, and after half a day working one free, Ronan had peeked through to see a village warrior there, waiting. Any attempt to distract the front-door guard or lure him inside had been met with derision and mockery. So the only option was up.

Ronan had spent half the night working at roof tiles. Now it was Ashyn's turn. And she wasn't nearly as enthusiastic about the task as one might imagine.

It wasn't merely the low chances of success that discouraged her. She was being held captive, with no idea what fate lay in store for her. Of course she'd escape any way she could.

The problem was Tova. He could not possibly take this route. Earlier, when Ronan came in through the roof, she'd presumed he was going to lead them out some other way. If he'd intended to go back up onto the roof, she never would have followed. Not without Tova. When they'd hatched this plan, she'd said as much, and he'd brushed off her concerns, which made her suspect she was not making an escape route for three. She was making it for one.

She found the spot where he'd been working on the tiles. He had two loose already. She settled herself awkwardly on the rafters and set to work prying off another.

It was nearly breakfast when Ashyn descended, filthy and exhausted, her nails broken, her fingertips aching.

"It's done," she said. "The hole is big enough."

Ronan grinned. "Great. They'll bring food any moment. I heard the morning bell. We'll eat and take what we can. Then we'll go."

"And Tova?"

Again, he waved off the concern with a nonchalance that set her teeth on edge. "We'll figure it out. You should go get dressed." Another grin. "Not that I'd complain if you stayed like that. . . ."

She didn't crack a smile. Didn't even blush. She was too tired, too filthy, and too annoyed. She went into the bedroom with Tova, closed the door, cleaned up, and put on the simplest of the dresses her captors had brought.

Wenda's dresses were still there, shoved into the corner as Ashyn had tried to get them out of her sight. She'd figured out what had happened. Ashyn had been lured to Fairview by a spirit that had apparently possessed Wenda even before they'd left Edgewood. Ashyn cursed herself for not realizing it, but her connection with the spirit world apparently did not extend to recognizing one in a living body. Tova hadn't detected it either.

So Wenda had lied about seeing Moria leave Edgewood. Her charge against Gregor had also been a lie. She must have overheard Ronan and Ashyn talking about leaving together and accused Gregor, knowing it would keep the group together, so she could ensure Ashyn reached Fairview, which seemed to be her mission.

Was Wenda still alive? Or had she been consumed by that spirit? Was Moria alive? Their captors said yes. Their captors were cutthroats and thieves.

Ashyn could be the only survivor of her village. And here she was, putting on a pretty frock for breakfast.

When she came out, the meal had arrived. Ronan was stuffing pickled plums into his mouth as if he hadn't eaten in days. Which was, she'd learned, pretty much how he ate every time an unlimited amount of food was placed in front of him. Presumably food in this quantity and variety had not been part of his daily table, as it had hers. And perhaps that should soften her annoyance. It would later, when she looked back, after he'd made his escape. She'd think of his life and would not question why he'd chosen to leave her behind, to consider only himself. That was his life. She should expect nothing more. But for now, thinking of all they'd been through, she *did* expect more. She couldn't help it.

"We need to talk about Tova," she said as she took a bowl of rice porridge. "He can't go through the roof."

"We'll figure—"

"Do not tell me we'll figure it out." She struggled not to snap the words. "I think we have been through enough for me to expect a little honesty. There is no way to get Tova out through the roof. Therefore I cannot leave. You're waiting for me to realize that. First, though, you needed to make sure I helped you open those tiles for your escape."

He'd chewed steadily slower as she'd spoken. Now he swallowed and his eyes narrowed. "If I wanted to escape alone, Ashyn, I could have done that yesterday, when you were taken. I was outside the village walls. I could have escaped."

"Without a reward."

His face darkened, and he set down his plums.

Before he could answer, she said, "If my tone is harsh, I apologize. I'm tired and my fingers hurt from prying those tiles. But I would have done it for you. I only wish you'd show me the respect of honesty. I've never faulted you for wanting a reward. You deserve it. You helped me, and I do not expect you to suffer with me. As you said, you came back. The reason doesn't matter. The point is that you are leaving alone, and I wish you would not pretend otherwise."

"You could come."

"Without Tova? Even to suggest that—" —*shows how little you know me.* She wouldn't say that, though. It spoke of disappointment.

"I meant that you come with me, and Tova will find a way back to you. He can take care of himself, Ashyn, and he can do it better if he doesn't need to worry about you."

Ashyn stroked Tova's head. He lay beside her, quiet and still, as if not to interrupt or influence the conversation. "And what if, in trying to get back to me, he's killed? They'll not hesitate to kill him, which means I will not leave him. I did once and . . ."

She didn't say, "And look what happened." Ronan would tell her that the shadow stalkers would have risen even if Tova had been with her that day. He was correct, and yet it was one more small thing that added to the pile of what she'd done wrong, what she *felt* she'd done wrong.

She looked over at Ronan. "Go. I understand."

He argued, but it was clear there was no other way out of this quandary. She would not leave without Tova, so she could not leave through the roof. As for Ronan . . .

"I *must* go," he said, shifting, his gaze averted. "I know I ought to stay and look after you—"

"I don't need looking after, Ronan."

"I still would not leave, if there were no other considerations. But I have . . . responsibilities. In the city. People who need me."

Who? she wanted to ask. *You were exiled to your death. No one would expect you to return. They will have moved on with their lives and . . .*

She caught the look in his downcast eyes. The anxiety and the worry, and she realized what he meant.

You have someone there. A girl. You left a girl, a lover, and now she thinks you're dead, and you're anxious to get back and show her that you are not.

It made a romantic tale. The young rogue, cheating death, returning to his grieving lover. But in reality . . . ? Ashyn had always known that life did not resemble one of her book stories or Moria's bard tales, and yet there'd been part of her that hoped it did. The more she saw, the more she realized she was wrong. People made up those stories because it's what they wanted from their world. A place where goodness, kindness, and honor were rewarded. They were not rewarded. The people of Edgewood could attest to that.

Would Ronan's lover be waiting for him? There was a tiny part of Ashyn that wanted to point out the futility of that hope and the almost certain disappointment that lay ahead. The same tiny part that realized he had someone, and felt the crush of those words. A tiny part that wondered why he'd not mentioned it, and suspected it was because Ashyn would be more susceptible to his charm and his flirting—and more likely to argue that he deserved a reward—if he did not say he had a lover in the city. That was, she supposed, unfair and rather petty, but she thought it nonetheless before pushing all that aside to say, with conviction.

"Then you should go. If you can find a way to let someone in the city know what has happened . . ."

"I will."

THIRTY-NINE

As hard as Ashyn tried, she could not quite shake the lingering hurt over Ronan's . . . *betrayal* certainly wasn't the right word. Even *abandonment* felt too harsh. Just *hurt*, then, not so much that he was leaving, but that his agreement seemed to come so easily.

Still, she'd help him. That was the honorable thing to do. Assist him in any way she could. Be happy that at least one of them escaped.

She suggested a plan and he agreed to it. After breakfast, he gathered what food he could carry and took a makeshift bag he'd devised. Then he went up into the rafters while she took Tova to the door.

She rapped on it. The guard heard her—she'd knocked loudly enough—but he didn't answer. She rapped harder and said, "My hound requires meat."

The door opened then, the guard peeking in, his face screwed up as if he'd misheard.

"There was no meat with breakfast," she said, "save some pickled fish."

His face screwed up more. It didn't help that she'd spoken softly. Intentionally so, though her voice was never loud at any time. Now she stepped back and motioned at Tova.

"He cannot stomach pickled fish. He requires meat. Preferably fresh, though he'd settle for anything you have. Even fish, if it's not pickled."

The guard was one of the villagers. A warrior, given his dual blades. Not a high-ranking one—he bore no tattoos—but that was to be expected from a village guard. He was perhaps as old as her father, and she'd like to think that when he looked on her, there was kindness in his eyes, as if he might have a daughter her age. The kindness was, of course, rightfully tempered by caution and a touch of sardonic humor.

"Let me guess, Seeker," he said. "You would like me to go and fetch you some meat, leaving the door unguarded."

No, I want to hold your attention while Ronan escapes across the roof.

She smiled. "That would be nice, but I know you won't be so foolish. I simply want meat for my hound. His stomach has been grumbling, and I'm concerned. He requires more exercise than he's been receiving—and, no, I'm not asking to take him for walks. I understand our limitations. I only request that when the girls come to take our breakfast trays, you tell them to bring meat."

"All right, then, Seeker," he said. "Since you've asked nicely and haven't played any tricks—"

The guard pitched forward. He fell into Ashyn, and something hit the floor on either side of him. Pieces of a roof tile. Ronan stood behind him holding a second one, ready to smash it over the guard's head, but he was already on the floor, unconscious.

"Haven't lost the knack," Ronan said with a grin. "Come on, then. We need to pull him inside and go."

Ashyn stared at him.

"I saw an opportunity," he said. "Now quickly. Before someone comes."

Ashyn helped him drag the guard the rest of the way inside. They went out and closed the door.

"That way," Ronan said, pointing to a building across the way. "I could see from the roof and it's clear over—"

"Going somewhere, Seeker?"

Barthol rounded the corner, two of his men flanking him. Ashyn wheeled to see two more coming in the other direction. She looked straight ahead, where they'd planned to run.

"Go!" she whispered to Ronan. "They want me."

Before Ronan could run—or decide not to—one of Barthol's men had him with a blade at his throat.

"Oh, I think we want him, too, Seeker," Barthol said. "To keep you in line. Now, tell your cur to stop growling or we'll give him cause."

Ashyn laid her hand on Tova's head, but he stopped even before that. If there'd been a chance of overpowering the men, he'd have attacked already.

"Good girl." Barthol moved in front of her. "Turn around and go back inside your pretty little cage. I will count to three, and if you are not inside, the boy dies. One . . . two . . ."

She flung the door open, with Tova at her side, both of them stumbling over the body of the unconscious guard. Barthol shoved Ronan in with her, then strode over, lifted the guard by the front of his tunic, and slapped him hard enough that even Ronan winced. The man jerked awake.

"So . . ." Barthol said. "You let the Seeker and her brat boy escape."

"What?" He looked around wildly and when his gaze settled on Ashyn, she saw accusation there, and felt it, too, even as she told herself she'd done nothing wrong, that they were clearly the victims here.

"They bashed you on the head and escaped."

"I—"

"Are you going to tell me you let them go? That your conscience would not permit you to hold a Seeker captive?"

"No, of course not. I—"

"The alternative is that you were stupid enough to be fooled by two children. I would suggest, as a warrior, you stay with the first excuse. At least then you'll die with honor."

"D-die?" The guard scrambled to his feet.

Ashyn leaped forward. "It was my fault, not his. Please don't—"

"Silence, Seeker, or your boy dies. Back up three paces, or your boy dies. Do anything to displease me and your boy dies." He met her gaze with a chilling smile, silver teeth flashing. "Is that clear?"

She backed up. Ronan took her arm and tried to lead her into their quarters.

285

"No, boy," Barthol called. "She stays and she watches what she's done." He turned to the guard. "Take out your dagger, warrior. You know what to do with it."

"No," Ashyn blurted. "Please—"

She stopped as one of the other mercenaries stepped toward Ronan, his blade raised. Ronan put his arm around Ashyn, moving up behind her and whispering, "Keep your gaze on the wall beside him. Look, but don't look. Think of something else."

As Ronan whispered, the warrior pleaded.

"Please. I have a family. My wife, my children. My parents are aged, and I'm their only son. Give me any punishment, any at all. Please."

Barthol's men flanked him, one on each side, pressing down on his shoulders until he sat cross-legged, in the proper position. One took out the guard's dagger and put it in his hand.

"Do you know the point of ritual suicide?" Barthol sounded bored. "I may not be a warrior, but even I know it. You take your own life with honor, not beg for it like a dog. You want another punishment? All right. I'll take you into the village square, for all to see, and execute you. Cleave off your head in front of your wife and children and parents, so they may—"

The guard didn't even need Barthol to finish. He thrust his dagger into his stomach and sliced it open. Ashyn fell back. Ronan's arm tightened around her and he kept whispering, "Look to the side, Ashyn. Look to the side," but even if she did, she could see the blood and smell it and hear the man, still alive, breathing hard and panicked as he died.

"Finish it," Ronan said to Barthol, his voice a growl. "Finish the ritual."

"Finish?" Barthol sounded confused.

"The killing blow," Ronan said between his teeth. "That is how it's done. As soon as he plunges in the blade, you cut off his head. Show him mercy."

Barthol screwed up his face. "Are you sure?"

"Yes."

Barthol turned to the others. "Have any of you heard that part?"

They smiled and said no, they had not. Ashyn looked at the big man and she knew he understood the ritual full well. Writhing in agony, the guard whispered, "Please, please."

"Well, I suppose it makes sense," Barthol said. "This does seem slow. We'll be here all day." He glanced at one of his men. "Finish him off." He paused. "Drag him outside first, where it will make less of a mess. Leave the door open, though, so our Seeker can watch."

Two men dragged the dying guard out. Ronan kept whispering for her to not look, but she was still staring at the bloody floor when the killing blow came. She pressed against Ronan, breathing deeply, trying to keep calm and upright.

"There," Barthol said. "It's done. We'll drag him into the village square now, so the others may see what happens to those who neglect their duties." He looked at Ashyn. "I hope that was a lesson learned, Seeker. The same fate will befall anyone who assists your escape or allows it to happen. Go back inside with your cur and your boy, and be thankful I don't make you clean up the mess."

FORTY

Ashyn was playing capture-my-lord. The game was going nowhere and had been since they began, not because they were both astoundingly good players but because, frankly, neither had any interest under the circumstances.

It was an act. After what happened to the poor guard—and after Barthol threatened Ronan—Ashyn knew they had to convince their captors that they had settled in and would cause no trouble. Even now, as Ashyn moved her pieces, her fingers trembled, remembering the guard.

"Don't," Ronan murmured. "Don't think about it. You ought not to have witnessed that."

"I've seen worse," she said.

"You ought not to."

"It's not just seeing it. I feel as if I caused—"

"You didn't," Ronan said. "He chose to join them. Perhaps

288

he had no option. Perhaps his family is here, and they threatened them, but even if I give him the benefit of the doubt, it was still his decision to hold a Seeker captive. And it was mine to use him in our escape."

"I don't think it would have mattered," she said softly, gaze on the board. "Even if you escaped, Barthol would have killed him as an example."

"I think Barthol just likes killing," Ronan muttered. "And having others watch. He's a sadistic—"

Tova leaped up. Ronan rose, fingers slipping to his side, reaching for his missing blade. His hand clenched, empty, and he moved forward, gaze fixed on the door. It opened.

Something raced through the open door. Something long and black, and Tova bounded forward with a happy bark. The black blur hit him and took him down, and they rolled together, light fur and dark, as Ashyn stared.

It looks like . . . It cannot be . . .

She lifted her gaze slowly, almost not daring to look back at the door, certain she would not see what she—

Moria walked through.

There were others with her. Ashyn didn't see them. Her mind stopped there: *Moria walked through.*

She saw her sister's face, sweat-stained and hard, her blue eyes blazing fury. Moria spotted her and her rage evaporated in a flicker of shock. Then she raced across the stone floor.

Ashyn threw her arms around her sister. The fierce hug lasted a moment before Moria pulled back, holding Ashyn at arm's length, frowning again as her gaze traveled over her.

"Are you all right? Have they hurt you?"

Ashyn shook her head and started to ask the same of Moria, but her sister had already turned to the men who brought them in.

"Where'd the other one go?" she said. "The man in charge. I want—I *demand* to speak to him."

The mercenaries laughed and began to leave.

Moria started after them. Ashyn tried to hold her back, but she shook her off.

"You!" she said to the men. "Do you know who I am? In the name of the goddess, I demand answers."

"Then ask your goddess for them," one said as he continued toward the door.

Moria lunged. "Do not—"

A hand caught her by the shoulder. Ashyn hadn't even seen anyone standing there—she was too focused on her sister. She glimpsed the young man's face, curtained by braids as he leaned over, whispering to Moria.

Gavril.

Ashyn braced for her sister to throw him off, too, and march after the departing guards. But she only grumbled and Daigo snorted, both of them glowering toward the guards. Then Moria did pull from Gavril's grasp, but only to march back to Ashyn.

"You're all right?" she asked again.

Ashyn nodded.

"And Tova?"

"He's fine."

Moria's gaze flicked to Ronan. She didn't ask if he was

290

injured, but he seemed to understand the implied question and said he was fine, too.

"What happened?" Moria said. "And what's going on here?"

They sat to talk. Moria said she'd found Ashyn's letter, so she knew how they'd left and why. Ashyn skimmed over their journey through the Wastes, except to say that Beatrix, Gregor, and Quintin were dead. She did not tell them how the first two perished. Stories of death worms could wait. Finally she explained about Wenda.

"Spirit possession?" Moria said. "Yet she was not dead? Not possessed by a shadow stalker?"

Ronan answered. "Not unless they can keep a corpse fresh for six days."

He didn't mean it seriously, but Moria considered before saying, "No, the stories say possessed corpses rot slowly, but you would have noticed. It sounds more like . . ."

As she trailed off, she glanced at Gavril. Did he look uncomfortable? Or simply annoyed with the diversion? With Gavril, it was impossible to tell.

Ashyn went on to tell them about the children and the men who had control of Fairview.

Moria took a moment to digest it. "So it appears as if mercenaries were responsible for what happened in Edgewood, presumably working with"—she paused—"men of magic. They unleashed the shadow stalkers, among other things."

"Other things?" Ronan said.

"We saw a thunder hawk," Gavril said.

"We *fought* and *killed* a thunder hawk," Moria corrected.

She explained. Then Ashyn told them about the death worms.

When Ashyn finished, Moria fixed Gavril with a look. "Shadow stalkers, thunder hawks, and death worms . . . all just coincidentally appearing in the Wastes at the same time?"

"I agreed that the shadow stalkers suggest the arcane arts. But conjuring thunder hawks and death worms . . . ?" He shook his head.

"It would be the same principle, wouldn't it? Raising something that supposedly doesn't exist?"

Gavril paused. "I suppose so. It does seem unlikely the Wastes would be home to two legendary creatures and we see both shortly after the shadow stalkers."

Ashyn tried not to stare. Seeing Gavril and Moria speaking—without insults and barbs—was surprising enough. But exchanging ideas and actually listening to each other's opinions . . . ? Moria rarely did that with anyone other than her sister and father. And Gavril never seemed to do it with anyone at all.

"So the mercenaries appear to be responsible," Moria continued. "They unleash the shadow stalkers, take the children, and herd us here. Why not capture us at Edgewood, too?"

"Because it would have been sacrilege," Gavril said. "They may pretend they don't care about the spirits, but obviously they do."

"Or someone does," Ronan said. "Whoever the mercenaries are working for."

Moria and Gavril turned to Ronan, looking surprised, as if

they'd forgotten there were others there.

"He's right," Moria said. "Someone has hired them. Someone who respects the spirits enough not to lay hands on the Seeker and Keeper, but not so much that he fears holding them hostage. So they have us, and they have the children, and they've slaughtered the village of Edgewood. To what purpose? Have they told you?"

Ashyn shook her head. "We've only been here one night, and no one will speak." She did not mention the escape attempt. She told herself this was not the time, but in truth, she didn't wish this moment clouded by the memory.

"I want answers," Moria said, pushing up.

Gavril rose with her. He leaned over, whispering to her again. Ashyn heard enough to make out the gist of it, which was nothing terribly private. Gavril wanted Moria to let him get answers.

"At least allow me to try," he murmured. "If it doesn't work, you can do it your way."

Moria waved for him to go ahead. He bent to say something else. As he did, Moria turned her head to listen and Ashyn noticed the odd way her hair was bound, with small braids at the sides, pulled back with a dark strip of leather. She looked at Gavril, leaning over, one of his braids loose at the end, the tie gone.

Ashyn remembered back in Edgewood, the village girls vying for lovers among the guards. It was not easy to marry into a higher caste, but it was possible, and for the girls of Edgewood, those warrior guards were their best chance of bettering their lives. If they managed to catch one even temporarily, they'd parade trophies like the plunder of war. Most prized of all were beads. If their lover wore braids, they'd persuade him to part with a few and weave them into their own hair.

Ashyn looked at Gavril, at that unbound braid, the strap now binding her sister's locks.

She knew it did not mean the same thing. Her sister was too private a person to ever flaunt a conquest. And yet, was it still a lover's gift? There *was* something between her sister and the Kitsune. There always had been, even when they were at each other's throats. Now even Ronan saw it, given the way he watched them whisper.

Was he sad to see it? He ought not to be, considering he had a girl in the city. Perhaps, though, he still had feelings for Moria, and she felt no pleasure at seeing him disappointed.

As for Moria and Gavril . . . Ashyn knew her sister was curious about what happened between men and women, and she made little secret of it. But that was a curiosity to be pursued when nothing else required her attention. She would not escape her massacred village, set out on the Wastes with a handsome warrior, and decide it was the perfect opportunity to find out what all the fuss was about.

Yet they had spent five days alone together, in the wake of a tragedy, relying on each other for survival and . . . comfort? Perhaps.

She looked at her sister's hair.

"Yes," Moria said. "It's a mess. Just be thankful I didn't cut it after it almost got me killed."

"Your hair?" Ronan said.

"Did I mention the talons on that thunder hawk?" she said.

"They liked long hair."

Ronan moved closer. "You truly killed it?"

"Gavril struck the fatal blow."

Ronan started to ask for more, but Ashyn cut in. "So your hair, that's why it's pulled back like that."

"Yes, he"—a wave at Gavril, now at the door, talking to the guard outside—"wouldn't let me cut it and risk angering the spirits. So I made him figure out an alternative."

That explained the strap then. Expediency. Which Ashyn should have known—while she thought it quite romantic to wear a lover's beads, her sister was far more practical. Still, there *was* something between them. . . .

Gavril came back. "We'll have an audience before sundown."

"Thank you," Ashyn said.

Gavril nodded, but Ashyn could tell he was waiting for a response from her sister. Moria grumbled about the wait, but she didn't blame him or try to do better, which Gavril seemed to recognize as a sign he'd done well. He walked to Daigo and bent to examine the wildcat's wounds.

"We should get water for these," he said. "One is oozing a little."

Ashyn retrieved a bowl of water and helped Moria clean Daigo's wounds. She took a closer look, too. Gavril was right. One showed signs of infection. The surrounding flesh was hot to the touch. Yet the wounds were otherwise healing well. She'd keep an eye on it.

As they finished their work, Ashyn gestured to the bowl. "Daigo isn't the only one who could use some cleaning. There's a tub in back, and they'll bring all the hot water you want."

Her sister opened her mouth, but Ashyn cut her off. "Yes, I know you consider it a waste of time under the circumstances, but we have time to waste. You ought to spend it getting rested and fed."

"And clean," Gavril said. "You could use the bath, Keeper."

"No more than you, Kitsune. Did you notice I've been sleeping upwind?"

He shot his fist at her. Moria only laughed. It was a good sound to hear. Ashyn went to ask the guard to bring water. When she returned, Gavril was following Moria into the bathing room.

"Um, there's plenty of water," Ronan said. "You don't need to share."

Gavril gave him a hard look. "As the water is not yet here, I'm clearly not taking any liberties. I simply wish to speak to Moria."

"Then speak here."

More of that expressionless stare. "I don't know you, and I would prefer not to share my thoughts with you." He turned to Ashyn. "No offense meant to the Seeker."

"None taken," she murmured. "Go on."

Gavril closed the door behind them.

FORTY-ONE

Guards came shortly after Moria and Gavril had bathed and changed into fresh clothing. Before they arrived, Ashyn and Moria finally had a chance to talk. Yet they discussed nothing important, nothing about all the things they ought to be talking about—Edgewood, their father . . . Ashyn had raised the subject of their father, but Moria had only asked how *she* was coping.

Gavril had spent the time prowling. Pacing the room, checking everything, trying to look through the battened windows. Which meant Ronan had to do the same, lest it seem as if he was content to wait for rescue while the warrior found it. Ashyn wanted to tell him to sit. Just sit. They already knew there was no way out, so leave Gavril to it. But she knew it would do no good.

Then the guards came and escorted them through the

village. Now it was Ashyn's turn to look all about, getting a fresh picture of Fairview, should they have an opportunity to escape. Ronan did the same, but Gavril and Moria kept their gazes forward. Empty gazes, each lost in thought.

There was, Ashyn admitted, nothing to see. Even Tova and Daigo didn't show more than cursory interest in their surroundings. The village was locked up tight. This time, no one even opened a window to peek out.

An entire village held captive. How was it even possible? True, Fairview didn't have a garrison, but they had guards and able-bodied men. Women, too, would fight, if their homes and their men and their children were in danger.

There was no sign that the capturing force was simply too large to conquer. She'd seen perhaps a dozen mercenaries. She could hear the spirits whispering, but as always their messages were vague and unhelpful.

The guards led them into the village hall. It was a simple affair—just a long, whitewashed building. As they passed through the doors, she saw Barthol, the big leader of the mercenaries, and his confederate, the small man, Fyren. There were also four guards—mercenaries, all of them, she was sure, like the men who'd escorted them here. And the governor. He was the only one sitting. She presumed it was "his" chair, an ornate one big enough to hold his weight. But he shifted and fussed, as if he couldn't get comfortable. Then he saw them and went still.

"By my poxed ancestors," Fyren said, sliding forward. "They truly are alike in every way." A chortle. "Or every way I can see."

Ronan stiffened beside her.

Fyren continued forward. "Feast your eyes on this, my brothers. Can you imagine both of them in your bed? I know I can."

He leered. Moria reached for her waist and stopped as Fyren pulled a dagger from his belt.

"Looking for this, pretty one?" He twirled it, metal flashing. "A lovely blade. I thank you for it."

Moria lunged. Ashyn didn't have time to react—didn't even have time to see what truly happened. She heard Fyren let out a grunt, saw the blade swing, only to stop abruptly. Fyren twisted to see who had him by the arm. It was Gavril. He plucked the dagger from Fyren's fingers and handed it to Moria. She thanked him. Ashyn looked at the mercenaries. They all stood watching, as if amused.

Gavril pushed Fyren aside. The smaller man reached for his sword, but before he could pull it out, Moria had her dagger at his throat.

"You've been bested," she said. "Don't embarrass yourself further by pulling a blade on an unarmed man."

Snickers now, from the others.

"The girl is right, Fyren," Barthol said. "Step back."

"You aren't going to let her keep it, are you?" Fyren said.

Barthol shrugged. "I don't see the harm. It is but a dagger."

And one dagger would not help them against so many. Leaving it with Moria was more a statement than a concession—even if they were armed, they could not escape.

Ronan moved forward. "As long as you're handing out weapons, I had a blade—"

"You'll get them when you leave. Which will be soon."

"Leave?" Moria said.

"Yes, I know, you just got here," Barthol said. "I'm sure you'd love to stay, but we need you to take a message to the emperor."

A moment of silence. Moria broke it. "What message?"

Barthol took an envelope from under his jacket. "A sealed missive for the emperor's eyes only. If the seal is broken or tampered with in any way, we'll find out. We have eyes in court."

"Then get them to deliver your message."

Gavril shifted as if he knew why they wouldn't. Ashyn did, too. She had read enough stories about the court to realize that Barthol was referring to spies, who would never reveal themselves by handing notes to the emperor.

"Would you rather stay here?" Barthol asked Moria.

"I'd rather know what the blazes is going on."

Barthol laughed. "Quick with your blade and quick with your tongue. I'd be inclined to make you an offer of employment, Keeper, if I thought you'd entertain it. The message is for the emperor only. However, because it might speed your steps, I will share part of it with you: the stakes. Fail to deliver this note—or tamper with it—and every child from your village dies."

Silence. Even Moria didn't speak.

Barthol continued. "What you saw in Edgewood was only a demonstration. If the emperor does not agree to our demands, this lovely town—and all its people—will suffer the same fate."

It was Ashyn who found her voice first. "You mean the . . ."

"Shadow stalkers. Yes, that's what they were. They wait just beyond the town walls, as the good governor can attest."

The governor looked as if he might be sick. Fyren walked over and kicked his leg. "Come now, old man, tell the children what happened."

"It was . . ." The governor swallowed. "A traveling party. A few warriors and their families. The shadow stalkers set upon them at dusk. Our people were . . ." He paused now. "Taken from us."

"Now, governor, be truthful," Fyren said. "We didn't take them. We brought them back. Right here to Fairview. The next night."

The governor grabbed the sides of his chair, as if he might launch himself at Fyren. Two armed men stepped forward. The governor lowered himself and turned to the captives.

"They brought them, as shadow stalkers, to show us what they had become. To show me what my son and his family . . ." He could go no further.

"But you have other sons," Barthol said. "With other families. And you will continue to have them if these children do as they are told."

Ashyn watched her sister's hand grip her dagger hilt, so tightly her knuckles whitened. Gavril tensed, as if ready to stop her. Ashyn knew he wouldn't need to. Her sister's blue eyes blazed hate, but she was not foolish enough to attack.

Ashyn looked at the governor and tried to imagine—

Her knees quivered just watching the grief on his face, the remembered horror. To see your child returned to you, not dead and not alive, but something far worse. It was beyond—

Ashyn's breath caught. She slowly turned to her sister, but Moria was facing resolutely forward, her chin up, her whole body stiff.

To see your child that way was terrible. And to see your *father* that way? To run home, certain he was dead, then to watch him rise, to feel the joy of relief, and then . . .

There was something more horrifying than what the governor had suffered. Seeing Moria standing so rigid, holding in her grief and her pain and her rage—now Ashyn understood, and when tears filled her eyes, they weren't for the governor, however sad his plight.

"What say you, Keeper?" Barthol's voice rang through the hall. "Will you take the message? Or would you like to tell the good governor here to bid farewell to the rest of his family? We can take you to tell the children they'll die, too. They'd be delighted to see you. They hold you in such high regard. *The Keeper will save us.* That's what they said when we told them you were coming."

A round of chortles from the other mercenaries.

Barthol stepped forward. "So, Keeper, will you save them? Or will you tell them to prepare to meet their ancestors—"

"Enough."

It was Gavril, his voice low. Barthol only snorted a laugh.

"Yes, Kitsune. At your command, my lord Kitsune."

Barthol strolled closer. Then, in a flash, he had his dagger at the young warrior's throat. Moria pulled hers.

"Sheathe your blade, little one," he said. "I'll not hurt the boy . . ." He dug the tip of his dagger in, drawing blood. "Unless he interrupts me again."

He lowered the blade and turned to Moria. "So what say you, Keeper? Will you take the message? Or does another village perish?"

Ashyn saw her sister's jaw flex. But her lips didn't open. It was as if she'd been holding herself so still, biting her tongue, that now she could not answer at all. Panic flashed in her eyes.

"Yes," Ashyn said quickly. "We will deliver your sealed missive to the emperor."

Barthol turned, as if just noticing her now. He looked from her to Moria.

"Does your sister speak for you, Keeper?"

Moria managed to nod.

"She speaks for all of us," Gavril said. "I will accompany the Seeker and the Keeper to court and protect them and the message."

"As will I," Ronan said.

"Excellent choice," Barthol said, flashing his silver teeth. "You will leave at dawn."

FORTY-TWO

They'd been riding since sunrise with no guards other than Gavril and Ronan. There was no need of more. They were plainly dressed and armed, making them a poor target for bandits. Having no guards also meant there was no one to ensure they went to court. Again, unnecessary. Barthol's threats bound them to their task.

The mercenaries had sent them on a less-traveled road. It was the same one Ronan had marched to Edgewood—they used it for the exiles, so the criminals would pass as few travelers as possible. Ashyn and Moria met none that morning. Then, just past lunch, they'd seen clouds of dust ahead, announcing the approach of a wagon train. Traders, Ronan said—those bypassing villages on the main road, uninterested in their amenities or business prospects.

Other travelers presented a problem—namely that fair-haired twin girls would not pass unnoticed. Nor would a young warrior bearing Kitsune ink. It was easy to hide Gavril's arms. Disguising the girls was harder. They wore their cloaks, with their hair tucked in, hoods tented over their faces. It would still draw attention—there was no need for cloaks in the spring sun of midday—but Ronan said that two hooded girls accompanied by young warriors would be presumed to be headed for the city, likely to one of the courtesan houses.

The real problem was Tova and Daigo. Even the most jaded traveler would realize they weren't simply exotic pets from a far-off kingdom. The best way to handle it was to send the beasts off into the wooded roadside. Daigo was quite willing to go—he'd happily avoid people if he could. Tova was harder to convince—if they were about to encounter strangers, he wanted to be at his Seeker's side, to protect her. Ultimately Daigo convinced him—or drove him off, herding him until they were in the trees, following alongside their girls, keeping an eye on them.

They passed two wagon trains and four carts without incident. When it came time to stop for the night, they found a place far from the road, so no stray travelers would see their fire and decide to join them.

They'd tethered the horses near the stream, where spring grass grew in abundance. Then they made camp a hundred paces away. Now Ashyn watched her sister crouch beside Daigo, examining his leg. The infected scratch seemed to be worsening. Ashyn had already done what she could, helping Moria wash and drain it. Now her sister was fretting, and Ashyn wanted to be there, sitting with her, comforting her, and reassuring her. She tried, but it was like talking to a spirit, one who may respond, but only vaguely, remaining hidden and distant beyond the veil.

Moria tugged impatiently at her cloak as it slid over her shoulder. It was obviously new, and Ashyn had asked about it, but her sister had stiffened at the question before changing the subject.

Ashyn presumed she'd taken it from Edgewood. Moria's own had clearly been—Ashyn winced at the memory—unusable. So she'd likely removed one from the tailor's shop. Completely reasonable, but perhaps to Moria it seemed like theft. Ashyn wanted to offer comfort, but for once in their lives, Ashyn couldn't reach her.

As she watched Moria, she noticed Ronan heading her way. He slowed and looked from her to Moria. Then he made his choice. It was—she sighed—the expected one.

Ronan crouched beside Moria. He pointed at her dagger and made a motion, as if throwing it. Moria lifted one shoulder in a half shrug. Ronan took out his blade and gripped it, as if to throw it, then gestured at his hand. Asking her if he was holding it properly. Trying to entice her away from Daigo for a lesson. Again, though, Moria only gave a half shrug.

She clearly just wanted him to go away, and those lackluster shrugs—instead of telling him point-blank—only proved that she wasn't herself. But Ronan would see it as rejection. Ashyn could take no pleasure in seeing him hurt.

She stood and walked over, with Tova trailing silently after her.

"Can you throw both?" Ashyn asked as she approached

them. "I know you've practiced with your off-hand, but can you throw them both at once? Like . . ." She motioned.

Ashyn thought she'd pantomimed it quite well, but Ronan choked on a laugh. Even Moria managed to find a smile.

"If I threw them like that, I think I'd lose both my feet," she said.

Ashyn shot her fist at her sister. Moria sputtered, a real laugh now, then turned to Ronan.

"What did you teach her on the road?" she asked. "She usually squawks every time *I* do that."

"I don't *squawk*," Ashyn said.

"Yes, you do." Moria raised her voice to a falsetto. *"Moria! That's rude!"*

Ronan laughed and Moria grinned, and Ashyn didn't care if they were laughing at her, only that her sister was smiling again.

Moria leaned over to Ronan and mock-whispered, "Just don't tell her what it means."

Ashyn shot her fist again before motioning her away from Daigo. "Ronan wants to learn to throw a blade. Go teach him so he'll stop pestering me about it. Tova and I will look after Daigo."

A throat clearing behind them. They looked over to see Gavril returning from his patrol.

"Given how you just pantomimed throwing a blade, Ashyn, I would suggest you join the lesson. At the very least, your sister ought to teach you how to handle it better. You draw it as if you're preparing to slice an apple."

Ashyn's cheeks heated.

"Martial arts aren't a Seeker's focus, Kitsune," Moria said. "*You* don't use *your* dagger for much more than slicing apples."

"Because I have my sword. While fighting may not be her strength, I'd like to see her better able to defend herself."

Ronan got to his feet. "Ashyn is—"

Ashyn rose. "Gavril's right, even if he could use a few lessons himself—in diplomacy." She gave him a pointed look, which he chose to ignore. "I'll spar with Moria later. For now, she can go with Ronan while I tend to Daigo."

Gavril shook his head. "I'll stay with the cat. I need no lessons on holding my blade."

"No," Moria said. "You just need lessons on how to release it. Preferably before you fall from a thunder hawk and dash out your brains on the rocks." She paused. "Though that might not be an overly debilitating injury."

He turned a cool look on her, but Ashyn swore she saw a flicker of warmth in it before he knelt beside Daigo.

"Go, Keeper. I'll tend to your cat."

Now Ashyn was sure a look did pass between them. She was almost as sure Moria mouthed *thank you*, but that seemed too great a stretch of the imagination.

"Come, then," Moria said. "Time for class."

The lesson did not last long. The sun had almost dropped before they even began. They continued by the light of the moon and the campfire, but when Tova nearly got his tail lopped off, it became clear that throwing daggers in the dark was not, perhaps, a wise idea. They should have settled in for sleep then. Yet no one was tired.

They sat around the campfire, talking. Or Ronan and Moria talked. She had brought out sharp quills from her bag to show them, which necessitated the tale of where the quills came from. Then Moria and Ronan discussed the ways they could be used as weapons, poisoned or not. Ashyn had tried to slip away and give Ronan time with her sister, but he'd kept her there, pulling her into discussion.

It would have done little good to give them privacy anyway. Gavril sat across the fire, as silent and still as the rock he'd settled on. But he was listening to the conversation. When Moria stretched out her arm, explaining something to Ronan, and her cloak swung a little too close to the fire, it was Gavril who noticed first, scrambling up with, "Watch it!" and sweeping it away from the flames.

"You don't want to damage that," he said as they both moved back a step.

Moria murmured, "I know," her gaze dropping slightly.

Gavril hesitated. He glanced at Ashyn, then he bent and whispered something to her sister. Moria shook her head. Gavril said something else. She hesitated and then nodded.

"Ashyn?" she said. "I need to stretch my legs. Will you come with me?"

Tova was on his feet even before Ashyn. Moria made a stop at her pack and pulled something from it, then they began to walk.

FORTY-THREE

They headed toward the horses. At night, Ashyn could look out at the landscape and think she was still in the Wastes. It was flat land, with distant, irregular shapes that could be heaps of stone and rubble. But the ground here was soft underfoot. Earth, not lava rock. As they walked, their steps swished through new grass, and those shapes were trees and distant mountains.

This was what the Wastes had looked like before the Age of Fire. It was so different. Normal for other people, she supposed—the rich smell of grass and soil, the chirp of crickets and night birds, the unseen creatures that scampered out of Tova's path. There were spirits here, too, quiet ones whispering past. She ought to revel in her surroundings, in the sense of life swirling all about them, so unlike the Wastes, so unlike her home.

But it wasn't home. It felt odd and alien, and she knew part of that owed to the circumstances—there was no way she could enjoy her surroundings given the situation. Whatever the reason, it was not what she'd expected. She'd always dreamed of rich, vibrant, living land, and now she almost yearned for hard rock underfoot.

When Ashyn shivered, Moria started undoing her cloak. "Here, wear this."

Ashyn shook her head. "It was just a breeze."

Moria stopped walking and pulled her cloak off. Ashyn protested again, but Moria didn't pass it over. She just stood there, fingering the supple leather and fur lining.

"It's beautiful," Ashyn murmured. "I'm glad you found it."

Moria nodded.

Ashyn pressed on. "Whoever was supposed to have it would be pleased that you found it, too. That it went to such good use."

"It's mine," Moria whispered, gaze down.

"Exactly. It's yours now and—"

"No." Moria raised her head, eyes meeting her sister's. "It truly is mine. I found it in Father's shop, with a . . ." Her voice clogged and she cleared it. "With a note. It was my Fire Festival gift. There was . . ." She tugged a small package from her pocket, and when she held it out, her fingers trembled. "This is for you."

Ashyn stared down at the wrapped parcel.

"I'm sorry I didn't give it to you earlier. With everything . . . I didn't forget. I just . . . I wanted it to be a better time. But I don't know if there will be a better time, not for a while, so you—you ought to have it."

When Ashyn took the package, her own fingers quivered. Moria started to back up.

"I'll give you some privacy—"

Ashyn reached out and caught Moria's cloak. "No. Stay. Please."

She untied the paper and folded it back, then folded it back again and again. She managed a small laugh. "I don't think there's a gift in here. It's all paper."

She kept going until, finally, she reached the middle and found a ring. A thin silver band studded with garnets. As she lifted it, she saw a note underneath. She picked it up and turned her back to the moon, letting the light spill over the page.

> *To my child whose heart shines as bright as these stones,*
> *It was at a Fire Festival that I met your mother, and I later bought her this ring as a reminder. It's time to let it shine again, a reminder of the love that brought me my two greatest treasures.*
> *All my love, always,*
> *Father*

Ashyn put the ring on. It fit perfectly, and she swore the stones glittered in the moonlight.

"It's beautiful," Moria said.

Ashyn nodded. "It was . . ." The words caught in her throat and when she looked down at the note again, she couldn't read it through the haze of tears.

She passed the note to Moria.

Her sister lifted her hands. "No, I shouldn't. It's a private message for you."

"It's for both of us," she said, and pressed it into Moria's hand.

She watched as her sister read it. Watched as her face crumpled, as her shoulders shook. Ashyn caught her and held her, and they fell against each other as the tears came.

When Ashyn and Moria returned to the campsite, Moria went straight to Daigo, who was again resting under Gavril's care. Ashyn headed to the stream, to check on the horses and wash off some of the day's dust. She was cleaning a spot of dried mud from Tova's ear when Ronan appeared.

"Is Moria all right?" he asked. "She was happy when we were practicing and talking, but when you two headed out . . . she seemed upset."

"She's fine. We talked about our father. Finally."

"Good." He hunkered down beside her. "So you feel better?"

She nodded.

"I'm glad. You have enough to worry about."

He crouched there, looking at her as if she was supposed to make some kind of response, but she wasn't sure what.

After a moment of silence, he said, "If you want more lessons with your dagger, I can give them. Your sister is an excellent warrior but a lousy teacher."

Ashyn sputtered a laugh. "Patience is not her strong suit."

"I can tell."

"It doesn't help that she's distracted."

"We all are. Understandably."

"I meant that if she seems . . . cool, it's just the circumstances."

He frowned, as if confused. "All right. But I'm serious about the lessons. We'll be on the road a few more days, and

313

I'm happy to give them."

"Thank you." She glanced over. "I'm sorry if I've been sharp with you."

He frowned. "You were sharp with me?"

"Distant or . . ." She could tell by his expression that he had no idea what she was talking about. Apparently, unlike Moria, she did not convey her feelings well. "I've been as distracted as anyone, I fear. I only wanted to say thank you for all you've done, and I'm sorry your return to the city was delayed. I know you have someone waiting for you."

"Someone . . . ?" He gave her an odd look.

"You said you had someone waiting."

"I said I had . . ." He sputtered a small laugh. "You think I have a girl waiting?"

"No, of course not. I just said—"

"You said *someone* in a tone that leaves no doubt that someone must be young and female. Truly? I was exiled to my death, Ashyn. If there was a girl—which there was not—I'd hardly expect her to be waiting for me." He sat a few moments in silence. "I have a younger brother and a sister. They're the ones I need to get back to."

She glanced over. "Then why would you not simply say so?"

He shrugged. "There was enough to worry about. I wasn't going to burden you with my life story."

"Telling me you have a brother and sister is hardly your life story."

Another shrug and when she looked over at him, she knew there was more to it. She saw guilt there, and discomfort, as he shifted and kicked at a small rock.

"How old are they?" she asked. "And no, I'm not prying. I'll ask that and nothing more."

"Aidra is six summers and Jorn is almost ten. They're staying with my aunt. She'll take care of them well enough, but . . . they are of an age where she'll want them to start earning their keep, and I'd rather they did not. If I can help it, they will not."

Ashyn suspected that "earning their keep" did not mean sweeping shops. She noticed he'd made no mention of a mother. Presumably she was dead, then. Ashyn had promised not to pry, though, and she would not, as dearly as she might wish to know more.

"We'll get you back to them," she said. "As quickly as we can."

He looked over. Their eyes met. His hand dangled there beside hers, and she wanted to give it a squeeze. A friendly squeeze, reassuring, nothing more. But she could not breach that gap.

He cleared his throat and rose. "Let's get to bed, then. Gavril's made a guard schedule. I'm on second shift. You get early morning." He grinned over. "Less chance for you to drift off."

"I did not—"

"Oh, yes, you did. I could hear the snoring—"

"I don't snore."

He continued teasing her all the way back to camp.

315

FORTY-FOUR

Ashyn woke as Tova rose. While the night wasn't nearly as cold here as on the Wastes, she noticed the loss of his warmth and lifted her head. He nudged her cheek, telling her to go back to sleep while he went to relieve himself. But now that she was awake, she realized she could stand to do the same.

She glanced over at the small rise they'd agreed to use for watch. She could see a light-brown cloak and dark, tousled curls. Ronan was on duty. She started over to warn him where she was going, but his head was lowered, as if he'd drifted off. She didn't doubt it. He'd not seemed to sleep at all during their two nights in Fairview. She'd wake him when she returned and insist on taking her shift early, though she'd still tease him about it come morning.

She wasn't going far anyway. Just down by the stream, where the shallow gully offered some privacy. The horses were downstream, asleep. She gave them wide berth.

Tova wandered off, looking for a place to lift his leg. As she was unclasping her cloak she heard a faint whistle. An insect zipped past, as long as a finger joint. It hit Tova in the side. He snorted and twisted, biting at it, as if it had stung him, but it was too far for him to reach and clung in his thick fur. She walked over to pull it off. He took a step toward her. Then he teetered.

"Tov—!"

She didn't even get the rest of the word out before she felt something hit her neck with a sharp jab. She clawed at her neck, and something fell into her hand—too hard to be an insect. As she peered down at it, she had to struggle to focus, forgetting for a moment all about Tova and wondering why she was staring down at this odd little tube with a pointed end.

It looks like the quill that Moria had. Not the barbed tip, but the tube, hollowed out and . . .

Her legs gave way, and she was unconscious before she hit the ground.

Ashyn woke on a soft pallet. She lifted her head groggily to peer around the dark room, and spotted a figure sitting beside her.

"Moria?" Her voice sounded odd, like a frog's croak.

Her sister turned, but it was so dark Ashyn could only see the outline of her head.

"You better not be going out," Ashyn said. "You know Father hates it when you and Daigo . . ."

Father...

The thought caught in her mind, and she could feel it buzzing there, trying to push past her sleep-stupor. *Something about Father...*

She couldn't focus. Her throat hurt and her head throbbed. Had she drunk too much honey wine? No, she was always careful since the last Fire Festival, when Moria wanted to know what it felt like to be drunk and Ashyn had spent half the night nursing her.

Fire Festival...

Again, the thought caught, and her gaze went to her hand. There was a ring on her finger. Silver with red stones.

Where did that...

Father. Fire Festival.

"Moria?" she said.

"Shhh."

Ashyn hesitated. Her sister sounded odd. Was her throat hurting as well? Ashyn struggled to rise, her hands gripping the coverlet. Only it wasn't her silk coverlet from home. It was coarse hemp cloth.

She heard a distant noise. Men's voices, speaking in a tongue she didn't recognize. She pushed up on her sleeping mat and peered around, her heart hammering now, mind struggling to put the pieces together.

As soon as she looked around, she knew something was missing. Something she ought to be able to see even in the dimmest light.

"Tova?" she said.

No answering scrabble of claws. Ashyn blinked hard. She

318

caught sight of a drawn curtain, moonlight seeping in on all sides. She scrambled over and yanked at it.

"No!" whispered a voice beside her. "Don't—"

Ashyn turned and let out a shriek. A hand clapped over her mouth and when it did, she screamed all the louder, feeling that hand, covered in hard bumps that rasped against her skin. She struggled to get away, but another hand grabbed her by the shoulder, holding her fast.

"Be still," the voice said. "I'm not going to hurt you. You need to keep your voice down, child."

A nightmare. She was having a nightmare. Nowhere else could she wake to see such a thing and hear it speak like a normal woman.

As Ashyn struggled for calm, she looked up into that terrible face. It had the shape of a human head, but instead of skin, it had overlapping reddish scales all over its bald skull. Where there weren't scales, there were warts—on the nose, the ears, the lips, even the eyelids.

Shadow stalker.

As the thought came, her mind stuttered. It seemed to latch on to an idea—a memory—that wouldn't quite form.

Shadow stalkers. Death worms. Thunder hawks.

The words passed through her mind and brought the rest tumbling after, all the memories of the last days, of why she wasn't at home in Edgewood, of what happened there. It all rushed back, and she started to shake.

"Shhh," the creature said. "Don't make noise or they'll beat us. They have no sympathy for tears."

Ashyn stared at the thing. Not a shadow stalker. Some

new monster raised by sorcerers, unleashed on the empire?

A monster that talks? Kindly? Comforts me and warns me?

"W-what are you?" Ashyn asked.

Anger flashed in the thing's dark eyes. "A girl, like you."

Ashyn glanced down at her own hand, as if expecting to suddenly see it covered in warts. Of course it wasn't.

The creature's voice softened. "It is a deformity of the skin. I am a girl, even if I do not look like one. My name is Belaset. I am nearly eighteen summers. I live in the imperial city."

Ashyn's cheeks flared red hot. "I—I'm so sorry. I . . . I have never met . . . I was confused."

"And your name?" Belaset prompted.

"Ashyn of Edgewood."

"Edgewood." Belaset frowned. Then she nodded. "The village that guards the Forest of the Dead."

Gone now, Ashyn thought. *All gone.* But she did not say that. There was no reason. Instead she only nodded and lowered her gaze so the girl wouldn't see the pain there. Then her head shot up, and she looked around wildly.

"Where are we? I . . . There was a dart. Tova. Where's—"

"If you mean the great dog, I saw them bring him on a cart with you. Where did you get such a huge beast?"

"He's a . . ." Again, too much to explain under the circumstances. "He's a special breed. But where are we?" She looked around again, focusing. "A wagon. We're in a wagon. But it's not moving."

"They're preparing to return for your sister."

"My sister?"

"They want both of you, of course. Alone, you are exotic,

320

but no more so than dozens of Northern girls in the city. It is the pair that is unique—because you look so alike. Some believe you're twins, which isn't possible, of course, but I'm sure that's what the trader will tell King Machek."

Machek. King of Denovoi, a small land to the west of the empire. There were dozens of such kingdoms beyond the empire's borders. Lands the empire did not care to—or could not—conquer. So why did she remember this particular one?

She heard Moria's voice, talking to village children she'd caught stealing or striking a smaller one.

Do you know what happens to little savages who mistreat others? They grow tails like monkeys, and then they're sold to King Machek. For his zoo. Have you heard of the Denovoi zoo? They say he keeps monsters there, locked in cages, and people come and pay money to see them.

Ashyn looked at Belaset, at her scaled face and arms.

"No," she whispered.

"You know who he is, then?"

"The zoo. They mean to sell me and my sister to him. For his zoo."

Belaset laughed softly. "No, child. You're bound for his harem. King Machek collects oddities of all sorts. Some for his zoo. Some for his bed. As for where I'll end up, that has yet to be seen. While the choice should be obvious, the king apparently has . . . unusual tastes."

Ashyn tried to process all that, gave up, and shoved it aside. "They've made a grave mistake. I have to tell them who I am."

"It won't matter who your family is, child—"

"No, who I am. Who my sister is. We *are* twins. The Seeker and Keeper of Edgewood."

"Seeker and . . ." Belaset stared, much as Ashyn must have stared at her moments ago. "The hound. I . . . had forgotten the stories."

"There are a Seeker and Keeper in the imperial city as well. Have you not seen them?"

"I'm casteless, child. I would not dare show my face anyplace they would be."

"Casteless?"

Ashyn had heard of such a thing, though there were no casteless people in Edgewood. They were the lowest of the low—those not permitted an occupation.

"My parents cast me out when my skin began to harden. I was allowed to live but stripped of my caste, as I was clearly cursed by the goddess for some sin or other, though I was but five summers old."

Deformity *was* believed to be a punishment. But a child of five could not possibly have committed a sin grave enough to deserve this.

"We need to tell them who I am," Ashyn said. "Harming me is an affront to the goddess."

Belaset laughed. "You truly are a child, aren't you? Do you think the king of Denovoi cares for the goddess of our empire? Now I suspect the slave trader knows exactly who you and your sister are. He would not speak too loudly of it, for there are men in his employ who might object, but he will be rubbing his hands, imagining the fortune that is to come. King Machek has no love for Emperor Tatsu. How much will he pay to be able to tell the great man that a young Seeker and Keeper warm his bed?"

"We need to escape, then."

"And we will, when we reach Denovoi. This is my plan, and I'll gladly take you and your sister with me if you help."

"No, we must escape now."

Belaset shook her bald head. "It sounds as if the other men have left to fetch your sister, but there is still an armed warrior outside our door. To escape, we would need—"

Ashyn pulled her dagger from beneath her cloak. "It seems they did not think to search a mere girl."

"A blade? And you can use it?"

"Adequately."

Belaset nodded slowly. "Yes, then. We can call the guard in. I will create a distraction, and you will slit his throat."

"S-slit—?"

Belaset's eyes flashed with impatience. "You said you can use it, did you not?"

"Yes, but I have never killed a man." *I've never stabbed anything more than a pig carcass.* "Perhaps we could just disable him."

"So he can cry for help? No, child, he must be killed. I'll do it while you create the distraction. When the guard brought you in, he clearly found your looks pleasing. I caught him stroking your hair as he laid you on the mat. That's how you'll distract him. Use your wiles."

"Wiles?"

Ashyn was sure she looked almost as shocked as she had when Belaset suggested she slit the man's throat. *I truly am a child. I can't even save myself.*

Ashyn took a deep breath. "I can distract him."

FORTY-FIVE

As they prepared, Ashyn got a better sense of the situation from Belaset. They were in a wagon from one of the trains they'd passed earlier that day. Apparently, the slave trader had spotted the girls and realized they were alike—in his profession, he would have a much keener eye than the average traveler.

He'd cut Belaset's wagon from the train and returned with a few mercenaries, planning to take the girls at night. That's why Ronan seemed to be asleep at his post—he'd been unconscious from a dart. They'd likely planned to use darts on the others as they slept, but then Ashyn and Tova woke. They'd brought them back and returned for Moria and Daigo.

Now Belaset had Ashyn remove her cloak, pull her hair over her shoulders, and undo the top button on her tunic. Ashyn would have been fine with all that, but then Belaset insisted on a second button and tugged her tunic down until

Ashyn was certain if she leaned over, her breasts would be on full display. That was, she supposed, the idea, but her cheeks still blazed at the thought.

"How do you do that?" Belaset said.

"Do what?"

"Redden your cheeks."

Belaset reached over and pinched them hard with her scaly fingers. Ashyn tried not to shrink at her touch.

"There," Belaset said. "You look very sweet and shy. Men like that. I worked at a brothel doing chores for the women, and men were always asking for virgins."

"Brothel?" Ashyn said. "Is that like a courtesan house?"

Belaset laughed. "Not exactly, child. Come now. We must move quickly, before they take your sister."

Ashyn knocked on the wagon door. "Hello? Is someone out there?"

It took a moment for the guard to answer.

"Yes?" he said.

"I'm unwell," she said.

"It's the dart," he said. "It will wear off soon."

"I—I'm going to be ill. Do you have something for me to . . . use? I don't want to be sick in here. I'm afraid I'll wake . . . the thing in here with me."

Ashyn hadn't wanted to say it that way, but Belaset insisted. If she called her a girl or used her name, it would be clear they'd been speaking, and the guard would be wary.

"Is there a bucket?" Ashyn asked. Belaset had said there was, hanging from the wagon, so the captives could relieve themselves.

The guard grunted. She heard the bucket clatter against

the wood. He opened the door just enough to pass the bucket through. Ashyn pulled it into the gap so the guard couldn't close the door.

Now it was time to use her wiles. Did she even *have* wiles? She doubted it, but she could feel the guard's gaze fixed on those opened buttons, on the pale skin beneath.

Pretend I'm a maiden in a tale, and this is my warrior love, slipping to my door for a few stolen moments.

She leaned forward, letting her tunic open more, her hair tumbling over it, and she didn't need to fake the blushing cheeks or shy gaze as she looked up into his face. He was not much older than she, his own cheeks darkening as he stared at her open tunic.

He's only a boy. We can't do this.

I'll find another way.

"I . . . I thought I heard something in here," she whispered, as if trying not to wake Belaset. "A snake or a rat. Could you take a look?"

She gazed up into his eyes. Not that there was much use in it. His attention hadn't left her open neckline. She steeled herself and leaned over farther.

"Please," she said. "I'd be so grateful."

He nodded, his gaze not lifting until she backed onto the pallet. The move was not so much seduction as necessity—the wagon was only big enough to hold the wide sleeping mat. But when she backed onto it, his breath caught and he started forward, as if she were pulling him into her bed. He glanced over at Belaset, who was feigning sleep.

"Where did you hear the noise, miss?" he asked, his voice thick.

"Up here. At the head of the mat."

He knelt on the pallet, his gaze on her. Then he put his hands down carefully, ready to crawl onto it, watching for any sign that she was going to stop him. When she gave none, he started forward.

I'll pretend I'm going to let him kiss me. Then I'll grab his hair and knock him unconscious. We won't need to kill—

Belaset sprang up and grabbed the guard by the hair.

"Knock him—" Ashyn began.

The blade slashed.

"No!"

It was too late. The guard's throat split before he could pull his blade. He gurgled blood. Ashyn stared in horror as Belaset grabbed her arm and yanked her toward the door.

"Hurry, child!"

Belaset pulled Ashyn outside. Ashyn resisted at first but quickly realized there was nothing she could do. She tumbled out the wagon door, hitting the ground. The night was silent and still.

"Tova," she said. "I need to find—"

"Your dog? We can't worry about him. Hurry!"

"No, go on. Keep the dagger. I'll . . ." She swallowed. "I'll take the guard's."

Belaset shook her head. "There's no time. Find your dog quickly. He can't be far."

Tova was right under the wagon. Sound asleep, still

unconscious from the dart. As Ashyn shook him, her heart pounded.

He leaped up with a snort, and she threw her arms around his broad neck.

"There's no time for that," Belaset said. "Hurry!"

Belaset raced off. Ashyn untied Tova and caught up. She had no idea which way to go—the plains all looked the same to her—but she trusted Belaset. They ran until they reached a patch of scraggly bushes. Belaset crouched behind them.

"Here's where we part, child. The road is that way." She pointed. "I trust you can find your camp?"

"Come with me," Ashyn said. "You'll be safer. We're all armed. My sister is well trained with a blade, and we have a warrior escort. We'll take you back to the city."

"There is nothing for me in the city."

"Then we'll take you someplace safe."

"You've been kind, but I'm going my own way, Ashyn of Edgewood. I trust you'll allow me to take this blade."

The request caught Ashyn off guard. It was a fine dagger, one she'd used since she was a child. If Belaset wanted a blade, she should have gone back for the guard's, when Ashyn mentioned it. As soon as she hesitated, she felt shamed. Ashyn could easily get another.

"Of course," she said. "Take it. Please."

"And that ring?"

"Ring? I . . . I am sorry, but I cannot part with that. It was my mother's."

"I think I have earned it, child."

"My father left it for me. When he died. Barely seven

nights ago." Ashyn heard the edge in her voice and the snap in her words. Yet there wasn't an inkling of understanding in Belaset's eyes, much less shame.

"You can buy many rings," the girl said. "I will take that one, in payment for my services."

"No, you will not—"

Belaset lunged. Ashyn staggered back. Tova grabbed Belaset by the blade arm, and she let out a hiss of shock, as if she'd forgotten the hound was there. He whipped her off her feet, Ashyn's blade bouncing to the ground. Then he retrieved the dagger gingerly by the handle and returned it to Ashyn.

"I deserve that ring," Belaset said. Her voice remained calm, as if simply requesting her due. A simple act of necessity, devoid of emotion. "I deserve it. I rescued you."

Ashyn gave a short laugh. "No, you helped me escape, using my blade, and in return, you earned your freedom, which you would not have gotten otherwise. I owe you nothing but my thanks. However, I will give you the dagger. Stay where you are. I'll walk away and leave it on the ground between us. When I whistle, you may retrieve it. If you make a move before that, I will set Tova on you, and this time, he will not be so gentle."

"All right."

Belaset's agreement came quickly—too quickly—which made Ashyn certain the girl was planning to trick her, but Belaset stayed still as Ashyn walked away and set down the blade. Even when Ashyn whistled softly, Belaset only rose and walked toward the dagger. When Ashyn glanced back, the girl was bending to retrieve it. She saw Ashyn and lifted a hand, as if in farewell. Then she turned and loped off across the dark plain.

FORTY-SIX

As soon as they left Belaset behind, Tova started off, presumably heading for camp.

Ashyn kept looking about, creeping quickly, until she saw a figure crouched behind a bush. It was not apparent at first, and she was certain he thought the bush hid him, but spring had not yet brought the bush into full bloom, and she could make out a crouching figure through its half-bare branches.

She froze. Her fingers fumbled under her cloak for her dagger . . . before she remembered she no longer had it.

"Tova!" she whispered.

He glanced at her. She motioned at the bush, where the figure was now rising. Tova looked over at it, then back at her, as if to say, *So?*

The faint moonlight lit the figure. It was Ronan.

"Ashyn?" Ronan's whisper crossed the distance between them.

"Who else would it be?" she whispered as she walked over. "Tova gives me away nicely."

"It was not a question so much as a greeting, lest you decide to put Moria's dagger-throwing lessons into practice."

"I doubt you'd be in much danger even if I did."

He chuckled softly. His hand went out, and she thought he was going to take hers and draw her to him, but he only beckoned her close, then laid his hand on her arm.

"It seems I fell asleep at my post." He flashed a wry smile. "But if you don't tell Gavril, I won't tell Moria that you got lost relieving yourself."

"Got lost?" She gave him a hard look. "Is that truly what you thought?"

Tova harrumphed, equally offended.

"You were knocked unconscious with a dart," she said. "I was kidnapped."

"Kidnapped?"

"How long was I gone?" Ashyn shook her head and waved for him to follow Tova, who'd started back toward camp. "I'll explain to everyone at—" She stopped and spun on him. "You did not realize I was taken?"

"I didn't, and I apologize—"

"No, I mean—Moria and Gavril. You didn't wake them?"

"I wanted to find you before they realized I'd—" He swore. Ashyn was already running.

* * *

331

The slave trader's men were at the camp. Ashyn could hear the commotion before they were close enough to see anything. When she tried to race ahead, Ronan caught her cloak.

"We'd do better to surprise them," he said. "Come this way, along the stream."

They ran down into the shallow gully. Ronan told her to follow in his footsteps, on the hard ground, so their boots wouldn't squelch. The gully was neck high, meaning Ashyn could still see over the edge. It seemed forever before she spotted the horses, looking about as if startled. When she gazed over the field, she saw figures at the camp.

Those figures had gone silent now. Their early oaths and curses seemed to have been Moria and Gavril as they were woken from sleep. And perhaps the raiders as they realized they'd lost the element of surprise.

Ashyn and Ronan continued running silently until the figures became clear—Moria, Daigo, and Gavril, surrounded by armed men. Ashyn tried to dart past Ronan, but again, he held her back.

"Race in there, and you'll distract Moria and Gavril as much as those mercenaries."

Causing a distraction hadn't actually been her plan. She'd had no plan at all but to run in, armed with Ronan's dagger. Even that would be pointless—they were still several hundred paces off.

Ronan resumed moving, quickly. Ashyn followed, her gaze fixed on her sister. Four men surrounded them. Daigo was at Moria's side, while Gavril stood with his back to her, their blades raised as they faced off against the raiders.

"Give us the girl," a man said. "And we'll let you live."

The words came from a fifth man, one Ashyn saw only now. He stood off to the side, well out of the fight. The slave trader.

Gavril didn't even acknowledge the offer. Moria did, saying, "I'll let *you* all live, if you return my sister."

"Take them!" the slave trader shouted, and the raiders surged forward.

Ronan raced up the stream gully onto clearer ground. Ashyn could barely even see the fighters; they seemed a seething mass of dark forms and flashing metal, their clangs of steel mingling with Daigo's snarls. Every now and then, though, she'd catch a glimpse of Moria and Gavril, still back-to-back as they fought.

Tova raced ahead. Already a man lay on the ground under Daigo, and another was fleeing. By the time Tova reached the fight, Daigo's prey lay unmoving. Moria's target was staggering back, and the wildcat was leaping for him. Gavril fought the last raider, but Tova circled past him, instead heading for the slave trader, who realized the fight was lost. He began to flee, with Tova at his heels. Once he was far enough gone, Ashyn whistled Tova back.

Moria spun to help Gavril, but he was already drawing his blade back as his opponent rushed him. The man's charge left him open, and it took only one solid swing to end it.

Ashyn saw Gavril's expression as his sword struck the man's side. Anger and resolve as he swung. Relief as the blade sliced into the man. Then horror as the raider hung there, nearly cut in two, held upright by the sword.

Gavril stumbled back and yanked his blade out, as if he hoped he could somehow undo the fatal blow. Moria wheeled from the raider Daigo now had pinned to the ground. She took hold of Gavril's elbow and pulled his attention to her as she said something.

Ashyn caught Ronan's arm, slowing him. Moria seemed to be asking Gavril if he was hurt, and he was shaking his head. Then he reached out, one hand going to the back of Moria's neck, under her hair, the other rising to her cheek. The young warrior leaned over her sister's upturned face, his braids falling in a curtain around them.

He's going to kiss her.

He never even came close. And unlike Ashyn with Ronan several nights before, Moria gave no sign that she ever expected a kiss, given that she kept talking. Instead, it seemed Gavril was examining a cut on Moria's cheek, and she was brushing off his concern.

Gavril continued checking the wound, his voice low, and as Ashyn watched them, she knew it didn't matter if he kissed her sister or not; there was something between them. A deep concern for each other's well-being that went beyond blossoming friendship.

She glanced at Ronan. He watched them, looking uncomfortable.

"I'm sorry," she murmured.

He glanced over, brows gathering. "About what?"

She paused. "Are you all right?"

A short laugh. "I'm not the one who just fought off armed kidnappers. Though I might feel like I did in a moment. Moria and Gavril aren't going to be pleased with me."

"It was an honest mistake," she said. "You thought—"

"Ronan!" Moria's voice rang out, and they looked up to see her striding over. "I hope you have a good excuse for being captured on guard duty."

Ashyn stepped between them. "He does. They used darts with some sort of sleeping potion, and we were taken captive—"

"*Ashyn* was taken captive," Ronan corrected. "While I was unconscious. I woke and thought she'd wandered off."

Moria snorted. "Wandered off? I should hope after all these days together you'd know her better than that."

"Moria?" Gavril called. "We'll speak about this later. We ought to leave before that trader decides to return."

Moria turned. "And the other mercenaries?"

"Daigo killed one," Ronan said. "Another fled. The third is unconscious. I've taken his blades. Gavril's right. We ought to gather the horses and go."

As they rode, Ashyn explained what had happened—but only to Moria. Given the fate that had awaited her in King Machek's court, she'd been too embarrassed to tell Gavril and Ronan. "What's the shame in being kidnapped for a harem?" Moria had said. "It wasn't as if you volunteered." Still, Ashyn was more comfortable letting her sister tell Gavril and Ronan, which she did, riding behind with them while Ashyn went on ahead.

As for *their* reaction, they had none—to the harem prospect, that is. To them, it seemed as unremarkable as a young man being captured for work in the mines. It was simply another terrible fate that could befall unprotected youth.

They reacted more strongly to the actual kidnapping. Gavril

was furious at the affront. To kidnap the Seeker was an unforgivable insult to the goddess, and even if one did not follow the laws of a neighboring land, one ought to respect its customs.

Like Moria, Ronan was more concerned about how the ordeal affected Ashyn. She assured them she was fine. Yes, it had been a shock, but it had ended so quickly that she was quite recovered. Which was untrue, yet not something she wished to burden them with now.

They continued through the day, but Moria and Gavril were obviously finding riding difficult, having taken several hard blows and blade slices during the fight.

Finally, as the sun began its descent, Ashyn persuaded them that the horses needed to stop. Having decided not to risk camping on open ground again, they found an inn for the night.

FORTY-SEVEN

The inn was a two-story wooden building with communal dining and bathing areas. Stairs led up the side to a balcony that stretched across the front and back, with rooms along each side. The inn was not large, and it was already crowded, the four of them needing to cram into one small room with a sleeping mat for two.

"It was that or the stables," Ronan said after he'd secured lodgings while they waited outside. "The girls won't mind sleeping on the bare floor, I'm sure."

"You won't mind sleeping in the stable, I'm sure," Moria said. "Which is where you'll end up if you attempt to put me on the floor."

"Moria should be on a mat," Ashyn said as they tramped up the outside steps to their room. "After that fight and a long day's ride, she'll be stiff and sore. Gavril, too. They should both take the—" She realized what she was suggesting and stopped short.

"I'm quite fine," Gavril said. "The girls ought to take the mat. Particularly you, Keeper. The fight was much harder on you."

Moria shot her fist at him. When they reached the balcony, she said, "If Ashyn's offering the bed, we ought to take it. They'll have one tomorrow night."

Ashyn's cheeks heated—and she was sure Gavril's did, too, even if she couldn't see it. Ronan seemed to be biting back a laugh.

When Moria caught Gavril's expression, she rolled her eyes. "Daigo can sleep between us. To keep you on your own side."

"*I'm* hardly the problem, Keeper. You flail. And snore."

"How would you know?" Ronan asked.

"She does," Ashyn cut in to save the young warrior from a reply. "She takes all the covers, flails about like she's in battle, and snores almost as loudly as Daigo."

The wildcat was not there to defend himself. They'd asked Tova and Daigo to remain below for now, in the adjacent stretch of forest. They'd sneak them up after dark.

They reached their room. When Moria opened the door, it was even smaller than they'd anticipated, barely big enough to fit the sleeping mat.

"I'm not sure we can get Tova or Daigo in here with us," Ashyn said as they crowded inside.

"It was honestly this or the stables," Ronan said. "That's where the traders behind me ended up."

"They truly rent room in the stables?" Ashyn asked.

"And the kitchen and the dining room, and probably the bath if they get an offer."

"I would suggest that Ronan and I find room in the

stables," Gavril said. "But after last night, I'm not certain it's wise to separate."

"It isn't," Ashyn said. "We'll squeeze in. For now, you and Moria rest up here, in whatever configuration suits you. Ronan and I will go down to dinner."

When Ronan and Ashyn went back downstairs, Ashyn lowered the hood on her cloak. Dining with it on would call too much attention to them, and Northerners were hardly unknown in the empire. The problem was only if the girls were seen together.

Indeed, their entrance into the dining hall attracted little attention. There was an entire trading party of Northerners there who nodded when they saw Ashyn, their gazes taking in her manner of dress and deciding she was not truly "from the North," and therefore required no more greeting than the nod.

Ronan guided them to one of the long, communal tables. As they knelt on coarse pallets, the innkeeper's wife came out. She paused and gave Ronan a hard look. The serving girl snickered as she laid down their bowls of rice and pork.

"Are we doing something wrong?" Ashyn whispered when they were gone.

"Not at all."

She looked back at the girl, whispering to the woman, who was now favoring Ashyn with that hard look. "What did you tell them when we arrived?"

"Only that my brother and I needed rooms for ourselves and our sisters."

"Sister?" she sputtered. "I no more resemble you than Gavril does. They're going to think . . ." She stared at him. "They think we're lovers."

Now it was Ronan sputtering as he laughed. "I would take more offense at your expression if it was not so adorable, Ash."

Ash? He's never called me— She pushed the thought aside, refusing to be distracted. "You let them believe—"

"Yes, because that is the best explanation for two young men and two young women to be on the road, and it's the one they'd likely arrive at whatever our story. Would you rather deny it and make them wonder who you truly are?"

"Oh." She settled back on her heels. "I suppose—"

"That I was correct in doing so, however much the implications might embarrass you?" He grinned, leaned forward, and whispered. "It's a good thing you were not taken to that harem. It's not just blades you require lessons in, is it? I would happily offer instruction in that as well if . . ." He trailed off, still smiling. "I'll stop before your face lights on fire. Drink some water. Just don't choke on it."

She was indeed blushing furiously. Furious, too, with him for teasing her, and with herself for reacting. *Like a child,* she thought. *I'm sixteen summers. Out here, in the real empire, I would be a woman now.*

I am a woman. The Seeker.

Not like that. She'd be more mature, perhaps no more experienced with men, but at least not blushing and stammering when the subject was raised.

"I apologize," Ronan said. "I was only teasing."

The apology only stung all the more, erasing any doubt that she'd reacted like a child.

I don't want you to see me as a child.

"I forget sometimes that you're a highborn girl," he said.

"I'm not highborn. My family is—"

"It doesn't matter. Whatever your family's caste was, you've been raised above that. I ought not treat you like a normal girl."

"But I *am*—"

"I don't mean that as it sounded." He sighed and pushed back from the table. "I'm making a mess of this. I only meant to apologize if I sometimes forget my place."

"You don't have a *place*, Ronan. Not with me."

He waved off the denial. She tried to continue, but her insistence only seemed to make the situation worse. It certainly drove Ronan to silence, eating his meal as she struggled for something to say, something worldly and interesting.

She was gazing around at the other diners, looking for a comment to make, when Ronan said, "I know you're bothered by what happened last night." He paused. "Well, obviously, being kidnapped *would* bother you, but I mean the . . . girl. What she did. Helping you and then demanding payment."

"I'd have happily given her the dagger," she said. "Even a ring, if it wasn't this one. But . . . I helped her, too. Perhaps I couldn't kill that man, but it was my dagger she used and my distraction. Without me, she would not have escaped."

"You felt betrayed."

Ashyn considered that. "I think, in some ways, I would *rather* feel betrayed. Then I'd be upset with myself for getting tricked, but this . . . I'm just confused. She didn't seem angry. She just expected the ring, no matter how important it was to me."

"Her own family cast her out; she would not understand that your mother's ring would hold any importance. It is"— he waved his eating sticks—"beyond her comprehension.

Demanding the ring was not an insult to you. It was not even an expectation. She was simply seeing if you would give it up. If you did, that was your loss and her gain." He ate another mouthful. "You said she was casteless. They must take everything they can get. They have no choice. The empire *allows* them no choice."

"You know people who are casteless."

He made a noise in his throat and ate a chunk of sticky rice, swallowing before answering. "On the streets, you cannot help but know some."

"How do they make a living?"

"Begging. Thieving."

"Belaset said she worked in a, um, brothel. Doing odd jobs. That's employment, isn't it? Better than beggary or thievery."

"I don't know." He met her gaze, his dark eyes serious. "Would you find it more honorable to steal for a living? Or to clean shit buckets for whores?"

Her gaze dropped.

He sighed. "I'm sorry. Again. I didn't mean to be so blunt—"

"No, it's not that. I see your point and I feel shamed for not knowing more. There's no one . . . like that in Edgewood."

He grunted and took another bite of pork. They ate for a few moments in silence, then he said, his gaze still on his plate, "There's something I ought to tell you."

"All right."

"I . . ." He looked up. Indecision flickered in his eyes. Then he blinked, pulled back a little, and cleared his throat.

342

"When we get to the city, I'm going to leave. Before we enter the gates."

"What?" Ashyn tried to hide her surprise. "Do you think that's necessary?"

"Under the circumstances, I can no longer expect anything but suspicion from the emperor. He'll think I may be involved with these mercenaries. You'll be safe once you're there, and I'll be safer if I go my own way."

"Where?"

"Into the city. Just not through the main gates."

"Will I see you again?"

"I don't know." His gaze met hers. "Do you want to see me again, Ashyn?"

Her heart hammered, and she searched his expression. He just sat there, gaze shuttered, waiting.

"I do," she said carefully. "After all this, I wouldn't want you to vanish into the city forever."

"Well, I'll need to vanish for a day or two. To be safe. Before I go, I'll speak to Gavril and determine the best way for you to contact me. All right?"

She nodded.

"You'll contact me when you want to see me?" he said.

Again she nodded, and he seemed to be waiting for some other response, but she didn't know what.

Finally she said, "Have you told Moria you'll be leaving?"

"No."

"I can get her alone, so you can tell her."

He laughed softly. "I don't think I need to inform everyone

individually. I'll tell her and Gavril on the road tomorrow. I just wanted you to know first."

"Thank you."

He picked up another chunk of sticky rice. "Better finish up here. There's a mob at the door, and they're eyeing our table."

FORTY-EIGHT

They started before dawn the next morning, and Ashyn saw the imperial city as the sun rose. The wall soared twice as high as those of Edgewood, yet she could still see the tops of buildings beyond it. Buildings unlike any she'd ever seen—towers of blocks, every story smaller than the one below it, each with a sweeping, curved roof. Atop that was a rod. For lightning, Ronan explained. Being so tall, the rod attracted it, and thus kept it from the wooden buildings below.

The city itself was built into the base of a mountain, one as green as the Forest of the Dead. Beautiful, though, with the sun rising behind it.

Ashyn tried not to gape. Ronan rode close beside her, pointing out what they could see. Her sister seemed more interested in the wall, and was asking Gavril about it—how many gates, how many guards.

"Are you planning your invasion, Moria?" Ronan called.

"More like planning my escape," she said, looking at the city and shuddering. "I can smell the place from here."

It was true—the stink of the city was ill-contained by the walls. Ronan said it was because they were near the stables—only imperial horses were permitted on the roads within—but Ashyn was sure that wasn't all they smelled. It was said ten thousand people lived in the imperial city. When she'd imagined it, she'd pictured a town stretching as far as the eye could see. Except she could see from one end of the wall to the other in one sweep. It was many times the size of Edgewood, but still much smaller than she'd envisioned. Which would explain the smell. And the noise. Even at dawn the cacophony rolled out to greet them.

They were approaching along a tertiary route, through one of the many villages that had sprouted along the city wall. They were all together now, Tova and Daigo having joined them.

As their horses' hooves clopped along the empty street, a man staggered sleepily from a house. He turned at the sound, his gaze passing over the riders, then stopping as he gaped at the massive hound and wildcat. He went back inside as if deciding he needed more sleep.

"This is where I take my leave," Ronan murmured, leaning toward Ashyn, not loud enough for Gavril and Moria.

"Already?"

He smiled. "You're almost in the city, Ashyn."

Ronan pulled his horse to a halt and slid from the saddle. Ashyn got down, too, to say good-bye. Moria and Gavril didn't notice, caught up as they were in their conversation. Ashyn was about to call to them, but Ronan stopped her.

"They won't get far before they notice," he said as he handed her his reins. "I'll leave you here, but if you have any troubles in there, any at all, contact me. All right?"

"And if . . ." She swallowed. "If I don't have troubles, may I still contact you? Or would you rather—"

He stepped forward, his hand going to the back of her head, his mouth lowering to hers. And he kissed her. Not a long kiss, but not a light one either. His lips pressed firmly against hers for a moment, before he backed up.

"I would like it very much if you contacted me," he said, his hand still behind her head. Another kiss, this one little more than a brushing of the lips, before he released her, murmured good-bye, and left her there, standing in the middle of the road, holding the reins of his horse.

Her sister and Gavril had not seen the kiss. They hadn't realized that they'd left Ashyn behind until Ronan ran up alongside them for a quick farewell. Ashyn had still been standing like an idiot in the road, holding the horses. It was only when Gavril returned for her that she climbed back onto hers.

Gavril took the reins of Ronan's horse without a word— and without any suggestion that he would notice her condition even if she'd been swooning, flushed, and half-dressed on the roadside. He was not unkind. He simply paid her little heed at the best of times, and now, as they approached the city, seemed lost again in his thoughts.

* * *

Ronan had been right to leave when he did. Shortly after that, their tiny lane joined with the Imperial Way—the road heading to the city gates. That was where, as Moria said, things got interesting.

It was a massive road, big enough for six carts across, lined not with forest or even houses, but with walls, funneling traffic to the gates. So the wildcat and the hound had to remain at their sides, meaning there was no reason to hide Ashyn and Moria.

Gavril didn't hide his identity either—if he appeared to have snuck into the city, it would smack of shame or treachery. So he removed his cloak, revealing his inked arms, and the girls took off their cloaks, and they rode onto the Imperial Way.

It was, as Moria joked, an effective method of dealing with the solid streams of people. They noticed the riders first. Two identical Northern girls with long red-gold hair, riding side by side. Then they saw Gavril, riding slightly behind and between, his blade drawn, his inked arms bare. Finally, they noticed the beasts. That was usually the point at which they decided they were too close to the riders and stumbled out of the way.

And so, despite the crowd, Ashyn and Moria cut easily through to the gates, where there was a line of those wishing to enter the city. It was generally a quick process, Gavril had said. Travelers paused, ostensibly to state their business, but in truth so the guards could get a look at them. Exiles were marked by a brand on the side of their neck. As well, there were travelers from outside the empire who did not follow its laws and attempted to carry weapons into the city. And, of course, there were criminals whose faces the guards had been told to watch for, though considering that Ronan knew another way in, Ashyn suspected it was a rare and truly foolish criminal who attempted to use the front door. Ronan himself, fortunately, did not bear the exile's brand—if a convict survived the Forest of the Dead, his exile was considered at an end, so no permanent mark was given.

As they approached the line, their magical crowd-clearing powers proved useful again. They'd stand behind someone who would look back, see the girls and the beasts, and wave them ahead. Sometimes they would be met with lowered eyes and a murmured, "Blessings to you, Seeker and Keeper." Most just moved aside quickly.

As soon as they drew close enough for the guards atop the wall to see them, one hurried down and spoke to his comrades. Then the line truly did part before them, as two armed guards strode along and ordered everyone back.

Ashyn started to dismount, but Gavril murmured, "No," and Moria seconded it with a nod. As the guards drew close, Ashyn could see why they stayed on their horses—because it meant they towered over the guards, putting them in a position of power.

Gavril moved his horse forward. "I bring the Keeper and the Seeker of Edgewood." He didn't shout, but his voice carried, and around them, a hush fell. "They bear a message for the emperor."

The guards exchanged a look. Clearly this was not an occurrence for which they had been trained.

"We were not informed of this visit," one said finally.

"Because that was not possible," Gavril said. "We bring urgent tidings. *Grave* tidings."

Another look between the guards.

"These are clearly the Keeper and the Seeker of Edgewood," Gavril said, his voice hardening. "No more ought need to be said. You will let them pass."

The crowd behind the guards was parting again, this time for a gray-haired man, an inked warrior. Likely the commander of the gate.

"My apologies to the young Seeker and Keeper. This is unexpected and—" The old man stopped. His gaze went from Gavril's face to his arms. Then his weathered face broke into a smile. "Gavril Kitsune. Welcome home."

A murmur rippled through the crowd. Few would have been able to recognize the tattoos at a distance, and even those who had would likely presume it was only some distant relation of the former marshal.

Gavril discreetly waved for the girls to stay seated, but he dismounted and, for a moment, Ashyn thought he meant to embrace the old warrior. Which proved, she reflected, that she didn't know Gavril nearly well enough. He only dismounted and bowed.

"Commander Alain," he said.

The commander clapped Gavril on the back as he straightened. "It is good to see you, son."

"I would say the same, sir, were it under other circumstances. As I was telling the guards, I'm escorting the Keeper and the Seeker of Edgewood with a message for the emperor, along with ill news."

350

He lowered his voice, and Ashyn knew he was telling the commander about Edgewood. The other guards moved closer to eavesdrop, but Ashyn could tell from their expressions that they heard none of it.

As Gavril finished, Commander Alain's face paled and his gaze shot to the girls. "My sincerest condolences," he said, with a deep bow. "The imperial city welcomes you. My men will escort you to the court."

Gavril murmured something, again too low for anyone to hear.

"Yes, of course," the commander said. "Understandable." The old man clapped Gavril's back again. "It *is* good to see you, Gavril. Welcome home."

A buzz ran through the crowd, and Ashyn realized this was more than an old warrior welcoming a young one. There was a subtext to the words and the effusive greeting. A dangerous subtext, given the crowd's whispers and murmurs. In welcoming the son of the disgraced former marshal, the commander was making a very public statement.

Ashyn knew that when the emperor exiled Marshal Kitsune, his family was permitted to keep their rank and live in the city, and were accorded all due respect in the court in acknowledgment of the marshal's long service. It had seemed simple enough. Yet given Gavril's concerns about appearing to sneak into the city—and now the commander's reception and the bystanders' reactions—Ashyn could tell it was not simple at all.

As Gavril walked back, he leaned over to Moria and whispered, "I asked for a small escort kept at a distance. Otherwise, by dusk, people will be saying we were taken to the court under armed guard."

Moria nodded. "Good idea."

The commander gave their packs to guards to carry, and two boys led their horses away. No one asked about the riderless fourth horse.

FORTY-NINE

The commander accompanied them to the gates, talking as they went, mostly to Gavril, though he included the girls. It was idle chatter, yet not meaningless, Ashyn decided as they passed through into the city proper with the commander still at Gavril's side, still talking to him. It was another statement. So, too, were the actions of other guards, older than the ones who'd first met them, warriors coming out from the gate garrison, welcoming Marshal Kitsune's son home.

Was it simply a sign of respect for their old leader? Ashyn hoped so. She knew from her studies that no enemy, no plague, no natural disaster was more dangerous for an empire than a schism between its emperor and its army. She'd heard her father and other villagers speak of the current marshal, saying he was not the man his predecessor had been, and she'd heard relief in their voices. He was a competent marshal and nothing more, and that seemed to be the way most liked it.

At least, it was the way the villagers of Edgewood had liked it. For the average citizen, peace was good. She looked at the armed men greeting Gavril. Were they as fond of peace? Did they chafe under a "competent" man?

The commander took his leave of them at the roadway, and they walked into the city, followed at a distance by the two guards with their packs. There was no need of anyone to lead them. While Gavril knew the way to court, the path was clear—the Imperial Way, now paved with brick, cutting clear through the city, ending at the palace.

It was still quite early in the morning, but the Way was more crowded than the main thoroughfare in Edgewood on market day. Carts and makeshift booths lined the roadway as traders hawked everything from fresh chicken eggs to petrified dragon eggs. Gavril assured Moria that the latter were simply pretty rocks, but Ashyn was certain her sister was making a note to come back later for a closer look.

There was no time for dawdling at merchant carts now. It did not take long for people to see them, and for whispers to snake along the street and spread. Soon it was as if they were leading a victory parade, as onlookers lined both sides of the Way and watched and whispered.

The spirits came, too, those whispers an undercurrent of the air itself. At home, they were mostly just that—an undercurrent, the spirits conversing, rarely to her. These ones were talking both to and about her.

You ought not to be here, child.

Not your place.

Beware.

"Beware of what?" she whispered under her breath.

Everything.

She could tell Moria was hearing the same messages. Her face was tight with annoyance.

"Tell me something useful for a change," Moria muttered. "We could truly use some help here."

Beware and be safe, the spirits whispered.

Moria grumbled and Daigo snorted.

The onlookers' whispers had grown now. Cries of "Bless us, Seeker," and "Protect us, Keeper," rang out. When a group of children pushed to the front of the crowd, Moria reached into her pocket and pulled out copper coins, blessing them and throwing them. It was almost instinctive, Ashyn thought, and when the children dove for them, Moria hesitated. Ashyn saw grief flicker across her face, and she knew Moria was thinking of the children of Edgewood.

She caught her sister's hand and squeezed it.

"You ought not to throw coins here, Keeper," Gavril said. "I know you mean well, but these are not the children of Edgewood."

"I can see that," Moria said dryly. The children looked as if no one had bathed them in a week, and most wore clothing so tattered that even the thriftiest mother in Edgewood wouldn't have attempted to mend it. "I'm not sure we can trust the emperor to care about the plight of Edgewood's children when he apparently has so little regard for those of his own city."

Ashyn hushed her, but it wasn't necessary—Moria was wise enough to keep her voice low. When an older child grabbed a coin from a younger one, Moria flipped the bereft little one another, her aim perfect. The crowd cheered.

"Your advice is noted, Kitsune," she said. "But I will give coins where I choose."

"As expected," he said. "You'll do as you choose and learn your own lessons."

"Is that not the best way to learn them?"

Gavril shook his head and prodded them to pick up the pace. People continued to join the throng along the roadside. Few ventured onto the actual road, and those who did moved back at a growl from Tova or Daigo.

They were halfway along the road when a voice yelled, "Kitsune!"

Gavril didn't turn, only letting his gaze flicker that way, as if to reassure himself it wasn't someone he knew.

"Gavril Kitsune!" the voice called. "Did you meet your father in Edgewood? Does that son-of-a-whore haunt the Forest of the Dead?"

Someone shouted for the man to be silent. Gavril's hand tightened on his sword hilt, but he kept walking, gaze forward.

"If it was *my* father, I'd do the honorable thing," the man shouted. "Drive my blade between my ribs. If you'd like, I can do it for you."

Moria stopped then, swinging around.

"Don't," Gavril said.

Moria didn't stop, but only because silencing the man wasn't necessary. Someone had done it for her—with a punch to the man's jaw. Others had joined in, and a brawl erupted.

The group continued on, but this time they didn't get more than twenty paces before someone else shouted, "Kitsune!"

Gavril kept walking. This man didn't settle for shouting from a crowd. He elbowed his way to the front, coming out behind them and jostling the sheath on Gavril's sword as he passed. In previous ages, to knock against a warrior's sword, even by accident, was an insult punishable by a lethal swing of that blade. Today, such a response broke the empire laws, but the insult remained, and could be answered with a scarring blow.

Gavril turned a cool glare on the man and rested his hand on his blade hilt. For a moment, it seemed the man intended to stand his ground. Then, slowly, he eased back, just enough to let Gavril ignore the insult with a nod and continue on.

Ashyn saw her sister tense as they passed. She also let her hand fall to one of her blades. But the man made no move and said not a word. He simply spat, loudly, spittle landing on Gavril's arm.

Moria threw her blade so fast neither Gavril nor Ashyn had time to stop her. It sailed under the man's arm and pinned his cloak to the cart behind him. Then, with a snarl, Daigo ran at him. The man let out a high-pitched shriek, arms shielding his face, but the wildcat simply plucked out the dagger, giving him a disdainful look, and bounded back to Moria. As she took it from him, the crowd laughed and let out a cheer as the man slunk back into the crowd.

"Keeper! Keeper!"

"What's your name, Keeper?" a young man near them shouted.

Moria sheathed her weapon. "I am Moria of Edgewood. My sister is Ashyn."

"Welcome to the imperial city, Moria!"

"Ancestors bless you, Moria!"

Gavril sighed as they resumed walking. "So much for a quiet and subtle entrance."

"If you wanted either, you needed to give her a sleeping draught," Ashyn said.

Moria rolled her eyes. "The street is lined with people gaping at us. We were hardly passing unnoticed. Gavril couldn't respond to the insult, so I did."

"Which I appreciate," he murmured. "But I'm going to ask you not to repeat it, Keeper. You would do well not to align yourself with me."

"I already have."

"I'm serious, Moria," he said, voice lowering as he moved beside her. "You cannot—"

"Ashyn, is the city what you thought it would be?" Moria asked.

Ashyn glanced at Gavril, but he only shook his head. He'd have the conversation with Moria at another time, she was sure. For now, he let the subject drop, and they continued on to the court.

MORIA

FIFTY

Moria looked at the palace ahead. It was imposing—she'd give it that much. The wall around the compound was said to take four thousand steps to circumvent and it was so high they could only see blue-tiled roofs beyond. Ashyn had always talked about wanting to see this, not because she was truly interested in court life, but because she'd read of it and heard of it so often that she wished to see it for herself.

Moria wondered if it was what Ashyn expected. Or if Ashyn still cared. No matter what their message brought, it would not return their village.

The Imperial Way ended at the Gate of the Crimson Phoenix. Which sounded terribly impressive, until one realized that it simply meant "the south gate"—the crimson phoenix being the guardian of the south. It was not even a proper gate, but rather a gatehouse two stories tall, with flared roofs at each level, in the imperial tradition. It was made of cypress wood, painted red, with a red tiled roof. The first floor was for the guards. The second was a tearoom, where the emperor would meet dignitaries from enemy nations, which allowed them to be on the palace grounds but not truly within the palace proper.

Once again, guards spotted them long before they arrived. This time, though, they stayed inside the walls of the gatehouse as if they didn't notice the party approaching, though Commander Alain had sent a runner ahead.

When the party reached the gatehouse, the men bowed deeply and respectfully to Moria and Ashyn.

"Welcome, Seeker and Keeper of Edgewood."

There was no greeting for Gavril. Not a glance his way. He'd told her to expect that, as he'd told her to expect the overly warm greeting from some warriors, like the commander, and an uglier one from some bystanders, like the man who'd spat and jostled his sword.

Moria was not sorry she'd thrown her dagger and caused a scene. It wasn't even about avenging an insult to a comrade. Truly, if the man had spat at Gavril over some misdoing, Moria would not have gotten involved. While she'd never felt the urge to spit at Gavril herself, she certainly understood the underlying sentiment. But the insult wasn't about Gavril—it was about his father. That was unacceptable.

She wasn't much happier about the commander's greeting. At first, she'd thought perhaps Gavril had trained under him or spent a season learning his trade at the wall. But as they'd walked Gavril had said he knew the commander only slightly. He'd been a general under his father, demoted to wall commander after the marshal's exile. Just as the spitting man had said, "I stand against your father," the commander had said, "I stand with him," and had simply used Gavril as a tool to do it. Unacceptable. She could certainly understand now why he had been in no rush to return to the imperial city.

When these gate guards ignored him, Gavril didn't react. He'd said this would happen—no matter what their position on the matter, those at court would keep it to themselves. Truly, Moria didn't see why there ought to be any "position" on a marshal exiled ten summers past, but there was, and there was little she—or Gavril, apparently—could do about it.

"We come with a missive for the emperor," Ashyn said to the guards. "We ask that you allow us to take it to him."

"That is, I regret, impossible, my lady," the older of the guards said. "We must ask that you give us the message, and we will convey it to his imperial highness."

"It is not an invitation to lunch," Moria said. "Do you have any idea—?"

"They do not, I'm sure," Ashyn cut in.

Ashyn gave her sister a look. Moria glowered but held her tongue.

"Our missive must be given to the emperor himself," Ashyn said. "Those were our orders, and I fear we dare not disobey. There are lives at stake. Many lives."

Gavril had warned them to tell as few people as possible about the fate of Edgewood and the threat against Fairview. It would only lead to panic.

"We cannot let you in, my lady," the guard said. "Our Keeper and our Seeker are in court. The spirits would be disturbed and offended if we permitted you onto the grounds."

"Then tell Thea and Ellyn to leave," Moria said. "Better yet, call them here, and I'll tell them myself."

Her sister stiffened at her tone. The younger guard's eyes flashed in something like amusement.

"We know your Keeper and your Seeker," Ashyn said. "They trained us in Edgewood. Ask them to come, please."

"I would, my lady, but they are the ones who gave the order not to open the gates."

"Did they?" Moria stepped forward, Daigo moving with her. "Go tell those old—"

Ashyn cut in. "Please ask Thea and Ellyn to come speak to us so that we may properly explain the situation. Under normal circumstances, we understand their concern, but the situation is far from normal."

The older guard nodded and sent the younger to fetch the city's Keeper and Seeker. Then he murmured, "It is good to see you, Gavril."

"Thank you, sir."

An awkward pause. "Your lady mother is well. She was at the palace last moon for the Cherry Blossom festival."

"Good." A pause, and Gavril seemed to struggle, finally asking, "Is she in the city?"

"No, son. She is not."

Gavril didn't seem surprised by the news. He turned his attention beyond the gatehouse, inside the walls to the palace grounds. Moria followed his gaze to see two warriors sparring. They were on a raised platform, which would have suggested they were performing for an audience, except the dais was uceremoniously placed at the rear of a government building. It was for training, then—get knocked off the narrow platform and the young warrior would suffer a bruised rump and ego.

In the silence, she could hear the faint click and clash of their blades. She moved to the fence for a better look. The two were dressed in battle armor. They wore sleeveless tunics and loose-fitting breeches, as Gavril did, but were also dressed in sleeve armor, shoulder plates, shin guards, and neck guards; all were made of fabric and covered in overlapping lacquered wood scales.

One of the warriors wasn't much older than Moria. From here she could see little of him except dark hair tied back and arm tattoos, though only two pairs of bands, rather than full sleeves—one band circling his upper arms and one his lower, like ornamental cuffs.

"Is that how they sometimes do the tattoos?" she asked Gavril. "In stages?"

He shook his head.

Ashyn moved forward and murmured. "It signifies that he is a . . ." She seemed to struggle for a word, and her cheeks flushed. "He is not born of a wife, but a courtesan."

"That's Tyrus," Gavril said. "He's one of the emperor's bastards."

Moria watched the young man. His instructor was having a hard time keeping up, the youth's sword flashing like quicksilver.

"Do you know him?" Moria asked Gavril.

"We trained together."

"He's very good."

Gavril grunted. "Decent enough. We used to spar."

"Until you weren't enough of a challenge?"

He gave her a look. When she resumed watching the fight, Gavril tried to nudge her from the fence. She ignored him. This was a distraction and she was happy for it. Also, admittedly, she was enjoying it. There was something to be said for watching an expert swordsman in training, particularly if he was young and, at least from this distance, well formed.

When Tyrus wheeled to avoid a blow, he noticed that he had an audience and gave a small bow. His instructor's sword flashed, nicking the youth's cheek to get his attention. Moria would have expected a prince—even a bastard prince—to take the rebuke badly, but she heard Tyrus laugh as he called something to his instructor. Then he resumed the fight.

"Keeper," Gavril said.

She was about to brush him off again when she saw what he meant—the court Keeper and Seeker were coming down the walk.

FIFTY-ONE

The Seeker—Ellyn—came first, walking with a warrior's haughty stride, despite her age. The Keeper—Thea—followed behind, her hands folded in front of her. It was said that when a Keeper and Seeker were chosen, the beasts determined which would be which. Then the babies were quickly given bracelets. Moria was convinced that some early nursemaid had switched Thea's and Ellyn's bracelets.

Even their beasts didn't seem as bonded to them as Tova and Daigo. When Ashyn was little, she'd say it was because Thea and Ellyn hadn't named their beasts. They were simply the Hound and the Wildcat. That was, however, the tradition. It was their father who had let the girls break it—one of his small, quiet rebellions.

"Moria," Ellyn said as she strode through the gate. "What is the meaning of this, summoning us?"

"She didn't," Ashyn said softly. "I did."

The old Seeker turned a disdainful look on her student. "Don't take the blame for your sister, Ashyn. I know which of you is the impetuous one." She turned to Moria. "And the disrespectful one."

"I'm sure Moria meant no disrespect, sister," Thea said as she caught up.

"No, she didn't," Ellyn said. "She's simply thoughtless. As demonstrated by coming here, knowing the danger it puts our city in, having two Keepers and two Seekers."

"We haven't even passed our seventeenth summer," Moria said. "Our combined powers should barely add to one of yours." She paused. "Unless you're concerned that we're more powerful than we ought to be. Or that you're weaker."

Ashyn elbowed her to silence. "We've had a long journey. My sister is tired and even more impatient than usual. However, we bring an urgent missive—"

"Which you will give to us. Then you will leave the city."

Moria stepped up to the old woman. "Edgewood is gone. Our village has been massacred by shadow stalkers—"

"Shadow stalkers?" Ellyn laughed. "Your village was massacred by figments of your imagination?"

Moria gripped her blade, and it took everything in her not to draw it. "No, my *father* was killed by *shadow stalkers*, as Ashyn and Gavril will attest—"

"Your sister and a traitor's son? Those are your witnesses?"

"My witnesses are the dead of Edgewood. My father and the governor and the commander—"

"This will be investigated. In the meantime, you shall not—"

"I will pass!" Moria roared, Daigo snarling beside her. "My village is gone and its children are held prisoner, and you will let me pass, old woman, or I swear by my ancestors—"

Thea drew her blade, lunging forward, still spry for her age.

Gavril stepped between them. "This is unreasonable. They ask only to see the emperor. It is their right to do so. If you will allow us to explain . . ."

"Yes, ladies," said a voice behind the women. "Please let them explain."

It was the young prince, Tyrus. He'd sheathed his sword and was walking toward them from the palace gardens.

He looked—as she would have expected from the emperor's son—empire-born. Of course, they were all born in the empire, but the term was used to denote those who came from the original kingdom that had eventually conquered the surrounding lands and formed the empire. His skin was the color of golden sand, his hair straight and black, his cheekbones high, and his dark eyes slightly tilted. It was, within the empire, considered the highest standard of beauty—a standard, Moria suspected, set by those who ruled it. She was not herself given to preferring any regional "look" over another, but even she would admit the boy was very well formed from face to physique, and she allowed her gaze to linger as he approached.

"Hello, Gavril," he said with a genuine smile. "It's good to see you back."

Gavril managed a stiff bow. In turn, Tyrus bowed to Ashyn and Moria.

"The Keeper and Seeker of Edgewood, I presume. I'm Tyrus Tatsu. Welcome to the imperial city."

"This does not concern you, your highness," Ellyn said. "It is a spiritual matter."

"Oh?" He stopped before them. "It sounded like a martial matter from where I was standing. Do you always discuss the spirits with shouts and drawn blades?"

"Your highness—" Thea began.

"Have the young Keeper and Seeker come for guidance? Additional training?"

"No, your highness," Ashyn said. "We bear a message for your imperial father. One that we have been instructed to deliver to his hand."

"Oh?" He gave a feigned look of confusion for the old women. "That does not seem like a spiritual matter at all."

"The spiritual matter is that they ought not to be in this city. Two Keepers and two Seekers ought not to occupy the same location."

Again he faked confusion. "But it's been done, hasn't it? I seem to recall that one of the traveling pairs visited court last summer."

Moria bit her cheek as Ellyn's face darkened. Challenges and arguments posed as innocent questions were not Moria's style, but she could see the advantage of the strategy. There was no way the old Seeker could argue without seeming rude, particularly when the one asking was an imperial prince.

"Your highness," Ashyn said to Tyrus. "If we could explain the situation—"

"There is no need to bother the young prince—"

"The village of Edgewood is no more," Moria said. "The people of Edgewood are dead, massacred. The children were spared, but if we do not get this missive to the emperor, their lives are forfeit, as are the lives of every villager in Fairview."

Silence. Tyrus stared at her, stunned. "Your entire village . . ."

"Yes, your highness. Every man and woman. Now mercenaries hold the children in Fairview, under siege."

"We have only their word, your highness," Ellyn said. "Three children, one of them the son—"

"One of them a *warrior* in service of the empire," Tyrus said. "A boon companion who trained with me. Although given that Gavril is several moons my senior, I suppose that means I am merely a child, too."

"Of course not, your highness."

Tyrus turned to the two guards. "Would you leave us, please?"

Once they'd walked out of earshot, Tyrus turned to Moria and Ashyn. "The deeper problem, I fear, is that my father is not in the city."

"Your highness!" Thea said.

"It is, as you see, a matter of some secrecy. The people do not like their emperor to leave, yet my father feels the occasional need and does so unbeknownst to his subjects and most of his staff. I will, of course, have my brothers send a party to retrieve him. In the meantime, I would like to offer you the hospitality of the court. It has very richly appointed guest rooms for visiting dignitaries, which you are. Our Keeper and

Seeker will remain in their quarters, in the Chambers of the Divine, suitably separated from you, should the proximity make the spirits uneasy."

Ellyn grumbled but allowed that this was reasonable.

"You ladies may take your leave, then," Tyrus said. "I will escort the young Keeper and Seeker to their quarters. The less time you spend in their presence, the safer it will be."

Thea and Ellyn withdrew with their beasts trailing after them.

"My apologies for that," Tyrus said when they were gone. "Things have been . . . difficult this last moon, which is why my father needed a rest."

"Problems?" Gavril asked.

Tyrus shrugged. "Tensions. Internally and externally, with mountain tribes. Do not ask me for details." A flash of a smile. "You know how I hate politics."

"But you're good at it," Ashyn said as they began walking. "You handled that admirably."

"A bastard must have some head for political wrangling. If not, he risks losing the head he has."

Another affable smile, as if the prospect of assassination was simply part of everyday life. Moria supposed it was, for him. The children an emperor fathered by official concubines were recognized, like Tyrus. They were raised in the palace as princes and princesses. They received their father's name and, apparently, modified clan tattoos for the sons.

While bastard princes could not succeed as emperor, they could attain any other high office—even marshal. The problem was that the emperor had several sons by the empress, and only one could succeed him, so the others would need to fight the bastards for court appointments. It was an old joke that emperors bred like rabbits because, like the rodents, so few of their offspring survived. It would not be nearly as amusing an analogy if you were one of those young rabbits.

Tyrus continued, "My place of choice, as Gavril knows, is the battlefield."

"I saw you practicing," Moria said. "You're very good."

"I had an excellent sparring partner," he said, with a nod toward Gavril. "But thank you, my lady. You are . . ." A glance down at Daigo. "The Keeper. Of course."

"Moria," she said. "My sister is Ashyn. This is Daigo and that is Tova."

"Ah, yes. I'd heard the Edgewood twins named their hound and wildcat. They are magnificent beasts." He paused, sobering. "About Edgewood. You said *all* except the children were killed."

Ashyn nodded. "We suspect they only spared us because they feared spiritual reprisals."

Moria snorted. "I think they spared us more because we're useful. We could get their message to the emperor, and Gavril could help us survive the journey across the Wastes."

"Across the Wastes?" Tyrus paused. "Yes, of course. If the village was massacred, you had to cross. I cannot imagine . . ." He shook his head. "Do you know who killed your people? Tribesmen? Sending missives seems very well organized for tribes—"

He cut himself off with an audible click of his teeth. "And that is none of my business."

371

"We'd be happy to tell you all we know," Ashyn said. "We appreciate what you've done for us."

A wry smile her way. "No, I mean it is truly none of my business, and it's best if I leave it as such. My brothers will already find fault with my involvement. They are always looking for a sign that I take an interest in court politics. I'll hear the rest of the story when my father does. He ought to be back before dawn."

"Dawn?" It was not even midday.

"When my father leaves, he doesn't stay close. It may be nightfall before the riders even reach him. But he will come, and he will come swiftly. You have my assurances on that."

FIFTY-TWO

The court was comprised of two dozen buildings, as Tyrus explained. The Chambers of the Divine were at the back, near the storehouses and the tea garden. "The tea garden is magnificent," he said. "Particularly now, as the cherry blossoms begin to bloom, but I'll ask you to stay away from that end for now."

"So Thea and Ellyn have no cause to complain," Ashyn said.

"Yes. That seems best."

He pointed out the Hall of the Eight Ministries—the large building he'd been sparring behind. To the side was a small, lushly landscaped garden, centered about a pond. He left them there on the bridge overlooking the pond while he went in to make arrangements for their visit.

"Will you stay here?" Moria asked Gavril once Tyrus was gone.

"I will," he said. "They require my statement on the matter, and they'll not want to waste time fetching me from my mother's house."

Moria nodded. Ashyn wandered along the bridge, leaning over to look at the koi fish sparkling in the clear water below. She continued off the bridge, heading for a collection of unusual rocks arranged beside the pond.

"So Tyrus," Moria said when her sister was out of hearing range. "You don't like him."

Gavril stiffened. "If I gave that impression, I apologize—"

"Stop politicking, Kitsune. There's no one to hear you."

"We are in the imperial city. There is always someone to hear us. Remember that, Keeper." He lowered his voice. "As for Tyrus Tatsu, he is the emperor's son. I cannot afford to have a personal opinion on him. If you are asking if I suspect him of ulterior motives, I do not. Tyrus is as he appears. When I knew him, he had no interest in politics, and I cannot imagine that has changed. He knows it's not in his best interests, and it doesn't suit him anyway. He lacks the guile to compete in that snake's nest. He is best suited for his chosen profession: a warrior."

"So he can be trusted."

"No one here can be trusted, Keeper." He gave her a stern look. "Remember that, too."

"I misspoke. Is he honorable?"

A pause. It didn't seem as if Gavril was considering the matter, but more as if it pained him to speak the words. "Yes," he said finally. "Tyrus is honorable."

Moria realized *that* was Gavril's problem with the young bastard prince. He respected him. He might even like him.

Which was unacceptable, because Tyrus was the son of the man who had, in Gavril's eyes, betrayed his father.

They were taken directly into a large chamber, where they were seated on cushions and given food and drink, and then told that the chancellor and one of the three major counselors were on their way. Gavril had warned them to expect a delay— the men would be briefed first, and would not rush, for fear of seeming panicked.

Politically, the chancellor ranked just below the emperor and marshal. He was in charge of all matters of state. Major counselors were the emperor's advisors. Sending both showed that their situation was being taken seriously.

Gavril and Moria decided Ashyn would speak for them. Letting Gavril do so would be politically dangerous. So would letting Moria, though in a much different way.

There was little need for restraint. When the men arrived, with their scribes and their attendants, it was nothing like their encounter with Ellyn and Thea. The chancellor and major counselor listened to their story with incredulity, but they did not question its veracity. Or, Moria suspected, they did not question that the three young people *thought* it was true.

Whether the village had truly been massacred by shadow stalkers seemed dubious to them, but clearly a large number of citizens were dead and the children had been taken hostage by mercenaries, who threatened the people of another town. These were events on too grand a scale to be wholesale fabrications.

They had, of course, dispatched fast runners to Fairview to "assess the ongoing situation," and to Edgewood to "search for survivors." Moria would argue with neither. Their story was indeed incredible, and the chancellor would be a fool to take it at face value.

Ashyn said nothing of death worms and thunder hawks. That would come later. Adding more sightings of presumed legendary creatures would not aid their cause.

So they told their story, and then were escorted to their quarters, where they would await the return of the emperor.

Moria wandered about the confines of their room. It was large enough, though the design was not truly to her taste. It was done in the imperial style, starkly white, with "windows" made of thin paper that let in light, but were impossible to see through. Bright, colored pillows decorated the floor and the sleeping mat, adding enough color to ease the chill of the white, but Moria still found herself shivering as she walked.

"Stop pacing," Ashyn said. "You're making Daigo dizzy."

Moria glanced at the wildcat. He was on a bed of pillows like a sultan, sleeping soundly, his wounds cleaned and tended by the court doctor.

"Fine," Ashyn said. "You're making *me* dizzy. And Tova."

The hound grunted in agreement.

"Go to the library and fetch a book." Ashyn lifted the one she was reading. "You've never seen such a collection. They're sure to have new ones for you, with new beasts you can use to scare children."

Ashyn smiled, but Moria was in no mood to think of fantastical creatures. At this point, it seemed as if merely to consider them would be to conjure one in their quarters. She had no interest in new tales of wild adventure either. She would be quite happy when this one was done.

"Let me see the envelope," she said, walking to Ashyn.

"And let you nearly set it on fire again, holding it to the flame trying to read the message inside?" Ashyn shook her head. "You'll find out soon enough. We cannot risk tampering with it."

"I'm not tampering. I'm trying to learn more. Once we hand it to the emperor, we have only his word on what's written within."

Ashyn's brows shot up. "You think he would lie?"

"Perhaps not, but I don't like knowing so little. Let me see the seal again."

Ashyn sighed and took the envelope out. Moria examined the wax seal.

"It looks like a family crest," Moria said. "But there is no creature in it, and Gavril did not recognize it."

"Because if it is a family crest, it is not from a family of the empire. These are mercenaries. They must work for a foreign king."

"If we could identify it, then . . ."

Another sigh. "Then what? What difference does it make?"

"It would be knowledge. Insight. Before we hand it over."

Ashyn shook her head and pocketed the envelope. "You're bored, Moria. Go for a walk. Visit Gavril. He'd be happy to see you."

"No, I'm quite certain he's enjoying the respite."

"Oh, I'm not so sure." Ashyn smiled. "I think he'd welcome a visit, particularly if your sister is not tagging along."

"Do not play matchmaker, Ash. Or, if you must, find a more suitable target for me. Gavril is a valuable ally. I respect him."

"Meaning you do not find him attractive? Because I'm sure I caught you watching at the stream when he took off his tunic to bathe."

Moria shrugged. "He was doing so within view; it was no invasion of privacy, and it was a sight worth watching. So is a pretty sunset. It does not mean I wish it for my own. I respect Gavril. I admire him. Therefore, he is not a potential lover."

"*Because* you respect and admire him? That may be the most ridiculous thing you've ever said."

"Not wishing to dally and amuse myself with someone I hold in regard?" Moria sat cross-legged on the end of the sleeping mat. "I think that is perfectly reasonable. I like Gavril. I enjoy his companionship. He infuriates me, but he challenges me, and I appreciate that. I can talk to him honestly. That's rare."

"And all qualities you ought to seek in a lover."

"Why? I don't want a lover so I can talk to him. That would defeat the purpose. I can think of much better uses for a lover's energy. And his mouth."

Ashyn's cheeks colored. "I'm going to pretend you didn't say that."

"You keep your notions of romance, Ash, and I'll keep mine. Just understand that they do not include Gavril Kitsune." She crossed the room and peered out the window into the courtyard. "Is the sun not even down yet?"

"Go to the library and get a book."

"I don't want—" She stopped. "Give me that missive again."

"You're not—"

"I want to draw the seal. Perhaps I can find references in the library."

"An excellent idea." Ashyn sat up. "One that ought to keep you busy and allow me to finish my book. I'll copy it for you."

FIFTY-THREE

The buildings of the imperial court were quiet, the walkways linking them empty. The library was almost clear across the grounds. The most direct path to it cut dangerously close to the Chamber of the Divine, meaning Moria instead had to head through the smaller garden and the warren of buildings that followed. She took a wrong turn, and as she retraced her steps to the garden, she saw Gavril sitting on a bench, staring into the koi pond. Lost in thought. She wouldn't disturb him.

She started retreating, but he seemed to sense her. He rose and gestured, too subtly for her to figure out what he wanted. Then he began walking away. She hesitated. He looked over his shoulder, jerked his chin, and mouthed, "Follow me."

She did, keeping her distance. They wound through the manicured garden, eventually coming to a shed. Gavril glanced around and then went inside. She followed, entering as he lit a lantern. He motioned for her to close the door and keep her voice low.

"Is this a secret meeting?" she whispered.

"You should not be seen conferring with me," he said. "I warned you about that. You cannot risk appearing to have aligned yourself with me. I must seem merely your escort from Edgewood."

"And as I told you, I'm not concerned—"

"You must be," he said, his voice harsh. "I mean it, Moria."

His use of her name told her he was serious.

He peered down into the darkness. "Where's Daigo?"

"Resting."

"Is his infection worse?" He sounded alarmed.

"No, but the doctor advised him to rest, and he's sleeping so soundly he never noticed me leaving."

"You should have him with you at all times, Keeper."

"In the imperial court?"

"Particularly in the imperial court."

She peered at him. The flickering lantern light cast shadows on his face, but she still noticed a faint sheen of perspiration and a tightness to his features. Gavril was usually so good at hiding his emotions that she sometimes wondered if he even had any. But now the worry and fear was so thick she could almost smell them.

"I need to leave," he said, before she could speak. "That's why I called you in here. I'll be gone before the emperor returns."

"What?"

"I've realized my testimony may actually do more harm than good. I shouldn't be here."

"So you're *abandoning* us?"

She'd only meant to get a reaction from him, to break him out of this odd mood and back into the Gavril she knew. But he stiffened before saying, "You'll be fine. Just keep Daigo with you."

"You're running away, then?"

If he did not react to an accusation that he was failing his duty, surely an insult to his honor would work. But once again, there was only that brief flicker of tension, quickly dowsed.

"I am retreating. Yes."

"What's wrong, Kitsune?"

"I am uncomfortable here, and you do not require my services any longer—"

She looked up into his face. "What is wrong, Gavril?"

Sweat trickled down his face. She swore she could feel his heart pounding.

"Come with me," he said quickly, closing the gap between them. "We'll go away from this. Bring Ashyn."

"What?"

"War is coming, Moria. You know it is. Whatever that letter demands, the emperor will not bow to threats. War will come, and we're caught in the middle of it when we don't need to be. We'll give the missive to Tyrus. He'll take it to his father. I trust him to do that. We can leave."

She stared at him. "What have you eaten?"

She reached up and touched his forehead. He jumped back, but not before she felt his skin, burning hot. "You're fevered. Someone has poisoned you." She gripped his arm. "We must get you to the doctor—"

"I'm not poisoned."

"Then you're possessed, like Wenda. The Gavril I know would never abandon his duty. Would never run from a threat. You are a warrior, Kitsune, and to even suggest fleeing ahead of a possible war . . ." She couldn't finish the sentence.

"You don't under—" He stopped and he looked at her. Then he swallowed and took a slow step back, his hand going to his forehead. "Yes, I am fevered. I have not eaten or drunk anything but . . ." He took a deep breath. "I'm sorry. You are right, of course. I'm unwell, perhaps from the strain of the journey."

"And perhaps *from* not eating or drinking."

He nodded. "I apologize for my outburst. It was . . ." A sharp shake of his head. "Madness. I ought to speak to the doctor."

"So you aren't leaving the city?"

"No. I'll stay the course. I must." Another deep breath, his gaze lowered. "I must." He rolled his shoulders and shoved back his braids, and when he spoke again, his tone had returned to its usual clip. "But I was quite serious about you wandering without Daigo, Keeper. You shouldn't be poking about at all."

"I'm not poking about. I'm heading to the library."

"To read? Or do you just look at pictures?"

He rewarded her glower with a twitch of a smile, and she began to relax. This was the Gavril she knew.

"Both." She took Ashyn's drawing from her pocket. "I want to find out what this is."

There was a heartbeat of silence. "I believe it's a seal. In fact, it rather resembles the one from the letter, though it's hard to tell. Someone should not trade her daggers for drawing pencils."

"I'll tell Ashyn that. She drew it for me."

Another pause, and she wondered if he was about to apologize for the unintended insult to her sister. He simply said, "So you plan to research it."

"Yes. Or ask the scholars."

"And if I said you were wasting your time on frivolities . . ."

"I would say it was my time to waste."

"Perhaps instead you would care to waste it in the training yard with me? Or touring the grounds? I know a few secret spots that might be of interest." When she looked up, he shrugged. "You aren't the only one going mad with boredom, Keeper. Either activity would be an acceptable excuse for you to be seen with your guard and escort."

She hesitated and then looked down at the drawing. "Can we do it later?"

He paused, and she thought he'd say he wasn't waiting on her convenience, but he merely murmured, "You are resolved to your research, then?"

"I am."

When she looked up, his expression seemed odd. The lantern light, she decided.

"Of course you are," he said.

"So we'll meet afterward? I'd like to see these secret places you mentioned. In the meantime, since you need to eat and drink, you should pack us a picnic."

"Should I?"

"Yes. We'll 'poke about,' and we'll have sweets and honey

wine, and perhaps, if we don't have too much wine, we'll spar afterward. Does that sound like a good way to pass the time?"

"It sounds like a perfect way to pass the time." His voice was strange, almost wistful, and she looked up sharply, but he only turned his face and bumped her shoulder. "Go on, then, Keeper. Look up your seal."

Moria found the imperial library. It seemed the busiest place in the court at this time of evening. Or perhaps *busy* was not the right word. It was simply the most populated. There were six or seven scholars there deep in study, the room so silent that her footfalls echoed like thunder when she entered.

A man came hurrying out from behind stacks of books. He seemed only in his third decade but was already slightly stooped and graying, as if from a lifetime of poring over books. When he saw her, he stopped and smiled.

"Did you finish your book already, my lady?" he asked.

"That was my sister, Ashyn."

He blinked. In Edgewood, it was rare even to be mistaken for each other—their manners, their stances, their speech, and even their style of dress was different.

"Of course," the man said. "You must be the Keeper." He bowed deeply. "I am the master of the library. Are you looking for an adventurous tale? Your sister did mention you are fond of them." His dark eyes twinkled. "We have several new translations from beyond the empire. You likely will not have heard them."

"I would be interested in those another time, master. Tonight I wish to identify a seal."

His brows rose. "A seal?"

"A family crest, I believe." She took the paper from her pocket, smoothed it, and showed him. "I am curious."

"Curiosity is what lets a young mind grow and keeps an old mind young." He peered at the paper. "Yes, it does appear to be a family crest. A secondary seal, if I'm not mistaken."

"Secondary?"

He waved her to accompany him into the stacks of books. A few other scholars—old and young—glanced up, but only briefly, before returning to their studies.

"A noble family's primary crest bears its emblematic beast. As such, it is easily identified." He waved to a wall hanging, showing a dragon circling on itself. "The Tatsu crest. There is no mistaking it." They continued walking. "However, there are times when the family wishes to send a message that is not immediately recognizable to all who see it. So they have secondary seals."

Which made perfect sense, given the nature of this particular missive.

"I myself am not familiar with the secondary crests, but there's someone here who will know. The old master of the library."

He led her to an elderly man sitting at a long table, transcribing a crumbling text onto new pages. The younger man cleared his throat and then gave a slight bow when the old man looked up.

"Master, this is the Keeper of Edgewood. She brings a family crest that she wishes identified. It appears to be a secondary one."

"Oh?" The old man's gaze settled on Moria. "The Keeper of Edgewood. I heard you were in court. Welcome." He began to rise stiffly from his low seat to bow, but she stopped him and he settled back with a grateful sigh. "Thank you, my lady. My old bones prefer the shape of a cushion these days. Now, you bring me a crest?"

She handed him the drawing. As he took it, he reached for his looking glass. Then he glanced at the page and set the glass down again.

"I have no need of that," he said. "I've seen this one often enough, though not in many a summer. Where did you—?" He stopped himself and smiled. "Ah, yes. I heard you came with the Kitsune boy. Did he have it on him?"

The old man didn't seem to expect an answer, and Moria wasn't sure she could have given one, her heart was pounding so hard. Finally she managed to say, "It is . . . the Kitsune crest?"

He nodded. "A particular one, for a particular man. The boy's father. Marshal Kitsune."

FIFTY-FOUR

As Moria stumbled from the library, no one came after her, so she presumed she had thanked the library masters and said good-bye, but she could not remember doing so. Nor could she remember how she got out the door or, moments later, how she arrived in the gardens.

The man who sent the letter was Marshal Kitsune.

No, that was impossible. Someone else was using his seal. Pretending to be the man who'd perished in the Forest of the Dead.

He *had* perished, hadn't he?

When Gavril came to Edgewood, the villagers had wondered what to tell the boy of his father. Should they mention that they recalled him? Should they not? Then there was the matter of the body, which had not been found. They feared Gavril would discover that, and it would only make matters worse for the boy, knowing his father's spirit roamed the forest, trapped between worlds. So they'd decided to lie. They'd told him his father was at rest. It was a small kindness he deserved.

But the body had not been found.

Because there was no body to find?

Again, impossible. You could not simply walk from the Forest of the Dead. Even if you managed to make it to Edgewood, you would be seen by the guards. No man could escape his fate.

Not even one who had been, arguably, the most powerful man in the empire? She had seen Gavril's reception among the city guards. He had not been nearly so respected in Edgewood, where many were too young to have served under his father. But there had been those, like Orbec and the commander, who'd treated Gavril with deference and respect. Honor, duty, and loyalty—the tenets of the warrior code. Loyalty to one's lord. One's warlord. And the warlord of all warriors was the marshal. Whether Marshal Kitsune had been disgraced or not, there would be men who would risk their own exile in the forest to help him escape it.

Marshal Kitsune wasn't merely a warrior either. She remembered Gavril at the campfire in the Wastes, arguing that the raising of the shadow stalkers did not seem the work of a sorcerer. Eventually he'd allowed that it might be, but they both knew it was—it could be nothing else.

Her stomach clenched so hard she doubled over and had to grab a bench for support.

Does Gavril know? He must.

But he'd said he didn't recognize the seal.

He lied.

That was even more impossible than his father escaping the forest. Hadn't Gavril refused to believe those things in the forest were shadow stalkers? Hadn't he refused to believe that the people of Edgewood had been massacred? Hadn't she seen the shock and horror on his face when he discovered it?

Gavril knew nothing of this.

She'd found him in the forest, injured but alive. *Left alive. The sole survivor.*

Because his father had spared him, as any father would. Which did not mean Gavril knew his father lived. Or that he knew anything about this terrible plot.

But would the former marshal allow his only child to unveil that terrible plot to the emperor? When the emperor discovered who was behind it, Gavril would be lucky to escape with his life. What father would do that?

Not one who had made sure his son had survived thus far.

As Moria sat on the bench, she looked to the garden shed and heard Gavril's voice in her head again. *I need to leave. That's why I called you in here. I'll be gone before the emperor returns.*

She inhaled sharply. No. Gavril had played no witting part in this. He'd simply been uncomfortable in the emperor's court and wanted to leave. Or perhaps, on reflection, he *had* recognized the seal. He came to recall it later and knew he had to flee. Flee quickly, because Moria was about to uncover the identity of the man who had sent that message.

She ran for the guesthouse.

***

Moria was almost to Gavril's quarters when his door opened. She crouched behind a squat statue. He stepped out, pack in hand. Then he paused and went back inside, as if he'd forgotten something.

She hurried to his door and nudged it open. He had his back to her as he stood at a tray of food, stuffing fruit into his pockets.

She watched him, the way his braids swung forward as he bent, the way he pushed them back impatiently, a motion so familiar it quelled the turmoil in her gut.

Gavril had played no part in his father's plan, if it was his father at all. Gavril was stubborn and difficult and prickly and arrogant, but he was, above all else, honorable. He had fought by her side. He had confided in her, about his sorcery and his fears. He had trusted her and she had trusted him. That meant something.

He must be another victim of this tragedy, used by his father. He'd recognized the seal and known that he could not say, "I am innocent" and be believed. Moria had seen how people treated him. He'd spent his life paying for the treachery of his dead father, punished for events he'd clearly played no part in. How would he be treated now, if his father was no longer dead? If Gavril had—however unwittingly—played a role in this new treachery? He had no choice but to flee.

She pushed open the door. Gavril spun, hand on his sword hilt. Then he saw her and . . .

He saw her, and she caught his expression, and she didn't see worry or fear. She saw guilt and shame.

He said nothing. Just stood there, watching her.

"So you're leaving after all?" she said.

"You know I am." His voice was low.

"You're not even going to pretend?"

He straightened. "You know me better than that, Keeper."

"No." She closed the door behind her. "Clearly I do not know you at all."

Something flickered on his face, but he hid it quickly.

"So he's alive?" she said. "Your father?"

He said nothing.

"And you knew that? All along you knew that?"

Still nothing. Her heart hammered so hard she could barely draw breath. This was not possible. She must have fallen asleep in her quarters and was having a nightmare.

"You knew what he was going to do?" she said. "You took part in it?"

Another flicker of emotion, too fast to decipher. His mouth opened as if he was going to speak. Then he clamped it shut, jaw held tight, and said nothing.

Moria stepped forward. Her hands were shaking. Rage pounded through her, and she had to struggle to keep her gaze on him, struggle to speak to him.

"You raised shadow stalkers. With your father. *For* your father. You raised them, and you commanded them to massacre my village."

His eyes rounded. "No, I would never—I did not realize—"

Again he clamped his mouth shut, so hard she heard his teeth click. She could still see more in his eyes, more he wanted to say, but he blinked hard and when he looked at her again, his gaze was shuttered.

"You let them kill my village. Kill your comrades. Kill my *father*."

She heard his teeth grind and the muscles on his jaw worked, as if he struggled to keep silent.

"What?" she said. "You have some excuse? Some explanation?"

He took a moment to open his mouth, just enough to let words out. "I have no excuse, Keeper."

"Do not call me that!" she roared, yanking her blades from their sheaths.

"Moria, I—" He swallowed hard, and he seemed to pause, as if considering. A flicker of something like pain. Then anything in his expression vanished, his face going hard as he pulled himself straight. "Yes, I have done whatever you believe. I have deceived you. I have betrayed you. Remember that. Whatever happens, remember that."

"Remember that?" She whipped a dagger at him. "I remember my *father*, you son of a whore!"

Gavril spun out of the dagger's path just in time, and it passed just under his arm, ripping through the fabric before hitting the wall. He stared at it, as if shocked. She charged him, the other dagger raised, and it was only at the last moment that he feinted. He pulled his own sword. Her charge was clumsy, rage-blind, and his sword broadsided her arm, knocking her blade flying. She scrambled out of the way, but he didn't strike at her, just stood there, sword half-raised.

"I'm going to leave now, Moria," he said. "You can't fight me."

"By the spirits, I can. And I will, if I need to wrap my

hands around your throat and choke the life from your body."

She dove for the nearest dagger. He tried to intercept her, but she twisted and went for the other one instead, yanking it from the wall. She spun. He lifted his blade.

"You cannot fight me with a dagger, Moria. You're outmatched and—"

She threw it, but she was too angry, every lesson evaporating from her head. The dagger flew off-target, Gavril easily dodging it. She went for the second blade, but his sword struck her again, broadside, knocking her into the wall. Then it was pointed at her throat.

"Enough, Moria."

She stepped forward, the edge of his sword touching her throat.

"Enough!" he said.

She met his gaze and moved a little more, letting the edge dig in.

"Moria! *Stop this.* Are you mad?"

"If you want to stop me, you'll have to kill me." She met his gaze and eased forward again, feeling blood trickle down her throat.

Gavril's eyes filled with fury. "Blast you, Keeper. A pox on—" He snapped his mouth shut. "You will not do this."

"Is it so hard to kill me?" she said. "Perhaps it's not the same when you aren't ordering dead men to do the deed."

"I would not kill you, Keeper. Not kill you. Not harm you. Not ever." He looked her in the eyes. "I regret any hurt I have brought to you. Most of all, I regret what I had to do to Daigo."

"Daigo?" Her heart thumped. "The infection? You caused—"

"No, not that. What I did tonight. After we spoke in the garden. I went to your rooms, hoping to take your sister as a hostage, but Ashyn was not there. Daigo was. He knew something was wrong." Gavril looked at her. "He attacked me, Moria. I would not have harmed him, but I had to defend myself. I hope . . ." He paused. "He was alive when I left him, though barely."

Rage blinded her. She reached to grab his sword, not caring if it sliced through her hand, but he'd already lowered it. She dove for her blades. Then she felt something hit the back of her head. Everything went dark.

FIFTY-FIVE

Moria bolted upright, pulse racing, mind on fire, knowing she had to do something, had to get somewhere, but she was momentarily dazed. She looked around.

Where am I?

An empty room. Her gaze snagged on one of her daggers lying on the floor, and it all rushed back.

"Daigo!"

She grabbed the dagger and ran. She tore across the gardens and threw open the door to their quarters. As she raced through, she could see Daigo lying on the cushion, a pool of crimson beside him.

"Moria?"

It was Ashyn, but Moria barely heard her. She flew to Daigo as the wildcat rose, stretching and snarling a yawn. He let out a chirp as she dropped to her knees, running her hands up and down his sides.

She could see and feel no injury.

Her gaze shot to the crimson pool. It was a bright-red cushion he'd been lying on. She kept patting him down, certain there was something. He rubbed his cheek against hers as a purr rumbled through him. Behind her, Tova whined and Ashyn hurried over.

"Moria? What's wrong?"

"He's hurt. When you were gone. He came in and hurt him."

"What?" Ashyn's hand closed on her shoulder. "When did I leave?"

Moria gulped breath as her heart slowed. She couldn't find any sign of injury on Daigo. In fact, he seemed rested and recovered from his infection.

"Moria?"

She turned to Ashyn. "Did you leave the room?"

"No, I've been in bed the whole time. Reading my book."

Moria stood. "Gavril lied to escape. He said he'd hurt Daigo so I'd come straight here before raising the alarm."

"Gavril?"

She turned to her sister and told her everything.

"I—I don't understand," Ashyn said when Moria had finished. "That's not possible."

"The Seeking party never found Marshal Kitsune's body, did they?" Moria paced the floor, fury and rage fresh again.

"No, I *can* believe the marshal survived. I *can* believe he would strike against the emperor. While I find it difficult to believe any person could do it in that way—raising shadow stalkers and annihilating a village of innocents—I do not know the marshal. But I do know Gavril, and that is what I cannot believe. That he was part of this."

"He admitted it. He used us and betrayed us, and he played a role in the massacre of our village and the death of our father." She gripped her dagger. "For that, I'll kill him."

"Moria, don't talk like that."

"Like what?" Moria spun on her sister. "Don't threaten to kill the boy who helped massacre every person in our village? Who helped murder our father? Gavril Kitsune's life will end by my hand, Ashyn. I swear it."

Her sister dropped her gaze, mouth setting in a way that told Moria she would resume the discussion at a more suitable time. Moria continued pacing the room.

"Now that we know this, we need to decide how to handle—"

Ashyn leaped up. "We must tell someone. Immediately."

"All right. We'll summon—"

"No." Ashyn gripped her arm. "We must raise the alarm. You said that is why Gavril tricked you—so he could escape. If anyone finds out that we *allowed* him to escape, that we discussed the matter and merely summoned a servant to request an audience . . ."

Ashyn was right, of course. They'd delayed too long already, and every extra moment would count against them.

Moria raced for the door.

A fast rider had arrived, saying Emperor Tatsu was on his way, coming quickly, and he expected all parties involved to be in the throne room when he arrived. Moria and Ashyn had been there since shortly after they'd burst from their room, calling for help.

It had been chaos—the court steward convinced the girls were hysterical, waking from some nightmare. Then they discovered Gavril was gone. And the young master of the library confirmed that the seal on the letter did indeed belong to Marshal Kitsune.

The steward, clearly out of his depth, summoned his superior—the minister of the imperial household. Not the correct choice, he'd discovered, as he'd been soundly rebuked in front of the girls, while the minister sent word back to the palace.

The chancellor was brought, along with two of the major counselors and the marshal's head general—the marshal himself was with the emperor. Ashyn had gotten only partway through her story before they were joined by the crown prince and the whole tale had to be retold.

So it was chaos, and Moria could not decide whether to be infuriated or relieved. Had Gavril still been in the city when all the confusion began, he clearly was not by the time the guards were properly alerted. However, those delays meant no one could blame his disappearance on her own delays in telling someone of his treachery.

And so they waited. People came and went. Tyrus was there. She'd seen him slip in, and he'd nodded to her, but he kept his distance. Being cautious around his brothers. Based on her conversation with the library master, Ashyn had said there were four princes in the imperial family. Several princesses, too, though all were married and living elsewhere. Of the official bastards, Tyrus was the only son. Or the only one still living—Ashyn said the master had not elaborated on that. Moria did not, then, blame Tyrus for avoiding his half brothers.

Apparently all four were there, though only the crown prince had been introduced. There was a steady stream of others, too, ministers and such, and when the doors opened again to admit yet another group of men, Moria was beginning to wonder where they'd fit them all.

This last group looked much like the others. Middle-aged men, all warriors, all moving briskly, heads high. The one in front was the shortest of the group. A broad-shouldered man with a severe face, well formed for his age, empire-born and perhaps in his fifth decade, his dark hair entwined with gray. He had flashing, dark eyes that reminded her of a hawk's, scanning the room as he moved fast. His sleeves were pushed up and she could see his tattoos. They looked like . . .

She glanced over at Tyrus and the dragons circling his forearms. Then she looked at the man walking in . . . with dragons inked on his arms. Her gaze dropped to his breeches and boots, both filthy with the sweat and dust of a hard ride.

It was only then that everyone else seemed to notice the newcomers. The room went silent. Then men rushed forward to take Emperor Tatsu's cloak and offer him cold water and hot tea, but he waved them off impatiently. They lined a route to the emperor's seat—a raised chair at the head of a long table. The man ignored them, instead striding into the room and looking around. His gaze fell on the girls.

He gave a short laugh. "You two are easily spotted, even in this crowd."

As he walked over, Ashyn bowed as deeply as she could, and Moria tried to emulate her. She was not as adept at social graces, but she also had to struggle not to keep staring at the man.

This is the emperor. Our emperor.

In the days before, she'd prepared for this moment. She would be polite, despite her feelings about the man who had exiled Gavril's father, and exiled Gavril, too, in a way, cruelly sending him to guard his father's death place.

Except Gavril's father hadn't died. And whether Marshal Kitsune was innocent or guilty of the charges that had led to his exile, the blood of Moria's entire village stained his hands.

She wasn't even sure now whether Gavril had been sent to Edgewood or volunteered for the post, to aid his father's plan.

"The Keeper and the Seeker of Edgewood," Emperor Tatsu said. "I am so sorry for your loss."

Ashyn dropped her gaze and Moria could see her eyes filling. She kept hers on the emperor.

"We will have justice for Edgewood," he said. "And we will free the children."

Ashyn lifted her head and held out the envelope. One of the ministers rushed forward, pulling her arm back, glowering at her.

"The emperor has just arrived," one snapped. "You will not shove that at him—"

"She did not." Emperor Tatsu returned the man's glower tenfold as he took the envelope. "She handed it to me as quickly as possible, because she is well aware of the urgency of the situation. Unlike those who would have me take off my boots and sip tea first." He shot his glare around the room. "What are all of you doing here? This is not an acrobatic performance."

"We thought you might need us, your imperial—"

"I sent word telling who I needed in this room. The rest of you will hear what is in this missive when I am ready to share it. Now, begone. Quickly."

The mass of ministers and counselors started for the door. When the crown prince tried to remain at his father's side, the emperor snapped, "You, too. Begone." He paused and then turned to the mass of exiting men. "Tyrus? Where's Tyrus?"

The young man was almost out. He backed into the room.

"Come back, boy. You know Gavril Kitsune, don't you?"

"We trained together, Father, though it has been almost two summers—"

"Good enough. You'll stay." Tyrus ducked his brothers' glares as he approached. The emperor continued snapping orders, expelling men from the room.

"I am sorry," Tyrus whispered to Moria. "About Gavril. I could tell you two were close."

"You misjudged, your highness. He was merely a traveling companion."

"Yes," Tyrus murmured. "That is for the best. Say that to all who ask. I am sorry for it, though."

"But not surprised?"

He seemed confused by the question. "It is his father. He must do as he is told. Filial piety comes before everything, even obedience to the empire."

"Even obedience to one's conscience? Slaughtering innocents is acceptable if your father commands it?"

Ashyn tried to shush her, eyes wide with alarm, but Tyrus said, "No, which is why I am certain there is more to it. Gavril is prickly, but he has a true heart. He is always honorable."

"There's no mistake, your highness. He accepted full responsibility."

"There is more. I am certain—"

"Tyrus?" the emperor said. "While I do hate to pull you away from a pretty girl . . ."

Tyrus turned to his father, gaze dropping as he murmured an apology. The emperor clapped him on the shoulder and waved everyone to the table. As they walked, Emperor Tatsu opened the envelope and pulled out the missive.

The men who had stayed were the chancellor, all three major counselors, and one of the warriors who'd arrived with the emperor. He was short, slightly squat, breathing heavily as he tried to keep up with Emperor Tatsu. An older man, the summers weighing heavily on him. From the way he dogged the emperor's steps, she presumed he was an attendant, until Tyrus leaned in and whispered, "Marshal Mujina."

He did not look like a man of war, and she wondered briefly if Tyrus was referring to someone else. But she could see the man's tattoos were marks of the Mujina—the badgers. He did rather resemble one. An aged badger, toothless and slow. Not a man Moria could imagine leading an army. Perhaps that was the point—after Marshal Kitsune, the emperor wanted a man he could control. This marshal certainly looked controlled, hurrying after the emperor and then sliding past him to quietly take his seat at the man's left hand.

The chancellor sat at the lesser, right-hand position, with

the major counselors beside him. Tyrus tried to seat Moria beside the marshal, but she motioned for Ashyn to go there instead—she ought to speak for them. Tyrus gave Moria the next seat, and pulled out the one beside her as Daigo and Tova wedged in beside their girls.

No one had spoken a word on the walk to the table. No one spoke now either, the room silent as the emperor read. When he passed the missive to the marshal, his face was unreadable, his gaze distant.

"This is—" Marshal Mujina said. "He cannot expect—"

"Of course he doesn't." The emperor snatched the letter and handed it to the chancellor, motioning for the major counselors to read it after him.

When the last counselor handed it back, his face somber, the emperor folded it, then held it out across the table. He was clearly passing it to Ashyn, but she sat there, looking confused, until Tyrus nudged her. Even then, she took it carefully, gaze on the emperor, as if waiting for him to rescind it.

"You brought it this far," he said. "You ought to read it. Seeker, is it? Ashyn?"

She nodded.

"You and your sister will read it, so there can be no question that what we claim is in that letter is true. Otherwise, I suspect there will be those who think we must be misrepresenting the situation."

"It is the old marshal, then?" Moria said. "Marshal Kitsune?"

"It is. As you will see, he includes information known only to the two of us. We grew up together. It is he. He threatens to destroy Fairview if I do not step down immediately and cede the imperial throne to him."

"Cede—? But that is—he cannot expect—" Moria inhaled sharply. "He does not expect it. He is asking for what he cannot have. He means to incite war."

"Yes, apparently even a child can see his true purpose." The emperor shot a glare at his marshal. "It would be difficult for me to make any concessions to an exiled traitor. If he were, however, to ask for something reasonable, such as a pardon, negotiations could be held. This is beyond negotiations. He will have war. The destruction of Fairview and the death of Edgewood's children would lie at my feet."

"But . . ." Ashyn's head shot up from her reading. "Fairview? The children? Are they lost, then?"

"No, child. Rescuing them will be our first priority, one that can hopefully be accomplished before Alvar Kitsune realizes we've refused his generous offer."

"But war?" the marshal said. "How does he imagine he'd win that? His mercenaries cannot outnumber our troops."

"I'm quite certain he hopes to win some of his former men to his side. I'm equally certain he already has, and they are merely awaiting his signal." He gave his marshal a hard look. "You have told me that your warriors are content. Now we will see the truth of that."

"But war?" the chancellor said. "Against shadow stalkers?"

"And more," Ashyn said quietly.

They all turned to her, but she seemed unable to go on.

"He has raised more than shadow stalkers," Moria said. "Ashyn encountered death worms in the Wastes. I fought a thunder hawk. I have a feather in my pack to prove it. That may mean he has plans to do battle with more than men and shadow stalkers."

"Then we must be prepared," the emperor said. "For a war unlike any the empire has seen."

TURN THE PAGE FOR A SNEAK PEEK
AT THE HEART-RACING SEQUEL!

ONE

I n retrospect, Moria should not have pulled her dagger when she was attempting to pass through the imperial city unnoticed. In truth, the pulling of the dagger was not so much a mistake as the throwing of it. Even the throwing of it wouldn't have been as grievous if her blade had missed its target. But if Moria pulled her dagger, she would throw it, and if she threw it, she would not miss, so the problem, she reasoned, could be traced back to the man responsible for the throwing of the blade.

Of course, there was a reasonable chance she'd have been recognized even without the incident. All the city knew that the Keeper and Seeker of Edgewood were at the palace. Northerners weren't exceedingly rare, but when people were watching for a pale-skinned girl with red-gold hair, it was difficult to affect a sufficient disguise. And then there was the matter of Daigo . . .

"I need to go into the city," she'd told him earlier as she'd fastened her cloak.

He'd walked to the door and waited.

"No, I need to go by myself. Quickly. Before Ashyn gets back."

Daigo had planted himself in the doorway and fixed her with a baleful stare. The huge black Wildcat of the Immortals was her bond-beast, as much a part of her as her shadow. A very large, very conspicuous shadow. Luckily, unlike her sister's hound, Daigo didn't feel the need to stick to Moria's side like a starving leech. He'd kept pace with her along the rooftops.

Moria was to meet Ronan in the third market, where merchants traded among themselves and with the casteless. He'd said to meet by the perfume stall. Presumably her nose would lead the way . . . except the crush of people meant she could smell only the stink of overheated bodies. The din of shouted barters didn't help. For sixteen summers, she'd lived in a village where "market day" meant four carts along an open roadway. This was enough to make her head ache.

Taking a moment's break, she spotted a man following a girl of no more than twelve summers. He made her think of the children of Edgewood, held hostage by the former marshal. Orphaned and terrified, children who trusted her—and she was forced to trust the emperor to save them . . . while he entertained dignitaries from some kingdom she'd never heard of.

As frustration flared, Moria watched the child. A merchant's daughter, her simple dress adorned with mismatched beads and crooked embroidery. The girl went from booth to booth, picking out the cheapest baubles and bargaining with the merchants.

The man following her had leathery skin and the squint and rolling gait of a fisherman. Eyeing pretty young girls two castes below him and thinking them unlikely to complain, perhaps even welcoming his attention.

Moria drew closer, her hand under her cloak, fingers wrapping around her dagger. She would let the man see that she was watching, in hopes that would frighten him off. If it did not, she would allow him to see the blade. A plan so devoid of her usual recklessness that even her sister would approve.

Then a large woman—her arms loaded with goods— waddled into Moria's path. Moria swung around her, and by the time she did, the fisherman was right beside the girl, whose attention was fixed on some trinket.

As the man's hand snaked into the folds of the girl's dress, Moria launched her blade. Her second blade followed so fast they seemed to fly as one. The daggers pinned the man's cloak to the stall behind him. There was a near-comic moment as he ran in place, pinned by his cloak. When he realized what bound him, he slipped free of his cloak.

Before he could get more than two paces, a shadow landed in front of him and let out a snarl that reverberated through the square. People screamed. People fled.

It was not, Moria mused, an inconspicuous entrance.

Daigo pounced. The fisherman let out a scream and dropped to his knees, hands shielding his head. The wildcat plucked one dagger from the wooden stall, took it to Moria, and returned for the second.

"He touched you?" Moria asked the girl.

"Yes, my lady." The girl flushed. "Inappropriately."

"I saw." Moria waved to two men standing nearby. "Deal with him."

She turned to walk away, as if she could make such a spectacle and then slip into the crowd. It didn't help that there was no longer a crowd to slip into, most having fled the huge wildcat. Those who remained closed in as they realized who she was.

"My lady . . ."

"Keeper of Spirits."

"Moria of Edgewood."

"A blessing, my lady?"

Moria reached into her pocket for a handful of coppers, blessed and threw them, hoping to slide away in the scramble that followed.

A woman caught her cloak. "My thanks to you, Keeper. He has bothered girls before."

"He won't anymore. I truly must—" She looked over her shoulder, but people pressed in, blocking her escape.

"I heard your wildcat has a name," a little boy said as he squeezed through. "The court Keeper's cat has no name, but they say yours does."

"Daigo."

The boy reached out to pat the wildcat. Someone yelped a warning, but Daigo sat there, ears back, bracing himself to suffer the attention. Soon a half dozen children were patting and poking him.

"We must go," Moria said. *Before someone tells the guards*

I've left the palace court. She was not a prisoner, but she'd been ordered to stay within its walls for her own safety.

"Did you truly throw those daggers?" one of the girls asked.

"Like bolts of lightning," an old woman in the crowd said.

"Spirit-blessed," someone said. "My uncle saw her when she entered the city. She threw her blades at a man who insulted Marshal Kitsune's son. He brought them here. Gavril Kitsune, returned to the city. Fortune shines on us."

Fortune? Oh, no. That is not what shines. It is death and destruction, and Marshal Kitsune is at the center of it. Your hero is a monster. His son no better.

"I—I must go."

"Yes, you must," whispered a voice at her ear. Fingers wrapped around her forearm and a firm hand tugged her through the crowd. A young man held her. Seventeen summers of age. Light brown skin. Dark curls hanging in his face.

"Ronan," she murmured.

"Hmm. Daigo? Help me get her out of here."

TWO

Daigo cleared a path through the crowd, bumping people and growling when they didn't move fast enough. Ronan nudged gawkers aside from the rear. Moria allowed herself to be led, well aware of the scene she'd caused and the trouble she was in. More important, she was aware of the trouble Ashyn could catch for not realizing her twin had left. If there was one thing that could melt the steel from Moria's spine, it was the prospect of causing her sister grief.

Only once they were out of the square did she regain her stride. Ronan took the lead, and they wound down two alleyways before finding a dark corner behind a bakery, the sweet scent of honey cakes wafting out.

Moria asked about his young brother and sister. After four moons of exile in the Forest of the Dead, he'd been anxious to return to his orphaned siblings, left in the care of an aunt he feared would have them picking pockets for their keep. But now he answered with a quick, "They're well," before saying, "You don't know the meaning of inconspicuous, do you? All I had to do was follow the commotion and there you were, in the midst of it."

"I have no training in stealth and disguise," she said. "Nor any reason to learn. I'm the Keeper of Edgewood. I should walk where I wish."

His look said she knew full well why she couldn't do that, but she only settled onto a crate. Daigo took a seat beside her, leaving Ronan standing.

"How is your sister?" he asked.

"As fine as can be expected, being held a virtual prisoner and worrying about the people of Fairview and the children of Edgewood."

Ronan sighed. "You have no gift for the art of conversation, Moria. All right. I take it Ashyn is well. Please tell her . . ." He struggled long enough for words that Moria sighed with impatience.

"I'll tell her you send your undying love and cannot wait to see her gentle face again."

From the look on Ronan's face, you'd think she'd suggested telling Ashyn he wished her a slow and tortured death.

"Fine," she said. "I'll tell her you asked after her and that it would be pleasant to speak with her, once she is permitted to do so."

"Yes, thank you. I have great regard for your sister, but she is a Seeker, and I have good reason for not . . ."

Moria peered at him. "Not what?"

"I . . . have great regard for your sister."

"Yes, yes, you said that. I didn't come to play matchmaker. I asked you to meet me—"

"Summoned would be a better word." He crouched against the wall. "Is it about Gavril? I heard that he has left the city."

"Yes, but that is not—"

"I wouldn't have thought him quick to leave your side. He seemed to have appointed himself as much your loyal guard and companion as Daigo."

Daigo growled, as if understanding enough to not appreciate the comparison. Bond-beasts were said to be the reincarnations of great warriors, and the wildcat comprehended more than might be expected of an animal.

"I did not come to speak of—" she began.

"What happened?"

She'd truly rather not speak of it, but he'd need to know if he agreed to help with her plan.

"You'll recall the message we bore from Fairview?" she said. "For the emperor, from those who held the children and villagers captive. It bore a seal. One that Gavril claimed not to recognize."

Ronan nodded.

"It was the Kitsune seal."

Ronan pulled back. "Gavril must not have known—"

"He did. It was a secondary seal used by his father. The former marshal did not perish in the Forest of the Dead. He is alive, and he is responsible for raising the shadow stalkers that destroyed Edgewood. He's also responsible for the death worms and the thunder hawk. The rumors are correct. The

Kitsune family knows sorcery. Gavril confirmed it in the Wastes. I forced him to, having caught him at it."

"But Gavril—"

"—betrayed us. After Edgewood was massacred, his task was to escort Ashyn and me to the emperor with a firsthand account of his father's power."

Ronan shook his head. "I cannot believe that. Gavril might be one of the least companionable people I've ever met, but I would want him at my side in any battle. He's steadfast and loyal—"

"—to his *father*. That's the warrior way. Filial piety above all else. Even integrity and conscience, it seems. Now you know why he's gone, and I would like to leave the subject alone."

"But—"

"I insist. I came to speak of Fairview."

Ronan studied her expression and then nodded. "You don't believe the emperor is taking the threat seriously?"

"I have no idea if he is or is not. I only know that the children are still gone and there is no army marching from the imperial city to rescue them. Which is why I need to return."

"To Fairview? Did Gavril not say they would be moved elsewhere?" He paused. "Oh."

"Yes, *oh*. Given that Gavril was lying from the start, the emperor believes the children are indeed at Fairview, and I agree, which is why I'm going there."

His lips twitched. "To rescue them yourself?"

"If I must. But I hold no illusion that I can swoop in and set them free like birds from a cage. I merely wish to assess the situation. Confirm that the children are there."

"You don't think the emperor has already done that?"

"He deems it too dangerous."

"Too dangerous for trained warriors and spies, yet you plan to do it? That's madness, Moria. Brave and bold and utterly mad."

"I agree," said a voice.

A young man walked into their alley. Like Moria, he wore a disguise. His was more elaborate—and less obvious—than a cloak with the hood pulled up. He'd dressed in a rough tunic and trousers, with a loose jacket to hide his dual blades. On his feet he wore a peasant's simple thonged sandals. His long, black hair was plaited and he wore the rice straw hat common to farmers, oversized to shade one's eyes from the sun.

Yet even with the hat shadowing his face, his disguise was as poor as her cloak and hood. It wasn't his coloring or his features. He was empire-born—the golden skin, high cheekbones, and dark eyes that were the most common look even in this cosmopolitan city. He was well-formed and strikingly handsome. What made him stand out was something no hood or hat could hide. The face of an emperor. Or, at least, an emperor's son.

Ronan's mouth dropped open in a very unattractive gape.

Moria narrowed her eyes at the newcomer. "You followed me."

"I tried. I'm not very good at it, though. I left too large a gap, and I lost you. Luckily, it's not easy to lose you for long. Just follow the sounds of chaos."

He grinned and tugged off his jacket. Ronan's stare dropped to the matched dagger and sword hanging from the young man's waist, the silver handles inlaid with flawless rubies. Then Ronan's gaze lifted to the red-and-black tattooed bands on the young man's forearms—the intricate dragon design of the Tatsu clan.

"Your highness," Ronan said, bowing so deep Moria expected him to fall over.

The young man made a face and waved him up. "That's for my brothers. One need not be so formal with a bastard prince."

Which was not exactly true. An emperor's bastard sons were treated little different from those born to his wives. They could not ascend to the throne, and they had tattooed cuffs rather than the full sleeves of highborn warriors, but otherwise Tyrus was as much a prince as his brothers. He just didn't like to act the part.

Tyrus picked up a crate and plunked it down closer to Moria's.

"Take off that cloak before you melt," he said. "It wasn't disguising you."

"Nor is that"—she waved at his peasant outfit—"disguising you."

"It isn't supposed to. It merely conveys the message that I'm attempting to pass incognito."

"That makes absolutely no sense."

Ronan cleared his throat. "Actually it does. His highness—"

"Tyrus."

"Um, yes. If people see him dressed like that, they know he wishes not to be recognized, so they grant him the courtesy."

"I'll teach you how to do it," Tyrus said to her. "For the

next time you sneak off, because expecting you to stay in one place is like trying to cage that wildcat of yours." He lounged back on his crate. "So, we're discussing the issue of Fairview."

"No, we are not. This is a private conversation."

Ronan sputtered and shot her looks of alarm. She ignored him. She'd spent enough time with Tyrus to take liberties—and to know he'd allow them, even enjoyed the informality.

"How can the meeting be private," Tyrus said. "If you're holding it in a public place?"

"Because I don't have a private place. Not even my suite. I was bathing yesterday and a maidservant brought in fresh towels."

"They're very attentive."

"Which is fine. Just not while I'm bathing."

Tyrus grinned. "I don't mind them."

She rolled her eyes.

He turned to Ronan. "Since Moria refused to extend proper courtesies, I'll presume you're Ronan?"

Ronan nodded mutely.

"I apologize for dragging you into this, but if Moria had asked me what my father was doing, I'd have said he has sent spies to survey the situation in Fairview. He must determine an appropriate course of action since he cannot meet Alvar's demands for their release."

The former marshal had demanded nothing short of the throne. As Emperor Tatsu said, Alvar Kitsune didn't expect him even to consider such a thing. It was not a negotiation but a declaration of war.

Tyrus continued. "If Moria had asked me, I would have

happily answered her questions. But she refuses to speak of the matter."

"Because you shouldn't be pulled into it," Moria said. "Your brothers have spies watching to see if you're paying attention to me because I'm a young woman or because I'm part of a situation that could further your position in court. The latter would suggest an interest in politics, which would suggest a *lack* of interest in a long life."

Two of the emperor's bastard sons had already died from paying an unhealthy amount of attention to matters of court. Tyrus aspired to be a warrior—a great one. Nothing less and nothing more.

"Yes," Tyrus said. "But I suggested finding a place where we could speak privately. Which you refused."

"Because I won't involve you."

"I said I wish to be involved."

"And I said I would not allow it."

They locked gazes, but she would not back down. If he wanted to give her sword lessons, she would not object to that. If he wanted to befriend her, she would not object to that. If he wanted to be more than a friend . . . well, that was open to consideration. Her sister deemed such matters affairs of the heart, to be approached with great care and forethought. To Moria, the heart did not enter into it. If Tyrus fancied her and she fancied him, she could use lessons in more than fighting techniques.

There was only one role she would not allow Tyrus to play: her champion. In court, everyone wanted something from you. She would not be part of that. She enjoyed Tyrus's company because his company was worth enjoying, not because he was a prince. She would do nothing to suggest otherwise.

"My father has sent spies," Tyrus said. "Two, to take separate routes, in case one is captured. He expects word from them at any moment. You may have noticed he is entertaining guests?"

Moria said nothing.

"I'm sure you're fuming at the emperor for throwing lavish parties while the children of your village suffer. He does no such thing, Moria. He entertains the Sultan of Nemeth and the King of Etaria. Minor principalities near the Katakana Mountains, where the Kitsunes once ruled. Both men were close friends of Alvar Kitsune. Someone has been sheltering him since his escape from the Forest of the Dead."

"Your father thinks it's one of them," Ronan said. "That's why they're here. So he can decide which is guilty."

Tyrus nodded and watched Moria, waiting for her to ask questions. She had a hundred of them. And to protect Tyrus, she'd ask not a one.

"He's doing what he can," Tyrus said. "He's not a perfect ruler, but he is a very good one. I know you think I'm only saying that because he's my father. But did he seem incompetent when you spoke to him? Did he seem uncaring? Did he seem to underestimate the threat?"

She shifted on the crate.

"I know you are frustrated," he said. "But there is no reason for you to go to Fairview. If it would help you to speak to my father, I can arrange an audience."

"No."

"I would be discreet about it. Allow me to—"

"No," she said, getting to her feet. She turned to Ronan. "I'll convey your regards to my sister. Please convey mine to your family. Thank you for meeting with me."

She glanced for Daigo, but he was already at her side. She walked off, stiffly, leaving the two young men behind.